wj/22

MW01143971

Just Call Me Maggie

a novel by

Marjorie Page

authorHOUSE®

AuthorHouse™
1663 Liberty Drive
Bloomington, IN 47403
www.authorhouse.com
Phone: 1-800-839-8640

This book is a work of fiction. People, places, events, and situations are the product of the author's imagination. Any resemblance to actual persons, living or dead, or historical events, is purely coincidental.

© 2009 Marjorie Page. All rights reserved.

No part of this book may be reproduced, stored in a retrieval system, or transmitted by any means without the written permission of the author.

First published by AuthorHouse   8/6/2009

ISBN: 978-1-4490-0423-1 (e)
ISBN: 978-1-4490-0421-7 (sc)
ISBN: 978-1-4490-0422-4 (hc)

Library of Congress Control Number: 2009907279

Cover photograph by Marjorie Page

Printed in the United States of America
Bloomington, Indiana

This book is printed on acid-free paper.

For Olive

and Rose

I

Monday, November 27, 1978

"NO WONDER THEY call it Winterpeg," she grumbled. Her face still ruddy from the cold, she brushed the grainy snow from her shoulders and the bottom of her black coat, unbuttoned the top two clasps and loosened her red scarf. She marked herself 'In' with a magnetized black dot on the silvery board behind the receptionist's desk. She scanned the purple waiting room for clients and, finding none hidden behind the greenery, continued on her way.

She stepped back onto the elevator to ascend to the eighth floor, watched the numbers light up as it passed each floor and counted, six, seven, eight. At her office door, she stopped a few seconds to admire the brass wording, 'Margaret L. Barnett.' Head a little higher, she entered her spacious but Spartan work space. After she hung her coat on a well polished tree in the corner and placed her boots side by side on the floor, she opened the beige vertical blinds to let in the winter sunlight. She stowed her bag lunch in the bottom drawer of her teak desk. It was completely bare except for a glass beer mug engraved in gold with *University of Manitoba*, filled with black pens and sharpened yellow pencils, and a desk calendar in its faux leather box.

Before she settled down to work, she put a pot of coffee on to brew and allowed herself a few seconds to check her surroundings, nothing out of place, no errant papers left on tables and filing cabinets, no coffee mugs on the work table, no telltale rings left by wet cups. Shortly after ten o'clock Maxine, the receptionist, called to inform her that a Miss Sandra MacNair wished to speak with her.

"Sandy. What a surprise. Good to hear from you."

"Hi. Maggie, thank God I found you. I need your help. I need a lawyer. Jim left me this morning."

Maggie gave no hint of surprise or shock. "I am sorry to hear that, but family law isn't my specialty. Did you try David?"

Years before, David Abbott was in the same grade as Maggie and Sandy in both elementary and high school.

"Jim retained him. Several weeks ago."

"Oh, really. So this wasn't a spur of the moment thing. Tom Henton might be able to handle your case. Wait a minute and I'll see when he's free." Seconds later, she was back. "He could see you at eleven this morning or at three this afternoon."

"I'll be there at eleven."

"I'll pass on the message, but I have an appointment at eleven and won't be able to meet you at reception. It's on the fifth floor of the gray tower on Broadway. Yes, that's the number. Just give your name to the receptionist and say you are meeting with Tom Henton."

As she scanned the documents that she had prepared for this appointment, she forgot about Sandy and her problems. At five minutes before eleven, Maxine rang to say her client had arrived. Maggie, her heart-shaped Scottish face devoid of makeup, ran a comb through her short black hair, smoothed the wrinkles from her woollen dress, and then hurried downstairs to meet Rodney Thomason, one of her regular clients. He was a tall, rotund gentleman actively involved in trading commodities world-wide. His handshake was firm but at least he didn't squeeze hers until it hurt. As they shook hands, she heard a familiar voice off to the right.

"Maggie. Hi." Maggie turned to see Sandy advancing towards her with a baby dressed in pink balanced on her left hip. She nodded hello. The two women stared at each other for a few seconds. Eleven years had elapsed since their last meeting. Maggie recovered first.

"Hi. Sandy. It's hard to believe we haven't seen each other since your wedding. Um, Tom," she addressed a slight blonde-haired man leaning on the receptionist's desk. "I would like you to meet Sandy, uh, MacNair Borden."

She and Rodney took the now-crowded elevator back to her office. Her floor counting was interrupted at six.

"How are you wintering?" He was an all-business type of man, not given to much small talk.

"Alright I guess." She smiled at his old-timers' greeting, "But then what can we expect? This is Winnipeg."

"Could be worse – could be forty below."

A superb hostess, she showed Rodney to a captain's chair padded with off-black nubby cushions at what she called her business nook. She offered him a coffee with real cream and sugar by the cube, served in black and tan pottery mugs. She switched on a black desk lamp, opened her file folder and started the discussion.

After his departure, she ate a working lunch at her desk, a salmon and romaine lettuce salad, a whole wheat roll, a small piece of dark chocolate, an extra-special treat she always brought back from London, and a yellow pear. Just as she opened her mouth wide to bite into the fruit, she heard her father's angry voice, "You slut, you little tramp, Margaret Lynne. Get out of my sight."

Shaken to the core, she swivelled around to look out the window at Broadway Avenue below, as if looking off into the distance would bring some understanding to her situation. The city was white with snow, trees barren silhouettes, cars of various colours, buses, trucks slipping and sliding on the icy streets, clouds of exhaust fumes spiralling upwards, pedestrians scurrying here and there wrapped in bulky winter wear against the minus twenty-five degree temperature.

She couldn't imagine or recall a situation where her father would have spoken to her in that way, but the disgust in his voice was all too real. A slut? She didn't have one boyfriend in her high school years. What on earth was he talking about?

She jumped up and paced around her neat and sparsely furnished office in her leather boots, banging her hip twice on the desk, checked her appearance in the full-length mirror in the en suite powder room, combed her hair again since she had this tendency to run her fingers through her dark locks when deep in concentration. She made a pot of fresh coffee and drank two cupfuls, one cream, one sugar, in rapid succession, then she forced herself to sit back down and prepare for her two o'clock appointment. Maxine rang for her promptly at two and she met importer Ted Foxworthy in the waiting room.

"Margaret Barnett?" He was well over six feet tall and gray-hound lean, his hand cold and clammy and limp in her grasp, and her first instinct was to withdraw her own hand and wipe it on her dress.

"Just call me Maggie," she replied.

She couldn't bring herself to initiate any social chatter but he said, "Cold enough for you?"

"Yes, it most certainly is." She smiled at that question, never knowing how to respond.

He was apparently too pre-occupied with his current problems for more conversation, so they rode the rest of the way in silence. She counted the floors, six, seven, eight. After he left, she finished up the paperwork his visit had engendered and entered her appointments in the log for November 27, 1978. On her notepad she drew an oval, scribbled lines here and there and all over the inside of the shape, picked out triangles and ellipses and filled them in with ink until she had a pattern, a mosaic. She leaned back in her black chair to relax, placing her left ankle on her right knee, awkward because of her long dress.

Suddenly she and her brother Rob are running up the four wooden steps to MacNabb's Crossing School, a one-room country school that resembles a small church without a steeple. It is long and narrow, white with black shingles and red trim around the windows, topped with a peak roof and sitting high on a stone foundation.

She hangs her blue cardigan on one of the hooks in the lower row in the hallway, pleased that a six-year old can reach them, and follows Rob into the airy classroom. A tall thin teacher introduces herself as Miss Lindsay and shows her a row of four pint-sized desks of varnished wood.

"These first three are for you grade ones," she says. "You may pick the one you want."

Little David Abbott sits in the one at the back. She chooses the second one with the initials P.T.S. carved in blue next to the inkwell, and unpacks the books she carries in a brown paper grocery bag. She glances up to see her friend Sandy MacNair entering the classroom with Miss Lindsay. Always the performer, Sandy twirls around to show off her empire-styled dress whose pink flowers accentuate her blonde hair. Maggie doesn't understand why her friend is wearing such a pretty dress for playing baseball. She is dressed in red pedal pushers and a sleeveless blouse of red and white cotton, which shows off her deep tan and a scab the size of a quarter on her left elbow.

"Hi. David took the last desk," she informs Sandy. "Is the front one okay?"

"Hi, yourself. Sure, I'll sit up front."

"Good." Maggie stows her blue reader and other textbooks, all hand-me-downs from Rob, and her scribblers and school supplies in the drawer beneath the seat.

With a jolt Maggie came back to the present and shoved the memories back down where they belonged. She wanted to forget the Crossing School and everything about it. After work, she took a cab to the dealership to pick up her Buick and then drove to the Blue Rose Bar. A flashing neon sign over the door featured the name of the bar and a huge flower, the colour of faded blue jeans. She thought the place was tacky rather than trendy, but it was the ideal place to meet people. She handed her coat to an anxious valet and looked around with some distaste. The high ceilings were open to the rafters with black pipes and ersatz studio lights hanging from black straps. The dull blue walls and ceiling were barely noticeable as recessed lighting behind the long counter and at strategic spots along the walls reflected on unframed mirrors and a collection of antique glassware behind the bar.

Anton sat alone at a centre table nursing a draft beer. To her dismay, he was casually dressed in a white golf shirt and black jeans, showing off his muscular build, dark hair and olive skin. She bent to kiss him lightly on the lips before she sat down.

"Hey, what's with you? I tried to call you three times today and your receptionist said you were busy."

"I was busy. I had clients with pressing issues. Why aren't you dressed up? I thought we were going out to dinner." Her forest green sheath with its cowl neckline and long sleeves now seemed too formal. She wanted to cut it off above the knee.

"This'll do. But why didn't call me back?"

"Never mind. I need to talk to you about something important."

"Are you dumping me? Have you found someone else?"

"No. No. Nothing like that."

Before she could explain, his friends Joe and Gary joined them and the topic of conversation turned to their upcoming ski trip to Whistler. She was somewhat annoyed that Anton hadn't invited her. She was bored, too, listening to them making plans that didn't include her. She glanced around the crowded bar and spotted Rebecca, a classmate from law school, having a drink alone at the counter and decided to join her. Maggie ordered and drank a Brown Cow while she talked to Rebecca about her preparations for the spring marathons, but Anton still showed no signs of spending time with her. An intense jab of rejection struck her mid-section. To cover her embarrassment, she played with a cardboard coaster decorated with a blue rose. A cloud of pain descended onto her left eye and the left side of her forehead. She tried to shake it off but it was not about to leave her alone. She said good-night to Rebecca and got up to leave.

At home in her luxury apartment, she kicked off her snowy boots, threw her coat on a chair, flopped down on the couch, and looked around. The living room was almost as barren as her office, except that all the furnishings were in black and white with ornaments and vases of hot pink blown glass artistically placed on black lacquered shelves. Pink throw cushions decorated the black leather couch. The sofa and two matching side chairs were placed around a furry white rug, and another pink glass piece was set on a black coffee table made of wrought iron with a smoky glass top. She couldn't bear to look at the room and she closed her weary eyes.

She hears banging from outside as if something is hitting the exterior walls, or maybe it is gun shots that make the noise. The telephone awakened her from a restless sleep.

"What are you doing?" said Anton in a loud whisper. "Why did you leave without telling me?"

"I have a headache."

"That's no excuse. I do have reservations for dinner. Are you coming?"

"No. I can't. I'm sorry. I told you I have a migraine. I'll talk to you tomorrow." Maggie hung up without waiting for his reply.

Not one to spend much time in the kitchen, she heated a can of chicken with rice soup, ate it all with some salted crackers, and chased it down with a cup of green tea. The pain over her eye intensified and she wished the soup was still in the cupboard. A search in her kitchen cupboards and the bathroom cabinets for painkillers yielded nothing so she opted for more rest. She changed into navy track pants and T-shirt and cuddled up on her queen-sized bed. Her bedroom was a mirror image of the living room with black lacquered furniture and a black and white watercolour bedspread, pink throw cushions and a white carpet. Feeling a bit chilly, she started to pull back the bedspread, but changed her mind and reached for a blue crocheted afghan, one of Grandma MacDonar's creations, tucked away on the top shelf of her walk-in closet. She wrapped it snugly around her and was soon sound asleep.

Sometime after midnight, she dreamed that she is playing catch with her older brother in the crowded farmyard near the Crossing. A two-storey house with its peaked roof and lean-to kitchen stands off to the right, and to the left is an oval-roofed steel machine shed. In front of her is a row of poultry houses of various styles and construction, and chickens, ducks and turkeys wander about the yard searching for insects and seeds in the cropped grass. A small clump of straggly Manitoba maples provides little shade to the fenced vegetable garden west of the house.

A brown turkey gobbler struts toward her, its back feathers ruffed and tail feathers standing on end, glaring with its black beady eyes. Suddenly it charges towards her and Maggie screams and runs toward the farm house, the closest safe place. Rob laughs at first and then he too screams for help. The big turkey pecks her bare calf and she races faster and faster but the irate bird keeps up. Then a brown streak of fur passes her and she hears a dog barking as if from outer space. The turkey turns and runs two or three steps, then flies for a few feet, then runs some more, until it is out of harm's way inside a chicken coop. The German Shepherd sidles up to Maggie to get his reward. She puts her small arms around his thick hairy neck and hugs him tightly. "Good dog, King, good dog," she whispers in his ear.

2

Tuesday, November 28

THE NEXT DAY Maggie tried to concentrate on her work but the long-forgotten memory of the turkey's attack bothered her. She didn't know why she had forgotten a small incident like that from years ago, and the venom in her father's voice also haunted her. She'd never had a good relationship with her father, but she didn't remember such hostility from him. She was trying to puzzle it out when she heard a timid knock at the door.

"Oh, Sandy. Good morning. Come in."

"Hi. Are you busy?"

"Of course, but I have time to talk. Make yourself comfortable. Would you like a cup of coffee? Or something else?"

"Coffee, please. One cream, two sugars."

"So. Are you and Tom a good team?"

"Yes. I think we can work together on this thing. I came by to thank you for helping me yesterday. Your office is great. May I check out the view?"

Sandy peered out the window at the stalled traffic on Broadway and the government buildings and the powder blue sky in the distance. She turned to admire the office and a horse's head carved from ebony wood caught her attention.

"Where did you find that?"

"In a craft sale in a small town near Ottawa. I like to explore that area when I am there on business."

"Just what is your line of work? Your specialty?"

"I'm in international law and I travel a lot – mostly to London and New York."

"Do you enjoy it?"

"Yes. Most of the time. It's challenging. I have to keep abreast of all aspects and changes in laws that affect the countries where our clients do business. The downside is time spent in airports and airplanes."

As the two young women chatted, they eyed each other to assess how the past decade had treated their appearance. Maggie's face was still youthful and clear, and her eyes gleamed with ambition and hope for a promising future. Dressed in a well-cut gray pant suit which suited her slim tomboyish figure, her black hair cut short, professional and efficient, she looked like a stereo-typical lawyer, sombre, serious and focussed, yet there was a hint of a red blouse under that jacket and the well-polished laced oxfords on her small feet featured a three-inch heel.

Due to her present emotional trauma, Sandy's eyes were shadowed black with fatigue and the whites had turned to red, possibly from crying. She missed being a classic beauty because of her turned up nose. Her still lovely golden curls now reached down to mid-back, but her hair had an unkempt, un-styled look. Still pretty and optimistic, she was clad in a pair of tight blue Levis, obviously hiding a muffin top under a black sweater, its zippered front open a few inches at the neck.

"I don't know what I am going to do, for work, I mean."

"Jim persuaded you to give up on university, didn't he?"

"Yes. He insisted we get married as soon as I was graduated from high school. He said he just couldn't wait, why I don't know, and it was out of the question for me to attend school after we were married. No. He wouldn't let me do that. He wanted babies right away."

"Did you mention that to Tom? You could ask for assistance for post-secondary training in your settlement."

"Yes, I did tell him. Do you remember what I was planning to do? Did I say anything about a possible career?"

"I can't say I remember much about my childhood. I thought you wanted to teach elementary school."

"Oh. Really? That is an idea, but how can I go to university with three kids to chase after?"

"I don't know. It would be difficult. You have three children?"

From her leather shoulder bag, Sandy took out a small photo album with 'Brag Book' etched on the pale blue cover. Maggie's eyebrows flew up as Sandy opened it to the first page. A professional mommy.

"This is Caroline – it rhymes with wine. She's ten. Here she is in her first dance competition." The photo showed a young girl in a red tartan kilt standing in second position with her right toe in point and her left arm high in the air.

"Oh. You're teaching her to dance. Good for you. She looks like your mother."

"Yes, brown, but I think she'll be a bit taller than either Mom or me." Sandy puffed up with pride. "This is Daniel, we call him Danny. He's eight now and heavy into hockey, as you can see. And here's one of the baby, Melissa."

"They are truly lovely kids. Has Jim seen them since he left?"

"No. He has not. Not even a phone call. He's actually been planning to leave for over a year."

"How do you know that?"

"I've been going through our bank statements and investment reports and I found out that he has been withdrawing assets from our joint accounts for over a year." Her voice choked with outrage.

"A year. Huh. He won't get away with that. Where did you meet him, anyway? How did the rich industrialist's son meet the little farm girl from MacNabb's Crossing?"

"We met when I was on *Reach for the Top*. Our team played against Winnipeg in the semi-finals. Remember? We lost, but I met this dream boat named Jim. Love at first sight, as they say."

"How did you get together after that?"

"His father bought him with a Chevy for his win in the TV show and he came to see me almost every Sunday."

"Never noticed. Wonder what I was doing."

"Preparing for law school, probably."

They both laughed. Maggie's social life disappeared the day she committed to a career in law.

"The other thing that really bugs me is that Jim insisted we have a third child. I don't get it. He planned to leave, but he wanted to father another kid? It's just crazy."

"It sounds as if he wants to pen you up like a prize steer. Or else he wants to hurt you."

"Well, if hurting me is what he wants, he's succeeding admirably. If it weren't for my parents, I'd be destitute, and all I've ever done is everything he wanted – never what I wanted. He didn't want to know what I thought or felt."

"So David is Jim's lawyer?"

"Yes."

"Traitor."

"Jim apparently retained him several weeks ago."

"Must be another woman. You should get a good settlement from that dickhead."

Sandy's mouth dropped open at the suggestion that Jim was unfaithful and she seemed on the verge of defending her husband.

Maggie twisted the silver watch on her slim wrist so that she could see its large face. "I'm really sorry, but I have to run. I am going to London tonight and I still have to pack and get to the airport in time to sit and wait to fly away again."

"Hurry up and wait?"

"Definitely. Come by again when I get back. We'll do lunch."

"Okay. Have a good trip."

After Sandy disappeared, Maggie packed the documents for the trip in her briefcase, double-checked that she had everything she needed, and then quietly left the office. While she was folding her business suits into her Samsonites, she decided that she should call Anton. Usually they talked during the day, but he hadn't called. She didn't know what to say to him and she hadn't phoned him either.

"How long have we been seeing each other, anyway?"

"I don't know. Four or five years."

"It must be that long. Why haven't we discussed marriage or even living together?

"Can't answer that either. Of course, one is us is usually in the air somewhere over the Atlantic. Why the questions?"

"I was just thinking. I live in this swank apartment high in the sky and I work up in the clouds too. I want to come down to earth and plant a garden, get my hands dirty. Maybe I should buy a house. Want to buy a house?"

"Shouldn't we be married to buy real estate together?"

"I don't know. Should we?"

"I'll think about it. Was that what you wanted to discuss at the bar last night?"

"No. But listen. I have to go. Will you be able to meet my return flight?"

"Probably. Call me from London. Have a safe journey. Love you."

Maggie responded, "Love you too," and hung up the phone. She went into her bathroom to collect her toiletries, and looked at the black fixtures, white tiles, and pink towels and bathmat. No clutter here either, not a thing was out of place. She shuddered. Deliberately, she entered a second bedroom, this one piled high with books, bookcases on three walls, books on the desk and table, on the side chairs, on the floor. She chose seven or eight of her favourites and the one she was currently reading, and lugged them to the living room, where she placed her current object of interest on the coffee table and the rest in a shelving unit. She didn't have time to do more. She called a cab and dashed off to the airport.

After she checked in and ceded her luggage to the attendant, Maggie found a comfortable spot in the waiting area and reached into her shoulder bag for her reading material, only to find she'd forgotten her novel. Annoyed at herself, she strolled over to the bookstore and browsed through the selection. One paperback seemed to jump out at her, actually begged to be picked. It was a new Taylor Caldwell, *Bright Flows the River*.

She sat down to read while she waited for her flight. Several sharp pains pierced her crotch and lower abdomen and she couldn't sit still in the well-padded furniture in the waiting area. She was afraid she would vomit. An elderly woman with gray hair pulled back in a small bun stared at her with disapproval. Maggie thought she resembled her mother Mary Ellen and had to look twice before she was able to ignore her. When the young lawyer boarded the plane, the sensation passed, however, and she wondered if she had picked up a urinary infection. She prepared for her appointments, watched a movie, and read a few more chapters of the novel during the long trip on the 747. On her legal pad, she wrote, Boeing, Bing, being, binge, big, bin, bog, nib, neb, nob, gob, bone, one, on, o, I, beg, gin, Ben, gone, no, go, Bo, in. She thought, wow, nab, nib, neb, nob, nub.

Then she relaxed into a deep sleep. Her dreams were fleeting images of a green tractor pulling the harrows in a cloud of dirt, a red combine spewing out dust and chaff, a house resembling a Swiss chalet, a ribbon of yellow roadway, a cement bridge, her brother Rob driving a grain truck, the inside of an old church, herself up to bat, Sandy on the swings with her long blonde hair flying in the wind, King following a scent through the wheat field, a university lecture hall, a red Nova automobile.

3

Wednesday, November 29

HER TRAVEL ARRANGEMENTS were flawless as usual and soon after her arrival she was settled into her hotel room in the City. The room was a cozy space decorated with some interesting antiques, the walls, bedding and flooring in gold, deep reds and matte white, and dark wood furniture and wainscoting. The first order of business was to meet a client, Abe Waterston, for lunch in the hotel dining room. She was rather hungry since she'd eaten lightly on the plane. An obese, almost repulsive gentleman, Abe hid a razor-sharp mind for business under his balding head, and they covered a lot of ground in between bites, sips of an excellent black tea, and his smelly fat cigar. Their meeting lasted for more than two hours, and after he left, Maggie went for a walk to relax her cramped and sore muscles after the long flight. The gray skies and drizzle matched her mood. She wanted to stay outside for an hour or more, but she had forgotten her gloves and her cold hands took her back to the hotel. Curled up on the queen-sized bed, she slept for a couple of hours.

The telephone rang, an odd sound, and awakened her. Groggily she said, "Hello. Maggie Barnett."

"It's Abe. I have another issue that I forgot to mention. Do you have plans for dinner?"

"No, I don't."

"I could meet you at seven in the dining room?"

"Seven would be fine."

Hot and sweaty from her nap, she showered in the gleaming white bathroom with the gold faucets, washed her hair and dried it with her fingers. Over creamy silk lingerie, she dressed in her wool slacks and dress boots, a long-sleeved white shirt, the top buttons left undone, and gold stud earrings and a matching pendant, a smooth circle straddling a fine chain. She was drinking her second glass of white wine when Abe joined her. While they consumed dinners of fish and chips, they discussed his trumped-up reason for the unscheduled meeting. Huffing and puffing, he paid for their meals from a wad of bank notes stashed in his right pants pocket. When they stood up to leave, he grabbed her left elbow and hustled her upstairs.

4

Thursday, November 30

THURSDAY MORNING, MAGGIE awakened refreshed from a good night's sleep. She had no memory of the previous evening's activities. She did notice that her breasts were tender and she thought her period must be due.

Always focussed on the task at hand, she attended her appointments and business lunch with her normal professionalism. As soon as she was free, she changed into a track suit and strolled for an hour through London's busy streets with no destination in mind, admiring the architecture and people-watching. Back in her room, she ordered a salmon dinner from room service and reviewed her notes and documents from the day's business while she sipped on her green tea. She jotted down her thoughts about the meetings and acquaintances she'd met and perused the materials for the next day.

"What kind of a life is this? Airports, airplanes, hotels. Airports, airplanes, hotels. Lonely nights, lonely days, not a friend in sight." She spoke out loud but there was no one to hear.

She checked her schedule for the next few days. With weeks of holidays banked there was no reason she couldn't have a few days off, so she called her boss Jared at his personal residence in Winnipeg and made her request. He gave her the okay without hesitation. She called the office, left a voice message for the receptionist to reschedule a couple of appointments and then rescheduled her flight. Anton wasn't in when she called; she left him a message too. She knew he'd be upset by the sudden change of plans, but she wanted some time off so badly she shrugged aside any concerns he might have. With a city map and a bus schedule, she figured out how to get to the Tate Britain Gallery, and then picked up the Caldwell. She was disturbed after three pages.

She is back at Crossing School in mid October. Most of the crops have been harvested and the fall work of preparing the land for spring seeding done. The rolling fields are dull and gray, and the few leaves left on the maples, poplars and oaks and the wild grasses have turned from gold to brown.

Miss Lindsay asks her to read aloud from *Fun with Dick and Jane* for the first time, for the entire student body to hear. She usually daydreams during reading class and doesn't bother to do her homework. She is not prepared. Besides, she doesn't like the reader, although at the time she couldn't have explained why.

"Read 'Spot and the Blue Ball,'" Miss Lindsay shows her the page.

She begins. "Come up, Sally," said Jane. "Get the little t t t t ..."

"Can anyone help Maggie?"

"toy," answers Sandy.

"Get the little toy d d d d ..."

"Anyone?"

"duck," David knows that one.

Maggie starts to read again. "Get the little toy duck and the little cars. Get the toys and come with me.' 'Come, Spot,' said Sally. 'You can come, too. Get the little blue ball. Get it and come with me.' 'Here, Spot,' said Jane. 'I want the blue ball. Do not play with it now. I want to p p p putt ...'"

"Sandy?"

"put."

Miss Lindsay's hazel eyes flash with anger. She paces back and forth in front of the young students. "Were you not paying attention in class yesterday, Maggie? We went over those new words for this story yesterday." On the blackboard she prints 'toy, duck, put, did, he.' All the other students stop their work to listen.

"David, read them please." He does so with ease.

"Maggie, now you read them." She falters on 'put' again.

"Did you not read this story for homework?"

She has to admit she did not and her chin sinks to her chest. She has the sensation of falling into a deep hole.

"Well, I'll send a note home to your parents. Don't let this happen again."

Maggie stares at her in disbelief. She is in trouble and she knows it. She is afraid of the consequences if her father finds out that she got in trouble at school.

"Sandy, please read to the end of the next page, then David finish the story."

Maggie's face turns crimson and she is sick with embarrassment. Tears well up in her eyes and she brushes them away with her sleeve and swallows her need to cry. When the story is completed, Miss Lindsay lights into her again.

"What do you have to say for yourself, Maggie?"

"I am sorry, Miss Lindsay. I will pay attention, really I will."

The teacher makes her stay in the classroom during recess to practice reading the story. Besides being sick with humiliation Maggie is annoyed because she wants to be outside and she misses her favourite activity, playing baseball.

5

Friday, December 1

ALTHOUGH SHE FELT off balance, Maggie managed to conduct herself normally during the second day of meetings, and she had a delicious lunch of fish and chips with a colleague from Glasgow who wanted to know all about her Scottish and English roots. When she was finished for the day, she took a leisurely walk, window shopped, browsed in stores that appeared interesting, listened to the accents, observed the shapes of the faces in the crowds. While she was waiting for room service to deliver her dinner, she picked up the Caldwell novel, a book that held her attention and wouldn't be put down. Caldwell's protagonist has become so fed up with his life that he attempts suicide by crashing his automobile into a tree. Now in a mental hospital, he has healed from his physical wounds, but cannot or will not speak to anyone, not even his doctor, and he is remembering his life, just as she was.

She and Rob are on their way home from school, riding their bicycles the two miles to the farmyard along the smoothly worn gravel road. It is the same day that she embarrassed herself in front of the class and she is in poor spirits. Rob vents his anger at her. "You listen in class, you dummy. And do your homework." He pedals as fast as he can and soon leaves his little sister far behind. He takes off just as they turned off Sampford Road to go south into the farmyard, a half mile distant. Since there are very few trees in the bleak yard, she can see the gray roof and twin chimneys of the house and her mother's pink hollyhocks. The two-storey house looks large and foreboding and she is in no hurry to get there. She dismounts from her red boys' bike with the annoying crossbar and walks for a distance, watching the ducks and loons in the reedy slough by the lane.

When she finally gets home, Maggie pulls the crumpled note from her pocket and shows it to her mother. Mary Ellen doesn't read it out loud so her daughter doesn't know what it says. Mary Ellen doesn't scold or slap or make threats, she just says, "Okay, young lady, get up on this stool here at the table and read your story for tomorrow. I'll get you some milk and cookies."

Maggie isn't sure whether her mother is angry or not. Certainly there is no understanding smile to greet her. Without any argument, Maggie does as she is told, three times. To her relief her mother says nothing to her father about the note when he comes in from the field for his evening meal. After supper, she takes a glass of red Kool-Aid, her apple pie and her school books upstairs to her bedroom, and closes and locks the door behind her. She does her arithmetic assignment and tackles that reading lesson three more times before she goes to bed, still angry with the teacher because she missed her ball game.

6

.

Saturday, December 2

THE NEXT MORNING, Maggie found her way to the Tate Gallery, an institution she had longed to visit on her many trips to London. She spent the majority of her time examining and admiring the works of the masters and perennial favourites, Turner and Constable. She was enthralled by the treatment of skies, the vivid colours, and the depiction of ordinary landscapes.

She is in her tiny bedroom on the second floor of the old farmhouse. She sits down on the wooden chair at her desk where her homework is waiting but she can't face it. Instead she picks out a colouring book full of horse pictures and sets to work. After doing three or four pictures, she takes some scrap paper and begins to draw, trying to make an image of a pinto horse standing on its hind legs. It turns out fairly well, so she tries one of a Shetland pony running in a grassy field. Released somehow, she falls on her bed but she chokes back her tears and anger.

Maggie wept silently as she continued to view the surprisingly large and magnificent paintings in the gallery. She felt the heartbreak of that day but she had no memory of the event that triggered it. On her way out she admired the ten-foot tall, beautifully decorated Christmas tree in the entrance, and decided that the next day would be a good time to shop for gifts. She ducked into a dark wood-panelled pub for a satisfying dinner of shepherd's pie on her way back to the hotel. Later she made a cup of tea in her room and settled down to read the novel that kept beckoning to her. Two chapters later, the past came bounding back.

The night of the Christmas concert is finally here. It is held in St. Andrew's church, a yellow brick building with a high sharp spire, across the road from the school. Maggie rushes in to see the decorations. Stage curtains of forest green velvet are hung across the communion rail and a magnificent tree decorated in red and gold and silver stands next to the stage. She can smell the pine from the doorway. Quickly she runs downstairs to hang up her jacket. She gets in line behind David for the procession upstairs to the stage and while she is waiting impatiently, she smoothes the creases from her green kilt.

The entire student body assembles on stage and waits for the signal to begin. A hush falls over the crowd. The piano plays the opening bars and everyone, students, parents and guests sing *O Canada.* Then the three grade ones step forward to recite the welcome recitation. David, serious and manly in his new eyeglasses, Sandy, breathless and nervous, afraid to make a mistake, and Maggie with her normal what-do-I-care attitude each have one verse to recite. She looks with envy at Sandy in her new red velveteen dress with white ribbon trim.

When they are finished, the grade ones are allowed to sit in the front pew to watch the skits, the square dance and more recitations. Maggie, restless as always, sees Miss Lindsay waving to them to join the rest of the students for the choir act. Wearing crepe paper choir gowns with white bibs, they sing their unique renditions of *Rudolph the Red-Nosed Reindeer, Jingle Bells, Santa Claus Is Coming To Town* and *Frosty the Snowman*, ringing handfuls of metal bells for accompaniment.

In the basement again before the pageant, Maggie hears the first strains of *Silent Night* and visualizes the curtain opening in the darkened church. Then she listens with her eyes closed as the parents' choir sings her favourite, *O Little Town of Bethlehem.* She knows all the carols by heart. Diane, in the coveted role of the Virgin Mary is dressed in a blue robe and hood, and she and Peter, dressed as Joseph, creep up the stairs. Joseph wears a striped robe made of rough fabric in muted tones of brown and green, with a matching piece draped on his head like an Arab and tied with yellow twine. He is followed by a strange looking donkey - two giggling boys bent double under a brown horse blanket.

Through the floorboards, Maggie can faintly hear the drone of big Frank's voice as he tells the familiar story. She mouths the words along with the narrator. The floor creaks as Mary and Joseph walk slowly across the stage leading the donkey.

The curtain closes and reopens a few minutes later to the tune of *Away in a Manger*. Now Mary kneels in front of a doll's cradle covered in a burlap potato sack tending her baby Jesus. In the hallway, she has quickly added a yellow cardboard halo suspended on wire over her head. Jesus' father also sports a halo. A cardboard cow and donkey plus a bale of yellow wheat straw and one of green aromatic hay add realism to the scene.

On cue, David, Rob, George and Tom, the shepherds, dressed like Joseph but without the halo, tiptoe up the stairs. The angel Gabriel played by Rachel with her waist-length hair climbs the stairs followed by the heavenly host of angels, Carol, Sandy, Sarah, Beth and Maggie, dressed in white choir gowns with long pointed sleeves, cardboard wings trimmed with silver tinsel attached to their shoulders and more tinsel banded across their foreheads. The choir sings *While Shepherd Watched* and *Hark the Herald Angels Sing* as the angels walk among the shepherds and the cardboard sheep. Maggie is beaming, arms crossed at the wrists and hands over her chest. The curtains are drawn once more.

In the final act, the angels and shepherds crowd around the manger and the baby. While the choir sings *We Three Kings*, Grant, Joe and Marvin, the three magi, enter the stable dressed in gold and purple robes with shiny pointed gold and silver crowns, carrying their gifts of gold, frankincense and myrrh under their arms like footballs. Everyone on stage bows or kneels to worship the Lord, the choir and the children sing *Joy to the World*, and the curtains close during the final verse.

The audience of parents, grandparents and neighbours clap

enthusiastically. Maggie joins the rest of the cast on stage for *God Save the Queen* and then they file downstairs to change into their normal clothes. When they have all appeared upstairs, Santa, in his red suit and white beard, bounds into the classroom. He shouts, "Ho, Ho, Ho, Merry Christmas everyone," and seats himself on the teacher's wooden chair. Maggie waits in line, giggling with anticipation. Santa hands her a small gift that looks but does not feel like a book, but she waits until all the gifts are given out to every student and pre-schooler before she opens it. She tears off the red wrapping paper to find a zippered case full of watercolour paper and a set of watercolour paints with a selection of brushes. She jumps up and down with glee and calls, "Look, Sandy, look at what I got." Anxiously she waits for Santa to opens his white flour-sack bag. He chucks her a brown lunch bag full of chocolates, caramels in their plastic wrapping, ribbon candy, red and green gums, peanuts and Brazil nuts, and the best treat of all, a sweet juicy Mandarin orange.

She laughs as Santa's helpers throw the remaining bags into the audience. Mike gets one for himself and one for Mary Ellen. Then it is over. The fathers slip out to start their cold vehicles, and everyone calls Merry Christmas and Happy New Year as they bundle up against the frigid weather and leave for the evening.

7

MAGGIE HAD PLANNED to attend church at Westminster Abbey on Sunday morning to see the architecture, hear the music and experience the holiness of the nave, but she slept until after ten o'clock. She was aroused from a dream in which she was at a church service in St. Andrew's Church at the Crossing. She was aged seven or eight. She was sitting between Sandy and Rob and the choir was singing *Holy, Holy, Holy*, as they did every Sunday. Then she was in the same church, standing in front of the altar, and wearing a blue dress which was inches too short, she was confirmed into the Church. Suddenly she was again before the altar dressed in a prickly rose gown. She turned and watched as Sandy floated down the aisle in a cloud of white lace on the arm of her father.

As she waited for room service, she had her usual shower. She stood in the bathtub and allowed the water to run over her head and down her body for several minutes, willing the water to wash away the feeling of being dirty. She had planned to visit the London Museum in the afternoon but she was just too tired, so she ate her breakfast of toast and coffee and went back to bed. After sleeping for an hour, she woke up feeling worse than before. She lunched at a nearby pub, and on the way back, something internal pushed her.

She stepped off the curb and a red double-decker bus missed her by inches. Frightened, she ran back to the hotel. Then she choked back her fears in a desperate attempt to salvage her vacation, and used her map to gauge the distance and cab fare to the Tower and London Bridge.

A voice said, Yeah, maybe I'll just jump off it.

"Who are you?" she asked aloud.

No one answered.

Her energy flagged and she flopped back on the bed and turned on the television. Two women waving their handkerchiefs were standing quayside watching their sons ship out, crying in fear, smiling with pride. The tears filled her eyes, flowed down her cheeks, and soaked her T-shirt. She bawled until her stomach hurt. She cried until she could cry no more and she didn't know why. She fell asleep again. After she ate dinner in her room, she watched TV with an uncomprehending mind. She drew a sheet of paper from her briefcase and idly wrote, television, vision, nose, lose, vise, veil, vile, evil, tile, stile, Nile, silo, sole, vole, isle, oil, soil, toil, let, set, vet, net, veto, sit, site, nit, snit, lit, slit, sot, lot, slot, vote, not, note, lent, silent, lint, vent, sent, vest, invest, nest, lest, list, enlist, silt, invite, onset, inset, stone, tone, Eton, son, ton, one, on, o, to, toe, no, so, lo, I, seen, lion, loin, tin, tine, sin, sine, stein, Sten, Len, vine, ovine, lesion, sieve, live, love, stove, vie, tie, lie, lien, line, in, into, lone, snot, teen, ten, steno, steel, lei, is, it, its, tee, lee, see, nee.

Lonely and desperate she picked up the telephone to call Anton and then slammed the receiver down, no comfort there. A pain started in her left eye and spread throughout her head prompting her to sock back a couple of painkillers and go back to sleep.

8

Monday, December 4

MONDAY MORNING, SHE woke up restless and irked that she didn't have a chance to play tourist the day before. Putting all the memories and strange experiences out of mind, she shopped for gifts for her parents, an angora tartan stole for her mother and a curling sweater for her father, leather wallets for her brothers and golf shirts, of course, for Anton, and a package of dark chocolate, a treat for herself. She returned to the hotel for lunch in the dining room and ate alone thinking about the gift for her boyfriend, neither intimate nor extra-special, as brotherly as the wallets she bought for Mike and Rob. Later, she called Anton to see if she had a boyfriend at all, and he was very brusque and didn't seem ready to talk.

"Why did you take time off without me? I thought we would spend our holidays together."

"I just needed a couple of days off, that's all."

"So? You just wanted to avoid spending them with me."

"That's ridiculous. You're going to Whistler without me. Will you meet my plane? I get in tomorrow morning."

"No. I won't take the time off."

"Okay then, I'll see you when I get there," answered Maggie. He hung up without saying love you or good-bye or even okay, fine. Annoyed at her insecure boyfriend, annoyed at her childhood memories for spoiling her vacation, and annoyed at herself for forgetting her pre-university life, she packed her luggage for her return flight. Her right biceps hurt and her thighs hurt and her back mysteriously began to spasm. She lay on the bed writhing in pain, and then as quickly as it started, the pain disappeared. She finished her Caldwell novel while waiting for her flight at Heathrow, confident in the knowledge that she had no choice but to allow more memories to surface. During the return flight, she tried to relax and read another novel she had picked up at the airport, but her mind, leaking memories like a dam that had burst, wouldn't allow it.

Knowing she loves horses, Sam asks Maggie to his farm to witness mowing the hayfield near the buildings. She and Sandy and Trish perch at the edge of the gravel road to watch. For his own safety, Sandy has their border collie Mack on a leash, an indignity he bears with stoicism.

Wearing a filthy railroader's cap to shield his eyes from the sun, Sam handles the dapple-gray geldings as if he and the horses and the mower are one well-oiled machine – a 'hup' here and a 'ho' there, a slap with the reins on a lagging rump as he manoeuvres the team around the field. Buck and Butch pull the machine without hesitation despite its metallic rattles and clangs and the clicking of the knife as it nips off the long grass a few inches from the ground.

The freshly cut hay has to lay in the windrow for a day or two to cure, that is dry out, to be ready to rake and store in the barn loft. Sam again asks Maggie over to watch, and Trish and Sandy come along, of course, and this time Rob. The horses pull the rake around the field making big piles of hay. Then comes the hard work for Sam. With a pitch fork, he loads the hay onto a rack, a special wagon with front and back uprights of one by ten boards, but with no sides. On the floor of the rack is stretched a sling made of rope and steel pulleys and snaps and Maggie wants to know what possible purpose they have. The team of Percherons stands patiently, switching their tails and stomping their big feet to shake off horseflies, as Sam throws forkful after forkful of dusty hay onto the rack.

When it is full, he drives the team to the barnyard with the four children riding in the hay holding onto the upright so they won't roll off. Upon their arrival at the barn, Sam takes the ends of the sling up and over top of the load and snaps them tight, attaches the sling to the pulley that hangs down from the sharp peak on the barn roof, and unhitches the horses from the rack and hooks them to the whippletree on the sling. Then with a loud 'giddup,' he slaps the reins on the horses' backs. They take off at a gallop. The sling full of hay rises to the loft and swings along a steel rail to the end of the wall, the steel strikes against steel with a loud bang, stopping the load and tripping the mechanism that dumps the hay into the loft, amid flying dust and small pieces of flowers and grass. He re-assembles the sling and lets the horses drink from the water trough at the well, then he hitches them to the rack and goes off to get another load.

9

Tuesday, December 5

BACK IN WINNIPEG, Maggie entered her black and white bedroom to unpack and change her clothes, but she was so unhappy with the decor that she left the unpacking for later and drove her Buick Skyhawk to Sears, the two-storey department store at the Polo Park Mall. She browsed through the linens department until she found a lovely bedspread and ruffle in shades of indigo, forest green and purple in a geometric pattern, and she chose two pairs of fine percale sheets, one blue and the other green to match the rest of the bedding and picked up two sets of thick cotton towels in a sea foam green for her bathroom. After more searching, she found a ceramic bathroom set in white with leaves of a similar shade of green and tiny red roses on it. With her arms full, she went back to her shiny black car, lifted the hatchback to deposit her parcels, and returned to her apartment.

She tossed her old towels, bedspread and sheets in the wicker laundry basket to wash later, and hurriedly unwrapped her new pastel blue sheets and pillow cases and changed her bed, adding the new bedspread and pillow shams. She liked what she saw. She hung a set of her new towels in the bathroom and put the new bathroom set on display. She didn't know what to do with her old one so she left it in the dishwasher.

She called Anton to see if he was available for dinner but he was planning to attend a hockey game with his buddies. She could not understand why he didn't invite her to join him. He knew she enjoyed hockey, but he obviously wasn't in any hurry to see her. She ordered Chinese food, her old favourites, sweet and sour spareribs, chicken fried rice and chop suey, and had it delivered. As she ate, she tried to imagine married life with Anton, Anton mowing and watering and fertilizing the lawn, raking up mounds of leaves, shovelling snow from the driveway, barbecuing T-bone steaks in the back yard, but it didn't seem to fit. She thought of going to dinner with him, eight months pregnant with a balloon belly and swollen ankles, and she had to chortle because he'd probably insist she cover herself with a white sheet, two eyeholes like a Halloween ghost. Anton in the delivery room, coaching her breathing to manage the labour pains, Anton holding a newborn baby in his arms, Anton taking a son to hockey practice, none of those images seemed to work. After four years of dating, she knew he liked sports, football, baseball, basketball, skiing, and hockey, and anchovies and mushrooms on his pizza, and Labatt's Lite on tap in the bar, and that was about all.

Their teacher Miss Lindsay returns to school in January sporting a diamond ring, a white gold band with a sparkling solitaire stone, and the girls gather around her to admire her engagement ring – except for Maggie, who isn't at all interested.

"His name is David McClure," she tells them, "and he is a medical doctor in Brandon."

"When are you getting married?" asks Carol.

"We haven't set a date yet. Dr. McClure would like to establish his practice in Sampford and he's looking for an office and examining room and a three bedroom home for us. Perhaps it will be in the summer after school is out, and I want you all to come to my wedding. Then I'll be Mrs. McClure."

Maggie suddenly awakens, "Why? Why do you change your name?"

"All women change their names when they marry. Your mother did and so did mine. It's just the way it is, Maggie."

"I won't. I like my name. I am not giving up Maggie Barnett."

Miss Lindsay smiles and says. "We'll see."

Maggie can hardly believe it. Maybe her mother's name is Mary Ellen MacDonar. That would explain Grandma and Grandpa's names. She resolves to ask her mother as soon as she gets home.

The temperature outside has climbed above zero, a January thaw Mike calls it, and Maggie and Sandy along with Sarah, in grade two, go outside during the lunch hour to build a snowman – a big fat roly-poly Frosty. They find an old black pot in the junk pile in the bluff of maple trees and use that for a jaunty hat and a half dozen granite rocks make a pair of piercing eyes and the mouth. In the absence of carrots, they are stuck for a nose, until Sarah thinks of using a chunk of wood. After a brief hunt around the trees they find a broken branch which can be shaped to their satisfaction. While they've been creating their masterpiece, the boys have started a snowball fight and as always it is all out war, boys against girls, and the three little girls are drawn into the battle by the older ones.

"Help us," they cry, "we're outnumbered."

The boys especially Frank can throw harder than the girls and they also pack their snowballs harder, and so the girls are becoming overwhelmed. Suddenly Miss Lindsay appears and the storm of flying snow stops dead. "Who started this?" she demands to know. No one answers. They have never seen their friendly teacher so angry.

"How dare you boys beat up on the girls like that? Are there stones in those snowballs?"

"Yes," offers Rachel, "I got hit on the cheek with one."

"Whose idea was that?" The teacher stares into the eyes of Frank and Grant and Tom and Peter, one by one.

Grant and Peter mumble, "I did," at the same time, the twins as usual acting as one.

The furious Miss Lindsay orders the four boys into the school where she straps them with the foot-long black leather strap, three times on each hand. Whimpering, the boys sit at their desks, and as additional punishment they have to stay in the school during recess. The rest of the students are stunned into silence. The friendly atmosphere in the classroom evaporates completely. As if to make matters worse, their newly engaged teacher brings out a schedule of chores for the students to do. She explains she isn't doing all the work herself any longer.

Maggie whispers to Sandy, "What gives?"

Sandy shrugs, "I don't know."

"Maybe Dr. McClure is a meanie."

"Then why is she marrying him?"

"Girls, stop whispering and finish your arithmetic."

Maggie and Sandy are assigned cleaning the chalk brushes for their first job. They take them outside after school and bang them on the exterior walls of the school house until the dust stops flying.

In retrospect, it seemed obvious that Augusta Lindsay should have said, I don't, to her doctor friend, and maybe Sandy should have said the same thing to Jim, but how a woman was supposed to know what man would make a good husband was a mystery, thought Maggie. A guy could pretend to be a Dr. Jekyll before the wedding and show his true colours as Mr. Hyde afterwards. Anton wasn't even pretending to be a good guy, he ignored her most of the time and demanded she jump to his side whenever he called. He was king and Maggie should follow three steps behind, and on top of all that, he didn't listen.

IO

Wednesday, December 6

THE NEXT MORNING, Maggie awoke wondering whether it was Tuesday or Wednesday and wishing she could stay at home to deal with these demon memories that haunted her, but she had meetings arranged with clients and other work to do so she hauled herself out of bed, had her usual and essential shower, and no breakfast and went to work. The flashbacks seemed to come when she relaxed, so she made herself as busy as possible and arranged to have lunch with her friends Rebecca and Sadie at their favourite spot, the Italian restaurant Alexander's. While she was out, Maxine took a call from Anton, saying that he would come by her place that evening.

Her interest in art revived in London, she stopped after work at a new art supply store where she browsed, trying to convince herself that she was just looking, then grabbed a shopping cart and loaded it with half a dozen prepared canvasses of different sizes, a sturdy wooden table easel, several long-handled oil painting brushes and shorter water color brushes, a bottle of oil painting medium, a set of drawing pencils, an eraser and sharpener, a coiled sketch book, a bottle of black India ink and a straight pen, a pad of parchment paper, and paint – alizarin crimson, cobalt blue, Thalo green, permanent rose, titanium white, Payne's gray, cadmium yellow light, Naples yellow,

yellow ochre, burnt umber, raw umber, raw sienna, cobalt violet. She took her credit card from her wallet and handed it to the young clerk.

"Thank you, sir," said the pert blonde cashier.

"Excuse me."

"Sorry. Um. Miss Barnett."

It wasn't the first time that someone had mistaken her for a man and she had always shrugged it off without thinking too much about it, but now it seemed to be significant. However, she wanted to immerse herself in visual art, so she put her treasures in the back of the Buick and hurried home without brooding about gender confusion. She took a table from her library and placed it under the window in the third bedroom so that the light came over her right shoulder, un-wrapped the easel and set it on the table.

She was still missing a few things so she made a quick trip to the Woolco department store for a green plastic tackle box, a golden brown wicker stool and a gray metal floor light with three bulbs. No time to cook, she put a turkey TV dinner in the oven and while it heated, she stowed her paints and pencils in her new art box. She found a glass mug engraved with Riding Mountain National Park in her top kitchen cupboard and used that to hold her brushes. In her library she located some dusty and forgotten books on art and moved them into her studio. She removed all the cleaning supplies from the utility shelves and put them under the kitchen sink to make room for her books, paper and canvasses. Grinning with delight, she stood back to admire her work.

Quickly she downed her hot dinner and took her herbal tea to the studio. Choosing a how-to book on drawing, she sat down at the table to test herself, just in case she'd forgotten how. She was absorbed in a line drawing of an old dilapidated barn when the doorbell rang.

"Anton. This is a surprise." She had somehow forgotten he was coming.

"Didn't you get my message?"

"Yes, but you never come here, I don't know why, but you don't."

"I know, we always go to my place, but you really blew me away you know, all that talk about buying a house and getting married. I like things the way they are – I have my space and you have yours. I can go out with my buddies and you can see your friends. We take vacations together and we spend weekends together. "

"That's all you want?"

"I don't know, but it's uncomplicated this way. Maybe we could try shacking up. Maybe I could move in here with you." He dropped his brown leather jacket on a chair as if he'd already moved in and looked around the room assessing its possibilities.

"No. There isn't enough room for you here, you with all your sports gear and weight lifting equipment. Anyway I don't want to live together unless we're getting married."

"A tad old-fashioned, aren't you?"

"So what if I am?"

"Is it a legal issue, madam lawyer?"

"Madam lawyer? "

Putting his arms around her and nibbling her neck, he murmured, "I know what we need, a little loving. How about it?"

She stepped back, her dark eyes flashing. "You don't call me in London. You don't bother to call me when I get back. You're barely civil when I call you and you run like a scared rabbit when I mention some kind of commitment. Then you expect me to fall into bed with you. No."

"What?" His brown eyes flashed with shock and anger, but he made no move to relinquish his claim on her.

She had never refused to have sex with him, never said no about any issue, and she didn't want to deal with his anger. "Please go. Just go."

He stomped out of the apartment, slamming the door behind him. Maggie sank into a chair, shaking. The phone rang and she didn't want to answer it.

"Hi. It's Sandy. Would you like to come for supper tomorrow night? Mom and Dad are here and they'd like to see you. Come after work whenever you're ready and we can visit while we cook."

"Okay. That sounds wonderful. Thanks. I'll see you tomorrow."

Meg and Sam. Maggie didn't know until that instant that she missed Sandy's parents. She remembered them dancing at a whist drive and dance at the Crossing School, a fund-raiser for something or other. The live band was playing a slow waltz. The petite Meg danced on tiptoes gazing skyward and Sam seemed to turn his tall spine into rubber as he leaned down to look into her eyes. He touched her as if she is fragile and precious, and they ignored everyone and everything around them, engrossed in each other. She thought about the past evening at the Blue Rose when Anton spent all his time with his friends and ignored her. But then she was the one who walked away – she wasn't interested in their ski trip, mostly because she wasn't invited.

She is at the Brandon Fair in June, and since her parents have no interest in going, Maggie tags along with the MacNairs. Upon their arrival, they stroll through the barns to admire the show cattle and horses and Sam shakes hands and stops to talk with almost every horseman and cattleman he meets. Meg glares at him as she holds Christie tightly around the shoulders, afraid that the little girl will get kicked. The great beasts, however, ignore their spectators completely. By the time they are through the stable area, it is lunchtime and Maggie and Sandy share a foot-long hot dog with sweet green relish and oodles of ketchup and a tad too much yellow mustard, and golden corn-on-the-cob dripping with butter, and pink lemonade to drink because Meg insists that it has some nutritional benefit unlike soft drinks.

"Are you going to tell me what's wrong?" Sam asks.

"You don't know?"

"No. I do not."

"You don't introduce me to any of the people you know. What am I? The little slave girl who darns your socks?"

"I can't help it. You're walking away ahead of me. But I am sorry. What can I do to make it up?"

"Give me some time in the art display."

The art display. Maggie wants to go with her, but Sam calls her over and he and the four girls sit in the small grandstand to watch the heavy horse competition. Six horse teams trot around the ring vying for trophies - black and dapple-gray Percherons, ash blonde Belgians with creamy manes and tails, and Clydesdales with their big white hairy feet, all in gleaming black harness, ribbons in their manes and tails, coats shining. The girls bet with Sam on which team would win. Sandy picks the black Percherons with their fine heads and bearing. Maggie and Trish are more interested in how well they handled and pick the best behaved team. Sam watches for both appearance and handling and picks the winners every time.

When Meg rejoins them, they walk down the busy midway, where loud unidentifiable music is playing and barkers yell, three for a quarter, win a teddy bear here, but Sam doesn't stop at those booths even though it looks pretty easy to lop a sealer ring around a milk bottle or hit bobbing balloons with darts. They do stop at the kiddie rides for Christie and Trish to ride on the boats and miniature trains, and all four girls go on the kid-sized Ferris wheel and the merry-go-round, with its pink, grey, mauve and green horses. Sam asks Maggie if she wants to ride on the saddled ponies tied to a carousel of red steel, but she shakes her head, no, because they look so sad and lethargic walking around and around in the hot sun. Meg and Sam climb onto the big Ferris wheel, leaving Trish and Christie in Maggie and Sandy's care. Trish tries to run away to watch another ride and Sandy yells at her and she starts to cry and other people turn their heads to see why this child is bawling and making such a racket. Sam and Meg come back just in time to prevent a major war between the two sisters, and give each other that we-won't-do-that-again look.

They watch the 4-H beef club competition, where some guys they know from the Carroll club are showing their market-ready steers, and suddenly Trish is excited. "Can I do that, Daddy, please, please?"

"Okay," Sam answers, obviously pleased, "I think you have to be ten to join 4-H."

"What's 4-H?" Maggie has never heard of it.

"Head, heart, hands, health. I pledge my head to clearer thinking, my heart to greater loyalty, my hands to larger service, and my health to better living for my club, my community, and my country." Sam recites the pledge with his hand on his heart. "Want to join, Sandy?"

"Couldn't I do something else? I don't want cows."

"Well, you do have your dancing and piano lessons, but yes,

there's cooking and sewing and handicrafts, dairy cattle, horseback riding, poultry."

"I'd like to learn more cooking, alright. I'd like to learn to sew too, but I can't do everything, can I?"

Maggie listens carefully to all this.

"Did you want to join the poultry club?" Sam asks Maggie.

"No. I hate those stinking birds. Maybe Rob would though. I wish I could have a pony. Guess I'll stick with dancing."

Maggie said to herself, I am not going to have my evening ruined by Anton's behaviour. She returned to her new studio and went back to work on her drawing. She found that her skills had not diminished much by the passage of time as she transferred the outlines of her sketch to a sheet of parchment and began to work it in India ink, hatching and cross-hatching to indicate shadows and different textures of the weathered wood exterior of the hip-roofed barn. She lost all track of time and worked long past her usual bedtime.

Refusing to think about Anton, she fell into a deep sleep and dreamed she is still in grade twelve at Sampford Collegiate where she and Sandy and two other girls are studying in the library. She is struggling with Shakespeare - *Hamlet.*

"'To be or not to be – that is the question.' To live or not to live, that is a question and a half. To continue in this miserable world or to take one's own life, that's what he's asking. I wonder how many people ask themselves that."

"Don't go there, Maggie."

II

Thursday, December 7

AFRAID AND SWEATING, she awoke at six ten Thursday morning. She remembered the dream and shuddered to think that she had actually considered suicide and she wanted desperately to know what catastrophe had happened in her life. Maggie showered and dressed in a navy pantsuit with a white shirt, had toast with peanut butter and strawberry jam and ginger peach green tea for breakfast, and drove to work. During her coffee break, she called her family doctor's office to request a referral to a psychologist, and to her surprise, Dr. Dixon himself phoned her back.

"What's all this about, Margaret?"

"Maggie. Please call me Maggie. Um. I need someone to talk with about some problems I'm having."

The elderly doctor replied, "I could see you at three. You could tell me what's going on and then we can find the best person for you. Do you want to do that?"

"Alright. It's a place to start. I'll come by at three." She hung up the phone, thinking that from now on she'd close her door before making personal telephone calls.

Leaving the office early was not a problem – she packed the two contracts that had been occupying her attention all day into the black leather briefcase that usually accompanied her wherever she went, and drove to the medical clinic to see her friend the doctor. While she waited to be called into the examining room, she played a word game in her mind, trace, caret, crate, cater, carte, react, race, care, acre, rate, tear, tare, cart, art, are, era, rat, cat, ret, car, ace, arc, tar, act, eat, ate, eta, at, re, a. She was startled when the doctor called her.

"Now tell me what this is all about." The frail Dr. Dixon lost no time in getting down to work.

"Where should I begin? I have almost no memory of my childhood. It is as if my life started when I enrolled in university and everything else was left behind. I don't want to see my parents and I don't want to see my two brothers and I don't even know why. Well, last week I was contacted by an old friend, one I've known all my life, but haven't seen for eleven years. We were in the same grade at a one-room country school and we went to high school together. Since then I have been remembering bits and pieces, sounds, smells, feelings of anger and fear, and these memories come up at the most inconvenient times, when I'm driving, when I'm trying to go to sleep. And I know that something awful happened to me. I know it but I remember nothing."

"That is not uncommon for someone who has experienced trauma at some time in the past. There are a number of techniques we can use to help you retrieve your memories, the good ones as well as the bad. Do you feel comfortable telling me what happened to you? Or would you like to try someone else?"

"Do you have time to work with me? You're so busy."

"Actually I do. I'm not taking any new patients and I have been referring some to other physicians. I am cutting down so that I can retire sooner or later, but I will make time for this if you want me."

"Okay. Yes. I thought I would need a psychologist or psychiatrist, but if you can help, I would like that better." The kindly white-haired gentleman was the closest thing she had to a father or grandfather at that point.

"Fine. I'll have the receptionist make one-hour appointments for you once a week for the next three months and we'll get to the bottom of this." He opened a cupboard door to withdraw two notebooks with hard black covers. "In the meantime, I want you to keep a journal. Record your memories, your thoughts, your fears, anything that comes to mind. Now let's hear about these flashbacks. What has come up so far?"

Maggie was in such an improved state of mind when she left the doctor's office with the journals that she almost forgot about her dinner date with the MacNairs. She needed a gift, something to add to the meal. She knew that this family didn't drink wine with their meals but they might enjoy a treat, so she picked up a bottle of Bailey's Irish Cream for their coffee. Uncomfortable in her work clothes, she went home to freshen up and change into blue jeans, a white T-shirt and a taupe corduroy jacket.

She had no trouble finding Sandy's ranch-style house, located just off Portage Avenue, and she took the opportunity to drive through that area of St. James to look at the prosperous houses, the well-kept yards and the tree-lined streets. Even covered in winter's snow and ice, it looked like a community she might choose for herself, especially if the yard reached down to the Assiniboine River. The Borden home occupied, two, perhaps three, city lots, and the exterior walls were covered in patterned stucco in off-white with a deep red trim around the windows and eaves. It was surrounded by a good-sized lawn, neat flower beds waiting for spring, shrubs and ever-green trees shrouded in snow. She parked the Buick in the driveway next to a white Ford pick-up.

Sam answered the doorbell, his face lit with happiness in seeing her. "Look at you. Maggie. You've grown up."

Meg pushed past him and hugged Maggie tightly. "Oh, I am so glad to see you."

"I am glad to see you too. I brought a little Bailey's for our coffee. Hi. Sandy. Hey, you cut your hair. Looks good."

Sandy, whose new hair cut was almost as short as Maggie's, introduced her to Caroline and Danny. With a mischievous smile, Maggie refrained from gushing about which parents the children resembled and shook hands with them as if they were adults. She took two steps down into the sunken living room, sank into the soft cushions of an L-shaped sofa upholstered in aspen green suede and started the conversation.

"Trish, how is she and where?"

Sam responded, "Trish is doing very well. After she finished her agriculture degree, she married Tom Bannerman, as you know, and they are farming both the Bannerman place and the Munroe place. I expect they'll take over when I retire."

"I always thought Trish was a farmer. Do they have a family?" Belatedly she remembered that she had been invited to Trish's wedding but did not attend. She was away somewhere – London, perhaps.

"Oh, yes. They have two boys, Matthew and Samuel," said Meg the proud grandmother.

"And Christie?"

Caroline piped up. "Auntie Christie is a science teacher and she lives in Brandon. She isn't married – she's too busy curling."

Maggie laughed. "I wonder where she gets that from."

Everyone laughed with her - Sam was an avid curler.

"Is Rob still in Vancouver?" Sandy wanted to know.

"Yes. He is lecturing at U.B.C. in zoology. He's married but has no kids, at least not yet. And young Mike is still in the Air Force, stationed at Moose Jaw."

"How did you decide to become a lawyer? We were really young when you came up with that idea. Whatever was it that made you want to study law?"

"Oh, man, it was a long time ago. I don't know. I read as many Nancy Drew mysteries as I could get my hands on, and I read all of young Mike's Hardy Boys detective stories. Then I started watching Perry Mason on TV and I was attracted to the professional way he operated and – I don't know what else. Justice perhaps."

"You didn't want to be Della Street or Paul Drake?" said Sandy.

"Not a chance. I didn't want to be a secretary. Still don't. And it wasn't the detectives that were in charge. It was the lawyers."

"Ah, a control freak," Meg laughed as she spoke.

"Don't you ever want to be a doctor instead of a nurse?" Maggie asked.

"Yes. I have to admit it. Sometimes I'd like to take over, but most of the time I am happy doing what I do."

"We'll eat here in the living room. Dad and I are redecorating the dining area as you'll see from the mess. So, if you'll load up your plates and bring them back here . . ." Sandy ushered them into the kitchen. "I made chilli con carne, salad and my own homemade rolls. I thought it would be the easiest."

When they had reassembled in the living room, Caroline said, "What about you, Aunt Maggie, do you have a love in your life?"

"Just call me Maggie, please. Well, if you'd asked me yesterday, I would have said yes, but today I'm not sure. I've been seeing a guy named Anton for about four years. He's a sports trainer at the U of M and he works with the football and basketball teams mostly."

"How'd you meet him? At university?" Caroline was very interested in this new acquaintance.

"No. We met at this bar where all the lawyers congregate. He and his friends decided to check it out one night, and we got talking and we've been together ever since."

"So what happened? Oh, that is none of my business," Meg stopped herself.

"It's okay. I suggested maybe we should buy a house and settle down and he panicked."

"Oh," Sam said, shaking his head, "he's not in love with you."

"Maybe not. That's why I said I wasn't sure whether I had a boyfriend or not."

They talked until about ten o'clock when Maggie made her excuses and went home for the evening. She had just removed her boots and hung up her sheepskin jacket when the doorbell rang. She spoke into the intercom, "Who is it?"

"Anton. Let me in."

She could hear giggling and scuffling in the background. "Who's there with you?"

"Joe and Gary."

He sounded as if he had been drinking. Suddenly Maggie was afraid. Anton had been so angry when she refused to sleep with him and now he came to her place late at night, drunk, with two friends?

"I have some work to finish and then I want to get some sleep. Call me tomorrow."

"Snotty bitch."

She thought it was Joe who said it. "Good night," she choked and she staggered down the hall to her bedroom. She curled up on the bed with her back against the headboard and hugged a pillow for protection. The buzzer rang twice more but she didn't move. Finally there was silence. She relaxed and took a deep breath.

She's in her bedroom in the old house on the farm. She hears footsteps on the stairs and her body curls up like a foetus, a neonate with a stainless steel backbone. She is shaking and her heart is beating very fast. She wants to run and hide, but there is nowhere to go. She sees young Mike's face contorted in sexual desire.

The past wouldn't leave her alone. She wanted to shower away the filth from her body and wash the grit from her hair and her stomach ached with shame, but she didn't have time to process this new information.

Maggie gingerly approaches her busy mother. "Sandy has a new red dress for the Christmas concert. What am I going to wear?"

Mike's voice booms from the living room. "Ye can wear yer kilt. A girl like you don't need to think she's gettin' any special favours."

"Mike," protests Mary Ellen.

"No. No new clothes. You can't expect me to keep up with Sam MacNair. Everything he touches turns to gold."

"Well, I have to get her new shoes. These are getting too small for her."

"Alright. But that's it."

She felt her father's hostility like a blow to the chest, but didn't have a minute to think about it.

Maggie sits in the kitchen with her head resting on her left fist pushing apple slices and circular chunks of processed cheese around her plate. The Barnett kitchen shows the age of the house, a few plywood cupboards painted many times with thick coats of shiny white paint and a hand pump on the counter which draws water for washing dishes and clothes from the cement cistern underground, below the driveway. A clothes rack for drying bedding and clothing can be lowered from the ceiling when needed and a number of hooks protrude from the beams for hanging vegetables. The linoleum covered floors, chipped and worn from decades of traffic, are usually cold since there is no basement underneath, just a cellar for storing root crops.

"Can I have those?" Maggie points to a pile of junk mail left on the dull red kitchen counter.

"Yeah, take what you want," says Mary Ellen without looking up from her knitting. Her four steel needles click as she produces another pair of mittens, blue this time.

Her daughter takes all the paper that is blank on one side and carries the precious cargo to her bedroom, locking the door behind her. Before she is called to eat she has completed two drawings of horses, the outlines copied from her colouring book. After supper Mary Ellen is on her case right away. "Have you done your homework yet?" She addresses both Maggie and Rob. They shake their heads.

"Wal, you better get at it right after you eat," commands Mike. "Maggie you clear the table and help your mother first."

She nods in acquiescence, no point in arguing, no point in speaking. She watches her father pull his blue plaid shirt out of his waistband and hitch up his gray work pants as he leaves the table. He sits down on his black leather recliner and pulls out a yellow can of Vogue tobacco from his stash in the end table. From a package of papers, he withdraws three sheets and rolls three odd-shaped cigarettes. He lights one up with a wooden match and sits back to watch Don Messer on television. As soon as Maggie is finished with the dishes, she escapes to her bedroom and its locked door, saying to herself as she climbs the stairs, 'I hate him. I hate him. Three, four, five, six, seven, eight. I hate him. Nine, ten, eleven, twelve.'

Her bedroom walls are wall-papered in a beige tone with tiny clumps of pink roses and green leaves. The brown metal twin-sized bed is covered with a patchwork quilt handcrafted by Mary Ellen's mother, as was the rose-toned braided rug on the floor. She has a rickety antique dresser for her small supply of clothes and a small wooden desk Mike bought at the auction sale of another cash-starved farmer.

Despite its drabness, she enjoys being alone in her room. She draws more horses, large ones and small ones, pretending they come from a merry-go-round, and colours them and their tack in reds, yellows, greens and purples. She pins her works of art to the aged wallpaper and stands back to assess the workmanship. She makes a couple of small adjustments, and then she reluctantly turns to her homework, doing arithmetic problems twice to be sure they are correct, reads and re-reads about Dick and Jane's dream world, and carefully practices the alphabet, upper and lower cases. She is determined to keep up with Sandy.

Maggie stretched out exhausted on her comfortable bed in her bedroom in the sky and fell asleep immediately, but two hours later she woke up.

She is at MacNabb's Crossing school. Her friend Sandy turns around to talk to her. "Me and Trish are going to take Scottish dancing with Sarah's mom. Could you come too?"

Sarah overhears. "Are you? Really? Then I'll do it too."

"Why not? Then we'd have four of us. That would be just great."

Maggie thinks about that. "Everybody says I look like a boy, no matter what."

"Who cares? And anyway I don't think you look like a boy."

"What I really want is a horse, a pony of my own, but I don't know if my Dad would let me do both. I'll ask him."

12

Friday, December 8

AT EXACTLY ELEVEN fifty-six, Maxine notified Maggie that Anton in the waiting room, asking to see her. She had half a mind to tell the receptionist that she didn't wish to be disturbed. She hadn't planned to go outside since her usual lunch was waiting in the bottom drawer of her desk. He could wait till hell froze over. She decided to act the professional. After all, Maxine didn't need to know that she and Anton were having problems. She answered, "I'll be right down."

She slipped into her forty below coat and her sheepskin boots – if he didn't ask her to lunch, they should at least take a short walk. It was much too cold outside for a long one. Anton grabbed her arm and pulled her closer to the windows outside Maxine's hearing. "Why didn't you let me in last night?"

"Let go of me." She jerked her elbow from his grasp. "It was late and you were drunk. You had your friends with you. I was tired. Is that enough reasons?"

"You embarrassed me in front of my buddies."

"That is not my problem."

"Jesus Christ. You really think you're something, don't you?" His eyes were black with contempt and his lips curled.

Maggie stared at him for a long minute. "I never want to see you again." She turned abruptly and marched sedately past the receptionist's desk and into the stairwell, ran up to the eighth floor without getting out of breath and melted into a side chair. She rubbed her temples with her index and middle fingers, trying to avert the headache she felt coming on.

"Oh, Maggie, you are here." It was her boss, Jared Williamson, son of the firm's founder. "I can't make the conference in New York. Can you go? Are you free?"

"Perfect timing, Jared. I'd be happy to get outa town."

"What's going on? Okay. Tell me."

"I just broke up with Anton."

"I see. Okay. I'll take that as a yes and I'll change the reservation and bring you the agenda so you can get up to snuff. Okay?"

"Yes. That's fine with me."

She heard Rob's voice. "You rotten little bitch. You did it for Mike. Why not for me?"

When she and Jared discussed the issues being raised at the conference, she asked him for a few more days of her annual leave.

"Yes. Definitely. Take a whole week. I'll change the flight and make all the hotel arrangements. Be sure to get receipts for your cab fare and all the usual expenses."

"Thanks. I really appreciate this."

It is the second of September, the first Sunday of the month. The day begins clear and dry, a perfect day for harvest. The rolling prairie stretches for miles around the farm with only the blue outline of the Brandon Hills to the east and the occasional bluff or well-treed farmyard to obstruct the view. The wheat and barley nod in the breeze, thick and high, a bumper crop for sure.

Maggie spends the afternoon helping her mother to candle eggs and pack them in cartons to sell to the creamery in town. About four o'clock in the afternoon, Maggie is in her bedroom assembling her grade two books for school the following Tuesday. The sky suddenly turns dark and thunder rumbles in the distance and she hears her father's tractor approaching the yard. Sensing that something is dreadfully wrong, she runs to the kitchen where she can peer out the window. Mike has unhooked the swather and is speeding to the farmyard as fast as his John Deere can go. He drives up to the machine shed and slams the big doors tight. The chickens and ducks crowd into the poultry houses but the turkeys meander about gobbling and glaring at everything and everybody. Valuable as they are, Mike has no time to shoo them to safety since golf-ball sized hail is bouncing on the ground around him and a two chunks of ice hit the top of his head. He dashes into the new house, calling for Mary Ellen to shut all the windows.

Without any trees in the yard the house is unprotected from the hail except for the north side where the old house still stands. Mike takes the stairs two at a time. He grabs a pillow off their queen sized bed and holds it against the glass in their bedroom window. Hailstones hit the house from the west, bang, bang, bang, like guns going off, machine gun fire. Maggie stands as close to her father's right leg as she possibly can without touching him. He smells of grain dust and sweat, and every time he moves, gray dirt and chaff fall from the cuffs of his charcoal work pants onto the homemade rug on the floor. He still wears his yellow Stetson-styled straw hat, set at a cocky angle to the right side of his face. He lets go of the pillow with his left hand just long enough to toss the hat on the bed, revealing his creamy white forehead above the deeply tanned face. His jaws are clenched shut, lips drawn back to show tobacco stained teeth, and blue eyes blaze from his mask-like face. With a loud crack a window in Rob's room shatters and Maggie hears her mother and brother talking excitedly below.

Then as suddenly as it starts, the storm is over, along with their high hopes of a bumper crop. They slowly walk outside to assess the damage. The ground is covered with white ice, as if it had snowed, and the air smells clean and moist. The ducks waddle out scooping up the stones in their yellow bills and chattering away at their good luck. A few chickens follow, and then the regal turkeys. Three dead gobblers lay next to a coop and Mike picks them up ready to take them to the eviscerating shed to clean later.

Mary Ellen's garden is smashed to pieces. A few bare stalks of corn and one gladioli plant remain upright. The heavy crop of wheat to the east of the house yard is equally driven into the ground. There will be no need to swath.

"The great white combine," mutters Mike.

13

Saturday, December 9

IT WAS TOO brutally cold outside to leave the apartment, but Maggie couldn't stay indoors. Perhaps art would restore her soul. She parked the Buick in The Bay Parkade and, covering her face with her sheepskin collar, ran across Memorial Boulevard to the art gallery where she browsed through the gift shop on the first floor, and then climbed the stairs to the display galleries. Her heart rate accelerated as she strolled through the various galleries, not analyzing, just enjoying the impact of the colours and images, and her head filled with ideas for paintings.

When she had sated herself with artistic images, she hurried back to The Bay to have a toasted cheese and tomato sandwich and a bowl of chicken noodle soup and coffee. She spent an hour trying on clothes, and finally bought a shoulder bag made of blue leather and a pair of black corduroy pants. As she opened the door to leave the store, she bumped into a middle aged man wearing a black suit coat and an enormous gray scarf.

"Watch where you're going, buddy," he said.

"Buddy?"

"Oh, sorry, ma'am."

Maybe it was time to let her hair grow out. Or maybe it was

time she wore blue eye shadow and bright red lipstick. She groaned and so did her car as she started it. Despite the chills running up and down her spine, she sat inside and allowed it to warm up before driving slowly home.

Once in the warmth of her apartment, she went directly to her new studio and set to work. She painted all afternoon, stopping only to refresh her tea cup and eat a small container of yogurt. At times she thought she had help with the work, but dismissed the idea immediately. She missed Anton. Twice she picked up the telephone to call him, twice she hung up without dialling. She shed a few tears. Here she was, twenty-nine years of age, unmarried, childless, without a steady boyfriend, without someone to love. She thought of calling one of her friends but didn't. She needed to be alone to heal, or so she thought.

Perhaps if she expunged all traces of Anton from her apartment, she would be able to let him go. To that end, she filled a black garbage bag with sweaters and scarves and lingerie that he had given her and she tore up pictures of Anton and pictures of them together. She wanted to burn them, but because starting a fire was a safety hazard, she disposed of them in the trash can. She couldn't bear to throw out his gifts of jewellery so those items remained in her drawer.

At long last the tears came; first just a few dribbled down her cheeks, and then they came in a torrent. She had failed again. She thought she'd found a great guy and she was wrong. Apparently, her judgement of men was faulty. Maybe it was her fault the relationship ended, but damn it, he didn't own her. She still didn't know why she freaked out that night he came to her apartment with his friends. She wondered if she missed him, or if she missed having a boyfriend. She would have to go on alone, as always.

The day seemed endless. She grilled a frozen steak for dinner, but she didn't want salad. It was much too cold outside for equally cold food so she heated a can of pork and beans and ate the whole thing with her meat. Nor did she want to go to the bar as she usually did on a Saturday night. She didn't want to see Anton, so she relaxed with a book, this one a historical novel about the civil war in the United States.

Easter holidays are just over. She and Mary Ellen drive into

Sinclair's yard to attend a shower for Miss Lindsay. "Give me a hand here," says Mary Ellen. She carries a Tupperware container full of assorted dainties and a cardboard box in which she has carefully packed eight delicate china tea cups, saucers, dessert plates and the matching cream and sugar set – the pattern, Old Country Roses. Maggie totes another container full of crustless egg salad sandwiches.

Abby and Sarah have decorated the living room with pink and white crepe paper streamers, two pink bells hanging over the place of honour, a large wooden arm chair with a black leather-like seat. The serviettes waiting on the side table with the china are also pink to match the theme.

For the occasion, Sandy is outfitted in a pretty new dress made of pastel pink embossed cotton. It has a full skirt, squared neckline and puffy short sleeves tied with identical laces, and around her waist is a cummerbund of blue, green, red, purple and yellow stripes on a white background.

Maggie is upset, green with envy. She wears a full skirt with a green city scene on it and a white eyelet blouse, clothes she inherited from her cousin. The skirt is at least one size too large for her and she wants to hide.

Meg and Mary Ellen usher the new bride into the spacious but frugally furnished room where the ladies of the district have gathered. First on the agenda is a game in which the guests have to take the word 'marriage' and make as many words as possible with the letters. Meg wins the contest with thirty-nine words and receives a pair of tea towels as a prize.

Next Carol, the oldest female student, reads 'A Recipe for Living.'

Into each day put equal parts of faith, patience, courage, work (some people omit this ingredient and so spoil the flavour of the rest), hope, fidelity, liberality, kindness, rest (leaving this out is like leaving oil out of the salad – don't do it), prayer, meditation, and one well selected resolution. Put in about a teaspoonful of good spirits, a dash of fun, a sprinkling of play and a heaping cupful of good humour. Pour love into the whole mix with a vim. Cook thoroughly in fervent heat, garnish with a few smiles and a sprig of joy, then serve with quietness, unselfishness and cheerfulness.

All the wives nod in agreement as each ingredient is read. Maggie catches Sandy's eye when she reads good spirits and a dash of joy, things their teacher are obviously lacking. Maggie rolls her eyes in disapproval of the entire event, especially sandwiches with no crusts. She can't sit still and she wants to go outside to play, but she knows Mary Ellen won't allow it.

Then Sarah and Sandy pull a red metal wagon loaded with brightly wrapped gifts into the room and stop in front of the bride. In complete disgust, Maggie rolls her eyes again and stifles a giggle. Mrs. McClure opens each gift, gently folding the wrapping paper and placing it in the paper grocery bag provided. The bows and ribbons magically disappear. Rachel writes down the name of each giver and a description of the gift on a writing pad. As each gift is opened, it is passed hand to hand around the circle of ladies, so that each guest can see and admire each item – tea towels, a pickle dish, a brown teapot, a rolling pin and cookie cutters, an electric iron and ironing board, bathroom towels, muffin tins and pie plates, a Pyrex casserole dish, bone china cups and saucers, oven mitts, a red tool box containing a hammer, screwdrivers and a set of small wrenches.

When the last gift is opened, Mary Ellen and Abby Sinclair, laughing, show the new Mrs. McClure her bridal hat made of an aluminum pie plate decorated with all the bows and ribbons from the presents. Maggie's eyes meet Sandy's. They stare in disbelief, but all the women think it is cute and laugh as the hat is placed on the victim's head. A camera flashes as the teacher rises and, holding the hat to keep it from falling off, thanks everyone for coming and for the lovely gifts. She invites one and all to come visit her and her husband and she announces that they have rented the red brick house next to the post office while their new house is being built. She thanks again and sits down, obviously relieved that it is over.

Maggie gulps down a glass of orange juice and spies Sarah out of the corner of her eye. Sarah waves for her to follow. She and Sandy and Maggie play with paper dolls in her room until Mary Ellen is ready to leave.

"I'm not going to get married - ever," Maggie vows.

14

Sunday, December 10

ON SUNDAY MORNING, she treated herself by attending services at St. John's Cathedral, a church whose age and history and architecture attracted her. She arrived half an hour before the service so that she could examine the stained glass windows dedicated to early pioneers and the military, the carved oak pulpit and the white marble baptismal font. She wanted to explore the chancel, but the choir was having a last minute practice. Her first Anglican service, she was baffled by the use of the green prayer book and the congregation's role in the service, but she was enthralled by the choir and the celebration of the Eucharist. It made her feel blessed and strong, and she resolved to find a sister church closer to home.

On the way home, she picked up a chicken burger and fries and munched her lunch as she quickly packed her bags and then took a cab to the airport. On this trip, she had a lay-over at Pierson Airport in Toronto and then her flight to New York. During her wait times, she read the daily papers, did a crossword puzzle and the Scrabble challenge, and then turned her attention to a James Michener novel about the history of Hawaii. Before she drifted off, she wrote, patience, pat, pate, peat, neat, pet, ate, eat, eta, tea, pea, tee, pee, nee, pie, tie, pi, nit, pit, pita, Nat, cat, pint, pent, cent, pant, cant, pan, pane, pine, pin, tin, tine, tan, can, cane, acne, pain, Cain, cap, cape, ape, tap, tape, nap, nape, neap, nip, tip, apt, act, pact, ace, pace, ice, nice, pence, peen, teen, pen, ten, Pete, cite, paten, it, at, a, I, catnip.

The flashbacks had apparently taken the weekend off, and she landed at JFK International refreshed and ready for the meetings. A taxi driven by a young man with a Sikh turban whisked her to the conference hotel in Upper Midtown, to a spacious room decorated in off-white with medium blue accents, where she sipped on a large cup of herbal tea, unpacked and continued to read.

15

Monday, December 11

THEIR GRADE NINE home room and mathematics teacher is Mr.
Adamson, a black-haired somewhat paunchy fellow that Sandy
nicknamed Casey, after Ben Casey the television doctor. Maggie
sits second from the front in that crowded classroom beside the
windows with Sandy directly to her right. In their first year at
Sampford Collegiate, they and their classmates are the babies of the
high school and have survived the hazing called initiation and the
lost feeling and the claustrophobia brought on by being surrounded
by so many students. Today is the last day of school before Christmas
holidays and they have to endure fifteen more minutes with Casey
before they are free for ten glorious days.

The teacher stands up, raps his knuckles on the teacher's desk to
command attention and clears his throat. "I have two announcements.
The first is the results of your marks in fall term. The top marks
in science – Maggie Barnett, in math – a tie between Maggie and
Sandra MacNair, in all other subjects – Sandy MacNair."

Maggie and Sandy exchange grins and high fives.

"I am very concerned about you girls," Casey goes on. "Don't you
know? Statistics prove that girls who are good at math are freaks,
and I am recommending you two to a counsellor."

The girls look at each other. Neither believes their teacher. Maggie nods toward him as if to say that he's the freak.

"The second announcement is this. The school board has always had a rule that girls will wear skirts or dresses at all times. They have asked us to enforce the rule because they want you to look and behave like young ladies. You may of course wear shorts during gym and pants on the buses and while walking to and from school, but any girl who wears pants in class will be sent home. Class dismissed."

Sandy turns to Maggie. "What are you going to do?"

"Ignore them. Hurry up or we'll miss the bus."

Maggie remembered that scene as she dressed for her first day at the conference. She figured it was her right to wear whatever she wished, and she donned a black pantsuit with a bomber style jacket and a lacy royal blue shirt, grabbed her leather briefcase and strode to the conference with her head held defiantly. Her baffling memories left her alone for the rest of the day. As always, she enjoyed getting acquainted with other lawyers and discussing points of law, and had both lunch and dinner with some friends from law school. Back in her hotel room she felt the first symptoms of a headache, popped some pills and retired for the night.

She dreamed she is in the vegetable garden at the farm. She is raising several varieties of corn for her 4-H gardening project. Her father cultivates between the rows with the roto-tiller.

"Why corn, kid? Why not wheat?"

"Maybe next year. I love corn on the cob with oodles of butter and pepper and salt and I intend to plant my favourite next year just for the table."

"Actually my favourite is the tomato, tomato ketchup, bacon and tomato sandwiches, stewed tomatoes, broiled tomatoes. That's what I want you to grow next year."

"You don't choose. I do."

"If'n you want help with the watering and the weeding, you'd better grow what I want."

"OH, ALRIGHT."

16

Tuesday, December 12

ON THE SECOND day of the conference, Maggie took advantage of a cancellation to present a paper that she'd been preparing on her own time. It was well-received and she handled the question and answer period with aplomb. Afterwards, Alex Anderson, one of two J&W representatives in New York took her aside to present his compliments and he also asked her to attend the Wednesday night banquet with him. At lunch time, she sat alone, gathering her thoughts. Her mind seemed to be in a jumble, and worried that she might be getting another headache, she gobbled down a couple of extra-strength painkillers.

The afternoon session was especially interesting and she forgot all about her lunch-time malaise, but as soon as she returned to her room, the headache returned with a vengeance. With another dose of painkillers under her belt, she lay on her bed with a dampened hand towel over her eyes, the drapes drawn and the television off. She heard every noise in the next room and in the hallway intensely. Every sound seemed to occur right beside her left ear. She slept for an hour, had a bowl of soup courtesy of room service, dressed in her gray slacks and a red pullover and dress boots, and returned to the conference for another presentation, which she didn't hear.

Their neighbour Sam MacNair is sitting in the dining room of the new house, arguing with Mike about MacNabb's Crossing School. Maggie is now in grade six. The enrolment at the small school has dwindled to ten students and Sam tells Mike that it is time for the school to close. He argues that they will get a better education in Sampford. Mike yells back at him. He does not want the school to close and he doesn't want Rob and Maggie to ride a bus to school morning and night just yet.

Mike says, "How can you want it to close? You're the one always harpin' about the history of the Crossing and how you went to that school and how we're losin' everything to the larger centres – the elevator and the post office and everythin'. Now you want to close the damn school."

"Rob will be going to Sampford in another year. And George. We have to face reality. How can we afford to hire a teacher for ten students?"

From her bedroom, Maggie listens in horror. She does not want to go to school in Sampford, ever.

"Well, we still have your Christie and the Franklin kids to start."

"Yes, that's three more, but after that, there's no one that I can think of."

"Well, I'm going to vote agen' you, Sam. I don't care if you are the chairman."

"Okay. I've had my say. I don't want to cause any hard feelings here. I just want what's best for my girls."

Maggie felt her stomach knot up in fear. She didn't know why she was afraid to leave the Crossing School all those years ago but she suspected it was fear of the unknown, the larger school in Sampford with new teachers, new customs, different students and more difficult subjects. Her headache raised its ugly head again so she returned to her room and passed out as soon as her head hit the pillow.

17

Wednesday, December 13

THE CONFERENCE WAS into its third and final day when Alex volunteered Maggie to act on a panel discussing trade laws between Canada and the United States, a subject she knew well. One of the panellists had taken ill suddenly and a replacement was needed. She wasn't mentally prepared for it and at first she floundered for words, but that soon passed however and she was satisfied with her performance.

She escaped to her room at lunch time, the fight the high school girls had with the school board about wearing pants on her mind. The principal sent home the girls who lived in town. One of her classmates had to walk over a mile to school and she wore pants just to keep warm. The teachers said she should have changed in the washroom, but it was standing room only in the washrooms before class, girls smoking and talking and sharing experiences. It was just impossible. Then there was another friend whose family couldn't afford to buy panty hose and dress shoes. So, she didn't know who started it, but the country girls including herself wore pants – the principal couldn't make them walk home. She was surprised he didn't call her parents. Or maybe he did. Anyway it took them two years, but the school board finally gave up and let them wear pants, not jeans, but dress pants.

That memory acknowledged, she relaxed for a few minutes with a wet cloth on her forehead, and she barely had time to grab a chicken Caesar salad before the final presentations of the conference. She had packed two evening dresses, the high-necked green dress she wore on her last date with Anton and a black velvet number that showed off her bare back and slender shoulders. She chose the black one, adding a shimmering white knit stole and diamond stud earrings and bracelet, both gifts from Anton. A wave of sadness passed over her and she almost wished he were there. She pushed that idea from her mind and went downstairs to met Alex, who whistled boyishly when he saw her.

"Are you the lawyer Margaret Barnett?" he joked.

"Maggie. No one ever calls me Margaret."

"Maggie it is. Jared couldn't make it?"

"No. He didn't give me a reason, so I assume it was family related."

"That's too bad. I was hoping to talk to him."

"Is there anything I can take back to him?" Maggie looked around the banquet room, a confection of pale green, pale green chairs, pale green drapes, pale green dinnerware, amidst off-white walls and a light coloured turquoise carpet, a place for quiet dining and pleasant conversation at tables meant for four. The servers quietly and efficiently served the filet de mignon dinners and poured generous helpings from a bottomless bottle of red wine whose label she didn't see.

"No. I may come to Winnipeg before Christmas if I can get a flight."

Her conversation with Alex was interrupted by the introduction of the head table after which the conference chairman summarized the events of the last three days and praised everyone who had presented papers and made presentations. He thanked Maggie for pitching in at the panel discussion and for presenting her findings, she was grateful for the acknowledgement. She had barely finished eating when the guest speaker stood up to give his talk.

Alex sat to Maggie's left, but they didn't continue their

conversation beyond, 'Please pass the rolls' and 'Would you care for more roast beef?' As soon as the chairman said, "Thanks for coming. See you next year," all of her colleagues rushed off to catch their planes, and Maggie thanked Alex for his company and slipped up to her room.

She changed her clothes, picked up a number 4B pencil and her sketch book and remembered nothing more.

18

Thursday, December 14

THE NEXT MORNING a chunk of skin the size of a quarter peeled off her chin, leaving it red and raw, but not bleeding. It was rather bizarre but she put some lotion on it and forgot about it. After breakfast she strolled down the street from the hotel, window shopping, observing the people rushing by, the Latinos and blacks unfamiliar to her Winnipeg eyes. She admired the architecture, the old mixed in with the new, the tall and the taller competing for sunlight through the yellowy sky. Bits of snow and sleet stung her eyelids and her lips and the pavement was slippery underfoot, the cold air heavy with car exhaust and smog, yet breathing was not difficult. She slowly became aware that she was apprehensive of every man she met - whites, blacks, browns, it made no difference, but she paid no attention to men who were shorter than she was. She caught sight of a six-footer with shoulders made for football in the distance and ran across the street to avoid him.

She ducked into a book store where a volume about contacting the inner child jumped out at her, and she bought it and *The Affluent Society* and continued down the street. At an art supply store, she purchased a pad of water colour paper and a set of water colour pencils, but when she stepped outside the store, she didn't know which way to go. Where was the hotel? Left? Right? She didn't know. Nothing appeared familiar to her.

She had the sensation that she was very short, perhaps six years old. A child. She wanted to cry - a little lost orphan in the middle of New York City. She noticed an elderly couple, their white heads bent towards each other as they chatted, arm and arm, admiring the sights.

Tiring, she stopped and leaned against the door jamb of the next store – an arcade where perhaps a dozen pubescent boys were playing games, laughing and shouting, the noise frightening and confusing. Her brain felt like a tangled mess and she still couldn't remember whether she had turned right or left into the art store. She gazed up and down the foggy street. The telephone booth to the left looked a bit familiar and she thought there was a tall husky black man in it when she passed by. She crept along past the booth and farther down the avenue. Passersby simply ignored her but one aggressive woman in heavy makeup and gold earrings as big as golf balls bumped into her and strode on without stopping or apologizing. Maggie made sure the zipper was closed on her leather shoulder bag and hugged it close to her body. Her heart was beating so hard she was afraid it would explode and her ears would pop. The aroma of French fries and vinegar, she recalled smelling it during her mad dash. It turned her stomach, however, and her head began to throb.

She remembered crossing the street, but where? Was it the broad avenue with all the traffic or the narrower side street? It seemed to have been a long walk across with all the people running and fast-walking with her, so she chose the wide one and crossed keeping pace with the crowd, counting fifteen, sixteen, seventeen, eighteen. Instinctively she turned left and continued for perhaps five minutes. Her heart leaped when she recognized the suit she had admired on the way and she slipped into the store to check the price but decided it was too expensive. She inched along the street for another block and to her relief spied her hotel ahead.

With knees that felt like rubber, she entered the crowded lobby and fell into a plush green chair near the glowing fireplace. Safe in the refuge of the hotel, she warmed her cold hands and feet, her heart rate returned to normal and the panic receded. She thought it would be a really good idea to stay in a familiar locality and decided to stay for the rest of the week in the hotel, even though it was quite expensive. A smiling baby-cheeked man at reception assured her that Jenkins Williamson had booked the room for her entire stay and had paid her account by credit card.

"Really? Thank you. What a marvellous treat."

Back in her room, she sank into the down-filled cover on the king-sized bed. She didn't understand what was happening to her. She seldom, if ever, got lost, and she didn't understand why she felt like a kid. She was so afraid out on the street, confused about directions. She couldn't even remember the name of the hotel, let alone where it was. And the old couple, they were like grandparents to her. She wanted to take the stout woman's hand and join them on their walk, but she knew the lady wasn't her grandmother because Grandma MacDonar was tall and skinny like her mother and Grandma Barnett died before she was born. Why did she even need to think about it? It was a frightening experience.

She needed to talk to someone, but who? Anton? No. He'd shown his true character just when she needed him most. Rebecca? No. It wouldn't do to let a competitor know she was losing it. Jared? No. Sandy? No. Other friends? Lawyers too. Meg? Maybe. Dr. Dixon? Yes.

His name and number were circled in her address book in red ink. His receptionist told her that he was with a patient and took her name and number. Surely he'd call her even if it was long distance. To her surprise he called back five minutes or so later and she told him all that had happened to her. "And do you know what else? I can't remember any law. The materials from the conference may as well be in Swahili. They make no sense to me. I am not Maggie, doctor. I remember everything that happened, but I am not Maggie."

"Whoa. Whoa. Don't panic. Sit down. Take some deep breaths and listen. Do you lose track of time?"

"Yes. I seem to black out."

"What you describe … Well, it sounds like you may be a multiple personality. Do you get the sensation there's more than one person in your head?"

"A multiple what? Yes, that describes it exactly. What is going to happen to me? How will I ever cope?"

"Calm down. This is not something new. It is something you've always been. You are going to be just fine. Now this is what I want you to do. Write in your journal, sometimes with the left hand, sometimes with the right. Draw. Relax. Let the memories come. These alternate personalities are part of you and you want to make friends with them."

"Should I see a psychiatrist?"

"Well, maybe. But we'd have to find the perfect one. Some therapists don't believe there is such a thing as a multiple. Some would slap you in a mental hospital right quick and some won't believe what you remember. Others would fill you with drugs. How do you feel? What sounds right to you?"

"Working with you. I trust you."

"Alright. Take time now you're safe in your hotel room. Curl up like a big old cat and relax. Okay?"

She hung up the phone, relieved, scared. She leaned back on the pillows ruining their artistic arrangement, pushed off her wet shoes with the opposite foot and followed doctor's orders. She curled up like a cat. Suddenly she was a cat, a three toned tabby with the long hair of a Persian. She poured herself off the bed onto the floor and moved about the room with the grace and light-footedness of a feline. She practiced stalking and pouncing on imaginary prey, mice and rats and careless birds. She pictured long claws on her furry paws and she scratched young Mike's eyes out. She meowed and purred and rolled on the thick carpet. Maggie. Maggie the Cat. Meroooow.

Slowly she came back to her senses. Anger at young Mike coursed through her body beginning at the top of her head and ending at her big toe. She pounded the pillows on her bed. Anger spent, she lay back and cried. Her sobs wracked her stomach. She cried the tears of the artist who wanted to paint and couldn't, of Maggie the Cat who was powerless to defend herself against her older brother, of Maggie the lawyer who had to carry on for the good of the whole, and for the sad lost little girl. She cried because she hated her brother. She cried because he had taken advantage of her innocence. She cried because she wanted to kill him. She cried because she was totally alone to deal with a severe emotional problem, with Dr. Dixon to help and no one else.

She thought perhaps the idea for the cat's name came from the movie, *Cat on a Hot Tin Roof,* starring Paul Newman and Elizabeth Taylor. How she admired Maggie the Cat – feisty, articulate, defending herself and her husband, winning in the end. Beautiful. Sexy. Strong.

"Just call me Maggie," she whispered but there was no one to hear. When she ordered dinner from room service, she asked for a glass of milk. Afraid to go out in the dark and snowy city, she settled down to watch a movie on television but couldn't concentrate. Her chin was sore so she checked it in the mirror. Maggie the Cat had scratched it and it bled a little. She applied more lotion.

For a distraction, she chose to draw with her new pencils. A ready-for-slaughter turkey appeared on the page along with the old brick house on the farm and King watching from his favourite spot in the flower bed. She remembered the old house, two-storey, weathered yellow brick, hot in summer, cold in winter, sitting on the bare prairie without a single tree to shelter it. She also remembered the new house.

Mike bursts into the house one Saturday in March with news. "The Munroe place is vacant. They've up and gone to Vancouver where their son is – what's his name?"

"Ray. Raymond, I think," answers Mary Ellen, interrupted from her baking. Sitting on the kitchen counter, Maggie plops a tablespoon of dough on a metal cookie sheet. She flattens it with a fork and goes back to the clear Pyrex bowl for another scoop.

He plunks down on a white cane-backed kitchen chair. "I bin thinkin'. What if we were to move that house here to our yard instead of building a new one?"

"I don't know. Do you think Sam and Meg want to sell it?"

"Can't imagine they wouldn't. It'll just fall apart sittin' there empty."

"I wonder what it would cost to move it. We have to dig a basement one way or the other."

Mike reaches for the telephone, rings for the operator and gives her a number. "Mike Barnett here. Want to move a house. Kin you give me a ball-park figure?" He gives an approximate square footage. "And it's only a couple of miles," he adds. "Thanks – be in touch." He writes a number on the back of an envelope, adds another number and then puts a big question mark under it.

"What's it worth?" he asks himself as well as Mary Ellen.

"Call Sam and let's go look at it."

He quickly cranks the MacNair's number, two long and one short, and when Sam comes to the phone, Mike tells him he might be interested in buying the house that Sam and Meg have just purchased along with the six hundred and forty acres that surround the farmyard.

"Let's go. They'll meet us there in about ten minutes." Mike, Mary Ellen, Rob and Maggie pile into their Chevy. On the way there, her parents discuss what they might offer for the house.

The two-storey house looks like a Swiss chalet with its peaked roof and sloping roofline and two dormer windows on one side. Well built, it features a compact kitchen made for one cook, a spacious dining room and a good-sized living room, two bedrooms and a full bath on the main floor. The upstairs is divided into two rooms, the master bedroom and a sitting room. A washroom has been carved out of the area beneath the eaves, an ivory pedestal sink and matching toilet.

The two families look through the house moaning at the deep purple bedroom on the main floor and the orange shag carpet upstairs.

"Be ye wantin' to sell?" asks Mike.

"Yeah," answers Sam. "We've no use for it."

"Would the furnace and hot water tank go with it?"

"Sure. Whatever you can use."

Maggie watches from the dining room as the two men go off together into the tiny kitchen to talk turkey. Mike says something but she can't make out what he says, Sam responds. Her father speaks again. Sam nods. They shake hands and clasp each other on the shoulder and then come back to the living room.

"We got a deal, Mither," says Mike to Mary Ellen.

By this time Maggie is very distressed. "But it is a real long way to ride my bike to school," she wails.

Mike looks at her as if she had no brains whatsoever. "No, Mags. Didn't you hear me? We're gonna move this house to our yard and tear down the old one. Now which bedroom do you want?"

She certainly doesn't choose the purple one and she dances around the one she had chosen. It is so much bigger than what she has that she can't quite believe it could be hers.

Now it's Rob's turn to grouse. "So I'm stuck with that purple bedroom?"

"No," says Mary Ellen. "I'll paint it whatever colour you want."

"I don't want this pink," Maggie thinks out loud. "I like your room, Sandy, the colour of lilacs, but I don't want to be a copycat. I want mine white, Mom, then all my drawings will look good on it."

"I kin write you a cheque right now," Mike is back to business.

"Come on back to the house," invites Sam, "and we'll put on a pot of coffee. Are there any muffins and biscuits left?"

Meg nods, "Yes. There are. Do come. We haven't had a visit in a while."

"I can give you a receipt then and the house is all yours," Sam tells Mike as they lock up the house.

Maggie rides with Sandy to the MacNair's farm, so excited she can hardly sit still. She reads Ford on the dash of the maroon car.

"Uncle Sam," she always calls him that, "when do you think we can move it?"

"Oh, after the snow's all gone and the ground is dry enough, your Dad'll get the basement dug and cemented, and then the house can go."

She jumps up and down on the car seat, clapping her hands.

By now Maggie was exhausted. Following the instructions in one of her books, she filled the tub with water as hot as she could stand it and soaked until it was nearly cold. She wished she had some bubble bath or bath oil beads, even some Epsom salts. Still she couldn't free herself of feeling dirty. She shampooed her black hair twice and in the process noticed a few gray hairs growing near her left temple but she didn't really care. Depressed, she donned a silky blue nightshirt and lay on top of the bedspread, wide awake.

She is at a track meet at Carroll. Some of the students have left the fairgrounds to climb and slide on the school's fire escape, but she rests beside an overgrown caragana hedge, searching for four leaf clovers and waiting for the races to begin. Now twelve she is determined to win this year. The first race is the one hundred yard dash. When the starting gun barks, she starts out low just as Miss Adamson has taught her, and doesn't reach her full height until she is in full stride, streaking towards the finish line. She wins handily and pins her red ribbon to her white T-shirt. She also wins the fifty yard dash and the high jump. MacNabb's Crossing wins the baseball championship too, partly because Maggie pitched the first game. She is in heaven when she wins the top Female Athlete award as well.

19

Friday, December 15

TIME HAD LOST its meaning, she didn't always know if it were day or night, Friday night, Monday morning or Sunday afternoon. If it wasn't for the *Times* delivered to her door each morning, Maggie would have lost all knowledge of the time of day or the day of the week. She rubbed the back of her hand across her jaw and another chunk of skin came off. She couldn't remain within four walls, so she joined a guided tour that took her to Wall Street, the United Nations, and other points of interest and returned to the hotel in time to catch a movie on television.

While she was having lunch in her room, Jared called to tell her that Anton had visited the office, demanding to see her. "He was very rude, belligerent, wouldn't believe me when I said you were out of town. He threw a grocery bag containing your red sweater on the floor in the waiting room and stormed out, yelling, 'Well, here, keep her junk.'"

Maggie could easily imagine a confrontation between her mentally tough supervisor, tall, thin, receding hairline and all, and the heavy-set muscular Anton. Anton didn't have a chance.

"He's dangerous, Jared. He slashed the back tires on my car the day before I left."

"No. Really? You should have told me. How do you know it was him?"

"I have no evidence. I just know. I called the city police, told them how he's been behaving. They're going to look into it."

"Do you want me to draw up a restraining order?"

"Yes. Definitely."

"Okay. Don't worry about a thing."

"Oh, Jared. Thank you for covering my hotel bill."

"Oh, well. It was the least I could do for a promising lawyer such as yourself. Enjoy."

She went out for a walk. Snow was gently falling – big fluffy flakes landed on her nose and wiggled down the back of her neck. The stores and streets were decorated for Christmas in red, green, silver and gold. The people in the streets seemed to have slowed their pace and many carried packages wrapped in bright Christmas paper. She strolled past St. Thomas Church, a very old grey stone church with a tall square bell tower, and noted that it was an Episcopal church, a sister church to the Anglican, and that services were at eleven o'clock each Sunday. A chubby Santa stood at a street corner ringing a bell like the one at MacNabb's Crossing school. She drew out a dollar bill and just as she shoved it into the slot marked Salvation Army, she noticed that it was a ten.

"Damn American money. It's all the same colour."

The red-suited bell ringer laughed and she laughed with him. She felt suddenly generous. The smell of pizza, oregano, enticed her to a restaurant where she supped on meat lasagne and a glass of red wine. Normally she didn't enjoy dining alone but tonight she watched the people come and go, chatting and gesturing with their hands. She observed the clothes they wore, whether their hair was long or short, families, couples, business associates with their bulging briefcases and serious faces.

She felt lighter somehow despite the heavy meal, as if a burden were lifting from her shoulders. A young couple dressed in identical black toques and denim jackets necking in a corner booth reminded her of Anton. They did have some good times together and she was sad it was over between them, but angry too. It all started because she refused to have sex with him, as if she had no right to say no, as if she were his sex slave, and that was intolerable.

A sharp pain in her crotch like a red hot poker being shoved inside made her gasp. It seemed to scorch her all the way to her throat. She almost screamed out loud. She identified the pain - rape. Maggie made her way back to the hotel detouring at the dress shop where she bought the pant suit she coveted, anything to make her feel better.

20

Saturday, December 16

IN THE MORNING she couldn't remember what she had done the previous evening. Her documents and papers from the conference were now neatly packed in her briefcase and she found several drawings of the old brick house, the new chalet-styled farmhouse, the MacNairs' double house and MacNabb's Crossing School in the sketch book, signed Lynne Barnett in tiny letters at the bottom.

She now knew that other than herself there were four personalities, Maggie the lawyer, Maggie the Cat, the little girl and Lynne. She didn't know how many more were there, within her mind and body. Her life was becoming more and more complicated, and she got scared when she didn't remember what she had done. What if she did something really stupid? What if Maggie the Cat hurt someone? What if she got totally lost and couldn't find her way back to Winnipeg? What if? She had to stop that. She had survived as a multiple for twenty-nine years. She was sure she and her alters could get through that crisis, somehow.

She picked up the book about the inner child. Maybe she could find a clue in it about reaching Lynne. The book said to talk – out loud, say you want to speak to your inner child.

She lay down on the brown and gold bedspread and said aloud,

"I want to speak to my inner child. Lynne. Lynne. Could I talk to your please?"

Nothing happened.

"Lynne. Lynne. I like your drawings. They are very good. Why is the old house so dark?"

No answer. But her whole body began to shake and chills went up and down her spine. She heard a voice. She couldn't tell if it was inside or outside of her head.

I'm not Lynne.

"Who are you?"

Jane.

"Hello. I'm Maggie."

No. You're not Maggie. Maggie's a lawyer. You're Sally.

"Sally. Oh. I didn't know."

Do you want to know the truth? About young Mike?

"Yes. Tell me. Please. I need to know what happened to me. To us."

After school Mary Ellen takes Rob to Sampford to see the doctor about a possible ear infection. Maggie wants to go along, but her mother insists that she stay at home to set the table for dinner and do her homework, and she is sitting in the kitchen of the old house having a snack of cheese and crackers when young Mike, her oldest brother, grabs her by the arm and half carries his tiny sister into the living room.

"No, no, don't."

"Come on. You know you like it."

He pins her down on the couch and unbuttons her cotton blouse to gaze at her skinny undeveloped chest. He pulls off her slacks and underpants and spreads her legs wide, and despite her fear and loathing, her body responds. Maggie screams.

"What the hell is going on here?"

Maggie opens her eyes and sees her father's horrified and angry face. Young Mike pulls himself out and tries to yank up his shorts and trousers, but his father shoves him backwards and Maggie thinks they are both about to die.

"You slut, you little tramp, Margaret Lynne. Get out of my sight."

She cringes and curls up in foetal position on the couch, not wanting to get up without her clothes on.

Michael Barnett is a tall barrel-chested man with wide heavy shoulders and hips and large work-worn hands. Known in the community for his physical strength, he could crush his son with one blow but he does not. He sits on the coffee table, creating a bow in the centre, and glares at young Mike.

"I know it's bin hard for you. You was only four when your mother died and I wasn't much of a father. And you and Mary Ellen never hit it off, but damn it you can't take it out on yer sister. She's just a little girl and ain't growed up yet. You're supposed to look after her, not hurt her."

Mike obviously doesn't know what to do, but an idea slowly forms in his mind. "I need you here, Mike, but you can't stay. I'm sending you to Masonville. My brother kin use a good man and he ain't got no girls."

He strides to the phone and cranks the handle to summon the operator. He asks for the train station in Brandon. As soon as he has a departure time and an arrival time, he calls Jack in Saskatchewan, luckily catching him in the house. It is all arranged in less than fifteen minutes. While he is on the phone, Maggie wraps her slacks around her bare bottom and disappears up the stairs to her room and locks the door. Shaking, Maggie stays prone on her bed for probably half an hour, her entire body wracked with pain and fear.

"Jane, are you still there?"

No answer. She felt even dirtier than before – as if she'd been out in the grain field combining barley, itchy, filthy. She showered and washed her hair three times, rubbed her skin almost raw with the thick white hotel towels.

"Jane. Jane. Tell me. What happened next? Did Dad beat up Mike? Did they send him away? What happened next?"

Silence.

In her journal, Sally added Jane to her list of alters. She had finally found out what calamity had happened to her, her brother Mike had raped her in the living room in broad daylight and her father had caught him and it wasn't the first time it happened, and it hurt terribly. Her father called her a slut, as if she wanted it to happen. She thought, I am good for nothing.

Sally returned to the Italian restaurant where she lunched on spaghetti with thick slices of garlic bread, drowned in butter, a salad and a pot full of coffee. The world was a dark and unfriendly place. The day before, she saw people full of the Christmas spirit. Now she saw abusive mothers and Scrooges everywhere. Sightseeing was out of the question because it was snowing heavily. She spent an hour browsing through a small art gallery above the book store where she bought a thick book on Impressionist artists, a magazine and a *Globe and Mail*. Later in her sketch book, she tried to duplicate one of Monet's paintings, *Sunset on the Sea at Pourville, 1882*. She failed miserably. She ripped that page out of her book, crumpled it up and threw it in the garbage. The second attempt was better and the third she rather liked. She drew a pencil sketch of young Mike, his hair standing on end, his mouth drooping, his eyes black and hungry, his ears sticking out under a red baseball cap, worn backwards. He looked more like a clown that a bastard creep, but maybe it was appropriate after all.

The telephone rang bringing her back to reality. It was her colleague Alex who called and asked her to dinner. He apologized over and over for not asking her sooner, and they agreed to meet in the hotel dining room at seven. She didn't know what to wear. She had worn her black dress to the banquet. She had to choose between it and the long green wool she had worn on her last date with Anton. She couldn't make a decision, and her eyes filled with tears. She dabbed her red and swollen eyes with a damp facecloth. She wasn't Maggie, Maggie the lawyer. What if he wanted to talk shop? "Please come back, Maggie."

She had an idea. She removed a legal document from the briefcase and read the first two paragraphs. She understood nothing, but slowly it began to make sense. She continued to read, challenged, interested - Maggie again.

In her green wool, she counted the floors as she rode the elevator to the lobby, where Alex was waiting. He ushered her into the tidy dining room to a small circular table with a peach tablecloth which fell almost to the floor. A single white candle in a crystal holder gave off a shadowy light. The table was set with polished silverware in a baroque pattern, spotless china in white edged in gold lace, peach napkins of heavy linen. Waiters in short red jackets with gold buttons, epaulets and tails and black pants, served the many diners. Maggie decided on the grilled salmon – she'd eaten a lot of pasta lately and maybe this would keep her from gaining weight. Alex plied her with questions. Where was she from? Where did she go to school? Was she tops in her class? Where did she attend university?

"Hey, what is this?" she asked laughing. "An interview? Tell me about yourself now."

"Actually it is. I am sorry. If you're going to interview someone, you should tell them. I was hoping to recruit you for the New York office. Would you move here and work for me?"

"Oh, I don't know. I'm a little girl lost here. It's so huge, this city."

"No. You are not. You're just as at home here as you are in Winnipeg. I can tell."

"Leave Manitoba? Canada? Why? I don't have any reason to do that."

"Extra pay."

"No deal."

"Adventure. A chance to explore."

"Hmm. Now you're talking my language, but I don't think so."

"Well, think about it. I'll talk to Jared and I'll ask you again in the New Year. Will you keep an open mind?"

"Okay. Alright. I'll consider it."

They talked about the best places to live in New York, the cost of housing, life in the Big Apple. Maggie was complimented by the offer but she was ready to go home, home to her black and white apartment and her corner office, the familiar streets of Winnipeg. It would be lonely without Anton, she knew, and truth to tell, she was worried about her ability to focus on her work, cope with life in general and maintain an outward appearance of sanity.

That night, she dreamed about riding her bike to school in early spring, the ditches on either side filled with bright blue water, reflecting the sunlight and the cobalt sky, the air fresh and clean. The red-winged blackbirds and yellow breasted meadowlarks trilled from their perches on the cat-tails and mallards with their gleaming green heads swam about quacking at each other. In the distance she saw the ribbon of yellow roadway and heard Rob yelling at her to hurry up or she'd be late for the ball game.

21

Sunday, December 17

ON SUNDAY MORNING, she awoke full of excitement. Today was her trip to Yankee Stadium, home of her heroes, home of Mickey Mantle, Roger Maris, Yogi Berra, Whitey Ford. The #4 train found its way to the famous intersection of E 161 Street and River Avenue – Yankee Stadium. To Maggie, a diehard baseball fan, a diehard Yankee fan, this really was a cathedral, a sacred place, the house that Ruth built. The tour started at twelve noon on the dot at the press box. The view of the stadium was stupendous even if the infield was covered by a white tarpaulin, and worker bees were busy removing the previous day's snowfall. She wondered how the play-by-play announcers and reporters could identify the players from such a high perch – she preferred to sit behind the catcher so she could call balls and strikes. The group walked slowly down the stairs, three tiers of them, past the blue seats to the playing field and to monument alley. She ran her fingers over Mickey Mantle's face carved in bronze and remembered how she adored him, how she watched every game of the World Series and kept score on a make-shift scorecard.

She is back at Riverside Park watching the Canucks play the Brandon Cloverleafs. The hot sun strikes her face and bare legs and she knows they'll be sunburned. Located near the Souris River miles from any town, the ball field is silent, except for the crack of the bat, the ball smacking the catcher's mitt, the umpire yelling You're OUT, the chatter of the ballplayers urging on their team mates, Caw Babe, the spectators cheering on their favourites and shouting at the good-natured umpire. She picks up the aroma of oak trees and trembling poplars, the native grasses, hot dogs, fatty hamburgers, French fries and vinegar.

When the tour guide tapped her on the shoulder, she returned to the present with a start. He led them along the warning track around the field and back to the exit. On the way back to the hotel, she felt a presence taking over her body.

"Who are you?" she whispered, hoping no one could hear.

I am Sammy, said the voice. I played ball at Crossing School, scrub we called it. I rushed to school with Rob to be the first to touch home plate and declare my position for the game – second base. Rob always beat me there and took first base. Then as batters went out, I got to play first base, then pitcher, then back-catcher, then batter. When I went out, it was left field for me. We did it that way 'cause there weren't enough kids to make up two teams.

"Yes, I remember – I think. What are you doing? I'll miss my stop."

Never mind, says Sammy. I'm a boy and I can take care of you.

She looked around surreptitiously. Could anyone hear their conversation? If they could, her fellow passengers ignored her in New York fashion. The connection was made to her relief and she descended from the bus at her hotel, but her feet kept moving a block or two and into a men's clothing store. She tried on several pairs of blue jeans and chose a snug-fitting pair and a jacket to match. When she spoke to the shopkeeper, she discovered that her voice was no longer hers, that it had a deep masculine tone. The store clerk looked at her oddly but said nothing. She paid for her purchases and went back to her hotel room where she immediately donned her new clothes. Sammy took them back to the street where they had hot dogs, New York fries and root beer for an afternoon snack.

Maggie knew what was happening but she had no control over her body, an eerie sensation that she didn't like. She was being moved as if by magic by some other force that carried her along and she was too intent on feeling and observing that she didn't notice that she was afraid.

Sammy had his own agenda. He located a corner pub with several pool tables in the back. The one unused table attracted his eye. Soon he asked a pale looking youth if he'd teach him how to play and offered to foot the bill. His name was Roger and he turned out to be an excellent instructor. They played for a couple of hours until the place got busy and they had to give up the table. Sammy mounted a bar stool, swinging his leg over as if on a horse, a masculine move, and ordered a Budweiser and a plate of fries and gravy. He paid for Roger's supper too and then returned to the hotel. As they walked along, Maggie felt him slide away and she was herself again.

She ran as hard as she could without falling on the slippery pavement back to her refuge. She heard a voice say, You're going to kill yourself.

"What!" she cried aloud, starting two women on the street beside her. She waved them away. As soon as she was safe in her room, she flopped on the bed her heart pounding, her mind in a whirl. Slowly she calmed down enough to put on a pot of coffee. Sipping on her freshly brewed cup, Maggie picked up her journal to record the names of the alternate personalities for Dr. Dixon, and wrote #1. Something stopped her. Her hand was frozen. Then it wrote on its own.

'Don't put our names in your book. We don't want anyone to know our names.'

"Why?" she whispered.

She was scared to death because there were actually people inside of her who can take over whenever they wanted, it seemed, and one of them was a guy. She actually had a man inside her brain, one who played pool and had a deep voice and wanted to be in control. Perhaps that was why people mistook her for a guy, why she'd been told she looked like a boy. It was too crazy for words. How on earth could she go back to work at Jenkins Williamson? How on earth was she going to work without interference? She wanted to run away from herself. She didn't want to be Maggie Barnett. But then she guessed that was why she became a multiple in the first place. She moaned, "God help me." She turned on the large-screened television, too confused and tired to think any longer, and fell asleep watching a hockey game between the Rangers and the Montreal Canadians.

She dreamed she is driving westward on Portage Avenue in her black Buick. Anton is chasing her. The clock on the dash reads 2:33 a.m. The wide street is almost deserted. She is afraid of Anton and she goes through several red lights, narrowly missing a blue sedan. She pretends she's going to pass the off-ramp at Route 90, but at the last second she jerks the steering wheel to the right, braking sharply to reduce speed. She cruises around the clover leaf and heads south on Kenaston Boulevard. She checks the rear view mirror. Anton is right behind. "Damn," she says. She makes a sharp right turn at Grant but he keeps on coming. A red light, a semi - she has to stop. Anton hits her back bumper with his souped-up Nova as he also comes to a stop. She is trapped. He jumps out of his car with a giant screwdriver in his hand and he punches holes in her back tire. He leaps around the front of her car, jabbing the hood and leaving four or five dents. He slashes the other back tire several times. He comes back to her side of the car and leers into her side window. His face is contorted, his eyes black as coal, his mouth twisted in a cruel snarl. A Rottweiler. He raises the screwdriver over her head. It is dripping blood. He disappears. He takes off in the Nova, squealing his tires, and leaves her stranded.

Maggie woke up screaming. She checked the clock. It was 2:37. She knew then why she feared him and why she wouldn't let him into her apartment that night. She was afraid he would rape her. Did she have grounds? She didn't know.

22

Monday, December 18

MONDAY MORNING. HER last day in New York. Maggie picked up her Crest toothpaste and it turned into an erect penis with white semen squirting from its end. She gasped. The sight startled her of course but it was the deep anxiety that accompanied it that really took her aback. She couldn't remember being afraid of Anton's genitals. Or was she? It was hard to recall their lovemaking exactly, but she definitely didn't like his penis near her face, especially her mouth. Was she ever frigid, unyielding? Yes, there were times. There were also times when she was lusty, raring to go, looking for seconds, much to Anton's disgust, and there were times when she was playful, tickling him, and laughing – which he said was childish and stupid. There were also times when she didn't want to make love at all, but she went along anyways. That was a really stupid thing to do, she thought, and she wondered how many women he'd had sex with, thinking it was lawyer Maggie. She should have left him ages ago. A great lover he was not. She felt less burdened, as if some explosion or implosion has been averted, and at the same time more and more doubtful she could fulfill her obligations as a lawyer. She decided that she was not going to do anything that day that might trigger more memories. It was hard work.

She ordered room service for breakfast, eggs over easy, French toast, apple juice, coffee. As she drank her second cup of coffee, she read the newspapers but nothing in them seemed very important. She grabbed her journal and wrote:

New Year's resolutions (a trifle early)

1. Play slo-pitch or fastball or soccer in the spring.
2. Find a way to talk to Meg alone. I need support.
3. Find a winter sport – curling or skating or women's hockey.
4. Come back to New York during baseball season.
5. Get a dog.
6. See Dr. Dixon as soon as I get back.
7. Ask Sam (Sammy?) to teach me to curl.
8. Go to the farm for Christmas.
9. Confront Rob at Easter.
10. Keep on drawing and painting, maybe take a class.
11. Consider confronting young Mike.

She wanted to go to the farm, just once, to look at the stars since she couldn't see them in the city because of the streetlights and the lights in houses and other buildings. She also wanted her drawings and her kilts and dancing shoes and she wanted to find out why her parents hated her.

To accommodate her body's need for exercise, she spent an hour or so doing a yoga routine she'd memorized from a video tape with Ali McGraw, and instead of lying prone in relaxation at the end, she sat cross legged on the beige carpet, palms turned upward and resting on her knees. Ooohm. Ooohm. Her breathing and heart rate slowed. Deeper and deeper into her sub-conscious she went.

She is in her tiny bedroom in the old house. Her mother knocks on her locked door. She crouches on her bed not moving a muscle. She hears the Chevy leave the yard. Something is over. She hears another soft tap on her locked door.

"I made you some supper. I'll leave it here by the door. If you want to have a bath after you eat, go ahead. I'll keep Robbie downstairs. Don't let your ice cream melt."

She listens until she is sure Mary Ellen has left, then opens the door, picks up the tray of food from the floor, and puts it on her desk. She discovers that she is hungry despite everything, and eats most of the chicken noodle soup and egg salad sandwiches, and the ice cream from the top of the rhubarb pie, but decides to keep the rest for later. She takes her mother's advice about having a bath and fills the tub to the top with warm water and adds a generous amount of her mother's bath oil. She isn't supposed to touch it, but at that moment she doesn't care. She scrubs her skin with a worn face cloth and Lux soap until it is red and raw and shampoos her hair three times. She soaks in the warm liquid until it is almost cold, dries herself with a clean blue towel and puts on some newly-washed yellow pyjamas. Back in her room, she finds that the tray of dirty dishes is now in the way, so she removes it to the hall, keeping the glass of water and the pie. Then she locks the door.

Not ready for bed yet, she sits down on the wooden chair at her desk. Her homework is waiting but she can't face it. Instead she picks out a colouring book full of horse pictures and sets to work. After doing three or four pictures, she takes some scrap paper and begins to draw, trying to make an image of a horse standing on its hind legs. It turns out fairly well, so she tries one of a pony running in a field. She swallows her tears.

"Let me in, Mags," says Mary Ellen.

Maggie gets up, opens the door and then plops back on the bed.

"Are you okay now?"

She shrugs her shoulders; she isn't sure.

"Are you bleeding?" asks her mother as gently as she can.

Maggie shakes her head. Mary Ellen pats her on the arm.

"He's gone, gone out west. Your uncle Jack will pay him to work on the ranch and he'll be okay, and so will you."

After she's gone, Maggie locks the door again, and reads the story about Dick and Jane and their happy lives, tears streaming down her face. She finishes her arithmetic problems and then crawls into bed, but she is a long time going to sleep.

Long repressed anger took over Maggie's body and mind. She had been raped and humiliated and her cold and unfeeling mother made her some supper and asked if she was bleeding. Then she patted her daughter on the arm. That was all. No trip to the doctor. No call to the police. No cuddling in motherly arms. No words of support. Maggie didn't know the woman she called mother.

In an attempt to restore her soul, she spent her final day in the Big Apple immersed in visual art. Lynne did not reveal herself, but Maggie felt that happy glow within. She had another late dinner with Alex, but this time she wore her new pant suit instead of an evening gown. He didn't mention his offer of a position in the New York office again nor did he mention his wife. They took in a late movie after which she took a cab back to the hotel and he took another to his apartment.

She can hear Mike downstairs in the living room, roaring at young Mike, "Now you sit there and don't move. I gotta talk to your sister. Where'd she get to?"

Mike knocks on her locked door. "Let me in, kid."

Maggie doesn't dare disobey her overbearing father so she lets him into the small room. He doesn't say he was sorry for calling her names. He doesn't ask if she was okay. He doesn't say it wasn't her fault.

"Was that the first time?"

She shakes her head, not daring to look up into his eyes.

He doesn't take her into his arms to comfort her.

"Well, it ain't gonna happen again. I'm packin' him off to Masonville." He stomps back downstairs and enters the living room just as Mary Ellen and Rob arrive home. Then he hollers, "Mike, git your gear together. We're leavin' right now."

Maggie hears young Mike's footsteps on the stairs and she curls up on her bed hugging a pillow. He creeps past her locked door and goes into his room. She hears some smothered sobs and drawers being opened and shut again. After rummaging around for a few minutes, he lumbers past her door again, hitting the walls with his hockey sticks, crashing against the newel post, as if he were going off to play hockey as usual, and then he is gone.

23

Tuesday, December 19

BACK IN WINNIPEG Maggie's first action was to check her telephone messages. The first was from her mother asking her to come to MacNabb's Crossing for Christmas. The sound of Mary Ellen's voice filled her with fear but she let that pass. The second one of importance was from Anton in which he called her a frigid bitch and demanded a chance to talk to her. Not knowing how calling her names would make her more amenable to his requests, she resolved not to return his call. Amid the telemarketers' calls asking for donations to this and that, there was another from Sandy inviting her to lunch.

Settling into her favourite leather chair, she took a deep breath and returned Mary Ellen's call.

"You called?"

"Yeah. I did. Why don't you come for Christmas this year?"

"Is this invitation from Dad?"

"No. I want you to come."

"Okay. I'll be there Christmas Eve, late afternoon."

"Good. Rob and Mike are not coming, so it'll be just the three of us and Ross is coming and your grandparents."

Maggie was relieved to hear Mike wasn't going to be there. She remembered the fear her mother's voice brought out and couldn't talk any longer. She said, "I just got back from London and I'm kind of tired. I'll talk to you Christmas Eve." She had nothing else to say.

She then phoned Sandy and arranged to meet for lunch on Thursday and then asked to speak to Sam and approached him about giving her some curling lessons. He said he'd be delighted and promised to book some ice time at the West Town Curling Club where he was now sparing. She didn't call Anton.

You're going to kill yourself, forecast the voice.

I am going to kill you, said another voice, deeper, masculine.

Too tired to care what they said, she ignored them both, unpacked her bags, and snuggled down in her own familiar bed.

A few days before Christmas, the family receives a cardboard box in the mail full of gifts from young Mike, including a letter for Maggie. Since it is written, rather than printed, she is unable to read it and hands it to her mother to decipher. Mary Ellen reads: Dear Maggie, I am sorry that I hurt you. I have spent a lot of time talking with Uncle Jack and he showed me that I just didn't have my head on straight. I want you to know it was never your fault. It was all my doing. Uncle Jack insists that I go to school so I'll get my grade twelve after all. He also lets me use his half-ton truck to get to hockey practice and he and the boys come to my home games. I like the ranch with the cattle and horses but I miss you all. Merry Christmas. Mike.

"Did you hear that? You see. It wasn't my fault. Mikey didn't lie. He even said."

Her father has a strange look on his face. She doesn't know if it is contrition or something else, but he speaks not a word. The family gathers around the table to eat their steak supper, Mary Ellen and Mike at each end of the long table, Rob and Maggie along one side. Even though Rob is two years older than she is, Maggie is almost as tall as he is and with their black hair and tanned complexions, they could be mistaken for twins. The difference is in the eyes. Maggie's are dark blue hidden by long lashes, and her brother's bright blue, open and curious.

The empty side of the table might as well be set for the absent son, the conversation sadly lacking without him. Mike and his son "young" Mike have always dominated the discussions with man talk – crop rotations, types of fertilizer, machinery and its workings, weather forecasts, hockey scores, baseball statistics, football tactics. The rest of them have eaten quietly, seldom speaking, listening.

"So," starts Mary Ellen, "How are the practices going for the concert? Will you tell us what you're going to do?"

"Nope," answers Rob between bites, "the teacher said to keep it a secret. Then all the parents will be surprised."

"Don't you need help with your lines?"

"The older kids are helping us. Is there an old shirt of Mike's I can wear? Mine is a way too short in the sleeves."

"Probably. We'll see after supper." His mother gets up to clear the vegetables and meat from the table and returns with homemade saskatoon pie and ice cream and a pot of black tea.

Mike has been oddly silent during the meal. "You'd better git Maggie a new sweater to go with her kilt." He addresses his remarks to Mary Ellen, but his eyes are on his daughter.

"What colour, Mags?" asks Mary Ellen.

She almost chokes on her pie crust. "Green, I think green would go best."

"Pullover? Cardigan?"

"Turtleneck pullover with long sleeves."

"I'll see what I can find." Her mother looks happy for once. "I want you to look nice for the concert. How about pants, Rob? Did you try them on?"

Rob shakes his head. Mary Ellen nods to indicate they'll look into that too, although with Mike's heavy build, his pants don't fit the slender Rob.

"Son, when's your next game?" Mike has always been away with his eldest son and hasn't seen one of Rob's games.

"Friday night in town, seven o'clock against Bayville. Dad, could you come to practice? Right now there's only the coach out there and he needs some help."

"Okay, I kin do that." With no livestock to tend, Mike has plenty of time during the winter.

"What about Christmas? Should we invite my sister and brother and company?" Mary Ellen changes the subject.

91

"Mebbe we should go to Jack's. See Mike."

Maggie's stomach lurches. "Will he come back with us?"

"No. Maybe he can come back when he's eighteen and ready to live on his own," answers her mother. "Okay?"

Maggie nods. The fear hasn't disappeared and she can hardly finish her meal. She barely breathes while Mike calls his brother in Saskatchewan and the two men talk for more than half an hour. Apparently they decide it isn't a good idea. When he returns to the table, he tells them nothing about the conversation. He just says, "Call your kin. Invite the bunch of 'em. Let's have a houseful."

Rob and Maggie climb the stairs to their rooms to do homework. He stops at her door. "Mags, let me in for a minute."

"What do you want?"

"Nothing. This is great. We're not going out west. Mom's family is coming and we're going to have a big dinner with wine and everything and a real tree and we'll have to shop for presents for everybody."

"Yeah. It does sound great." She gives a big sigh of relief. Rob steps into the room.

He sees all her drawings pinned to the walls for the first time. "Hey, those are pretty good."

She feels rather shy about her work. He turns and goes off to his room to do homework and she picks up *More Fun with Dick and Jane*.

24

Wednesday, December 20

THE TELEPHONE RANG before Maggie had removed her coat and
boots on Wednesday morning, and since it was on her personal line,
she answered immediately. Rebecca didn't say hello, how are you, or
how was your trip? She just said, "I'm representing Anton this time,
and only this time. He wants to talk to you. Will you join us for
lunch at Alexander's at twelve o'clock?"

"Okay, I'll be there."

At exactly noon, she walked into the restaurant with its white
stucco walls and red brick arches and searched among the small
round tables filled with the lunch time crowd to find Rebecca and
Anton already eating their lunch in a hidden corner. Maggie could
tell from the embarrassment on Rebecca's slender face that the slight
was Anton's idea. The white-aproned waiter quickly offered her a
menu, but she put her hand up like a traffic cop. "No. Thank you. I
am not staying." She turned back to the table and addressed her ex-
boyfriend. "What do you want?"

"I wanna know why you broke up with me."

"I want to know if you slashed my tires."

"Sit down. You are making a scene. Why did you break up with
me?"

Maggie did not comply with his suggestion, but paused to consider her answer. She thought of saying that he had frightened her. She thought of saying he had acted like a total jerk. But no, she answered, "I don't believe that you love me and I do not love you."

"You said you did. Did you lie? Or were you just buttering me up?"

"I did feel something for you, but I don't want to share a home with you and I don't want to have children with you. Is that all you want to know?"

"No. You said there was something important you wanted to talk to me about. I want to know what it was."

"Well, you will probably never know. Bye."

She turned on her heel and walked out, revealing a pair of expensive looking blue jeans tucked into her sheepskin boots, and returned to her empty office and her cold lunch. Shortly before two, Jared called to ask her to join him in his office.

"How are you coming with your presentation on the conference?"

"I should be ready by tomorrow afternoon, if that's convenient."

"Okay. Let's make it for two. Now then, Alex called me twice asking if I would assign you to New York. Did he talk to you about moving down there?"

"Yes. He did and I told him I wasn't really interested. I have no reason to leave Manitoba or Canada, for that matter, but he insisted that I consider it until after Christmas."

"I see. He was very impressed at the way you performed at the conference. I was glad to hear it. Tell me. What do you want to do in your career?"

Maggie hesitated for a minute and then said, "When I joined the firm, international law was the area where you needed the most research, and I was quite happy to do it. But I have always thought I would be a criminal lawyer, arguing cases in court. I am somewhat restless, not quite bored, but I feel I need more action. Do you understand what I mean?"

"Yes. I do and I will discuss your assignment with the other partners."

Maggie returned to her office elated, glad she had spoken up. She slipped out of her office just before three and saw Anton's red Nova, its the orange and pink flames licking the side panels and hood, parked in the lot next to her office tower. She wondered if he was planning to accost her at her usual departure time of four o'clock, or whether he was still in Alexander's with Rebecca. She was late for her appointment at Dr. Dixon's office because she took a long route – she needed to think. At the medical centre, his daughter Charlotte called her in without much delay for her annual physical – checked her throat, listened to her heart, tested her reflexes, discussed her menstrual cycle, performed a PAP smear and internal examination (which Maggie hated), and ordered blood and urine tests. By the time she was finished, Maggie felt as if she'd been assaulted. Finally she had the chance to talk with her doctor.

"So how are you doing?"

"Well, I am getting over my panic, but I am still afraid I won't be able to cope with my job. It is really intense when I am remembering all that stuff from years ago and the others started to come out. It is a weird sensation."

"I am sure it is. Do you have any questions?"

"I hear voices, voices that say I'm going to kill myself. Or that I'm going to kill Mike. Should I ignore them? Tell them off? Talk to them? What do I do?"

"Was Mike the brother that assaulted you?" When she nodded, he continued, "I don't know for sure. I think you should try to talk to them, but they may not be able to hear you. You could try to address them in writing. Or look into the mirror while you speak. It is hard to say because I suspect each one is different."

"Will I ever be whole?"

"I don't know. I really do not. Do you have any idea how many there are? It's probably too soon to tell."

"Six or seven, so far. They don't want me to tell you or anyone else their names."

"I hope they will learn to trust me and then they may talk to me when you come to visit."

They talked for a quite a while about what Maggie had learned about the past and more importantly how she felt about the new information.

"Are you going to see your parents during the holidays?

"Yes. I decided to go, on a fact finding mission. My brothers won't be there. I will see my mother and father, my grandparents, aunts, uncles and cousins, perhaps some old friends. I am hoping being there will stir up some more memories. There's something more I have to remember, I am sure – something ugly."

"You have just begun this process. You have about eighteen years to recall so don't get in a hurry. Okay, it's probably a good idea to go home for the holidays, but if it gets too much, come back to Winnipeg immediately. Don't let it overwhelm you and keep writing in your journal."

"I will. Thanks. See you in the New Year."

On the way home she thought she caught a glimpse of a red Nova near her apartment block, but she was too busy with a new idea to worry about him. Rummaging through her drawers, she came up with two bathing suits, faded and ragged from hours in chlorine. She chucked them both in the garbage and, after a quick dinner of a pork chop and salad, went shopping for a new swim suit. The selection in Winnipeg in the dead of winter surprised her and she bought a black two-piece. Without doing any more shopping, she went home to search out a pool in the Yellow Pages. She changed into her jeans and a black sweatshirt, and shortly after seven, she left the apartment with Anton following her all the way to the pool but making no move to accost her.

In the women's locker room she checked out her surroundings, the walls two tones of blue that reminded her of a robin's egg rather than water, partitions composed of lockers with locks and keys hanging from the doors, and several women in various stages of undress who kept their eyes carefully averted so that they couldn't see the shape of another woman's breasts or the colour of her pubic hair. Quickly she changed into her new suit, one made for competitive swimming and not for the swimsuit edition of a men's magazine, showered the day's sweat from her hair and body, and walked slowly on the slippery floors to the pool area, and its smell of chlorine, the echo of voices in the high ceiling, the laughter of a group of boys playing with a purple ball in the shallow end. She swam laps for over half an hour, then challenged herself by diving off the side of the pool for ten or fifteen minutes and finally took five dives off the diving board.

She didn't want to leave the safety of the fitness complex, but she showered, dried her hair thoroughly to kill time, pulled her dry clothes over her damp body, and ventured out to the parking lot. The Nova was parked in front of the Buick, but Anton was nowhere to be seen. Quickly she stowed her gear in the back of her car and left, unable to believe her luck. She went back to the refuge of her apartment, and spent the rest of the evening wrapping her Christmas gifts.

She was so tired of looking over her shoulder for Anton wherever she went and it was not fair to be so afraid. Her muscles tensed, her heart pounded, her life changed because she didn't go out. She was depressed as always before Christmas. The gifts for young Mike and Rob and their wives would be late this year. She should have mailed them last week, but she didn't actually care. Mike never sent her a Christmas gift at all, and Rob usually sent a gift certificate of some kind, so why was she sending them expensive English wallets? It was a mystery to her what it was like to live in a warm loving family and what would it be like to wrap her gifts with love instead of bitterness.

She stowed the wallet she'd bought for Mike in the linen closet, high up and out of sight, hesitated and after more thought took the one she'd bought for Rob and put in on top of Mike's. She addressed a Christmas card to Rob and his wife and stuck it in her purse – she'd buy a gift certificate to somewhere – the Keg maybe, in the morning. That would have to do.

In an attempt to reach one of the voices, she wrote on the legal pad, 'Why do you say I am going to kill myself?'

Of its own volition, her hand wrote in a feminine script, very small and delicate, 'I want you to step aside and let me be in charge.'

'Who are you?'

'You don't need to know. Will you?'

'Who is going to earn a living for us?'

'Oh. I didn't think of that. Well, for tonight, I want to give myself a facial and manicure my fingernails and toenails and wash my hair and have a bubble bath. I'd like to put blonde streaks in my hair.'

'Blonde streaks? You're kidding, aren't you? That is not a good idea. We'd look like a punk, but you just go ahead with the rest of your plan.'

As she lay with hot cloths on her face, Maggie felt herself slip away and she didn't remember anything else until the next morning.

25

Thursday, December 21

ON THURSDAY SANDY was waiting for her in the lobby when Maggie stepped off the elevator. They decided on Italian food. Maggie told her friend that she had acquired a taste for it in New York. "So how are you? You look a tad stressed."

"Oh. I might as well tell you the whole story. Yesterday morning Dad and I were busy painting the kitchen when Jim barged in. He started yelling at me, something about turning down his offer, what a bitch I was, and I couldn't have his son and on and on. Finally Dad shouted right back at him, 'That's enough. I won't allow you to talk to my daughter that way. What is the matter with you?' Well, Jim calmed right down and he flopped down on a chair and said, 'Look. My father is really angry at me for leaving you and he has threatened to force me out of the company. I may not have any money to give you, not that you deserve any.' Of course, that made me mad. I kept my voice as calm as I could and I told him that he had married me and fathered three children and he was responsible for supporting us. He stomped out of the house. I don't get it. What happened to him? Why is he so angry at me?"

"I don't know. If he ever calms down, you'll need couples counselling just to parent your kids. Tell Tom about this, today."

"Yes, I will. And counselling is a good idea, if he'll agree to it. It is over and I have to move on. His parents came to see me last week and his father wrote me a cheque for ten thousand dollars and I'm so grateful and now I can live without borrowing from my own parents for a while. He also offered me a job – in one of his companies that Jim has nothing to do with. I would be an accounting clerk and I could take courses and move up as time goes by. There's a day care centre in the building so Melissa could come to work with me and my cousin has agreed to look after Caroline and Danny after school when Mom and Dad are at the farm. I was always good with numbers. Remember that teacher who said girls who could do math were freaks?"

"Yes, I do remember him. Jerk. He was the freak. That sounds great, but I thought you were going to teach dance."

"I am going to do both. I will have ten students after Christmas and Dad is fixing up a studio in the basement. All I have to do is figure out when to have the classes. Saturday mornings would be perfect but Danny has hockey games then – not every Saturday, but sometimes. I can't be two places at once."

"I'll tell you what. If Sam and Meg are at the farm, I'll take Danny to hockey, how's that?"

"Oh, thank you. He'll love it. You know, I was going to ask you if you'd like to help with the dancing. They're all beginners and I could use a hand getting them started. It would be fun to work with you."

"Oh, man. I hardly remember how."

"It would come back to you really fast, like riding a bike."

"I haven't ridden one of those in years either. I'd probably kill myself. Okay. Are you just having classes once a week?"

"No. Wednesdays at 6:30. Are you free then?"

"Yes, if I'm not in London or New York or somewhere else."

"Great. Thanks."

Maggie was back in her office before it occurred to her that she hadn't said one thing about herself during the entire meal, but she wasn't ready to share her problems with Sandy anyway. She took the opportunity to phone Meg. "I need to talk with you. Would it be possible for us to get together? Alone?"

"Of course. Give me your number and I'll call you." Meg didn't ask any questions.

That was easier than expected.

Her presentation went as planned that afternoon. Jared remarked that she was a good speaker and that all her supporting handouts were well thought out and appropriate and she was feeling pretty good when left the office. As she was leaving the office parking lot, she spied the red Nova, but Anton didn't follow her. At Canadian Tire, she bought some hockey skates - the large picks on the figure skates appeared much too dangerous. While she was waiting for the blades to be sharpened, she browsed through the hockey equipment, wondering if there was a women's hockey team she could join. She remembered being dragged to Rob's home games, whether she wanted to go or not.

She decided to test her new purchase. Maybe if she stayed really busy, the past would leave her alone. She hurried home, changed into new blue jeans and drove to an outdoor rink nearby. She sat on an ice covered bench, removed her snow boots exposing her feet to the frigid weather, her bare fingers numbing as she drew the laces tight. She pulled her toque over her ears, tied her knit scarf over her mouth and stood up expecting to fall at any moment. After two or three rounds, she found her stride and skated for half an hour. Her ankles were protesting by then.

It is Saturday afternoon. She is eleven. She and Rob and Sandy and her sister Trish are skating at the hockey rink in Sampford. Rob challenges her to a race, one lap around the rink. Trish hollers 'One, two, three, go,' and they start together. He is a strong skater now because he plays hockey and he wins by one stride.

"Okay, I challenge you, bro - once around the rink doing crossovers."

Again Trish acts as starter and this time Maggie wins. Sarah Sinclair and her twin brothers skate onto the ice surface. Right away Peter grabs Maggie's favourite ear warmers, handmade by Mary Ellen from light blue wool, and she chases him around the rink but she cannot catch him. He plays her as a cat plays a mouse, she almost catches him and then away he skates again, and she is furious. After a while she tires of the game and goes into the waiting room for an

Orange Crush and a chocolate bar and he sits on a bench twirling her ear warmers around his index finger, watching her and grinning.

"Come and get it, Maggsy."

She hates being called Maggsy but she doesn't let him know that. She finishes her snack and skates with the girls for the rest of the afternoon. Peter keeps her ear warmers until Monday morning.

Maggie thought she'd been a dummy. She didn't see that Peter liked her, but he surely had a funny way of showing it. He stole her things, pulled her hair, punched her upper arms until they bruised, hit baseballs straight at her - and always picked her for his team in soccer. Then the Sinclairs lost their farm to the bank and moved out of the neighbourhood. She missed Sarah and she missed their mother, but she missed Peter like a hole in the head.

She was worried about going home for Christmas. Would her father be as mean as ever? And her mother, would she show Maggie that she cared, just once? It seemed to Maggie that she was punishing herself by going to the farm, but then it was a fact-finding mission.

Shingle, single, sling, sing, sin, in, I. Danger, anger, rang, ran, an, a. Shoulder, holders, solder, older, role, ore, or, O.

26

Friday, December 22

WHEN MAGGIE PICKED up her pay cheque on the Friday, she was surprised to find that she had been given a substantial raise and also a Christmas bonus of five hundred dollars. Instead of going home, she deposited her cheques in the bank and then went to the Polo Park Mall. She searched through all the dresses in Sears and The Bay and every shop in between, looking for a little black dress for her date with Alex, but all those she tried on were so short that she felt uncomfortable. Finally she chose a sweeping black organza skirt that fell halfway between her knees and ankles and a low cut royal blue knitted top, not that she had much cleavage to show off, a navy skirt suit for work and church with a white satiny blouse to go under it, and a pair of navy pumps. She felt someone else's happiness with the new clothes.

Extra hungry after her shopping trip, she grilled a pork chop and boiled a few potatoes for supper and she was chopping up cauliflower for a salad when Meg called, offering to come by in about half an hour. She was there in twenty minutes.

"Thank you for coming. I really need to talk."

"Is it about Sandy? "

"Oh, no. I hope I didn't scare you. No. It's about me. Please sit down. I've made some green tea. Would you like some?"

"Yes. Please. I have to say your apartment surprises me. All black and white?"

"It was even starker than this until last week. I didn't even have the books in here before. What did you expect my place would look like?"

"Paintings. Earth colours. More books. Mementos of your travels."

"That's interesting. I am going to change it, or perhaps buy a house. But you didn't come to discuss my interior design. I don't know where to begin. I have forgotten just about everything that happened to me before I came to Winnipeg for university. My mind is a complete blank, or it was until I saw Sandy again. Since then I've been having these horrible flashbacks and I think I am going mad."

"Really? What are you remembering that is so difficult?"

"Well, the worst thing is . . . I remember young Mike . . . He raped me when I was in grade one."

"Oh, no. I am so sorry, Maggie. So that's why he left for the west so suddenly."

"Yes. Dad caught him and kicked him off the farm, told him he can't come back until he's eighteen and can live in his own place. Do you know anything about multiple personalities?"

"A little. Did someone diagnose you as a multiple?"

"Dr. Dixon. But I know it's true."

"Oh, dear. No wonder you want to talk. How can I help?"

"I don't know. I just need support, I guess."

"Well, you have it. And Sam's too. Are you going to tell Sandy? She can be a support when we're at the farm. You can't phone me there, well, you can, but you can't say anything too personal. Darn party lines. But you can write."

"Thank you. I feel better already. I needed to tell someone, but please don't tell Sandy, not yet."

"We'll see you through this." Meg touched her arm tentatively and then gave her a big hug.

Maggie felt less alone after Meg's visit. At least there was one person that understood what was happening to her. Alex called her later that evening asking her to go out with him after the office party.

"Are you a mind reader? I was just thinking about the party. I just bought myself some new blades. Um, Alex, I don't understand. Am I being recruited or courted? I was under the impression you were married."

"Oh. I assumed you knew. My wife died in a car accident some years ago. I have a little girl who just turned six."

"I am so sorry. I don't pay much attention to office gossip."

"Will you go out with me?"

"Okay. Yes. I have just recently broken up with someone. I don't know if I am ready for a new relationship, but I enjoy your company."

"Good. It's a date then."

27

Saturday, December 23

SATURDAY MORNING SAM, Meg, Sandy and her three children were waiting in the lobby of the West Town Curling Club when Maggie arrived dressed in a new navy down-filled vest over a red fleecy, blue jeans and the Yankees baseball cap she'd bought in New York. Sammy had come out to play.

An experienced curler, Sam showed them how to cover their left running shoes with duct tape to create a slider, and Brian the manager provided them with some cast-off brooms as well as some smaller lighter rocks for Caroline and Danny. Meg entertained Melissa in the lobby while Sam gave Maggie, Sandy and the two children instructions on throwing a rock, on in-turns and out-turns, scoring and brushing. Maggie noticed that her voice was much lower than normal, but Sam and Sandy didn't seem to notice. Caroline looked at her strangely, but she hardly knew the girl so how would she know there was anything different about her?

They practiced for a couple of hours. As they were leaving, the rink manager approached Sandy and Maggie. "The Monday night draw is for women only, and they are short a few curlers. Why don't you two sign up?"

Maggie agreed right away but Sandy wasn't sure she would

have time with dancing and working and caring for three children, but Caroline and Danny encouraged her to go so they signed up, enthusiastically. Sam took them to the pro shop where they were outfitted with stretchy black pants, proper curling shoes, gloves and brushes.

"Are you coming to the farm for Christmas?" Sam asked gingerly.

"Yes. I guess so," answered Maggie. "Why?"

"We could rent some ice in Sampford, I'm sure."

"My father hasn't retired yet?"

"No. Ice makers are hard to find."

"Oh. Okay. That sounds like a great idea. Christmas is on Monday. I will probably be there most of the week." She hardly noticed when Sammy left the scene.

That night she relaxed in front of the television, rubbing A-535 into her sore muscles.

It is Christmas at MacNabb's Crossing. In the living room of the brick farmhouse, Maggie and Mary Ellen have decorated the blue spruce Christmas tree with red ornaments and lights and gold tinsel ropes and under it a tree skirt that Mary Ellen made, red Santas on white fake fur, piles of presents waiting for the big day. Rob and Maggie awaken early and rush out to see if the real Santa showed up while they were sleeping. Rob plugs in the lights and by their red light they examine their gifts, shaking and listening and poking. Mike calls, "Wait for us," and a few minutes later Mary Ellen joins them in her flannel robe and Mike fully dressed. Young Mike is conspicuously absent. Maggie is surprised to find a six-foot easel, a beginner's oil painting set, a package of canvasses and new skates. She helps her mother prepare for the dinner, setting the table, mixing the dressing for the duck, and a hundred other errands. Then her mother shoos her out of the kitchen and she and Rob entertain themselves playing Parcheesi and Snakes and Ladders and Chinese checkers. Grandma and Grandpa MacDonar and Uncle Ross and Aunt Irene and their two children arrive about two in the afternoon to spend the day.

In the presence of her family, her mother talks and laughs and she and Ross tell stories about their childhood. Grandpa and Mike talk about the war and the depression, and Maggie drinks it in like water. Uncle Ross challenges her to several games of Chinese checkers, but she can't beat him no matter what she does and it is fun to try. She plays hide and seek with the twins Annie and Alex. For Christmas dinner they have one of Mary Ellen's ducks, roasted to perfection, with mashed potatoes, gravy and dressing, a green salad, corn and peas, homemade orange sauce and icy apple juice to drink, and for dessert, saskatoon upside down pudding with vanilla ice cream.

Later in the afternoon, Maggie rummaged through her disorganized jewellery box and end table drawers and found some diamond studs, a gift from Anton, but she didn't want to wear those. She did find a sterling silver pair that was a very close match to her blouse. She couldn't remember where they came from.

Alex rang the bell promptly at six thirty. He showed her to a yellow cab waiting at the curb.

"Oh, I never thought. We could have taken my car."

"No. When I take out a lady, I provide the transportation. Besides I can indulge in good wine if I don't have to drive. Is the Keg okay?"

"Yes, of course."

"So did you have a good time at the party this afternoon?"

"Yes. I really did. I met three lawyers and two paralegals from the firm that I didn't know before, since I spend most of my time with Jared and my clients. They play hockey on a women's team and they invited me to join them. They also promised to call me when they go out to lunch on Fridays. I spend so much time alone – this will be good. I saw you there with your daughter. Don't you skate?"

"No. I was too busy with my nose in a book to do any sports, really. But I want my little girl to learn."

"She's cute. What's her name?"

"Angie. She looks just like her mother."

"So what brings you back to cold old Winnipeg?"

"I came to talk to the partners. We have two choices - either expand the office in New York, or close it and form a partnership with another firm. It's becoming too heavy for me and Harry to handle."

"What did they say?"

"Same old. Same old. We'll discuss it at our next meeting. Thanks for bringing it to our attention. Actually I'm thinking of moving back. I'd like to raise my daughter as a Canadian, and here I have my mother and sisters for backup."

"Where do they live? They aren't in Winnipeg, are they?"

"No. Miami. By the way, I'd like to see you on New Year's Eve, too, if you're not busy already."

"Okay. Why don't you and Angie come to my place? We'll watch movies and play games and eat hot dogs, if that's what she likes."

"Actually pizza is her thing. That sounds great."

They talked until about ten and then he jumped up and said he had to get going. He had promised his daughter he'd see her in the morning and he had to drive back to Miami that night.

Later Maggie tossed and turned, and turned and tossed, unable to slow down her racing thoughts long enough to fall asleep. She remembered every instruction that Sam gave on curling. She thought about little Meg and big Sam and the double house on their farm and their Ford cars and their Ford trucks and the well-kept farmyard surrounded by trees and their herd of cattle and the work horses. She recalled by rote everything that Alex said about New York and coming back to Canada, and meeting colleagues that she'd never seen before because she was too busy with clients in her corner office.

Mike takes his John Deere combine and tractor to MacNair's as soon as Sam's crop is dry enough to combine following the hail storm. Maggie perches on the fender holding on for dear life. Mike slows down but doesn't quite stop so that she can jump off at the house. Sam grins and waves 'Come on' to Mike and the two outfits move down the lane towards the north field.

All morning, Maggie, Sandy and Trish play with dolls in Sandy's room, a treat for Maggie who is not allowed to have dolls, she doesn't know why. The two dust covered men come to the house shortly before noon for dinner, and Meg feeds them a rib-sticking meal of stuffed pork chops, mashed potatoes, corn, pickles and salad. For dessert she serves fresh peaches with plenty of cream and brown sugar and chocolate cake with chocolate icing and hot black tea to drink.

Maggie and Sandy eat quietly and listen to the man talk. Sam listens to the livestock market report at precisely twelve o'clock on the radio, while everyone else waits in silence until it is over.

"You have insurance?" he asks Mike without taking his eyes off his plate.

"Some. Not enough. Should be able to get by."

"Heard from the railroad?"

Mike answers, "Not yet."

"Hear we need an ice maker at the curling rink. Simmons is moving to Winnipeg. She doesn't like it here."

Mike stops with his fork in mid-air and stares at his host. Before he eats his dessert, he asks, "Use your phone?"

"Sure." Sam points to the old wood speaker phone on the kitchen wall.

"Yeah. Mike Barnett here. Word has it you need an ice maker."

The rest of the group can't help but eavesdrop but he lowers his voice and they can't hear the last part.

"Think I got it," he announces as he returns to the table.

"You're damn good at it," Sam says. "You should get it."

Before leaving, he asks Meg to bring supper to the field. "Just come north around the farm to the fence line here at the half mile. There's an approach there where you can come onto the field." He draws a rough map for her.

"Okay," answers a nervous Meg.

"And don't drive over the heavy straw. It can bunch up under the car and start a fire. Come towards us at a corner where it's thin. Just go to where it hasn't been combined and wait. The combines will come to you. Okay?"

"Yes, I guess so."

He fills a picnic jug with cold water and grabs some plastic tumblers from the cupboard. "See you about five or five thirty." As he leaves the house with Sandy and Maggie tagging along, John Sinclair drives into the yard in his three-ton Chevrolet. "Need a trucker?" he inquires, his white teeth gleaming from a tanned and dusty face.

"Glad to have you. Listen, I'll pay you guys," Sam offers.

"Won't take it." John and Mike speak almost in unison.

"Well then, make sure your truck's full of fuel when you leave,

John, and your tractor too." He looks at Mike. They nod once for okay – no need for words.

Maggie and Sandy beg John to let them ride with him, and he laughs and tells them to jump in. He seems happy to have company and climbs into the back of the truck to retrieve some wheat for them to chew like gum. Maggie keeps hers for quite a while, but Sandy says it's dirty and throws it out. The two friends watch the combines and ply John with questions. They stay in the truck because it isn't much fun to run around in the wheat stubble. The sharp ends dig into their tender ankles, right through their socks. Mack, Sam's Border collie, stays beside the truck in the shade, occasionally getting up to give a gopher chase or to track an unknown quarry.

It is hot and dusty and grasshoppers jump in front of the truck as they collect the grain from the combines. When the truck box is full, John drives to a row of steel cone-topped grain bins along the fence close to the farmyard and backs the truck up to the auger, which rests in a triangular shaped metal hopper and reaches up to the hole in the top of the bin. He lifts the hoist of the truck to make the box empty faster. The auger has its own sound, putt, putt, putt, and dust flies. A steady golden stream of wheat flows into the granary.

As instructed, Maggie and Sandy stay well out of the way so they won't get injured. They don't want to be in the dust storm anyway. They are getting rather hungry by the time Meg gingerly makes her way onto the field in her new 1955 Ford sedan. The trunk of the car serves as a smorgasbord table and Meg pours the tea for the guys and juice for the girls.

There is almost no conversation as the three farmers wolf down their food. Sam finishes eating first and before he is done chewing, he reaches into his shirt pocket for a blue package of Players cigarettes and offers one to each of his neighbours, who stick them over their right ears. Rummaging in his pants pocket, he comes up with a wooden match and lights it on the sole of his work boot. He sits back with his large mug of black tea and inhales the smoke deep into his lungs. As soon as he has smoked it to his fingertips, he goes right back to his tractor. Mike and John, now shy in Meg's presence, gulp down their tea and climb into the truck to smoke. Shortly thereafter,

Mike takes off on his John Deere and John drives the grain truck further down the field where he expects to be needed.

Meg sits for perhaps ten minutes watching the combines gobble up the swaths in their pickups. She watches the wheat streaming from the spouts on top into the hoppers below. Dust and straw and chaff spew from the backs of the combines leaving a row of yellow straw to be baled later. Maggie and Trish are as entranced as Meg.

"Let's go, Mom," says Sandy.

"In a minute. You know what?" she asks no one in particular. "For the first time, I am glad I am learning to drive."

Christie is getting fussy so they leave the field but instead of going directly to the house, they take Maggie home.

28

Sunday, December 24

MAGGIE ADMIRED THE purple sunset on the way to her parents' farm on the afternoon of Christmas Eve. She listened to the radio, sang along with her favourite songs, and tried not to think about her father or her mother or the reception she'd get at her childhood home. It was dark by the time she arrived about five, but she caught a glimpse of a snowy owl perched on a hydro pole as she passed, high beams shining on the blue snow. She parked the Buick in the driveway and looked around. Since she left home at eighteen, Mary Ellen had replaced the assortment of poultry houses with two long low chicken barns painted white to match the asphalt shingles. Her father had also invested in the farm – five shiny cone-topped grain bins formed a line from the machine shed across the yard. The farmhouse, however, needed a coat of paint.

The current King barked in frenzy and wouldn't let her anywhere near the back door until Mary Ellen called him off. She just opened the door for her daughter and returned to a tall stool in the galley kitchen to resume a telephone conversation. She waved at Maggie as she dropped her suitcase in the back entrance. After pacifying King with a doggie treat in an attempt to make friends, Maggie proceeded through the dining room to the living room, where she tucked her gifts for the family under the plastic Christmas tree decorated with blue satin balls. She went on down the hall into her former bedroom where she immediately delved into the closet and pulled out several kilts and blouses that she had worn years before. She tried on a purple Lindsay tartan and determined that, if she removed two tucks, she could still wear it. She laid that one on top of her luggage and was busy packing the rest in a Reitman's shopping bag when her mother joined her.

"Hi. How are you? What are you doing with all this?"

"Merry Christmas. I'm okay. Sandy is teaching dancing and I thought she could use this stuff. There's no point in letting it sit here. I wonder where the shoes are."

"Here. In this bottom drawer."

Mary Ellen Barnett was a slim beanpole of a woman whose prematurely grey hair was parted down the centre and held at the nape of her neck by an elastic band, and she dressed in worn shapeless cotton housedresses and aprons during the day even though she had newer smarter clothes in her closet. Her dark blue eyes had lost their sparkle and she had a permanently dour expression on her long square-jawed face. Despite the fact that she had invited Maggie for the holidays, she didn't seem happy upon her arrival.

Maggie tried on the largest pair, but they were quite tight on her slender feet. "Can you still get these in that store in Brandon?"

"I don't know. Are you dancing too?"

"Oh, she asked me to help out with the beginners – if I remember how."

"I doubt you could ever forget. You didn't bring Anton."

"No. We broke up."

"Oh. May I ask why?"

Maggie was almost ready to say it was none of her business or perhaps just avoid the question, but instead she said, "I suggested that we buy a house and settle down and he freaked out. I brought a bottle of white wine for tomorrow." She held it out for her mother to take.

"We've got plenty of wine."

"Oh, well, now you have more." Miffed, she brushed past her mother, set the bottle on the kitchen counter and went to check

Rob's closet. There she found several hockey sweaters with matching socks. She was about to pack up the Montreal Canadians' gear when she heard a voice that sounded like Sammy's say, No. I want the Oilers stuff.

She grinned and whispered, "Okay. If you must." She packed the Edmonton Oilers sweater and socks in her suitcase and then joined her mother in the living room. "Is there a service at the Crossing Church tonight? I would like to go."

"Yes, but I'm not sure the time. It's probably in the paper." Mary Ellen rummaged in the brass coloured magazine rack until she found the Sampford Gazette. She scanned the pages, located the notice and said, "Seven. You know, we may have to close the church. We can't afford to hire a minister and the Sampford minister is too busy to perform two services in one morning."

"That's too bad. Is Dad coming home for supper?"

"No. He's flooding the ice for the bonspiel on Boxing Day. Let's just have some frozen pizzas and go."

Maggie guessed that her father wasn't obligated to work on Christmas Eve and she concluded that he was avoiding her. She didn't normally eat pizza because of its high fat content and the cardboard crusts, but she didn't tell her mother that. They ate their pepperoni pizzas in silence, neither knowing what to say. The gulf between them seemed unbridgeable.

As they turned into the church yard, Maggie said, "Why do you hate me, Mother?"

Mary Ellen did not reply.

The century old church was filled to capacity for the Christmas Eve service. Maggie wished Merry Christmas to Sam and Meg, Sandy and her children, Trish and Tom and their boys, and Sam's mother Aggie MacNair before the service. Sam's brothers, Angus and George, took the pew behind him along with George's wife Augusta, Maggie's grade one teacher. To her surprise, Sarah, Peter and Grant Sinclair and their parents, who had left the Crossing while she was still in elementary school, were in attendance. Maggie was always glad to see Abby Sinclair, her dancing teacher. Frank and Carol and Rachel, also school mates, waved from across the nave.

When Mary Ellen and Maggie drove back to the farm after

church, they spoke not one word to each other. Maggie dropped her mother off at the door before she moved the Buick to the machine shed where she plugged it in with the blue electrical cord she carried in the hatchback. The hard-frozen snow crunched under her leather boots and she could see her breath in the beam of the yard-light high on a hydro pole in the centre of the yard. On her way back to the house, she stopped and gazed up at the stars, searching for the Big Dipper, the Little Dipper, the North Star and the Milky Way, remembered from an elementary school science book, the rest she couldn't recall except perhaps Orion. But it didn't matter, only that she could see them high and white and twinkling and beautiful in the darkened sky.

Maggie's heart was filled with the joy of good friends and the Christmas spirit, but Mike was waiting for her. "Well, if it ain't the prodigal daughter."

"Merry Christmas to you too, Dad."

"Where's the frog?"

Maggie suddenly remembered her father's stories about being raised on the cattle ranch that his brother now owned, and how hard it was during the dirty thirties, feeding Russian thistle to the horses, fixing the machinery with baling wire, shooting or trapping gophers to eat. He joined the army in 1940, not out of patriotism, but out of need for warm clothing, nutritious food and a leak-free roof over his head. He didn't talk much about his tour of duty in France, but he often said he wasn't going back to dry old Saskatchewan.

"What?"

"Anton. Ain't he a Frenchie?"

"No. He isn't. I am no longer seeing him."

"Not good enough for ye?"

"I mentioned getting married and he ran like a scared rabbit."

"Can't blame him. I expected you yestiday. You didn't have to work."

"Office Christmas party."

"What're you doin' with them kilts?" From the floor beside his chair, Mike picked up a tobacco can, yellow with the Vogue logo on the outside, took a pinch and made a line of in his palm, dumped it on a cigarette paper and lit his oddly shaped cigarette with a wooden match.

"I'm going to give them to Sandy. She's teaching dancing."

"Ye can't give away what ain't yourn."

"What do you mean?"

"I paid for them. Just like your fancy edication."

"You gave me the kilts. They are mine. And I paid for my university training. I took out student loans and I worked in the summers and I earned scholarships. You said that you'd give me a thousand dollars, and then you reduced it to five hundred, and you finally gave me nothing." Maggie struggled to keep her cool. Mike had paid for Rob's education but not hers.

"You still running around the world – loose woman." With his fingers, he picked a bit of tobacco from his tongue and placed it in the ashtray.

"I am an attorney doing my job. Mom, is Rob's hockey equipment in the basement? I could use some shoulder pads and some pants."

"It's his'n. You can't take it. Yer makin' the big bucks. Buy your own," said her father.

"Oh, I see. The hockey equipment is Rob's, but the kilts are not mine. That's fair." She could take no more. Her stomach knotted. They owed her. She could feel a headache arising over her left eye and she was afraid she'd explode at any moment. "I'm going to bed."

Mustering all the poise she could, she walked down the hall to her former bedroom and out of long habit locked the door behind her. She changed into her usual night shirt and lay on the bed, eyes wide open. Her body relaxed into the familiar mattress, but she didn't stay there for long. She slipped out of bed and quietly opened and closed every drawer in her dresser and bureau and looked in every cranny of the spacious closet, but all she found were two more pairs of dancing shoes, which she added to the kilts and blouses in the shopping bag. Not one of her drawings was to be found.

Maggie lay awake for a while, breathing in the familiar yet strange atmosphere of her former bedroom, snow white walls, the same white vertical blinds, the original pink shag carpet, her antique dresser and her child-sized desk. Her father's barbs were just as sharp as they had ever been and her mother's indifference as pronounced. Perhaps her emotional defences had been undermined. After a while, she fell asleep. Around three, she awoke with a start. Someone was turning the door knob. Maybe not. Maybe it was a dream or a flashback. There it was again. Someone was twisting the knob and jerking it, trying to force it open.

"Please hold," she prayed under her breath. "My father. It must be my father."

So. That was the truth she'd been suppressing. Her father was as guilty of incest as his son. She dreaded the inevitable when she had to bring out the memories of the actual events. Footsteps mounted the stairs to her parents' bedroom and she breathed again, but unevenly, and her stomach burned and twisted.

29

Monday, December 25

MAGGIE COULDN'T GO back to sleep. She waited until about six o'clock and then she quietly dressed and re-packed her suitcase. Taking the kilts and shoes and Rob's hockey sweater, she sneaked out of the house. The floor creaked with almost every step, but apparently her parents didn't hear. Fortunately King didn't awaken when she started the Buick and allowed it five minutes to warm up. Slowly she drove out of the yard, heavy with the knowledge that she would never return, not to the farm on the prairies that she loved, not to the harvest bustle, not to the community of MacNabb's Crossing with all her neighbours and friends.

Only a few other hardy travellers were on the road at that time of the morning, in the dark and on Christmas Day. The car radio played only cheery winter songs and Yuletide carols that didn't suit her mood so she turned it off and continued down the long highway in silence. She shuddered. If that lock on the door hadn't held her father would have entered into her room. What a scene that would have been. Perhaps she would have had a chance to scream, to fight back, to grab a weapon, if there was one to be had. The guy had a lot of nerve, coming to her bedroom on Christmas Eve, especially now that she was a full-grown woman, single and available in his mind apparently. Some part of her mind refused to believe it was true, but the evidence couldn't be contradicted. She didn't want to think about it any longer and she turned the radio back on and searched for another station, one that played retro rock and roll.

As usual, she made a pit stop in Portage la Prairie. Grateful a restaurant was open on Christmas morning, she sipped on a coffee as she left the town travelling east on the Trans-Canada highway. Slowly she became aware that someone else was pushing her foot hard on the accelerator.

"Hey. Slow down. You can drive if you want, but slow down."

No. A voice said. I want to go fast.

"The Mounties will stop us. We'll get a ticket."

I don't care. You have lots of money. You can pay it.

The speedometer was approaching a hundred and forty and there was nothing Maggie could do about it. "Slow down. For God's sake. You'll kill us all."

Oh, alright. You're such a woose.

The Buick cruised along now just above the speed limit. After a short time, she noticed the street lights at an intersection in the distance.

"Now. We have to slow down for the lights. The speed limit at the intersection is eighty kilometres per hour and we may have to stop. What's your name anyway?"

Miranda. I am sixteen. And I like to go fast.

"Okay, Miranda. The overhead lights are flashing. We have to stop – the light will be red in a minute. Do you know how to gear down and stop?"

Yeah, I can do it. It's such a pain.

"I like it myself. Okay. Now don't stall it when you take off." The car jerked and sputtered but kept on going. "This is a very bad time to be doing this, you know. We could have practiced in an empty parking lot somewhere. Let the clutch out. You don't ride the clutch. There. Now stay within the speed limit."

Why? No one else does.

"I am an officer of the court. I obey the law."

They went through the same performance twice more and finally made it to Headingly. "Turn right at the little black and white church. We can miss all the traffic and street lights on Portage going this way."

You drive then. Our next car is going to have an automatic transmission, if I have anything to say about it.

As she felt herself back in control of the vehicle, Maggie heaved a sigh of relief and drove to her apartment without further incident. Exhausted and shaking, she flopped down on the couch without removing her coat. Her first action was to call Dr. Dixon.

"I'm sorry to bother you. Merry Christmas."

"The same to you. I still make house calls. I'll be right over."

He gave her a mild sedative and left a couple more pills on the coffee table for later. He listened carefully as she related everything that happened at the farm and all about the wild ride from Portage to Winnipeg.

"Holy cow. No wonder you're upset. So you were right, you do have a lot more ugly stuff to remember, and it's not much wonder you suppressed it. Calm down. You survived it once, you can survive remembering it. As for the teenage driver, when you've recovered, go somewhere safe and call her. Let her learn to drive."

Maggie leaned back on the couch, her back straightened and she threw her arms over the back. Her left foot came up and the ankle rested on her right knee. Sammy spoke. "Doctor. You have to help Maggie. She ain't doing so good."

"Who are you?"

"I am Sammy. I play baseball and I skate – all the sports - because I have to live in the same house as Dad and Mike and Rob."

"Nice to meet you, Sammy. I understand your role in the family. How can I help Maggie?"

"We don't like the way she lives. All she does is work and sit in airports and fly around and read."

"She's going to curl and play hockey and she draws and paints now. What else do you want her to do?"

"Go to a movie once in a while. Go to church. See Sandy and her kids. Take more holidays. Have some fun. You know, I'm a man and I might have to take over this outfit."

"I'll tell her about having fun. How could you take over? You're a man in a woman's body."

"I am but that could be changed. Gotta go. Good bye."

"Did you hear that, Maggie? About having more fun?"

"Yes. He's right. Even with Anton I didn't have any fun, but I did have fun at the skating party and curling with Sam and Sandy." She lowered her arms and set her left foot on the floor. She slumped over the couch's narrow arm. "Take over? Could one of them actually take over?"

The doctor watched her closely. "I don't know. I suppose it's possible, but you seem to be the designated driver, if you know what I mean. Well. Obviously you have to do more activities - guy things and girl things. This is difficult and it's going to remain difficult for some time. You have to learn to cope. Now get some rest and write all this up in your journal. You might try writing letters to Sammy and Miranda." He checked his wristwatch. "I am sorry. I must go. Charlotte is expecting me for lunch."

"Thanks for coming. Say a prayer or two for me, would you?"

The sedative did its job and she slept until two in the afternoon. When she got up she made a pot of coffee, took her usual place at the coffee table, picked up her black-ink pen and the legal pad, and wrote: Dear Miranda, you frightened me today. It was quite a surprise to have someone else take over the wheel. I promise to let you drive, but let's go to an empty parking lot and practice first. You said you are sixteen. I hardly remember being a teenager. What do you want to do? What do you like to eat? What do you like to wear? I hope you will write here on this legal pad and tell me all about you.

She waited on the couch, pen in hand, but Miranda did not emerge. With a sigh, she turned her mind to other things, missing Christmas dinner for one. Her refrigerator was almost empty since she had planned to be out of town for a week. Ruefully, she took out the bacon and eggs and hash browns.

No way, said a child's voice. I want turkey.

"O. Kay. I'll see what I can do."

About five thirty, she changed into her New York blue jeans and the blue top that she wore on the date with Alex, and she and her inner friends drove the Buick around Winnipeg looking for a restaurant that was open for business on the Holy Day. The parking lot of a new one on Pembina Highway was quite full of cars, so she stopped there.

Rockin' Ronny's was a retro place decorated in fifties style, with red vinyl seats in the booths, each with a jukebox. The walls were covered with memorabilia – pictures of Marilyn Monroe and Elvis Presley, Mickey Mantle's baseball card, Coca Cola signs, black vinyl records, Vogue tobacco advertisements, a long picture of a silvery blue semi and trailer, and a large picture of a red and white fifty-seven Chevy. Someone was playing Elvis – *Jailhouse Rock*.

The sad-looking waitress wore a full black skirt, white bobby socks and a ponytail – a style that would have suited Maggie more than the stocky middle-aged matron who served her. Without checking the menu, Maggie ordered the daily special, a full Christmas dinner of turkey, white meat only, cranberry sauce, mashed potatoes, dressing and gravy, vegetables and a cup of coffee. The platter was huge – half of it would have sufficed. There she was, having her holiday dinner alone in a restaurant, a real loser, despite her expensive clothes and haircut. She wanted to hide under the table but she was too hungry and the food too good to miss. The waitress returned to ask if she wanted dessert, since it was, after all, included in the special.

"Do you have banana cream pie?"

"No. But there's coconut cream pie."

"Okay. Would you please wrap up the rest of this turkey and my dessert? I'll take them home with me."

The woman glared at her but did as asked. Maggie paid for her meal with a fifty dollar bill, just to prove that she wasn't a derelict who needed to take her leftovers home, and walked out to the tune of *Don't Be Cruel*.

Back in her apartment, she sorted through her library until she found a Nancy Drew book, *The Sign of the Twisted Candles*, a relic from her childhood. She read it in an hour or so, but it didn't bring back any memories, so she searched for and finally found young Mike's Hardy Boys books. She read *The Mystery of the Chinese Junk*. The same thing happened – no new memories. Then she realized that those were her books, Maggie's books, and she needed to find something else. She sat cross-legged on the floor in her library looking for children's books. She found two volumes of the Bobbsey Twins series, which she had never liked.

It is the first of May. Her birthday is in ten days. It is her ninth birthday. She wants to have a party. She wants to invite Sarah and Sandy and Trish for a Saturday night pyjama party.

"Mom, can I have a party for my birthday?"

"No. I am too busy. I have to get the coops ready for the chickens and ducks, and I have to cultivate the garden and dig up the flower beds and rake the lawn, and I have to plant the potatoes and the corn. And I have spring cleaning to do. No. I have no time. Your birthday present is there on my dresser, the latest Bobbsey Twin book, I won't bother to wrap it."

30

Tuesday, December 26

ON BOXING DAY, Maggie drove over to the curling club hoping there would be some practice ice, but to her disappointment, a seniors' bonspiel was in progress and all the sheets were taken. From a strategic seat in the waiting room she watched the games. She paid attention to the skip's placement of the broom as a target for the shooter, the motion of the different curlers as they threw their rocks, and the strategy of the skips. In the next draw, there was a sheet free, so she hunted down the rink manager to ask permission to use it.

Brian was talking to a tall heavy set guy with blondish hair and a big smile.

"This is Bob Hunter," he said with a knowing grin. "Why don't you help her out, Bob? She's a rookie."

"I'm Maggie," she reached out her right hand and he shook it slowly.

They made good use of the time. He had her practice draw shots and takeouts and he threw a few rocks for her to sweep. After about an hour, he said, "Want a coffee?"

"Sure. That's enough for one day."

As he stirred milk and sugar into his hot drink, he asked her what she did for a living.

"I'm an attorney." She checked his left hand – no wedding ring.

"A lawyer!"

"Yes. I work for Jenkins Williamson. And what about you?"

"I am one of the vice presidents of Borden International, a place in an uproar."

"Why? What's going on?" Winnipeg was a small world, after all.

"Oh, the young Borden up and left his wife and kids and the old man's ready to boot him out. Fired the secretary he's sleeping with. Now we don't know for sure what to do when Gus retires."

For some reason, Maggie wanted to be absolutely honest with this man. "Yes. I know Sandy, Jim's wife."

"You don't. How in blazes do you know her?"

"We were neighbours at MacNabb's Crossing, went to school together."

"Small world, as they say. Where is MacNabb's Crossing exactly?"

"Near Sampford."

"I don't know that country very well, but I guess it's like the rest of Manitoba - flat."

Maggie laughed. "Ah, but Sandy's mother always says flat is beautiful."

Bob grinned. "Guess it's all in your perspective. So why didn't you learn to curl? I thought everybody outside the Perimeter Highway learned to curl."

"Well. My father is the ice maker in Sampford and I don't like him very much, so I avoided the curling rink."

He stared at her as if reading her mind. "I'll be right back." He walked over to the office and talked with Brian for a few seconds and then returned with the coffee pot. "There's ice available tomorrow at three. Want to work on your in-turn?"

"I'd like that very much. And thanks. Thank you for your help."

They chatted a little longer and then Maggie left the club, hardly believing her good luck. It wasn't often that a complete stranger would volunteer his time and knowledge to show someone a new sport. In fact, no one had done something nice for her since Jared paid for her hotel room in New York.

Sammy's voice, Hey, I'm supposed to do the curling, but I can't come out when he's around.

"Sorry. You'll have to wait."

No. I can come out when no one will notice. And he will notice.

"I'll try to find other practice times when we can be alone then."

Let's go buy hockey equipment.

Since Boxing Day sales were in full swing, she had to park a long distance from the store and elbow her way to the sports department. She was able to buy what she needed at a reduced price with the help of a harried young clerk, who obviously thought hockey was a man's game and she should buzz off.

I should have punched him, said Sammy.

"Not worth it."

Let's go to MacDonald's for supper.

"No way. I want a bowlful of green salad and some seafood, crab or shrimp."

No. I want a Big Mac.

"Oh, alright. Drive-through here we come."

After she ate her dinner, Sammy was silent. She wondered what other memories she might bring out, and searched through her books for anything she had read at an early age. She found three westerns by Zane Grey, which actually belonged to her father. She picked up *30,000 on the Hoof*, a story about ranching in the early settlement years – all the hardships and reversals, the drought, the isolation of the wives, and the problems encountered in growing crops and gardens and raising livestock.

She is thirteen. She and Sandy are in a dance competition in Brandon. Her grandmother has given her a MacDonar tartan kilt in red, white and gray, and new ghillie shoes. Maggie is very excited and very confident. When her carefully chosen music starts, she forgets her mother and her chickens and eggs. She forgets her father and the farm and the price of wheat. She forgets Rob and young Mike. She ignores the audience and the judges. She listens to the music and she dances. Already five foot five, she is strong and athletic and her movements are precise and rhythmic, quick and sure. When the music ends, she is surprised to hear the applause. She curtseys to the audience and to the judges and leaves the stage.

To her surprise, she is declared the winner in her age group. Sandy comes in third. She is exhilarated when she is selected to go to Maxville in Ontario for the Canadian championships.

Mike says, "No. You can't go. I won't have ye gallivantin' all over the country."

Maggie set the yellow legal pad on the coffee table again and hesitated a few minutes, thinking. Then she wrote, 'I hate my father. Sammy. Sammy, will you talk to me?'

He wrote back in handwriting similar to hers, but larger and more angular. 'You talk, I'll write.'

"Okay. What would you like to talk about?"

He responded, 'I am tired of being a guy in a woman's body. Would you have a sex change operation? Take testosterone? Live as a man?'

"How could I live as a man? A gay man?"

'I don't know. I'm not gay, but I see what you mean. You have to admit – you're a tomboy. Why can't you just be a boy? You don't even dress like a girl.'

"Women's clothes are silly, and I feel vulnerable in a skirt – not that wearing jeans protected me from Mike. Tell me about your life."

'You are avoiding the issue. Okay. I played the sports and helped with the chickens because you hated them. Neither of us talked much so no one noticed whether it was me or you.'

"Are you aware of the others – Jane and Sally and Lynne?"

'No. I'm completely separate. There are others? That complicates things.'

"Yes. It is very complicated. Did Dad or Mike hurt you in any way?"

'Dad hit me. When I played for the school team, he would hit me if I made a mistake on the field – whether it was actually an official error or not. When we got home, I'd get a back hand across my mouth. I don't want to talk anymore.'

'Okay. Could I talk to Sally?' she wrote.

"Could I talk to Sally?" she asked out loud.

There was no response.

She made blueberry muffins and chocolate chip cookies in the hope that baking would arouse the cook or baker inside. She thought at times she had help in measuring the ingredients, but no one took over.

"Baker, talk to me."

No one answered.

"Cook, please talk to me. Write on the yellow pad."

Again she sat with pen in hand, but no one took hold. She noticed the word 'investment' on the front cover of the newspaper and idly made words with the letters – vestment, invest, vest, nest, test, mist, vine, tine, tin, mine, nine, stein, sine, sin, in, inn, I, mint, mite, emit, item, tit, nit, sit, site, mitten, met, meet, net, mete, vet, Sten, ten, teen, seen, nene, time, teem, vim, stem, tit, mien, intent, tent, sent, vent, invent, me, tee, nee, tie, ti, it, snit, smitten, mitt, smite, stint, tint, vise, vie, sieve, even, seven, eve, Steven, event.

She gave up and went to bed, only to dream that she and Mary Ellen are making dill pickles in the new farmhouse. There is hardly room for her in the tiny kitchen, but she perches on a stool and packs dill weed into each Mason jar and pushes as many small cucumbers as will fit on top of the dill. The smell of the dill and vinegar fills the air. Mary Ellen adds some spices and then fills each jar with hot brine. She brushes Maggie aside as she seals the hot jars and turns them upside down on the counter.

"You can start shucking the corn," says her mother, drying her hands on the tea towel. "We should be able to get a dozen bags or more frozen by suppertime."

"Did you keep my corn varieties separate?" asks Maggie in a panic.

"Yes, yes, yes. See, there are three tubs, one for each."

"Which is which?"

"God, girl, do you think I am dumb? Look. I labelled them."

Maggie fetches a measuring tape from Mary Ellen's sewing room to measure the length and circumference of a sampling from each wash tub, which she records on a discarded envelope. She examines the colour and size of the kernels and jots down her findings. Setting aside three cobs to taste at dinnertime, she begins the hard work of cleaning the hairs from the cobs for freezing. She counts the number of cobs of each variety and keeps the varieties separate so that she can test for taste after processing. Mary Ellen cuts the corn from the ears with an electric knife and Maggie labels each plastic bag as Mary Ellen fills them, and seals each one closed with a twist tie. When she is finished, she runs to her room to record her results in her fat 4-H book.

Mary Ellen says, "This is such a bother. Why don't you join the poultry club with Rob?"

3I

Wednesday, December 27

THE NEXT MORNING Maggie had an ugly purple bruise on her right cheek and a black eye. She could feel her head snapping back and the entire right side of her face hurt.

She said aloud, "I am so sorry this happened to you, Sammy. I'll get you some ice."

Maggie didn't want to leave her apartment until her face healed somewhat. She was determined to heal herself as well.

"Lynne. Lynne."

There was no answer, no response whatsoever.

"Lynne. Do you want to draw and paint this morning?"

She lifted a university certificate off the wall in the hallway, substituted her pen and ink drawing of the derelict barn and hung the frame back on the nail. Leafing through her how-to books, she discovered a technique for water colours in which the artist splashes very wet washes over the paper or canvass and lets the colours mingle as they wish. She taped two sheets of water colour paper to a backing, and using washes of Naples yellow, manganese blue and permanent rose, created two glowing pictures. It was fun and so freeing, just playing with the colours.

A force took over her hand and arm. It reached for some

parchment and the India ink and straight pen and placed them beside her. Then with an HB pencil, she sketched an old John Deere tractor with the front wheels together like a tricycle. Maggie wouldn't have remembered the detail, but whoever this was had it down pat. She worked with the pen, outlining, cross hatching the shadows, filling in the darks, leaving the lights white. By noon, it was complete and dry. She took down another certificate and removed the contents, carefully reframed the drawing, and hung it beside the barn picture.

Maggie hadn't finished chewing her last bite of lunch when she was moved back to the studio. Dexterously, she added detail to her wash pictures with water colour paint and brush to create two seascapes at sunset. That done, she cleaned up all traces of paint from her brushes and returned the paint to her tackle box. She then chose a sixteen by twenty prepared canvass. She took out her oils and the long handled brushes, and with a piece of charcoal began to sketch out an abstract picture. Maggie remembered nothing after that.

32

Thursday, December 28

SHE AROSE THE next morning disoriented, like a stranger in her own room. She didn't remember having dinner and looked for clues in the kitchen. Nothing was out of place; nothing seemed to be missing, except perhaps two eggs and some bread. In her studio, she found two sixteen by twenty abstract paintings in fall colours – oranges, yellows, browns, a bit of pine green, a little crimson, and near the bottom of all the pictures was the signature, Lynne Barnett, in small print. The studio was neat and tidy, not a drop of paint on the drop cloth, not one used paper towel in the garbage basket, not one tube of paint left on the table.

Because Lynne painted the edges of the canvass, a frame was unnecessary and Maggie hung the oil paintings as they were in the living room, changing the atmosphere of the room completely. She rolled up the white area rug and deposited it in the library. She would lay it out when she found the floor. She added 'frames' to her buyer's list along with groceries, dancing shoes and a new rug. After a quick shower, Maggie, dressed in Sammy's jeans and a black and white plaid flannel shirt, left the apartment to spend the entire morning making her purchases. She bought a variety of food hoping to please everyone on her list and a rectangular rug with a pattern of large squares in muted tones of green, brown and orange similar to the abstract paintings. She tried three stores before she found a pair of ghillie shoes to fit. Satisfied, she returned to her apartment. To her relief, no one seemed to have noticed the bruise on her face. Alex phoned just as she stepped inside the door, inviting her to lunch at Alexander's. She had just enough time to put the groceries in the cupboards and the refrigerator. Still dressed like Sammy, she met Alex in the restaurant.

"So how are you?" He began the conversation.

"Oh, we're doing fine."

Fortunately he didn't notice that she referred to herself as 'we.'

"I have a wonderful idea. I had to tell you right away. Suppose instead of you moving to New York, Angie and I return to Winnipeg. And live with you."

"Live with me?"

"Yes. Wouldn't it be great! You have three bedrooms so there's plenty of space for all of us. We could start our life together right now."

"No. No. That will not work. I am barely over Anton. I told you that I wasn't ready to start a new relationship."

"Think about it. You could see Angie all the time and we could be together at work and at home. We get along so well."

"You didn't say you love me. You didn't say anything about marriage. You just want a roof over your head and a babysitter for your daughter."

"That's a little harsh."

"Alex, we have had exactly three dates. It is too soon to share a home together. Alex. I am not in love with you."

"Then why did you go out with me?" He jumped up, grabbed his jacket and left the restaurant.

Without looking at the menu, Maggie ordered her favourite Italian dish, meat lasagne with a Caesar salad. It reminded her of Sandy and eating the same meal in New York. She wanted to contact her but didn't dare because she had a date to curl at three. She went home, laid out her new rug and tried out her new shoes: feet in first position - heels together feet at right angles, second position - working leg to the side with toe pointed, second aerial position

– working leg elevated to the side with toe pointed, third position – working leg placed on the toe of the other foot, third aerial position – working leg lifted close to the knee, arms in second position left one overhead, third position - both arms overhead, palms facing each other, and high cuts down the hallway.

Her feet needed strengthening and she remembered Abby Sinclair advising her students to tiptoe around the house. When they were beginners, she and Sandy and Sarah practiced during lunch hours at the Crossing school. If the teachers were annoyed, they never complained or told them to go outside to play.

Her new friend Bob Hunter was waiting when she arrived at the curling rink a few minutes before three. "You look angry," he said.

"Do you agree that accepting a dinner invitation from a guy is tantamount to accepting a marriage proposal?"

"God, I hope not."

"Well, I have had three dinner dates with this guy from work and he thought we were ready to live together – in my apartment. With his six year old daughter."

"No wonder you're pissed off."

"Um. If we're going to continue this, maybe I should get your number in case something comes up and I need to cancel."

They exchanged business cards, writing their home numbers on the back.

"Come on, time's a-wasting," he grabbed his broom and led the way to the ice surface.

The West Town Curling Club was a twelve-sheet curling facility in north-western Winnipeg. At this time in the afternoon, there were about six others taking advantage of the holiday lull to make a few practice shots. Again her coach asked her to make in-turn and out-turn draws and take-outs in various spots in the house. This time he asked her to place some guards as well. Maggie was beginning to get a feel for the amount of weight required to place her rocks where the skip wanted. He talked to her about the role of the sweepers and the effect that brushing had on the rocks and he threw several rocks, asking her to watch the rock to gauge where the rock would stop. He threw a few more that she swept if needed. She found it difficult but she was making progress.

Bob rushed off about four o'clock saying he had to be somewhere. Maggie was a bit disappointed, but decided to stay a little longer to let Sammy throw a few rocks; however he didn't make an appearance. While she worked, she pondered about how to reach Sally. If Sammy was completely separate from the others, then Sally must reside in an area of the brain different from his. Maybe she was ultra-feminine.

Back in her apartment, she had a cup of green tea – a girl thing. She changed into a white blouse with lace on the collar and cuffs and her kilt, and laced up her ghillies. She needed music. Her collection was gathering dust in the library and her stereo was hidden on the bottom shelf behind closed doors, unused, in the living room. She brought her cassettes from the library and sitting cross-legged on the floor, sorted through them and arranged them on the shelf above. Eventually she located her dance music and put in on the machine.

Immediately she was someone else, she didn't know whom, and she rose gracefully to her feet, bowed to an imaginary crowd and danced until her feet were sore. She sat gratefully on the couch, flipped the legal pad to a fresh page and wrote, 'Who are you? Please talk to me.'

There was no response, the moment had passed and she was a lawyer again. She changed the tape to some sixties music – Simon and Garfunkel, *The Sounds of Silence*, which was popular when she started university. She had felt so good at that time, over a hundred-and-fifty miles from her parents. Rob was also at the University of Manitoba but he was immersed in science and she never saw him, which was just fine with her. She dived into her studies surfacing only to eat and sleep. She didn't partake in university activities that first year, content to be alone, to think her own thoughts, to live without fear. She listened to music as she studied with the radio on in her tiny dorm room, morning, noon and night. Her marks were excellent, but she needed exercise and so she took swimming lessons and was soon doing lengths in the campus pool.

Again she sat at the coffee table and the legal pad. Jane, Jane, could I talk to you. Tell me more. What happened? Jane.

No answer.

She spoke aloud, "Jane. Jane."

No response. She went into the bathroom and looked in the mirror directly into her dark eyes.

"Sally. Jane. Where are you? Talk to me."

No response. Maggie gave up. She switched on the television and relaxed on the couch with her feet on one arm and her head on the other.

She is ten. Mike is coming home on holidays, on leave from the air force. It is the end of August and he is coming to help their father with the harvest. She is petrified. She wishes school would start so that she can disappear every day. She is alone in the house because Mary Ellen is driving the grain truck with Rob riding along for moral and practical support.

King barks. She hears the crunch of tires on the gravel in the driveway. Mike silences the dog with one "Shut up." He strides into the new house in his olive green uniform. She is paralyzed.

"Well, lookie, lookie. Who's here but the little brat? Been waiting for me?"

He grabs in her direction but she dodges and runs towards her room but he is too fast. He has her before she reaches the living room. With one powerful arm he holds her across the shoulders and she cannot move her arms to scratch him. She cannot reach his arm to bite. She kicks but strikes his high-topped leather boots and sharp pains run from her heels to her knees.

"Now where did we leave off, little sister?"

"Leave me alone." She tries to scream but chokes.

"Now. Now. Don't be like that. I know you missed me. Come here now. Is this your room? Let's try out your little bed."

She is desperate. "You're a disgrace to that uniform."

He drops her on the floor hurting her elbow. She has obviously hit a nerve. He stands up straight and tall. He has grown three or four inches since he left home at sixteen.

"Where am I supposed to sleep?"

"In the basement."

He turns on his heel as if on parade and leaves her in a crumpled heap.

Maggie runs into Rob's room and locks the door. From the window she watches Mike, now in jeans and a white T-shirt, climb

137

into his green GMC truck and drive out of the yard towards the south field. She has won a small victory but she is still afraid and she wants to shove his lying letter down his throat.

On the pad Maggie wrote, 'Thanks for telling me about Mike's visit.' Suddenly someone took control of the pen and scribbled in large irregular letters: 'Damn you. I hate you. I hate you. Why won't you let me do things? Why is it always the others who get to do things? I have never driven a car. I have never thrown a curling rock. I have never danced. I have never gone to university. I don't draw and paint. I never get to do anything. I hate you. I hate you all. When is it going to be my turn? How come I can't do anything? Let me out. Let me do things. You are all mean.'

Maggie spoke aloud, "Who are you? What do you want to do?"

But the writer went on as if she or he hadn't heard a thing: 'I hate you. I hope you roast in hell. I am a person too and I need to do things. Why won't you let me do things? I hate you. I hate you. I hate law. I don't want to be a stinking God damn lawyer. I don't want to dance. It is stupid. Why won't you let me do something?'

Maggie tried again. "What do you want to do?"

The writer obviously couldn't hear and Maggie let him or her continue. The writing went on and on, the swearing and cursing worsened, and there were threats of suicide and threats of murder. Whoever this was, she or he was certainly angry. The scribbling slowed somewhat, so Maggie tried to communicate once more. "I am sorry. I didn't know. Tell me. What do you want to do?"

'I want to bake a cake.' The lettering was much smaller now and more controlled.

"Bake a cake? You want to bake a cake? Well. Okay. Let's." Maggie felt light-headed, somewhat separate from her body, but she was able to walk into the kitchen. She reached into the cupboard for the devil's food cake mix she had inexplicably bought on her last grocery shopping trip. She opened and closed a few cupboard doors before she located a nest of blue Pyrex mixing bowls and a hand mixer and a nine by thirteen cake pan. She couldn't remember when or why she had purchased those items. She followed the directions on the Duncan Hines package and soon a chocolate cake was baking in the oven. When it was done she removed it from the hot stove, allowed it to cool, and topped it with French vanilla icing. She ate two large pieces before she covered it with aluminum foil and set it in the corner of the counter.

Maggie returned to the coffee table and yellow pad. She picked up the pen. She wanted to know the baker's name but no one wrote again.

She wrote Duncan Hines, Duncan, dun, Hun, shine, shin, sin, sine, dine, din, Dane, Dan, dean, den, hen, sane, Sean, dune, sun, can, cane, chain, chin, china, scan, nun, nine, disc, ace, ice, dice, iced, aced, nice, since, dunce, chained, caned, canned, scanned, case, chase, chased, cased, hie, die, hied, hide, chide, nude, side, shied, Hades, had, shade, head, shed, said, Ned, snide, dish, dash, ash, cash, hand, hind, sand, and, an, a, I, is, sea, sac, sic, hic, inch, inched, sec, sue, sued, due, hue, cue, cued, sad, Chad, cad, send, end, cashed, shun, shunned, sunned, aced, ashen, Cain, Ann, Anne, acid, Sid, Inca, acne, ache, ached.

Exhausted she curled up on the couch to watch television. Five minutes later she was purring.

33

Friday, December 29

SHE AWOKE IN the night, not remembering going to bed. She wore
a pair of burgundy silk pyjamas that had been hiding in the bottom
drawer of her six-drawer bureau. She didn't remember buying them.
Her mind was a jumble. Tiny fireworks exploded inside her head
and she was unable to think at all. "Who am I?" she whispered to the
darkness. She closed her eyes.

Her radio alarm roused her at eight o'clock. She had an
appointment with Dr. Dixon at nine so she hurriedly showered and
dressed in gray wool dress pants and a red cashmere pullover. In her
ears she put pea-sized pearl earrings. After a quick breakfast of maple
and brown sugar oatmeal and a tumbler full of apple juice, she left
her apartment, wearing her long black coat and high heeled boots.
She shivered while she allowed the Buick time to warm up before
she drove off to the medical centre. The wind whipped snow across
the street and cut her face as she ran from the car to the entrance.

Dr. Dixon met her at the door, studying her as unobtrusively as
he could. "Good morning. Come on in where it's warm."

"Good morning, Dr. Dixon," she replied smiling warmly. "It is so
nice to meet you."

"And who might you be?" he asked.

"I really don't know what my name is. You knew I wasn't Maggie, didn't you?"

"Yes. Your eyes seem lighter in colour. You have a more pleasant, less serious look on your face. You're dressed differently. She usually wears jeans and her sheepskin jacket and boots when she comes. You're just more feminine."

She hung her coat on a clothes peg on the door and seated herself on the chair like a prim lady, feet elegantly and modestly crossed under the chair.

"She's a tomboy, alright."

"So tell me about you."

"Yes. I am more feminine, and, therefore, rejected. I liked to play dolls with my friend Sandy. But then we never had any dolls at home. Dad wouldn't let me have any. And what else? I like to wear skirts and dresses and lace and stuff that Maggie hates. I like to bake cakes and cookies and muffins but Maggie never bakes at all. She spent as little time in the kitchen with Mom as she could."

"So Maggie was out most of the time?"

"Yes. Her and Sammy. Without her, we would not have survived, but it makes me very angry. I never got a chance to do things, although I did dance sometimes."

"Did your brother Mike hurt you?"

"I don't want to talk to you anymore. Call Maggie." She dropped her head to her chest.

"Good bye then. Maggie. Maggie. Are you there?"

A minute or so later she lifted her head and looked around. "Dr. Dixon! How did I get here?"

"You don't remember driving here this morning?"

"No. I'm having black outs where I remember nothing. It scares me to death. Who were you talking to?" She slouched a bit in the chair and crossed her legs.

"She didn't know her name. She was very feminine – said she like to bake."

"Ah. We baked a cake last night. That's the last thing I remember." She jumped up and paced back and forth in the small office. "These are my clothes and I wear them to work sometimes. Maybe they are hers too." She was clearly agitated.

"What is it?"

"Just as I was coming up I caught a fragment of memory. I am being photographed. I am wearing my red and gray kilt and my bum is bare. I am embarrassed and angry."

"Did you parents have a camera?"

"A small one. No. This was a large camera – a studio camera. Did they make me pose for dirty pictures? Pornography?"

"I don't know. Do you remember anything else?"

"Well, when I was at home on Christmas Eve, I picked up all my kilts and blouses and shoes, and there was something about the tiniest kilt, but I couldn't remember what it was."

"Well. You need more evidence before you jump to any conclusions. What else has been going on?"

She told him that Sammy wanted to curl and about the one who came out to dance, and about Lynne drawing and painting, and about the different clothing. "But this blacking out, that really bothers me. Is this really part of the deal?"

"I am afraid it is. This is difficult, Maggie, and it is not going to resolve itself overnight."

"That nasty baker said she didn't want to be a God damn lawyer yet she wore clothes that I wear to work. I don't understand. I brought you the writing." She reached into her purse and brought out a yellow legal pad. "Now how did it get here?"

"It is confusing. Let's see. It looks like your hand writing, yet different. Gee. She writes as if she is in a rage, yet when I met her she was sweet and charming. Maybe there's more than one baker."

"I don't know. I'm so confused. I woke up this morning feeling as if I was no one at all. My mind was a whirlwind."

"Can you describe it more?"

"Yes. When I was in school, including university, I used to make this thing in my notebooks. I would scribble in an oval perhaps two inches across – go in every direction. Then I would pick out different shapes and fill them in, a triangle here, an ellipse there, a square, more triangles, until I had a design. I think it was my mind." She showed him what she meant on a prescription pad.

"That is interesting. You know, you do look a little different than you did when I first met you. Do you agree?"

"Yes. I am less focussed on being a lawyer and I am getting some exercise, skating, curling and walking. I feel less likely to explode. Less tense. And perhaps less like a boy."

"Yes. I see it in your face. That's good."

They talked for most of the morning with a short break when the doctor excused himself and came back with two cups of coffee. Maggie felt much better when she left the clinic except that she couldn't find the Buick despite its distinctive appearance. Finally she caught the gleam of the silver hawk on its hood. It was a good thing the parking lot wasn't crowded on that holiday Friday.

After lunch she drove to the pool and swam lengths for half an hour before she tired. It felt really good to be in the water again. She was almost late for curling, but to her disappointment Bob didn't show up. Sammy practiced for half an hour and then told her he wanted to play pool. The Blue Rose Bar where she met Anton had two tables in the back, she remembered. She could think of nowhere else to go. She looked around the spacious pub, but saw no one that she knew. So Sammy played the best of three with a tall dark moustached guy who had been standing against the wall looking hopeful. Sammy won the first game, and the fellow, who called himself Paul, won the second game. Sammy lost the last game. It was very close and he was dejected as he bought Paul a beer. Sammy drank a Blue and talked for a while and then they hurried home.

Wearily she made supper, a grilled steak and scalloped potatoes, steamed peas and carrots, and chocolate cake with ice cream for dessert. The extra cooking seemed to make someone happy. She lay on the couch to watch television and write in her journal. No deal. Someone – probably Lynne – wanted to work in the studio. She picked up a ten by ten water colour canvass and placed in on the table, setting in on the edge of her coloured pencils box, and blacked out.

34

Saturday, December 30

THE NEXT MORNING Maggie was aware that she had spaced out the previous evening but she chose not to dwell on it. She admired the two new water colour paintings on display in the studio. She took them and her law textbooks to the entrance to take to her office on Wednesday.

She vacuumed and dusted her apartment with her shoulders slumped, the weight of the world upon them. Life had become very difficult, confusing and uncertain. She felt sharp pains from time to time in her crotch and lower abdomen, sometimes in her anus, but she didn't want to think about those. Her head ached. In fact, her whole body ached as if she'd been through the wringer on the old-fashioned washing machine her mother had in the old farmhouse.

Sandy and the children paid her a visit later on in the morning. "Maggie. Are you okay? Your father told us you'd taken off for no reason. What happened?"

"Oh, he was his usual pleasant self and I couldn't take it." She didn't tell Sandy about the hand on the door knob, at least not yet.

"Well, Trish figured that out. She yelled at him, right there in the rink. Mike Barnett, she said, what did you say to her now? And he told her that you'd stolen the kilts. Stolen! The kilts you wore for years. Imagine."

"Yeah. He said they weren't mine, but I took them anyway. I'm surprised he didn't call the cops. You'd think after twenty-nine years I'd be used to his hostility, but it still bothers me."

"If my father said those things to me, I don't know what I would do, but Mom and Trish were pretty snarky at Christmas time." Sandy sank into Maggie's leather couch.

"Gee, and I used to play at your house to get away from it all." Maggie sat down opposite her and addressed Caroline and Danny. "Sorry, I don't have any kids' things for you, but there are lots of books you might like. Just go down the hall, first door to your right."

"Yes. But you had the TV. I don't know why it took all those years for Dad to buy a squawk box but now it'd take a crowbar to pry it away from him."

They both laughed. Maggie dragged the shopping bag full of kilts from the coat closet and they sorted through them.

"This is great. With these and mine, I should have enough to outfit most of my class, but are you sure you don't want to keep them? You may have a daughter yourself one day."

"Well, if and when I do, I'll just borrow them back. Look at them. They wear like iron."

"Maggie, there's something you're not telling me."

"Yes. There is. But I can't say anything right now." She picked up Melissa, who had been exploring the kitchen and living room, and set her on her knee. She bounced her up and down, giving the little girl a pony ride. Melissa squealed with delight.

"Okay. In your own good time."

Danny and Caroline returned to the living room, carrying some Hardy Boys books and a couple of Nancy Drews. "Can we borrow these, Maggie?" asked Caroline.

"Yes, of course."

"I'm going to be a detective, a cop, someday," proclaimed Danny.

His mother laughed. "And you'll make a good one," she said. They left soon afterwards, leaving Maggie lonely in her empty apartment.

She thought about calling Rebecca or one of her other friends, but couldn't. Her world was upside down and she needed to be alone to deal with all the memories and alters. She didn't realize that she was isolating herself further. Grandmother MacDonar called, asking her to spend New Year's Eve in Brandon with them. She didn't want to go because it was too cold for travelling.

"But Maggie, we're moving to a condo soon and I have some things to give you."

Maggie remembered her tall red-headed grandfather teasing her about a pink house, and her willowy grandmother giving him that shut up look. "I'm sorry. I can't come this weekend, Grandma."

A pink house. What was the pink house? She ran down the hall to her studio and with coloured pencils drew a picture of a two-storey house much like the one on the farm, but it had white wood siding except at the bottom where it was a pale pink. She couldn't remember where this house was located.

She is in the pink house, on a black bed, round. Her tiny kilt is pushed up. Her skinny bum is bare and covered with goose bumps.

Maggie was certain then that she had been the star and victim of pornographic pictures and she was angry that her precious kilt was used. Dancing had made her happy, and her father, she was sure her father was involved, had twisted her dancing into something ugly. She wrote all this in her journal and then went for a swim. Maybe if she stayed in the chlorine long enough, it would cleanse her in body and in spirit.

After the swim, she stopped at her favourite art supply store and purchased more canvasses for both oils and water colours, and at a grocery store for some blueberries to make breakfast muffins and thyme, pot barley and other ingredients to make hamburger soup. This cooking was getting to be a habit. She had dinner and then went to a movie, which one she couldn't say because her mind was elsewhere.

Maybe she should have gone to Brandon. Maybe if she went she could find out something, anything about her childhood. She could ask her grandmother for pictures. She had only a few. Even being in her house might give her some clues. She bet Sandy had pictures.

The movie was over by nine thirty. She drove around the city warming up the Buick, admiring the Christmas lights, not ready to go home. She drove past her favourite night spot. Anton's Nova was sitting in the parking lot, but she decided to go in anyway.

He spied her as soon as she entered and joined her at the bar. "Hi. What are you doing here? Thought you didn't want to be anywhere near me."

"I saw your car outside. I don't care whether you're here or not. I was hoping Rebecca and Sadie would be here."

"Nope. Haven't seen them. Did you have a good time at the Crossing?"

"No. Same old. Same old. The old man pissed me off and I left."

"So why do you go?"

"This time I went to see if I could find out why he hates me so much. I still don't know. So maybe I'll go back for his funeral, maybe not."

"I miss you, Maggie. Can't we get back together?"

"No. You owe me for two back tires. No. If we really loved each other, we would be married by now with two or three kids."

Angrily he banged his beer mug on the bar and strode back to his table. The young bartender washed the counter with a red and white checked dishcloth and asked her what she would like to drink. She shook her head, "I've changed my mind. Nothing, thanks." She left the bar and drove off, watching in her rear view mirror for Anton, but he didn't follow her. She went home to her silent apartment and turned on the radio. She flipped through the stations until she found some retro music and turned it up full blast.

Grabbing the bag full of canvasses, she strode down the hall to her studio. Working in charcoal, she outlined a dark silhouette of her father's John Deere combine against a fiery red sunset. Then with oils, Maggie began laying in the sky and dark and dusty foreground. She was aware that someone was helping her, perhaps painting the picture, but she didn't black out and she finished the coat of paint around midnight. She couldn't stop. She picked up another canvass and the charcoal and laid out a three tall stalks of wheat against a golden field with a broad clear cobalt sky overhead. It was close to two o'clock before she noticed her eyes wouldn't stay open. She tidied up the studio and cleaned her brushes and her hands and fell into bed.

35

Sunday, December 31

SUNDAY MORNING MAGGIE was awakened at ten o'clock by the telephone. Groaning, she rolled over and picked up the receiver. It was her grandmother begging her to come for what was left of the weekend. Remembering her plan for another fact-finding mission, she agreed to travel to Brandon that afternoon.

As a precaution, she prepared an emergency kit of candles, matches, a blanket, some candy bars and a jug of water, a long knit scarf and toque and a sign which said, 'Please call the police.' According to the radio, the temperature was hovering around twenty-four degrees below zero when she turned the Buick westward. Fortunately there wasn't much wind. To her relief, the car purred along as if it were warm and sunny. Her eyes relaxed as she gazed at the distant horizon, the snow drifted in the fields like sand dunes, the contrasting blue sky, the skiff of high white clouds, the silhouettes of leafless trees and evergreen spruce, the yellow grasses in the ditches. She made one stop in Portage for coffee.

The word 'Portage' caught her attention – port, part, pert, art, pore, tore, ore, or, O, gore, gear, pear, pare, par, per, gar, great, rate, grate, rat, pat, pate, peat, get, gate, ret, pet, pot, opt, top, rope, grope, grape, rape, reap, rap, tap, tape, taper, gape, gap, apt, rapt, age, rage, page, pager, ager, tag, rag, a, gator, trap, prate, eta, tea, eat, ate, pea, Poe, Po, to, go, goat, oat, rote, rot, re, ape, toe.

Her grandparents owned a beautifully kept fifties-style bungalow off the well-treed twenty-sixth street in the west end. Usually Maggie felt quite at home and welcome in their home, but this time she wasn't quite as comfortable. She didn't know if it was because of her new knowledge or because there was something different about the elderly couple who met her at the door.

"You had a good trip?" asked her grandfather.

"Yes, I did," she answered. No one was more surprised than she was. "I need to plug my car in."

"I'll look after it before I turn in," said her grandfather.

They offered her a glass of sherry to ward off the chill. "Come in, come in. Sit down. So, you and your Dad had words again?" Her grandmother wasted no time getting down to it.

Maggie avoided her piercing eyes, set in a face so much like her own. "He said words I didn't wish to hear, as usual." She glanced around the cramped living room at the floor length drapes and the swooping valance, made from textured satin and backed by white lacy sheers. The thick carpet had a peachy tone a shade or two deeper than the drapes. She perched on the rounded cushion of a French Provincial settee, which was hard and uncomfortable. The upholstery had a texture similar to the petit point pictures of a Scottish lad and lassie in green kilts on the wall on either side of the window.

"Well. You are welcome here. Now then, let's get this done and then we can have a good visit. I would like you to have my silverware. There is a twelve-place setting. Sterling silver. Worth a fortune these days. And my dining room set. Do you have room for it in your apartment?"

Her grandparents had never travelled to Winnipeg to see her or Rob. "No. I really don't. My dining area is very small. I suppose I could put it in storage. Or could one of the other cousins use it?"

"I would like you to have it. Couldn't you put it in one of your bedrooms?"

"No. Not really. One is my painting studio and the other is my library. It is absolutely full of books." Through the door to the apple green dining room, she could see a line drawing of a rearing horse matted and framed. "That's my drawing?" She jumped up to look.

"Yes, of course, dear. Don't you remember giving it to me? I have some other examples of your work, if you want them."

"I would like them very much."

"Can you not make room? I know you like this furniture."

"Okay. I will do that. It's time I weeded out some of those books anyway. You arrange for the packing and shipping."

Her grandmother disappeared into the bedroom wing of the house. Maggie heard some books or something else hit the floor and her grandfather rushed to her aid. Eventually, her grandmother brought out an Eaton's dress box which she handed to Maggie. The navy cardboard was soft with age. She opened it carefully and found a dozen or more of her drawings.

"Thanks. My mother didn't save any of my stuff. What I would really like are pictures. Do you still have your photo albums?"

"Yes. Of course you may have them. I have four or five. Come, let's look."

They spent the remainder of the evening visiting and examining the family photographs. Maggie was appalled at the unhappiness she saw in her own face beginning at a young age. Despite her active athletic life, she actually appeared to be ill, especially around the age of six when she started school. She didn't, however, see any other images that would make her suspect that there was anything amiss. She packed them in a cardboard box and set them by the doorway to take back to Winnipeg with her.

Her grandparents talked about their recent trip to California and about their friends in the bridge club and about her cousins and their families, but when she tried to bring up her uncle Ross and his wife or her parents, they shut down completely. They would not say another word. Now that was strange.

She didn't stay up to see the New Year in. In the guest room, she climbed into the high bed, covered with a patchwork quilt made by her grandmother, this one in the log cabin pattern in multi shades of blue. The walls was painted a dusty blue and layers of white sheer curtains covered the narrow window. A portrait of her parents on their wedding day graced the chest of drawers, a picture that haunted her. The day was overcast and puddles of water lay on the sidewalk in front of the church at the Crossing. Neither of them smiled. Her father wore a rumpled brown suit and her mother a navy suit with a white shirt, which she probably wore to work at the insurance office. She carried no flowers and wore no veil, but her long hair was swept up in curls. Her mother told her once that Mike didn't want to spend money on a fancy wedding because they had to invest all the money they had in the farm.

Maggie felt some sympathy for her mother, perhaps for the first time. She lay on the bed, thinking about the day's events, slowly becoming aware that someone inside was repeating every word she and her grandparents had said.

"Who are you talking to?" she whispered aloud.

No one answered and she could no longer hear the recitation. She wondered if there was an alternate personality who informed the others about current events and she wondered how her mind was organized. After a while she fell into a dreamless sleep.

36

Monday, January 1, 1979

ON NEW YEAR'S Day, Maggie cooked a brunch of mushroom omelettes for herself and her grandparents, and then drove back to the city, laden with silverware, the photo albums and drawings, linens, a silver teapot and sugar and cream set, and a pinwheel crystal bowl. No one apparently wanted to take over the wheel, so she had an uneventful and enjoyable trip back to Winnipeg despite the frigid weather and ground drifting. As she entered the underground parking garage at her apartment, she spotted Anton's Nova parked in front of the building. He didn't ring the doorbell, however, and she forgot about him as she tucked her new possessions into storage.

She spent the late afternoon examining her grandmother's photographs. As before she could see nothing that might be wrong in the pictures, but then she realized that she wouldn't. The family was posing for those shots and would reveal nothing. She started looking for what was missing in the pictures, and she found it. There were no pictures in which her father showed his affection for her, no pictures of her seated on his knee, no pictures of him teaching her to ride her bike or play catch, no pictures of them rough-housing together, no pictures in which he touched her at all, no pictures of the two of them alone. As well, there were no pictures of her with her grandfather except those with the entire family.

Since it was New Year's Day, the curling rink and pool were both closed for the holiday, and she needed to move her body to get rid of the tension and fear and anger that abided there. She inserted a yoga video into her VHS and followed the routine on her purple mat and afterwards she felt more relaxed. After dinner she worked on the two pictures she'd started earlier. She sensed that she wasn't working alone but again she didn't black out.

Later, she packed two cardboard boxes of paperback fiction books she'd picked up in airports here and there, and placed them at her doorway to take to a used book store the next day. She moved some more of her favourite fiction to the black shelving in the living room and packed a third box with history books to take to the office, then changed her mind and deposited the history books in the recycling bin in the parking garage. She discovered four books on creative writing that she didn't know existed. She put three of them on the shelving in the studio and, although she had no desire to take up writing, curled up on her couch to read the fourth – *The Art of Readable Writing,* published in 1949, the year she was born.

She wrote on the yellow legal pad, Is there a writer in the house?

No one answered her question. If there were no writers inside, it seemed odd that she had those four books. Disappointed, she had a hot bubble bath and went to bed.

She dreamed that she and her grandfather are fishing below the MacNabb's Crossing Bridge. She turns her face to the sun. It warms her face and bare arms. It is early spring and the river is high; the fast moving current carries tree branches and debris as it foams and twists and gushes toward the sea. Her grandfather puts his right arm around her, ostensibly to help cast her hook into the cold water. She shrugs her shoulder, twists out of his grasp.

"Come here, Maggie."

"No. I am fishing. Leave me alone."

"I didn't come here to fish."

"Well, I did."

They are interrupted by a vanload of five children and three adults who descend on the riverbank, laughing and chattering to each other. They line up along the bank, bait their hooks and cast their lines into the water.

"Damn," mutters her grandfather.

"I have to get home, Grandpa. I have a 4-H meeting this afternoon."

"Come on then." He jerks her arm. "Get in the car."

He tramps hard on the accelerator and almost hits a tree as he takes off up the hill.

37

Tuesday, January 2, 1979

THE NEXT MORNING she woke up tired and feverish so she called Maxine to tell her she wouldn't be in that day. It was the second sick day she'd used since she started to work at J&W. She didn't feel bad enough to stay in bed, and she spent the morning continuing to tidy up her library. She placed more art books into her studio, and packed her political science and economics books to take to the office, changed her mind, and lugged them to the recycling bin. She had a nap and a couple of painkillers, and woke up refreshed. After lunch she packed a bath towel and her new swim suit into a sports bag and set off for the pool. She didn't notice Anton following her – she expected he'd be at work. As she was climbing the stairs to the complex, counting each step, he grabbed her by the arm.

"Alright. Who is he? You didn't come home New Year's Eve. Where were you? Who is he?"

"Where I go and what I do is none of your business. Let go of me." She jerked her arm free. Fortunately a group of people emerged from the building, evidently some he knew, because two voices called, "Hey, Anton."

In haste, Maggie ran into the building, changed into her bathing suit and swam laps for about twenty minutes, back and forth, back and forth, hard kicks off the ends, quick reverse, breathe in, breathe out, counting the strokes in the Australian crawl, use the arms to propel forward, kick and kick, and maybe the fear would dissipate. Afterwards, she searched the lobby area but didn't see him. She peeked out the exterior doors but couldn't see the Nova anywhere. Afraid to drive home, she called the city police from a pay phone in the lobby, reported Anton for violation of the restraining order, and waited until a patrol car could accompany her home.

As soon as she got home, she entered her studio, picked up her tackle box full of water colour paints, and blacked out.

Sometime during the night she dreamed that Anton chased her through the streets of Winnipeg. This time, he broke the side window of her car, cutting her face with flying glass. Then laughing like a hyena, he squealed his over-sized tires and left two strips of rubber on the pavement as he sped off.

38

Wednesday, January 3

WEDNESDAY MORNING MAGGIE didn't remember what she had done the evening before, but she wasn't aware of it. The first thing she did that morning was write on the yellow legal pad, 'Please let me do my work today.'

Not waiting for a reply, she just had her breakfast, dressed for the day in her red sweater and gray slacks, lugged the boxes of books and paintings to the Buick and drove to work. When she marked herself 'In' at Maxine's desk, she stayed a few minutes to ask the receptionist if she had a good holiday and to compliment her on the beautifully decorated waiting area. She didn't notice Maxine's surprised look as she pushed the button for the elevator.

She arranged the books in the teak bookcase, hung the pictures in the blank space above the small table, and surveyed the effect. Her office was much homier but it still lacked something. She asked Maxine to contact the plant lady. She wanted two or three spider plants and whatever else the green thumbed woman thought appropriate. She couldn't see Maxine's astonished face.

During the morning hours, she accomplished a great deal and thought she was home free, but as soon as she stopped for lunch, a hand insisted on writing on her yellow legal pad. It wrote, 'You think you're a real hot shot lawyer, don't you? Well, I don't want to be a lawyer and I am going to get us out of here. So there. I don't like you and I don't like this office. And you don't have any right to put Lynne's pictures in your office. Who do you think you are anyway? I am going to find us another job and get the hell out of here.'

The writing was similar to Maggie's but had a definite slant to the left. Initially it was quite large taking up four or five lines on the pad, but as he or she carried on the rant, the writing became smaller and more controlled. She spoke out loud, "What kind of a job do you want?"

The writer hesitated and then started again. 'I want to work outside even when it is cold. I want to grow things. I want to be a farmer. I do not want some lady coming in with plants. I want to get my hands in the dirt and I want to choose the plants and I want to transplant them. I don't want anyone else doing my job for me.'

"Did you belong to the garden club in 4-H?"

'Yes, I did. With no help from you I might add. I had to push my way between you and your books to get noticed at all. Sometimes Mother had to intervene or you wouldn't have done it at all. Man, you are stubborn. I don't like you at all. You think you run this show and you do not. Okay, so you are the one making money right now. Well, I can make money too and I am going to take over and get us out of this jail cell of an office and outside. I don't care if it is twenty below.'

Jared interrupted the conversation. "Is your schedule clear tomorrow afternoon?"

"Yes. It is." She slid the pad of paper into the top drawer of her desk.

"Okay. Let me see. Meet me in that small conference room across from my office at two o'clock."

"Okay."

To her relief, the writing did not start again after Jared left her office. Without stopping to speculate why, she ripped the pages off the pad, tore them in quarters and threw them in the garbage. But she was suddenly afraid the cleaning lady would read them, so she retrieved them from the trash can. She hoped no one was watching through the open door as she tucked the pages into her purse.

After work, she drove home, looking for Anton, but not seeing the Nova anywhere. She quickly changed into jeans, gobbled down a Red Delicious apple, and loaded the remaining boxes of books into the Buick. The owner of the used book store was only too happy to buy the books from her, but wanted to give credit instead of money. She was about to refuse when she noticed some children's books on the crowded shelves – *Anne of Green Gables, Anne of Avonlea* and *Little Women*. She didn't have those in her library but knew she had read them at one time. She placed them reverently in the back of her car, climbed behind the wheel. She couldn't go home, not yet. She was as restless as Maggie the cat. She swam for her usual half hour and drove home for supper. She thought she saw the red Nova, but she might have been mistaken.

She relaxed on the couch and with a sigh picked up the pen. The writing began slowly. The handwriting was certainly not the same as that of her noon hour visitor. It too was large taking up three or four lines, but it was a child's printing. It said, 'Thank you for taking care of me. I didn't want to stay with Mom and Dad. I am sorry that I got lost in New York. It is a big and scary place and I thought that big man was going to hurt me.'

"What's your name?"

There was no reply. She was gone.

She went back to *Little Women*, suddenly remembering that she had borrowed the book from Sandy.

Maggie is catching up on her arithmetic problems. Sandy runs to her desk, waving an over-sized book with a smoky blue cover. "Maggie, look at this. It's a horse story. Look at the colt's head on the front. See – Misty, *Misty of Chincoteague*. I think that's how I say it. But look. Look at the drawings. It's about ponies and a horse race."

Rachel with the long black hair is walking past. "What'd you find, Sandy?" She glances through the book. "I've never noticed this one before. Do you want me to read it to you?"

"Oh, yes, please," cries Maggie.

Rachel sits down on the floor with her back against the wall with one little girl on each side of her. She reads *Misty of Chincoteague*, the story of a wild filly on the east coast of Virginia. Maggie forgets all about her teacher and Dick and Jane and loses herself in the story.

She admires the pen and ink sketches and misses not a word spoken by Rachel's clear voice. Sarah and George stop by and sit cross-legged in front of the reader. It takes three noon hours to finish the volume but by then Maggie is hooked on reading. She takes Misty home with her after school and reads it herself, pestering her mother every few minutes to help with the harder words.

Dressed in her kilt and a black turtleneck sweater, she arrived at Sandy's at six thirty. Sam and Sandy had created a dance studio in her roomy basement, one wall covered with mirrors to allow the dancers to watch themselves – a good way to check for correct posture. A set of brightly coloured stacking chairs lined the perimeter and six posters showing the various dance positions were tacked to the wood-panelled walls.

Maggie enjoyed helping the little girls get started, first position, second position, the same old drill, Scottish music playing in the background, Danny watching with amusement. Melissa wasn't content to play with her brother with all that excitement going on, so Maggie picked her up and danced with the little one on her hip. After the lesson was over the two friends collapsed on the sofa laughing. It was so much like old times.

"Don't run away," urged Sandy. "I'll get these two busy with their homework and Lissa to bed and then we can talk."

"Where are your photo albums?"

"Upstairs in the hall closet."

Maggie leafed through the books while she waited for Sandy to join her. She was surprised at how happy she looked in Sandy's pictures compared to her Grandma's.

"Could I borrow these? I'd like to have copies made of a few of these. I have none of them, not even the ones of the competitions."

"Yes. Certainly. Now tell me."

"Well. I really don't remember much of my childhood. I have blocked it all out. Well. It is all coming back to me in bits and pieces. I have trouble sleeping and it is just really weird."

"Why on earth did you block it out?"

"Young Mike molested me when I was in grade one. Dad caught him and kicked him out of the house and sent him to Saskatchewan."

"Oh, no. You never said a word about it."

"I was too ashamed. But then how did I know? Maybe it wasn't abnormal."

"So you've been carrying this around all these years. That is awful. So you want the pictures to stimulate more memories."

"Yes, I do, if you don't mind. I went home at Christmas to do the same thing, and it did bring up some stuff, but Dad is such a jerk. I couldn't stay in his house."

"Does he blame you? Surely not."

"I don't know. I can't figure it out. Mike was sixteen and knew better and I was just a little kid. I don't know. I just don't know."

"Holy. I am glad you told me. I am sorry, but Danny needs help with his math. Don't forget. Pick him up at eight thirty on Saturday."

"Thanks for the albums. And thanks for listening. See you Saturday."

Maggie passed the remainder of the evening examining the pictures. She chose a dozen to have copied. She saw how loving and natural Sam had been with his three daughters and how happy they were in his presence and she felt a stab of jealousy. One of the pictures she wanted was of her and Sandy with Sam, sitting on their veranda with Mack their dog. She was just as loved, well almost as loved, as his own daughters. She felt a rush of gratitude.

She wrote photograph, photo, graph, pot, opt, top, got, rot, goat, hot, hoot, root, pat, apt, tap, rapt, groat, hat, oat, hop, hoop, pop, poop, hog, hag, pap, Pa, Po, pooh, go, ho, tao, par, rap, poor, oar, gap, too, to, harp, tarp, prop, hoar, port, part, art, hart, trap.

39

Thursday, January 4

ON THURSDAY MORNING she wanted to wear her new skirt suit for the meeting with Jared. She pulled on one pair of panty hose that were too small, pealed those off, tried another pair and put her thumb through the mesh. She gave up and wore her black man-tailored pantsuit with the red silky shirt and her dress boots. The morning turned out to be unremarkable but she had to rush home during her lunch hour to take delivery of the dining room suite. Her grandparents had hired a local handyman to deliver the furniture and he was prompt and efficient. She had forgotten that the suite included a side board as well as a tall china cabinet and seven chairs, six armless ones and another larger armchair. The handyman and his helper managed to squeeze it all into her library, while she quickly moved books out of the way. She offered them a tip but they refused to take it, saying her grandparents had paid them quite well, thank you.

She returned to work, aware that the firm's partners had met that morning. She was getting curious about the meeting with Jared. Promptly at two, she knocked on the conference room door and entered to find Jared and another lawyer Brad Kowalski sitting at the table deep in conversation.

"You know Brad, don't you, Maggie?" asked her boss.

"Yes. We've met. Nice to see you again, Brad," responded Maggie.

He nodded, ignored her outstretched hand, and stared at the documents on the table. Jared questioned him with a look, but carried on. "Brad is working on a case of breach of contract involving one of our clients and an American firm. As you can see by the pile of documents on the table, it is quite complex, and he could use some help along with your expertise in international law. The parties are far apart and we expect the case to go to court. Would you be interested in working with Brad? He will be senior counsel."

"Yes. I would." It was just what she was hoping for.

"Good, I'll leave you to it." Jared melted out of the room.

"I just want you to know that there will be no hanky-panky working with me. I am a married man and I plan to stay that way."

"What? Why would you even bring that up?"

"Well, everybody knows you've been playing footsy with old Jared all this time – you even spent a week with him in New York, didn't you?"

"Jared was not in New York. How dare you make insinuations like this?"

"Well, it all comes from having single women working here. It creates tension in the office."

"Is that so? You may rest assured that I am not interested in Jared. Nor am I interested in you. My social life is private and none of your concern. I'll take these materials to my office and work there."

Half an hour later she phoned Jared. "Is Brad still in the conference room? I need to talk to you without his knowledge."

"I'll come to you."

Still steamed, she repeated what Brad had said to her. "My reputation and yours are at stake here, Jared."

"Good God. We've never so much as had lunch together. Who starts these things? Well, for starters, you could put a blurb in the office newsletter wishing my wife Karen a speedy recovery from the surgery she had before Christmas. That should stop some rumours. Then I will talk to Brad. Keep working on the file. I'm glad you told me so quickly." He strode out of her office, obviously troubled.

At four o'clock on the dot, Maggie left the office. She had to be at the arena for her first hockey practice by six. Marilyn, a paralegal from J&W, introduced her to their coach Kevin and the rest of the women on the team, and showed her how to tape her sticks. When she first arrived, the women were talkative, bantering back and forth, but they soon settled down to the serious business at hand. She could feel Sammy's energy as she tightened up her skates. Completely dressed, she stood up and immediately sat down again, unaccustomed to the weight of the equipment.

Since this was a beginners' group, she fit in readily. She could skate better than many on the team, especially when it came to doing crossovers and skating backwards. The coach, a sandy haired man of medium height and undeterminable age, put his players through a rigorous practice. Maggie had difficulty handling the puck for the first time, but the coach told her not to worry. He seemed pleased to have another skater on the team.

When she got home, she immediately filled her bathtub with hot water and Epsom salts to release any stiffness from her muscles. As soon as she was ready for bed, she lay awake thinking. She was acutely aware that every move she made was being monitored by the ones inside, the alters, or alter personalities or whatever they were called. She knew that if she didn't please them, one of them could take over and she would be moved about like a puppet on a string, or else one could write in the legal pad, calling her names and ordering her to do whatever he or she wanted. She also knew perfectly well that the ones inside didn't agree with each other, so she was not at all sure how to approach life. She decided that the only approach possible was to live as she had always lived, but adding painting, curling and playing hockey, cooking and baking, and going to movies and dancing and seeing friends as well.

Her mind turned to her colleague Brad. Was he still back in the fifties? She hoped she could stay on that case; it would be interesting to be in a court room again, and she wanted to hear what the judge had to say about the contract Brad had written.

The voices started. You're going to kill yourself. You're going to kill your father. You're going to kill Mike. You're going to kill me. You're going to kill yourself.

"Who are you?" she said aloud. "Talk to me. Tell me something else. Stop talking about killing. Do you want to write?"

You're going to kill Mike. You're going to kill your father. You're going to marry your father. You're going to kill yourself.

Annoyed she ran to the living room and picked up the pen. 'Talk to me,' she wrote. There was no reply. She went back to bed. The voices started again.

You're going to kill yourself. You're going to kill Rob. You're going to kill your father. You're going to kill me.

She tried to ignore them, but they wouldn't let her sleep. Eventually the voices died down and she fell into a restless slumber.

40

Friday, January 5

FRIDAY. SHE NOW counted the days. Every day was an adventure, not always a pleasant adventure, but an adventure nonetheless.

Dressed in the royal blue coat dress she found hidden in her closet, she arrived at her office at her usual time, shed her outdoor clothing and checked her appearance in the mirror. To her astonishment, the face in the mirror was wearing eye makeup and her hair was streaked blonde. She stepped out of the powder room just as Jared shoved the door open and strode into her office.

"I thought for a second you looked a bit strange," he said seating himself on one of the accent chairs at the desk.

"I feel a little strange. All my exercise must be changing me somehow. Did you talk to Brad? Did he deny it?"

"Yes. I asked him about it, and he didn't deny it. In fact he said that he doesn't want to work with you."

"That is discrimination."

"I suppose you could interpret it that way, but he is a senior man here. He's being considered for a partnership. He has a right to choose his co-counsel."

"So I'm off the case?"

"Yes. We'll find you something else. By the way, Bob Armston is in town. You remember him, don't you? I would like you to take him out to dinner tonight and show him a good time."

"No. I'm curling at seven."

"Oh. Well. Tomorrow then."

Maggie's blue eyes blackened with anger. "No. I am a lawyer, not a call girl."

"Okay. Fine. Take these documents down to Brad's office." He rose awkwardly from his chair and turned to leave the room.

"If he wants them, he can come and get them."

"No. That's three times you've said no to me in three minutes. I am wondering about your future with this firm."

"Funny. I'm wondering the same thing."

He stared into her eyes for a full minute then left without saying anything more. A few minutes later a red-headed freckled boy knocked on her door and asked for the documents. She thought at first he must be a newly hired young lawyer, but then recalled that he was the grandson of one of the partners, which one she didn't know. She joined her new skating friends for lunch at Alexander's and had an unusually enjoyable lunch hour, although she was still furious at Jared. She took her time and arrived back at her office about one thirty. At two, she had an appointment with Rodney Thomason who was starting a new and exciting project and wanted her involvement.

She left a few minutes early to spend some time with Dr. Dixon. They talked for perhaps ten minutes about the recent events in Maggie's life and then he abruptly said, "I'd like to speak to Miranda."

The woman before him grabbed her purse from the floor and rummaged through it, obviously searching for something.

"What are you looking for?" asked the doctor.

"Gum. That uptight broad never has any gum."

"You are Miranda?"

"Ya. What do you want from me?" She found some dark red lipstick in the black leather handbag and applied a generous coat using the doctor's wall mirror. She sashayed around the office examining every item on his shelves and every piece of equipment he had. She moved as if she hadn't a care in the world.

167

"I wanted to meet you. That's all. How old are you?"

"Sixteen. I can drive a car. I drive all the time now and what's her face doesn't even know."

"Did something bad happen to you?"

"Ya. Might as well tell you I guess. I was seeing this guy Phil, not going steady or anything. We sometimes walked uptown at lunch hour if we weren't playing volleyball or some dumb thing like that. And in the summer we met at the movies when my Dad took us to town on Saturday nights. But he'd only kissed me, like once. Anyway, we were walking down Main Street in Sampford this one night and Rob and all his friends met us, and started jostling us, wouldn't get out of the way. Rob put his arm around Phil's shoulders as if they were real buddies and said, "Don't let my little sister pull one over on you. She ain't a virgin anyway." Then he laughed his stupid head off and he and his stupid friends took off down the street."

"That was mean. Did you know what he meant?"

"Ya. I did. I knew about Mike. Well, Phil wanted to know the truth and I wouldn't tell him. I was so embarrassed, so angry at Rob, so sure everybody in the entire school would know by Monday. I just found a place to hide and I stayed there. At least until I saw the chance to drive."

"I see. What do you want to do now?"

"Beat the stuffing out of Rob, but I can't do that. I want to listen to music and go dancing and have some fun. What's her name doesn't have much fun. Now that she ditched that Anton, maybe we'll do something fun. I want to go now."

She dropped her head to her chin. Maggie sat up and crossed her legs and leaned forward. "What did she say?"

"You couldn't hear? She said Rob teased her in public about not being a virgin."

"Did he now? That was horrible."

"Yes. Traumatic. You should add something a sixteen year old teenager likes to do. Get a new haircut, get your face made up, buy some new records, I don't know."

"A teenager? I don't know how to be a teenager. All I did when I was a teenager was make money however I could and study like a mad demon to get into law school. Well, tomorrow we babysit

Danny. That's a teenager's job, I suppose. Thanks, doctor. See you next week."

Before she went home, she scouted out an Anglican church to attend the following Sunday, using the phone book as her guide. There were several in the area near her apartment, but an old stone one in Osborne Village appealed to her, reminded her of the church she attended as a child, and was off the beaten path in a well-treed part of the city. She knocked on the varnished doors at the front and a green door on the north side and tried the intercom but no one answered. Either the office closed before five or wasn't open at all on Fridays. But it was a good place to start.

She passed the evening creating a pen and ink drawing of a horse's head using a photograph as a model. Her heart wasn't in it but someone else's was. She retired early but couldn't fall asleep.

The voices said, You're going to kill yourself. You're going to kill Mike. You're going to kill me.

"I'd like to kill myself just to get rid of you," she shouted into the dark room.

You're going to kill your father.

Out loud she said, "Shut up. Just shut up."

Her body writhed and twisted, trying to get away from something or someone and she shadow boxed with an imaginary foe, punching and kicking and feinting. She wanted to scream but was afraid her neighbours in the block would hear her. She cried, "Don't, don't, don't," into her pillow. Finally she fell asleep.

She dreamed she is watching television in the new farmhouse, laying on the couch with her feet up on the arm rest. She and her mother are watching *Perry Mason*, a sharp successful lawyer who owns a big black convertible, a Lincoln. The secretary Della Street wants to become a lawyer too, but Perry and Paul Drake the detective laugh at her. They think she is silly. Girls aren't lawyers. They have to be secretaries.

41

Saturday, January 6

ON SATURDAY MORNING, Maggie turned into Sandy's driveway promptly at eight thirty, where her new friend Danny was waiting impatiently at the door. She waved to Sandy, loaded his equipment into the hatchback and climbed behind the wheel. Danny was already seated with his seatbelt done up and ready to go.

"Okay, chum. Let's go. Will you need my help getting dressed?"

"Nah. Well, you could tighten my skates for me."

"Kay." As soon as they arrived at the rink, Danny lugged his sticks and hockey bag down the ramp to the dressing rooms in the lower level. Maggie bought a cup of coffee and wandered about the waiting room examining the photos on the walls and the trophies in the cases. After perhaps ten minutes, she descended to the dressing room to check on Danny. His father Jim stood in the middle of the room, arguing loudly with Danny's coach. She didn't believe that was appropriate, so she strode up to him and said, "Hello, Jim. I'm Maggie, if you remember. Danny's with me today. Maybe you should go out in the hall and let me help Danny get ready."

He glared at her, but the coach ushered him into the hall, and he had no chance to respond.

"Thanks," whispered Danny. "What's the matter with him? He's acting like a psycho."

"I don't know," answered Maggie in an equally subdued tone. "I'll be waiting for you at the top of the ramp after the game. Try to forget about it and have a good time."

During the game Jim watched from behind the glass in the lobby, but Maggie went out to the bleachers where it was more interesting, and when the game was over, she looked around for Jim, but he seemed to have disappeared. As promised, she waited at the top of the ramp. Danny hustled past her, straight to the Buick. She glanced around the parking lot as she loaded his hockey equipment, but didn't see any sign of Jim. They piled out of the car at the house and Danny ran in to tell his mother that they had won the game and that he got an assist on the winning goal. Maggie retrieved his equipment and followed him into the house. Suddenly the door flew open and Jim barged into the living room.

"Where's my boy? I want my son," he hollered.

Danny dashed down the hallway to his room and closed and locked the door.

Jim confronted his wife, Maggie at her side. "You can't have him. He's my son."

Caroline curled up on a green tub chair, staring at her father in disbelief. He marched down the hall and pounded on Danny's door. "Let me in. Let me in."

Sandy quietly retreated to the corner table, picked up the phone and dialled a number. She whispered something and then hung up. A minute or two later, a burly city police officer entered through the open door. Jim was still yelling in the hallway. With three long strides, the cop landed beside Jim.

"Jim. Jim. Calm down. What's the trouble here?"

Alan, the policeman and next door neighbour, guided Jim to the living room and forced him to sit on the couch. Jim's clothes were dirty and un-pressed, his hair was greasy and unkempt, and he hadn't shaved. His wandering eyes didn't seem to focus on anything, so it was no surprise to Maggie that Danny was afraid of him.

"Call his parents," Alan suggested.

Sandy did his bidding. No one spoke for several minutes.

"I want my son," murmured Jim.

"Jim. You have not called Danny since you left. You have not tried to see him. What is all this?" Sandy asked.

"I want my son," murmured Jim again.

Maggie and Sandy looked at each other and then at Alan. There was something very wrong with Jim. The Bordens arrived a few minutes later and Alan took them aside and explained the situation.

"Maggie, isn't it? Nice to see you again," Marion said. Gus nodded in Maggie's direction and immediately took charge of the situation. "We'll take him to his family doctor." They supported Jim on either side as they accompanied him to their waiting car.

As soon as the door closed, Sandy ran down the hall and knocked on Danny's door. "Come out, son. Your father is gone. Are you okay?"

Danny opened the door and hugged his mother. She kept her arm around him as they walked into the living room. He ran to Maggie and hugged her too. "Thanks. Maggie."

She ruffled his hair. "You are totally welcome."

They relaxed for a few minutes, without speaking, recovering from the shock and surprise of Jim's behaviour.

"Tell Tom Henton about this," lawyer Maggie advised. "Well, I'm going to take off. Call me if you need me."

She was too restless and stirred up to go home, so she swam for three quarters of an hour, counting her strokes as always, suddenly able to hear the count, fifty-six, fifty-seven, fifty-eight. She counted along, fifty-nine, sixty, sixty-one, sixty-two, sixty-three, and the unknown counter stopped, and she could think about something else.

Maybe Sandy was well rid of her husband and maybe she should sue for full custody of the children.

After she dried her hair and changed from her swim, she still didn't want to go home, so she wandered up and down the corridors of the Polo Park Mall, and stopped at a hairdressing salon. Her favourite hairdresser surprisingly had time to cut her hair, and she asked for something a bit different from her usual boy cut. Elana suggested that they let it grow out a little more to show off her natural curls. So after a trim, she continued to meander down the mall. At the Sears entrance, she remembered Dr. Dixon's advice about getting her face done. She propped herself on the high stool at the L'Oréal counter where a short blonde husky girl agreed to give her a makeup demonstration. A half hour later, she looked in the mirror and hardly recognized herself, her dark eyes highlighted in brown tones, her face covered in sheer foundation with a touch of blusher, her full lips sporting a subdued maroon, almost brown, tone.

Chuckling, she bought all the makeup – the mascara, the lipstick, the foundation, the blusher, the finishing powder, the eyeliner and the eye shadow. Someone inside was happy too. After dinner, she settled down on the couch to relax with *Hockey Night in Canada*. During the second intermission, she felt a strong urge to write, so she picked up the pen and wrote, 'Let's go out.'

"It's been quite a day. Let's stay home."

'No. Come on. New hair cut. All made up. For nothing? Come on. Let's go.'

"Well, okay. It is Saturday night."

Maggie changed into a clean pair of jeans, the ones she bought in New York, and her Arran sweater. She checked the movie listings but there really wasn't anything she wanted to see. She drove past the Blue Rose looking for Anton's Nova, but it was nowhere in sight, so she stopped in for a drink.

Rebecca and Sadie were perched on barstools at the end of the long counter. Rebecca said, "Maggie. Look at you. Makeup! I have never seen you wear makeup before. Did you turn a new leaf or something?"

Maggie grinned. "No. It's the same old me. I was wandering through the mall and had this fit. And here I am."

"Looks good." Rebecca tucked her golden brown hair behind her right ear and waved to the bartender.

"Really? I feel like a clown."

Sadie, who was gorgeous with or without makeup, tossed her long blonde hair and said, "Why don't you wear makeup?"

"I don't believe I need to hide my face behind a lot of gunk. Men don't. Anyway, to me it's gaudy. It looks good on anyone else, but not on me."

Rebecca said, "Didn't you play with your mother's makeup when you were young?"

"No. I don't remember doing that. All my mother ever wore was a touch of lipstick."

Maggie ordered a Brown Cow, as usual, and sipped on it slowly through the straw. Paul sidled up to her. "I thought that was you. You clean up good."

"Hi. Thanks. I think." It was a good thing she knew Sammy's friend.

"Want to shoot a game?"

Maggie won the first game but she didn't feel Sammy's presence. Paul was easily victorious in the second and he took the rubber match, but she wasn't far behind. She worried all the time whether she seemed different than the last time they met, when Sammy was playing. After the games, she returned to the bar to talk with her friends and have another drink.

"There's Anton," whispered Rebecca. "Don't turn around. Maybe he won't know you with your new haircut."

Maggie was not afraid of a confrontation, if unavoidable, and made no move to hide from her ex-boyfriend. He didn't stay, however, and the three friends moved to a table and ordered coffee and a plate of nachos.

"Becky, tell me. You spend most of your time defending clients in criminal cases, don't you?"

"Yes. Mainly. I also do pro bono work for Legal Aid. I like it well enough. Why? Thinking of making a change?"

"I don't know. Maybe. I may have just hit the so-called glass ceiling. Do you ever feel that way?"

Sadie answered, "I do. The men always seem to get the more interesting and more complicated cases."

"Does being single make a difference?" Maggie pushed for more answers.

"Yes. I think it does. Or possibly just being a woman does," Rebecca nodded as she spoke. "I am usually left out of conferences and golf games and lunch meetings."

Later in the evening, Maggie rested her weary head on her new green pillow case.

She is at a dance in the gymnasium at Sampford Collegiate. One of the grade twelve boys sidles up to her, rubbing his arm and shoulder on hers suggestively.

"How about it, toots?"

"How about what?"

"Ah, don't get cute with me. Your brother told us all about you."

"Get lost."

"What's wrong with me?"

"I don't know what's wrong with you. If there's something wrong with you, see a doctor."

He walks off, obviously angry, and disappears in a crowd of students.

She knows perfectly well what he wanted and the evening has taken on a sour note. Sandy and Linda accost her on the way to the washroom. "Maggie. Ralph's telling everybody that you're going to the gravel pit with him after the dance. You aren't, are you?"

"No. Definitely not. What's with that guy? I am getting out of here."

"How'd you get here?"

"Dad's car."

"Do you want us to walk out with you?"

"As chaperones or body guards?" asks Maggie bitterly.

"Body guards of course. What's going on?" Sandy says as they walk through the gravel covered parking lot.

"Oh, Rob was shooting his mouth off. Told the guys I wasn't a virgin. Now I'm a slut, don't you know? Some of the girls won't even talk to me."

"Nice brother you've got."

"Since when?"

"Well, here's your car. I'm sure it will all blow over before long. Good night. See you at church tomorrow."

Maggie slides behind the wheel of her father's new Chevy and takes off into the night, but she doesn't go home right away. She drives all the way to Brandon before she decides she'd better stop wasting gasoline and she makes a U-turn and goes to the farm.

42

Sunday, January 7

SUNDAY MORNING, MAGGIE stayed in bed until nine, not caring if she got up at all, and then had to hurry to make it to church by ten thirty. She was intrigued as soon as she entered the narthex of St. Luke's, the century-old stone Anglican church, where there was a mural of the risen Christ dedicated to the Winnipeg Grenadiers, painted by a member of the Group of Seven. The rich dark wood interior suited her need for comfort and she felt the sacredness of the place as soon as she stepped inside the nave. *The Book of Alternative Services*, which provided the congregation with the liturgy, the interactive service, the robes of the priests, and the lengthy Eucharist celebration, was all new to her, a girl raised in the United Church at the Crossing. She especially enjoyed the opportunity to sing along with the excellent choir. In his homily the bespectacled priest spoke on the hope that the birth of Christ brought to the world, both the Gentiles and the Jews. Something stirred deep inside.

After lunch she called the curling rink for practice ice but there was none available. She skated for about an hour on an outdoor rink. She might have stayed longer but there was a group of teenagers who interrupted her counting as they slapped a puck around. She wished she had brought a stick too but probably they wouldn't want her to join them anyway. She went home, puzzled that she didn't feel left out.

She sat down at her ever-present yellow legal pad and wrote, Sammy, Sammy. Talk to me. Write. Sammy, are you there?

There was no response.

She spoke out loud, "Sammy. Sammy."

Nothing happened.

She went to the bathroom mirror, looked directly into her eyes. "Sammy. Sammy. Talk to me."

Sammy did not emerge, did not speak, did not write. She turned on the television to watch a game of American football, but Sammy still did not appear.

She is back at the Crossing elementary school. The boys want to play tackle football – after all, that's how the game is played. Mrs. McClure comes out to check on her students and finds all of the girls hovering around the faded red wood-framed swings behind the school. Diane and Rachel sit in the long grass next to the page wire fence talking, and Beth and Carol bounce on the varnished teeter-totters. Sandy and Sarah are quietly swaying on the swings with their arms wrapped around the heavy chains that reach to the red seats while Maggie lies in the grass chewing a fresh blade and watching the clouds float overhead.

"Why aren't you playing with the boys, Maggie?" The teacher wants to know.

"I hate football. I don't like to be tackled."

Their small rebellion yields the desired result. Since there aren't enough boys to have a really good game, the boys relent and play flag football after that.

Although Maggie did enjoy football, her focus was now on healing her shattered personality. She paused, waited for inspiration from within, and felt the desire to paint. In her studio, she chose a sixteen by twenty oil painting canvass, and from Sandy's photo album, she picked a picture of the church at the Crossing. She outlined the building in charcoal and painted all afternoon, stopping at seven only because she was hungry. She had leftover hamburger soup with thick slices of bakery bread and Apple Brown Betty for dessert.

After she'd cleaned up the studio and her brushes and hands, she read a few chapters of *Little Women*. She searched in the library for something different to read, something that would take her to a different time period in her life. She found her forgotten wooden paint box under some university textbooks. In the studio she chucked the old dried up tubes of oil paint in the garbage and filled her box with her new oil paint, then returned to the library. She spied a tattered copy of *Black Beauty*. Without moving from her cross-legged position on the floor, she read the opening paragraphs.

When Black Beauty was mistreated, she felt the horse's pain deep in her own stomach. The book didn't bring up any memories, but that night as she tried unsuccessfully to fall asleep, her body writhed and twisted, responded as if in the throes of sexual intercourse, a hand on her mouth, the desire to scream.

43

Monday, January 8

MONDAY MORNING SHE had no desire to go to work. All ambition seemed to be gone, but she went anyway. Around ten o'clock, Maxine rang to say that a Mr. Gus Borden was there to see her.

"I'll be right down."

"Mr. Borden. Gus. Good morning. How nice to see you. Would you come up to my office to talk?"

"Good morning Maggie. No. This will only take a minute." He motioned her to follow her to the corner where she'd broken up with Anton a short time ago. "First I want to thank you for helping Sandy at this time. My son is not well, I'm afraid."

Maggie took a sharp breath and was about to say, No thanks necessary, but he kept on talking.

"I came to ask you if you'd consider joining Borden International."

Her mouth dropped open and her eyes widened.

"Come to the house for dinner tomorrow evening about seven? We'll discuss it further then."

"Yes. Thank you. I'll be there at seven."

Abruptly he turned and walked out.

Jared was waiting in her office. "What did Borden want? Is he going to bring some business here? Tell me. What did he want from you?"

Maggie had no choice but to tell him the truth. "Actually, no. He offered me a position in his company."

"Oh. Well. Let's talk about that. Did you know that Anton is Marshall Jenkins' grandson?"

"No. I did not. What does that have to do with anything?"

"Marshall is very unhappy that you accused Anton of slashing your tires without corroborating evidence. You then placed a restraining order on Anton for no reason and reported him for accosting you at the pool. Will you rescind the order?"

"No. I will not."

"Well, then. I suggest you take the rest of this week off – you have plenty of annual leave to cover it. Think about your future in this firm." He stormed out of the office.

Maggie wondered whether she was hired to be Anton's woman or to provide legal counsel. She left the office taking her black horse's head with her. She dropped by the pool but it was busy with aqua-cise classes, so she telephoned the curling rink. Several sheets were free for practice. She quickly went home to change into her curling pants and drove to the rink. Her coach was, of course, absent, but Brian the rink manager took his place. They worked together for about an hour before he was called to the telephone. She waited for Sammy to take over, but nothing happened. She practiced for another half hour, had a cheeseburger and fries upstairs in the cafeteria, and went home to her black leather couch.

She spent the afternoon reading, made a salmon salad for dinner, and was back at the rink at a quarter to seven. Sandy arrived as they were going out on the ice, so she didn't get a chance to speak to her. After the game it was a tradition for each team to have a drink with its opposition, but Sandy disappeared after perhaps fifteen minutes. Maggie stayed with her rink until everyone was ready to leave so that she could get to know the skip Angela, third (vice-skip) Betty and second Heather.

When she arrived back at her apartment, there was a phone message was waiting from her mother, "Call me at my mother's place."

Maggie knew from her mother's tone that some calamity had occurred. She dialled the number immediately. Mary Ellen informed her that her grandfather had had a heart attack. He was in hospital and asked to see her. Maggie hesitated. She wasn't sure she wanted to see her grandfather, but she promised to come first thing in the morning and hung up.

She tried to sleep but the voices wouldn't let her.

You're going to kill your father.

You're going to kill yourself.

You're going to kill Rob.

You're going to marry your father.

You're going to kill yourself.

You're going to kill your grandfather.

44

Tuesday, January 9

SHE LEFT THE apartment the next morning at seven o'clock. It was minus thirty-two degrees with a nasty little wind blowing. The windows on the Buick fogged up as soon as she left the parking garage and she had to park on the roadside and wait five minutes for the windshield to clear. It was dark and gloomy when she passed Assiniboia Downs, where horse races were held in summer, but she who loved horses had never gone. As the sun came up, it cast pink and purple shadows on the white snow.

A death bed summons from her grandfather wasn't something Maggie expected. She couldn't imagine what he might have to say to her. Why she'd obeyed his command was another mystery she couldn't fathom.

In Portage la Prairie she ate two slices of fried ham with scrambled eggs and hashed browns and downed two cups of coffee. The Buick protested when she started it so she let it run for a few minutes and then took off again. The miles slipped away quickly as she drove along listening to radio and humming along to her favourite tunes. In Brandon, she drove directly to the hospital, a red brick building with white trim. Maggie smelled that hospital aroma as soon as she entered the sterile lobby. The helpful nurses guided her to the room where her mother sat on a green recliner near the bed reading a magazine. Her grandfather's face appeared pale and fragile on the starched white bedding. Her mother leaned over to whisper in his ear, "Maggie's here."

The old man lying in that bed had very little resemblance to the tall virile man who was Maggie's grandfather. She approached the bed warily. He opened his rheumy eyes, still as blue as the sky, and murmured, "Maggie. I am sorry." Then he closed his eyes, turned his head to the side and relaxed. He was dead.

Mary Ellen frantically pushed the alarm button, and doctors and nurses rushed into the room, but it was too late to revive him. Grandma MacDonar was summoned from the cafeteria. Maggie hugged her grandmother, asked her mother to let her know when the arrangements were made, and walked out of the hospital. She wasn't sure whether it was Miranda or herself who drove back to Winnipeg, but they made it without incident.

What exactly was he sorry for? She was more depressed than sad. Her body demanded exercise. She phoned the pool. No. No public swimming. She called the curling rink. No. No sheets free. The outdoor skating oval, however, was empty. She skated for fifteen minutes all alone in the rink, just listening to the sound of her blades on the ice, not thinking, not mourning her grandfather's passing, not worrying about her employment crisis, counting her foot strokes, not caring if she had a hundred alters inside. She hears it again, ninety-seven, ninety-eight, ninety-nine, a hundred. She counts out loud, one hundred one, one hundred two, one hundred three, one hundred four, and the count ceases, she can't hear it. By now her nose and cheeks were white with frost and the tips of her fingers icicles.

She is so hot, lying in bed under a pile of Mary Ellen's homemade quilts with orders to stay covered or else. The curtains in her room in the new house are drawn tight with blankets over top to keep out all traces of light which could damage her eyes. Her skin is itchy and it crawls as if she's found one wood tick and now thinks there's another on her scalp, on her legs, on her back and in her ears, and the pustules of chicken pox ooze onto her blue pyjamas and the white flannelette sheets, the blue stripes across the top. Her unusually solicitous mother offers her some ice chips to ease her parched throat and chapped lips.

"Mom, could I have a radio in here?" she croaks.

Mary Ellen brings a white box of a radio with a circular dial of clear plastic and Maggie with what little strength she has, finds her favourite station and lays back on her pillow. Hearing a commotion in the hall, she opens her eyes to see Rob coming into her room dragging his bed covers with him.

"Move over. I want to hear the radio too. Did you get CKY?"

She moves to the edge of the twin bed, taking her own bed clothes with her, glad to have some company even if it is her brother, and they lay side by side, careful not to touch each other.

"Yeah. It's on KY58. I'm so itchy I could die," she says.

"What is that pink shit that she puts on our pocks?"

"Calamine lotion. It doesn't do much good but at least it doesn't stink like the vinegar and baking soda she was using."

"I feel terrible. How long are we going to be like this?"

"I don't know. Shut up. I like this song."

After the skate, she had a hot bath using three beads of bath oil and dressed for her dinner at the Borden's. She chose black wool slacks and her Irish Arran sweater purchased on a trip to London. Since there was a death in the family, she could have postponed the meeting but chose not to. Marion, a slight woman whose bluish white hair was cut short and permed, answered the doorbell and graciously welcomed her to their two-storey brick mansion on Wellington Crescent. The original walnut wood had been beautifully preserved in the lobby that opened to a curved staircase carpeted in beige broadloom. Her hostess, dressed in gray slacks and a white high-necked blouse, ushered her to the right into a spacious living room. The walls above the wainscoting were painted forest green to highlight four paintings of the English countryside. Gathered around the black marble fireplace was a heavily padded sofa and matching loveseat and chair of brown leather.

Gus, a tall but fit man dressed in a blue denim shirt and black jeans, offered her a small crystal glass of sherry, which she didn't care for, but drank anyway. They showed her to their dining room in the north-west corner of the house which featured a beautifully restored antique table and eight captain's chairs. The north wall was entirely of glass, looking towards their one-acre back yard and the Assiniboine River.

"Oh, what a lovely room," Maggie didn't want to gush, but did.

Marion smiled. "It is my favourite. Won't you sit down?"

Maggie relaxed immediately in the warmth of her hosts and the aroma of roast beef. Marion left the room and returned pushing a cart laden with the promised roast, peas and carrots, baked potatoes, sour cream and gravy and butter, a garden salad and crusty rolls.

"I do all my own cooking," she told her young guest. "I enjoy it and it makes me feel useful. I do get help for large dinner parties, though."

"How is Jim?" asked Maggie. "He seemed so unhinged the other day. Is he alright?"

Gus answered as he honed a knife on a silver-toned knife sharpener and carved the meat, "Unhinged is a good word. The doctors say he should take an extended vacation from the company. He started working for me when he was sixteen, even before that. Every day after school and all day Saturday he was on the job. Then he married at nineteen, was a father by twenty. He didn't take the time to be a kid. He grew up too soon, but it was his choice, not mine. I didn't force him to do it. It was all his doing."

"No one is blaming you," Marion interjected.

"So what's he going to do? If you don't mind me asking."

"I am going to maintain his salary, give him the spring and summer off, and then he's going to attend university in the fall. He can take business administration, commerce, or physics, or philosophy. It's up to him. So. What do you think of my offer?"

"I haven't had much time to think about it. My grandfather passed away this morning. How many lawyers do you have on staff?"

"I am sorry. We can talk about this on another day."

"No. Really. I am okay. Please, tell me about the job."

"We have four attorneys at present, but I am sending one to Ireland, where we are opening a new manufacturing plant. We are hoping to extend our markets in Britain and continental Europe, so your expertise in international trade would be of great benefit to the firm. The law division occupies part of the fifth floor of the head office tower. All the lawyers' offices have large windows facing east towards the sunrise, bright in the morning, cool in the afternoon and we might have a corner office for you. Let me see, what else? We have an exercise room with weights and treadmills and stationary bicycles, as well as a swimming pool with four lanes, perfect for doing laps. As for salary, we'll match or surpass whatever you are making now."

"That sounds very tempting. I'm sure that the corporate culture is quite different from that of an all-lawyer firm. May I come for a visit before I decide, meet the other attorneys?"

"Yes, of course. Are you taking some time off? Why don't you come to the office at two tomorrow?"

"I am on leave, yes. Tomorrow at two would be fine."

They spent a pleasant evening talking about business, travel, Maggie's home at MacNabb's Crossing, Caroline and Danny. She left about nine thirty, drove west on Grant to Headingly and back to her apartment along Portage Avenue. She stopped at a Shell station and filled the Buick with gasoline, then she turned around and sped back west on Portage to the Perimeter Highway and followed it south to St. Mary's Road, cruised north to the St. Vital Shopping Centre, which had closed for the night. Disappointed, she turned onto Grant and drove back to Headingly and returned to the city on Portage Avenue. She half-expected Anton to catch up to her, but there was no sign of the Nova. Finally, she parked in the garage below her apartment and took the elevator to her apartment.

Before she removed her coat, she grabbed the pen and wrote on the legal pad, 'Tell me about Grandpa MacDonar.'

A line of small childish print appeared on the page. 'He took me to have my picture taken, naked.'

Maggie wrote underneath – 'Tell me about it.'

There was no response.

'What's your name?' wrote Maggie.

Again there was no response. She wrote beauty, beau, but, bet, yet, bat, bate, beat, abut, tab, tub, tube, bay, buy, Bea, tea, be, by, a. Grandfather, grand, father, rand, hand, rend, trend, end, and, fan, ran, tan, then, than, thane, rag, rage, rang, nag, fag, tag, hag, raged, range, ranged, anger, danger, drag, dreg, fang, hang, hanged, hanger, tang, ad, read, red, grade, grad, gad, tread, trade, fad, fade, head, had, hard, heard, herd, nard, nerd, ear, are, era, Rae, rear, rare, gear, gar, tar, tear, tare, dear, dare, far, fare, fared, fear, hear, hare, deaf, raft, rafted, rafter, graft, grafted, draft, after, daft, deft, aft, earn, fern, tern, tarn, darn, at, ate, eat, tea, eta, feat, fat, fate, gate, agate, date, gated, hate, hated, heat, rat, rate, rated, grate, great, grated, grant, granted, rant, ranted, rent, gent, dent, fated, fart, heart, hart, art, farted, dart, grander, gander, dearer, gather, garter, err, he, the, re, death, dearth, earth, thread, a, drat.

She finished *Black Beauty* and fell into bed.

You're going to kill your grandfather.

45

Wednesday, January 10

ON WEDNESDAY MORNING, she woke up feeling refreshed, but without plans.

Sell that damn furniture. Get rid of the silver, someone suggested.

After a breakfast of scrambled eggs and toast, she phoned an antique dealer and requested an appraisal of the dining room set and the sterling. The gentleman who answered the telephone was eager to come immediately, before his store opened at ten. He offered to buy both the furniture and the cutlery for an excellent price. Maggie agreed immediately. She spent the remainder of the morning working on the painting of the church and sketched out another of the bridge at MacNabb's Crossing, an autumn scene with a flying V of Canada geese in the partly cloudy cerulean sky.

The truck arrived promptly at one thirty to load her grandparents' furniture. She felt a stab of guilt as she deposited the cheque in her bank account. Her mother phoned just before six to tell her that the funeral was on Friday at two o'clock. "You will come, won't you, Maggie? You and your grandpa were close when you were little."

Maggie wanted to scream. "Oh," she said. "Tell me more - I don't remember much."

"He would come by on a Sunday afternoon and take you off with him, to his favourite fishing hole or to Brandon for ice cream or wherever. Just you and him. I don't know why Rob didn't go. And you stayed weekends at their place."

Maggie choked, coughed. She croaked, "I need a drink of water. Okay, I'll see you Friday."

She is in the bathtub at her grandparent's farm. It has an old-fashioned white tub with claw feet and the walls surrounding it are lemon yellow. She is four or five, maybe. Her grandfather calls as he walks by, "You'd better look out. When I pull the plug on that tub, you'll slide down the hole and be gone."

"Watch her while I get her pyjamas," says her grandmother.

He enters the bathroom and sits down on the toilet. "You are a cute little thing." He starts tickling her armpits, down her belly and between her legs. His index finger touches a tender spot and she giggles and tries to escape. Her grandmother bustles back into the room and her grandfather saunters out.

She prayed out loud, "Lord have mercy. Christ have mercy. Lord have mercy."

As she slid behind the wheel of the Buick, she wished she could drive and drive and drive right out of her own life.

Sandy met her at the door. "Come in. Come in. I'm so sorry about your grandfather. You didn't have to come."

"Oh, thanks. News travels fast. It's okay. It gives me something to do." She threw her sheepskin jacket on a maroon chair. Sandy immediately picked it up and hung it in the hall closet.

They went to the basement where the girls were giggling and talking as they laced up their shoes. Caroline hugged her and insisted she sit beside her while she put on her shoes. Danny waved hello. He'd moved a small table into the room so that he could do his homework and watch the action at the same time. Sandy lifted Melissa into her play pen. She cried a little, but was soon occupied with her toys.

Maggie took the six younger girls and put them through their paces. Her feet and ankles were as sore as theirs by the time they finished. After the class, Maggie and Sandy had tea in her newly decorated breakfast nook.

"Are you going to take Gus up on his offer?" asked Sandy.

"I don't know yet. I'm going to his office tomorrow to meet the staff. I want to assess the atmosphere in the firm."

"Well, where I work, it's great. Did you hear? Jim's going back to school. The company's paying for it. Can you believe it? I get to look after the kids and work my tail off and he is the one going to school."

"Yeah, Gus told me. It doesn't seem fair to you, I agree, but at least you'll get your alimony and child support. You could go to school, too, couldn't you?"

"I suppose so, but I don't really want to right now. I am taking an accounting course on Tuesday mornings, paid by the company. And Melissa gets free daycare. So I shouldn't complain, I guess. I hope you come though. We could do lunch sometimes."

Maggie felt the room closing in on her. She liked being alone on her lunch hours. She didn't tell Sandy about Anton and the problem she had at Jenkins Williamson.

"I don't know yet. I can't make any promises. Changing jobs is a big step."

Later, she fell asleep on the couch watching television.

In her dream she is a bag lady. She walks down Portage Avenue pushing a wonky grocery cart that contains her kilts and her dancing shoes and a box of Ritz crackers. She wears her sheepskin boots and her unlined jean jacket and a black toque. It is forty degrees below zero and a stiff wind picks up snow and throws it in her face, but she is not cold. She has a thermos half-full of gin and 7Up. She has no money, not a nickel or a thin dime. She looks for a warm place to sleep, but all the good places are taken. She is very hungry. She eats the last three crackers. She lays down on the snow and closes her eyes.

46

Thursday, January 11

MAGGIE AWOKE AT seven, fully dressed, the TV still blaring. Wearily she switched it off and made some toast for breakfast. She spent the morning sorting through her books. She packed three boxes for the used book store, and delivered them, taking credit because she didn't have the patience to shop that day. She called Dr. Dixon to cancel their appointment Friday afternoon.

"Come Saturday morning," he insisted.

Promptly at two she approached Gus Borden's receptionist who was hidden behind a circular desk made of a light wood arranged in a vertical design which reminded Maggie of snow fence. On her green corduroy jacket, the receptionist wore a name tag that said Borden Intl. on the top line and Peggy underneath. This Peggy told Maggie that Gus was busy with a conference call and he wanted her to have a coffee in the cafeteria and he'd be with her shortly. Maggie made her way to the staff lunch room on the second floor. At this time of the day, it was empty except for three young, lean men in expensive suits seated at a window table. Carrying a tray with a white coffee mug and a metal teapot full of hot water, she sat down at a table nearby.

One of them called out, "Are you the lawyer Gus is meeting today?"

"Yes. I am," she answered, surprised that he yelled at her.

"Well. Hello there. We're the legal team. Check us out. Which one of us do you want to sleep with first?"

She sighed audibly and stared out the window.

"Maggie, is that you?" Bob Hunter, her curling mentor, approached her table.

"Bob. Hi. How are you?"

"Just fine. I heard Gus was talking to you. Are you going to make the move to Borden International?"

"I don't know yet."

"Well, I hope you do. Listen. Brian tells me you're a natural curler. Would you be free to spare on Wednesday nights?"

"On the nine o'clock draw, I could, I guess. But are you sure? There must be better curlers than me looking for some extra games."

"Actually there aren't many spares. Would you curl for me next week? My lead is going out of town."

"Okay. Sounds great."

"Mr. Borden asked me to show you around," Peggy was there to get her.

Peggy took Maggie to the executive dining room off the cafeteria, the exercise room and swimming pool, the conference rooms, and the lawyers' wing including an empty corner office meant for her. She pointed out the two manufacturing plants close to the head office, one of which was Bob's domain. Maggie didn't ask where Sandy or Jim worked. The two women walked through the building and back to Gus's penthouse office. Peggy disappeared inside.

Gus barrelled out of his office. "Maggie. I am sorry to have kept you waiting. Come in and sit down. Can I get you anything?"

"Thanks. No. I don't need anything right now." Maggie lowered herself into a swivel chair made of soft green leather.

"Peggy tells me you know Bob Hunter. How did you meet him?"

"I met Bob at the curling rink. He was kind enough to teach a rookie some new tricks."

Gus took his seat behind a mahogany desk a third again the size of Maggie's. "Sounds like him. Always teaching. He's a valuable guy around here. So what do you think of Borden International?"

"It's very impressive. I can see that you care about the well-being of the staff here."

"Yes. We find that our workers are happier and more productive if we make sure they have good nutritious meals and exercise and ample vacation time. It pays off in the long run. Our staff turnover rate is very low."

Maggie thought about Jenkins Williamson where she barely had time for lunch and about all the unpaid overtime she spent in airports and airplanes. "Do you expect me to travel a lot in this job?"

"Possibly. Sometimes it may be necessary, but normally you'll be working here in Winnipeg. And because our employees give up family time and evenings and weekends when they travel, we allow them to stay at their destination for a day or two at company expense, if they wish, to see the sights."

"That's very generous. I see one problem here. I was not impressed by your legal team." She told him what had transpired in the cafeteria. "I have difficulty working with unprofessional people."

"I'm sorry. I will have a talk with them. That's not right, whether they were kidding around or not."

"Thank you for seeing me this afternoon. I will give you an answer by next week at this time."

At home in her apartment, Maggie poured a mug full of coffee and relaxed in the living room. She didn't understand why the fact that she was a woman had suddenly become an issue and she hated it. She was a lawyer and she could see no reason why being a man or woman made a difference, except that men seemed more at ease with each other than with a woman, especially a single woman. But then maybe she seemed like a man when Sammy was around.

The job at Borden International appeared too good to be true. Gus said there were four attorneys on staff but he didn't mention one paralegal or one office assistant. She still hadn't made up her mind, not yet.

Later she worked hard at hockey practice, trying to increase her skating speed and her ability to handle the puck. She felt more at home among the women perhaps because she didn't feel Sammy's presence. If Marilyn knew about the situation at work, she didn't say anything.

When she got home, she tried to reach Sammy via the yellow legal pad, but he didn't answer. Acting on impulse, she printed, 'I want to talk to you.'

Her hand moved and printed, 'I want to play with a dolly.'

'I do not have a doll.'

'You have a teddy bear.'

Maggie knew there was a white plush bear somewhere in her things, but she couldn't remember where she stored it. She searched through the top shelf and the bottom of her closet, but it was nowhere to be found. She returned to the living room and printed, 'Where is it?'

'By the towels.'

The child was right. The sixteen inch bear was buried under a pile of towels on the second shelf of her linen closet. She cradled it in her arms like a baby and hummed softly as she carried it to the bedroom. Tenderly she placed the bear on a pillow. She pretended to change her baby's diaper and give it a sponge bath. She went back to the linen closet for a green and white striped bath towel to wrap the bear in. She cuddled it as she pretended to feed it milk from an imaginary bottle. Crooning a wordless lullaby, she curled up on the bed and was soon asleep.

47

Friday, January 12

THE NEXT MORNING she put on blue jeans, her Arran sweater, and a creamy toque and scarf that matched the lining of her sheepskin jacket and boots, packed her emergency supplies and left for the funeral just before nine o'clock. It was another brutally cold January day and Maggie gave the Buick plenty of time to warm up. It was so cold that frost was forming on the highway, and here and there snow drifted across the road. The traffic was thinner than usual, adding to her unease, but the sky was clear and the scenery was beautiful and she cruised along singing with the radio.

At St. Françoise Xavier, she considered turning around and going back to town. It was too bizarre. There she was en route to a family funeral, to pay respects to a man who had abused her since she was a young child, tiny, vulnerable, trusting and innocent. She wondered what it was that gave an adult male permission to molest his granddaughter. Surely incest was taboo in any religion or creed, but then maybe not. She'd read of an expression in Britain, 'Sex before eight, before it's too late.' Too late for what, she wasn't sure. Break the girls in early? Or they'd refuse later on? Before puberty? Before there was a chance of pregnancy? She wanted to be sick.

As usual, she stopped at Portage for coffee, which she drank as she continued her journey. She spilled a little on her jacket and vowed never to drink anything hot while she was driving again. The blown white snow obliterated the details of the rolling prairie but she gazed and stared anyway. Living in the city had its disadvantages, the crowds of people and the traffic noise, never seeing the horizon, no rest for the eyes, the inability to see the stars.

Possibly that was the reason she started to paint, to create something of beauty in an ugly world full of pain and lies and betrayal, a world where adults preyed on children, where fathers taught their children to lie to their mothers, where mothers didn't care anyway.

When she arrived in Brandon, she filled up on a hot turkey sandwich and black tea at a Smitty's in the mall before going to her grandmother's house, where she changed into her most professional black pant suit and her dress boots with the stiletto heels. She talked to her uncle Ross for a few minutes, but for the most part, the family was silent, staring at their hands, their feet, or off in the distance as they waited until it was time to leave for the church. Maggie went alone in her car, taking no passengers, refusing offers of rides.

Her uncle Ross with Grandma MacDonar on his arm led the procession of mourners into the church, followed by his wife and children. Mike and Mary Ellen followed with Maggie and Rob behind them. Maggie kept her eyes on the brick red carpet. She entered the pew after her mother, acutely aware of her father's presence next to her mother and Rob beside her. Neither her father nor Rob had acknowledged her presence. She paid no attention to the service but she was aware of the huge pipe organ behind the choir loft. She searched in vain for a cross. As a mourner she didn't have to sing and for that she was grateful. The long wood casket was closed, the smell of white lilies overpowering. When it was over, she walked out of the church with the rest of the mourners, again keeping her eyes on the carpet, and escaped to the Buick. She manoeuvred her car into the line up for the procession to the cemetery on Eighteenth Street, her black car matched the hearse and limousines provided by the funeral home. At Victoria Avenue, she abruptly turned to the left and returned to Winnipeg.

She couldn't help but cry, not for her grandfather, not in sympathy for her mother or for her grandmother, but for herself because she didn't have a loving family. She had a glimmer of an idea of what she'd missed. She felt a strong hand on the wheel as the tears flowed down her cheeks. She barely remembered the trip.

Maggie had a tuna salad (never egg) for dinner, watched a movie on television, and retired for the night. The voices came again. You're going to kill your father. You're going to kill Rob.

"No. I am not."

They started again, as if she hadn't spoken. You're going to kill yourself. You're going to kill me. You're going to kill your father. You're going to marry your father.

"You are driving me mad. Shut up."

You're going to kill yourself. You're going to kill yourself.

"Stop. Please. Stop." But they did not. Eventually, she couldn't hear them any longer and she fell asleep. If she dreamed, she didn't remember the next day.

48

Saturday, January 13

SATURDAY MORNING SHE braved the cold again to meet Dr. Dixon in his office at nine o'clock. She wore a pair of faux suede jeans, the tan a close match to her sheepskin jacket, and a white shirt, a deep brown leather vest, with a paisley scarf filling the space at her neck.

"How are you?"

"I have no idea how I am. My mind is spinning."

"How was the funeral?"

"My father didn't speak to me and I said nothing to him. My mother barely looked at me, even though I sat beside her at the service and Rob sat beside me on the other side, but we never spoke to each other. Such a close family. That was all. I talked to my uncle, Mom's brother, for maybe three minutes, and no one else. And I left right after. I didn't even go to the cemetery."

"How do you feel?"

"I am a bit depressed. I don't seem to care about anything. I'm having trouble getting up in the morning and I want to run away."

"You want to run away. No doubt. It would be great if we could run away from ourselves, but it is not possible. I am also not surprised that you are depressed, but I don't want to give you any medication for it, not right now. I think it is important that you feel, whether it is depressed or ashamed or sad or angry or joyous, but you must tell me if you have suicidal thoughts. Do you? Truth now."

"Sometimes. In London someone pushed me onto the street. It scared me to death and so I think there is a suicidal one inside."

"Okay. I will remember that. Try to reach her. How do you feel about your family?"

"I am ashamed of them and I don't even want to acknowledge that they are my family."

"That is quite understandable, but who should be ashamed? Them or you? Think about that. Is there anything pressing you want to discuss?"

"I keep having body sensations of having sex, being raped, wanting to free myself from an attacker. I have pain in my crotch and sensations of being choked. And the voices are driving me crazy."

"The body has a memory and it remembers just as your brain does. This is part of your healing."

"I guessed that, but it's difficult. I can't reach Sammy. I don't know if he's still there."

"Well, let's leave that for the moment. How are you coping at work?"

Maggie told him all about Anton and the restraining order and Jared and the job offer at Borden International.

"What do you intend to do?"

"I don't know."

"What do you feel tell you?"

"Leave Jenkins Williamson. Work where there are no Bordens."

"Why?"

"I don't want to be involved in all the family stuff."

"Okay. Think about it before you do anything. Now then. Sammy. Sammy. I would like to talk to you."

They waited a few minutes, but there was no response.

"Jane. Would you talk to me?"

From the serious harassed woman before him emerged an energetic smiling imp. "Hiya, Doc. About time you called on me."

She removed the scarf and stuffed it in her purse, undid two buttons her white shirt, got up, put her right leg on the chair and sat on it. "What do you want to talk about?"

"Well, um, you, I guess."

"You should have seen that Anton when I made love to him. Ha. Ha. He didn't know what hit him. I like sex. I really like sex. But he's such a dead head. He wouldn't even try for seconds. Couldn't get it up, I guess. Told me I was disgusting."

"Really. That's, um, very interesting. You aren't Jane. Who are you?"

"Jeanie. I'm Jane's twin."

"Nice to meet you."

"She probably won't talk to you. She's bent on suicide."

"I am glad you told me. Now I know. Would you tell me what happened to you when you were a kid?"

"I figured it out real quick. I didn't fight the creeps. My body wanted it, so I went along. Then it didn't hurt."

"But didn't you know it was wrong? Didn't you know that they shouldn't touch you?"

"No. Yes. I don't know. It didn't matter whether it was right or wrong. It just was."

"I see. Who were the creeps?"

"Dad. Sweet Daddio. Did you know he has a brown wart on his right testicle? Grandpa MacDonar. He's a tall skinny guy with a tiny little pecker. Ha. Ha."

Dr. Dixon obviously didn't know what to say. "What do you do? Do you paint? Or dance?"

"Nothing. I just lay around. Watch TV. Read. Do my nails. I like to read sexy novels but the prude won't buy them. And now she's not with Anton, I'm not getting any. I've got to find a new guy."

"So, um, do you help Maggie?"

"Well, what Maggie doesn't know won't hurt her. Maggie doesn't know that I had sex with her client."

"You didn't."

"Yep I did. He's a big fat tub of lard, but he knows what to do."

"You could get her in trouble."

"No. I won't. I just ignore her most of the time. I'm going to take over one of these nights and go out on the town and I'm not going to that ritzy bar she likes. I'm going somewhere else where I can pick up somebody cool."

"Cool? Like how?"

"A biker type."

"Isn't that risky?"

"The riskier the better. You're as bad as the prude."

"Can I speak to Maggie then? Maggie. Maggie."

"I'm here. I couldn't hear anything."

"That was not Jane. It was Jeanie, her twin sister. She is your sexy part evidently."

"Oh. Well, it's a good thing she is. I'm not, at least not right now."

"Could you take some time off work? A month?"

"I could take my annual leave and then resign."

"Don't resign. Not yet. We need time to work on this. It is absolutely essential."

"Okay. I'll talk to the boss on Monday."

Jeanie may have returned to wherever she came from, but her sexuality hadn't. As she drove to Sandy's, Maggie felt that twinge of sexual desire deep in her groin. Her small firm breasts itched for a man's touch and she wanted the weight of a guy on top of her and hugs, kisses, arms around her. She had never felt so desirable and horny in her life and she was almost late for dance class.

Sandy was too busy with the girls to notice any change in her friend. The six little girls were all ready and waiting. Quickly Mags changed into her kilt and laced up her ghillies. She counted slowly to ten before she emerged from the bedroom. She taught her students a new combination of steps and kept them working for an hour. Sandy had to leave immediately after the classes for Danny's hockey game, freeing Mags to leave without making excuses.

As she approached her apartment, she twisted the wheel slightly to the right into the turning lane and almost hit the Nova blocking the garage entrance. She stopped, backed up a car length, took the car out of gear, applied the parking brake and stepped out of the Buick. Anton climbed out of his vehicle and strode towards her.

"Anton. What the hell are you doing?"

"Waiting for you."

"What do you want?"

He stood very close to her, looking down into her face, trying to intimidate her. "If you don't drop that restraining order, you're going to get canned."

"Are you going to stop annoying me?"

Cursing he marched back to his car, backed the Nova out of the driveway, and turned so sharply he almost hit the Buick. Laying a strip of rubber ten feet long, he sped off down the street.

He didn't say no and he threatened her job. She phoned the city police to report the incident, but the officer didn't sound too alarmed by her ex-boyfriend's behaviour. Too stirred up to eat, she flopped on the couch and picked up the pen. 'Jeanie, talk to me.'

'No. You're the prude who wears long skirts and turtlenecks.'

'I try to look professional.'

'You're so professional you forget to be human. You forget to be female.'

'I don't want to be female.'

'I know. You want to be a nothing – not a man. Not a woman. A eunuch.'

'Not quite.'

'Ha. You expect guys to treat you like one.'

'Do I?'

'Yeah. You do. You're insulted when they come on to you.'

'I don't want to argue. Tell me about you.'

'Like I told the good doctor, I played along with Grandpa and Dad so it wouldn't hurt. It was stupid. I see it now. They thought I wanted it.'

'You did what you had to do. To survive.'

'I guess. That old creep. Grandpa. Saying he was sorry. Death bed apology. I felt like pounding him.'

'I wanted a baseball bat, but he died too soon.'

'Well, at least we agree on something.'

Maggie wrote. 'Yes.'

The pen stopped. Maggie stopped too.

She couldn't believe what she read. A nothing? Not male? Not female? Did that describe her?

"Lord have mercy. Christ have mercy. Lord have mercy."

She actually wrote it. She didn't want to be female.

She is thirteen. She is in the dining room in the new farmhouse.

A pile of fresh smelling laundry is on the table. Mary Ellen expects her to fold the towels and sheets and tea towels. She picks up a white pillow case. It has BOSS embroidered in black on the edge. She grabs its mate. It has SLAVE in bright pink cotton.

"Boss and slave?"

Her mother laughs.

"I won't be any man's slave."

"Then don't get married."

Maggie leaned back on the couch and exhaled audibly. She couldn't stay within four walls. She went swimming, lap after lap after lap for an entire hour, not bothering to count, pounding the water. She wanted a punching bag to hit. Or a soccer ball to kick. Or her father's face to punch. She remembered her mother's words, "I don't know why Rob didn't go." Didn't she know? Was she blind? Did she care?

Back in her apartment, she ran to her bedroom and pounded and punched her pillows until she was worn out. She collapsed on the bed crying, but didn't stay there long. She searched her kitchen cupboards, her closets and her drawers for anything given to her by her parents and grandparents – clothes, afghans, ornaments, books, her father's Zane Grey books, her brother's Hardy Boys books, her everyday dishes, two flaming pink vases, black leather gloves that were too large for her, a red beret she hated, the white rug from the living room. She packed the books in grocery bags and dropped them off at the used book store which was fortunately still open. She was rid of those. Back at her apartment, she threw the clothes into large-sized black garbage bags and took the Buick out again to dump them in the red Diabetes Society bins. She was rid of those. She would donate the rest of the stuff, except for the vases, to the Salvation Army.

At the mall, she purchased an eight-place setting of dishes, blue roses on a white background. As soon as she got home, she loaded them in the dishwasher and started it up. She turned on the vacuum cleaner to muffle the noise, placed the two vases on her new living room rug, and pounded them to tiny pieces with a hammer. Spent again, she cleaned up the mess.

She ordered a medium pepperoni and mushroom pizza and ate

most of it while she watched the hockey game. She watched the entire match without knowing which teams were playing.

She wrote, diabetes, dab, tab, stab, Deb, Abe, dibs, said, sad, ad, Id, bid, bide, side, seed, bead, bade, bad, abide, tied, tide, stead, steed, bed, Ted, Ed, teed, debt, diet, date, sate, seat, sat, set, sit, site, bit, bite, beet, bet, beat, eat, ate, bat, bate, eta, beta, tea, Bea, bee, tee, see, sea, a, I, beast, east, best, bait, bias, baste, staid, aid, dais, tease, ease, as, is, its.

Then she went to bed. She dreamed Anton was chasing her down Portage Avenue. She stopped at a red light and he disappeared.

49

Sunday, January 14

THE NEXT MORNING, she attended church services at St. Luke's again, her special place. She seated herself in a comfortable pew of dark wood on the left side and about halfway between the entranceway and the chancel. Before the service, it was quiet in the church, a sacred time, a time to prepare for the worship to follow, and she was surprised to observe that most of the parishioners kneeled to pray as soon as they were settled their seats, a practice not followed in the United Church that she attended as a child. Indeed she had never before seen a padded kneeler attached to the pew in front.

Feeling a bit self-conscious, she pulled the kneeler into position, knelt and prayed, 'Sweet Jesus, come to me. Help me in my time of need.' She sat back and glanced about the nave. She noticed the divided chancel, new and interesting to her with the stalls for the choir separated to allow the congregation to reach the high altar at the back. She didn't try to follow the service in the green prayer books this time, she listened, a little unnerved by what sounded like chanting, but she sang the unfamiliar hymns, easily picking up the tunes after the first verse. She was impressed by the music of the massive pipe organ and the obviously well-trained choir, and drank in the aroma of the altar flowers. The priest told the congregation that anyone who had been baptized into the body of Christ could partake of the Eucharist, so she followed the others to the chancel and knelt at the solid brass communion rail. When she took her sip of wine, real wine, not grape juice, a shock like an electric current, passed through her body, leaving her surprised and grateful.

After lunch, she took her position on the couch to write on the legal pad. 'Talk to me.'

'Why should I?' The handwriting was faint, similar to her own, but the letters were more rounded and the 'I' was an elaborate curlicue.

'I want to know you.'

'If I write I will disappear.'

'Tell me who you are. Are you a voice that says I'm going to kill myself?'

'No. But I want to kill myself. I no longer wish to live. This world is too tough for me. I just can't make it.'

'What do you want to do?'

'Just have a life like everyone else - family, friends, a good job, a husband, children, a dog, a nice house and a white picket fence.'

'Well, family is out. But if we find the right guy, we could create our own family. It's not too late.'

'I have tried so hard and now I am tired. I don't want to go on.'

'If you die, we all die.'

'I don't think so. I can just melt away.'

'Thanks for all you've done. But you don't have to go.'

'Bye.'

Maggie considered integration for the first time. She didn't know if that was what the writer meant, but it was a strong possibility. She had felt the other's fatigue, more mental than physical; she was world weary and jaded. To let her mind rest, she went for a swim, lap after lap, counting strokes, until she could kick no more.

She thought that meditation might calm her whirling mind. She sat cross-legged on the rug with her back against a well-padded chair. She placed her hands on her knees, palms up and her thumbs and index touching. Silently she repeated, 'Oohm, oohm,' while she listened to her own breathing, inhale, exhale, inhale, exhale. As her breathing slowed, she let all thoughts of the day leave her consciousness. Deeper and deeper she went, but instead of resting her mind, the practice released memories of being slapped in the face. Her head jerked back, the muscles in her neck stretched, and she felt the pain in her jaw and her cheeks and her ear. She immediately came out of the trance and allowed the memory to engulf her whole body. She took the yellow pad once more. 'Talk to me,' she wrote in large clear letters. No one replied.

She took the word 'meditation' and found made, maid, aid, node, nod, mode, toed, toad, tied, tide, amid, Ned, Ted, mate, meat, mat, met, neat, teat, tat, tote, tot, dot, dote, moat, oat, note, not, doe, toe, to, tea, eat, ate, eta, tone, ton, one, on, o, moan, men, amen, man, mane, mean, meant, dent, done, don, dine, din, mine, mined, toned, moaned, toted, mated, noted, tin, tine, in, I, a, me, no, do, edit, tit, mitt, mitten, mite, item, time, dime, dim, dome, Nome, tame, tamed, dame, dam, damn, tam, tome, Tom, timed, nit, diet, die, tie, edition, Eton, ant, tint, mint, Minot, Miniota, Minto, into, aim, aimed, am, emit, omit.

It was time to tell the doctor about playing that stupid game. She knew now why she played it. It was a way to stop thinking and feeling and remembering. It was another way to dissociate, to reach oblivion, just like painting, reading, counting, even sleeping. She was in a contest when she played the game, a competition in which she had to think of more words than anyone else. She even played the game when she was driving her car and she had to stop.

The problem of employment was not solved. She didn't know what she was going to say to Jared on Monday morning. Maybe she should resign. The doctor was right. She needed time off to deal with her emotional problems which she refused to call mental illness. She would not.

The solution came to her. She knew what to do about Jared. She would do nothing. She would wait for Jenkins Williamson to make the first move. Decision made, she relaxed with an hour of yoga and spent the rest of the day in the studio where she finished the painting of the bridge at MacNabb's Crossing. With her watercolours, she laid in a green pasture and a clear prairie sky and then used pen and ink to create an Appaloosa colt frolicking in the lush grass.

Later, she lay in bed. She tossed and she turned. She lay on her belly. She lay on her back. She went to the kitchen for a glass of water. She emptied her bladder. Still sleep eluded her.

A voice said, You're going to marry your father.

"Why don't you let me sleep? Why do you always come out at night? Anyway, that's ridiculous," she whispered. "What on earth are you talking about?"

She is fourteen. She desires to please her father. She irons his shirts and mends the tears in his work pants. She bakes his favourite cake – marble with chocolate icing. She digs horseradish from the patch near the garden to go with his roast beef. She empties and washes all his ashtrays. She draws a picture of his tractor for his Father's Day card. She cleans and polishes his dress shoes and brushes his suit and presses the pants. She prays he will be nice to her, just once.

She looks out the kitchen window. He is coming across the yard from the machine shed, shouting 'Maggie. Maggie.'

"What?"

"Why aren't you helping your mother clean the chicken houses?" He clouts her across the mouth with a backhand.

She sprawls on the gravel driveway. Both elbows and one knee are skinned and bloody. She wobbles to the shade next to King and sinks into the lawn.

Maggie came back to the present, hate for her father a lump in her throat. Maybe the voice was right - she should kill the bastard.

"I certainly won't marry the son of a bitch. So knock it off, voice."

You're going to kill yourself. You're going to kill Rob. You're going to kill your father. You're going to marry your father.

50

Monday, January 15

JARED WAS IN her office Monday morning before she had her coat off. He twisted and turned the file folder he carried. Maggie took her usual place behind the desk. Jared remained standing.

"Maggie. You have done some excellent work for us and we don't want to lose you. Will you cancel the restraining order on Anton?" He spoke the name Anton in a tender tone, as if he were a beloved son.

"It was your idea in the first place, Jared. What are you doing? The man is guilty of harassment and the answer is no."

"Then I have no choice." He laid a letter on her desk. "This is your termination notice." He dropped a cheque on top of the letter. "Your holiday pay." He fumbled with the folder and withdrew another cheque. "Your salary to date." He took out one more cheque. "Severance pay. You'll need to speak to Gladys in Human Resources about your pension funds. Do you have anything to say?"

"No, nothing."

"I'll have someone deliver your things."

"No. Thank you. I'll take care of them myself."

"Well, that's it then." He turned and left the office.

She was surprised that Jared did this, the guy she considered to be her mentor. She fought back tears of frustration. She picked up the top cheque. It was made out for $15,000. She phoned Maintenance to request three boxes and when the red-headed kid arrived, she asked him to wait while she packed her paintings and books and her U of M beer mug and to carry the boxes down to her car. She put her reference list and client list in her briefcase, checked the washroom, all the filing cabinets, and the drawers in her desk for personal items, took her shoes, her box of tissues, her coffee mugs and coffee maker and her kettle, her creamer and sugar cubes. As she left the office, she turned to read the lettering on the door. She wanted to scratch her name off with her fingernails. She handed Maxine her keys and left the building with deep felt regret.

As soon as she got home, she called Dr. Dixon.

"I have my time off. When do you want to start?"

"Just a minute."

Maggie waited, biting her nails, and wondered who had that habit. Dan, den, din, don, dun. Pack, peck, pick, pock, puck. Pap, pep, pip, pop, pup.

"Come at three this afternoon."

"I'll be there."

She hung up the phone with shaking hands. After she found a space for her text books in the library, she deposited the three cheques in her bank account at the Toronto Dominion, and then shopped for groceries, thinking she had enough money to eat for a little while. She waited in the line-up at MacDonald's drive-through and ate her chicken burger and fries in the living room watching the soaps. She wrote, terminate, term, tier, mire, tire, ire, mine, tin, tine, mien, train, rain, main, ran, near, mere, tear, tare, tar, mar, mare, mane, mean, man, men, ten, amen, teen, meant, tent, tint, mint, rent, rant, tater, teat, rate, irate, tat, trait, mate, mat, meat, met, meet, mete, net, neat, rite, nit, it, tit, mite, item, emit, time, tame, tam, team, teem, ram, arm, tram, ream, name, remit, timer, mater, meter, mitre, neater, meaner, miner, tern, tarn, earn, mart, martin, matter, mitten, mitt, merit, eat, ate, era, eta, Rae, tea, tee, me, nee, mi, tie, trite, trim, rim, rime, inter, enter, art, tart, are, re, a, I. She didn't move until a quarter to three.

Dr. Dixon called her into the office. "You're as pale as a ghost."

"I got fired this morning."

"Over Anton?"

"Yes. I displeased the senior partner and I am angry and I don't understand."

"No doubt. So now what?"

"I have some money saved so I'll take some time off. I want to work with you and get stable, if nothing else."

"Alright. That's a smart move. Let's get started. Have you felt Sammy at all?"

"No. Not at all."

"Sammy. Would you talk to me?"

There was no response.

"Okay. I believe he has integrated with you or someone else. Now there's Jane and Jeanie and some children."

"And Sally and Lynne the artist."

"Do you still black out when you're painting?"

"No. But I feel her presence. I am sure she's the one who draws and paints."

The doctor opened a lower cupboard and brought out a doll, a baby doll whose eyes blinked open and shut, dressed in pink sleepers and wrapped in a pink and white wool blanket.

"You see this doll. Would you like to play with it? You may have it. Take it home with you, if you talk to me."

In an instant Maggie's face changed into that of a frightened little girl. Her little mouth pouted. She wiggled at the edge of the chair. The doctor handed her the doll. She reached out her hand, then took it back. She was afraid to take it.

"Daddy says I can't have dolls."

"Daddy isn't here. It's okay. If you want, I will keep it for you and you can play with it when you visit. Would that be okay?"

She grabbed the doll and held it to her chest with her left arm and stuck her right thumb in her mouth.

"What's your name?"

"Mary."

"That's a pretty name. How old are you, Mary?"

"I'm free."

"You go ahead and play with the doll. I have some work to do."

He pretended to tidy up the office, but he watched every move she made.

Mary climbed down from the chair and laid the doll on it. She removed the blanket and picked up the doll. She stood the doll against the back of the chair and shook her finger in its face.

"You're a bad girl. But I won't tell Mommy. Don't you tell Mommy, okay?"

She put the doll back on the blanket. She patted it on the crotch and murmured, "It's going to be okay. Don't cry."

"What happened to the baby?" asked the doctor.

"A black monster hurted her peepee. I don't want to play anymore." She threw the doll on the floor and curled up on the chair sucking her thumb, her eyes shut tight.

"Maggie. Maggie."

The adult lawyer emerged, removed the thumb from her mouth and sat erect. "What happened?"

The doctor retrieved the doll and laid it on the examining table. "Her name is Mary – like your mother?"

Maggie nodded.

"She's three. She was molested by a monster. You weren't allowed to have dolls?"

"No. My father forbade it, but I don't know why."

"I suggest you buy a couple on the way home. Leave them in view, maybe in the kitchen or living room. Don't force it. Let it happen. That's enough for today. Here's a list of times – almost every day for the next two weeks."

Maggie waited in the Buick until it was warmed up and she felt like an adult again. She walked up and down the toy aisles in the stores searching for a doll. The selection was poor since it just after Christmas.

"Which one do you want?" she whispered.

Her eyes came to rest on a baby doll, smaller than Dr. Dixon's, but just as pretty. She placed it tenderly in a shopping cart.

"Anything else?"

She heard a voice inside say, A Barbie.

She chose a Barbie doll dressed in a long white evening gown and two packages of extra clothing. As she added those items to her cart, another doll caught her attention. It was more than a foot in height and could pass for either a boy or girl. She bought it along with a little high chair and a blue blanket. In her apartment, she placed the large doll in the high chair at the kitchen table and the baby doll between the pillows on her bed and the Barbie on a chair in the living room.

Wondering what would happen next, she turned on the TV and sat down on the couch. She reached for the Barbie doll and struggled for several minutes to free the doll and her clothes from the packaging. She removed the doll's dress and dressed her in a pair of red shorts and a white shirt.

"We're going to play volleyball," she said aloud. She pretended the doll was hitting a ball back and forth over a net. She took off the shorts and put on a pair of jeans.

"Now we're going to help Mommy with the chickens. No. I don't like chickens. They stink. I don't want to play that game."

She carefully put the doll and her things back on the chair and deposited the packaging in the garbage container under the kitchen sink. Then she returned to the living room to watch the news.

Maggie had a peanut butter and raspberry jam sandwich and a glass of milk for dinner, and then she changed into her curling gear and left for the rink. Hat, het, hit, hot, hut. Pat, pet, pit, pot, put.

Sandy grabbed her arm and pulled her out of earshot. "So have you decided? Are you going to work for Gus?"

"I don't know. I haven't had a chance to consider it," she lied. She knew she wouldn't take the job unless Gus could wait for a month or more. She needed time.

Maggie played a good game, by her own newly formed standards. As lead, her main job was to set guards in front of the house and to draw into the rings, usually the twelve foot.

"Hey, you're really catching one," beamed her skip.

They defeated their opponents by five points and Maggie stayed afterward for hot chocolate. She found out that Angela, the skip, was an investment counsellor, and Betty was a registered nurse at Grace Hospital and Heather was a dental assistant.

"And you," said Heather. "Let me guess. You're an accountant."

"Nope."

"You're a flight attendant."

"Nope."

"You're a professor or a teacher."

"No. I am a lawyer."

"I knew it."

Everybody laughed. Her guesses were revealing.

"By the way," began the skip, "There's going to be a fun bonspiel on February tenth, just before Valentine's Day. We play four ends in each draw. There are lots of prizes and games like cribbage and checkers between games, and a skills contest and a banquet at six followed by dancing, if you're not dead by then. You can sign up here." She passed a sheet of white paper to Maggie who signed it immediately and handed it to Heather.

Later, at home, she marked the date on the calendar in the kitchen. She also wrote 'curling' on every Monday square until the end of March, and 'hockey' on every Thursday square until the end of March. She wrote 'dance' on every Wednesday and Saturday square except for the bonspiel day – just to remind the natives within.

She propped the baby doll against the headboard on one pillow and climbed into bed. She awoke around two with a sharp pain in her hip. She had rolled onto the doll. She didn't remember how it got there, but she didn't worry about it and she went right back to sleep.

She dreamed her father gave her a stuffed teddy bear. "This is for being so nice to Daddy," he said. She tore the arms off it, then the legs, then the head, and scattered the insides all over the floor.

51

Tuesday, January 16

ON TUESDAY MORNING, the alarm aroused her from a deep sleep at eight o'clock. She had her usual shower and a piece of toast with orange marmalade and a small glass of juice for breakfast. She donned a pair of skin-tight black leggings and a black turtle neck, and over the sweater a long white man-tailored shirt, the sleeves of which she rolled up to three-quarter length. She slicked her hair back off her forehead with styling gel and in her ears she put gold loops an inch in diameter.

Dr. Dixon stared at her in disbelief. "Good morning."

"Dr. Dixon, I presume," she reached out her right hand, "I am Lynne Barnett."

"Ah, Lynne, the artist. Come in, Lynne. Please make yourself comfortable."

This woman was completely self-assured. She had none of Maggie's worry and stress. She sat leaning forward slightly, unsmiling, alert and confident.

"Are you taking notes on these sessions, doctor?" She glanced around the room and rejected the austere white walls and ceiling, substituted pastel greens and blues and yellows and dismissed them as infantile and unprofessional like the scrubs hospital personnel wear, and settled on an earth colour taupe for one accent wall.

"No. I am not. I don't want any written record of this case."

"Did Maggie ask you about that?"

"No. As a matter of fact, she did not."

"Some lawyer she is." On that one wall, an arrangement of small Norman Rockwell prints would serve to amuse the doctor's clients while they're waiting, or perhaps two or three of her own pen-and-ink drawings would be appropriate, but she wasn't about to offer them since the elderly doctor was close to retirement and her work could end up in the trash bin when the offices were cleaned.

"Well, she's a lawyer under stress. And you always took over when she was deeply stressed. Am I right?"

"Yes. That is true. Mostly I ignored her and Sammy. I wasn't interested in what they were doing."

"Are you going to work today?"

"No. Today I am going to the Winnipeg Art Gallery and then every other gallery in the city I can fit in before dinner." She bit her tongue. It was best not to volunteer to redecorate his work space but still, even one brightly coloured poster of fields and trees and a lake or a Claude Monet print would make such a difference to the atmosphere.

"Are you looking for a gallery to display your work?"

"No. I am not even sure my work would sell. No. I am just looking. Seeing what the art world is putting out these days."

"Were you abused as a child?"

"No. For some reason I was spared. I didn't share my work with anyone. My mother made sure I had art supplies, and for that I am grateful but I don't think my father ever saw any of it." But then she wouldn't tell him if she was, the whole idea was so tacky and common.

"What can you tell me that will help?"

"What is the purpose of this therapy?"

"I want to get the parts to work together, but in this case I am not sure it will happen. There are so many of you."

"Yes. You aren't looking for complete integration?"

"I don't know if that's possible, but yes, that would be the ultimate goal."

"I agree that it won't happen. I certainly have no intention of going anywhere. You'll need to do more work with the children since all the little girls were rejected or abused in one way or another. The dolls are good. Did you know I wasn't allowed to have a doll?"

"Yeah. There's a doll on the counter. Do you not feel a child inside wanting that doll?"

"No. I don't feel anyone inside, child or adult."

"I sense that you are a strong woman."

"Thank you. May I go now?"

"Yes. Have a good day, Lynne."

Lynne spent the day as planned, examining paintings for brush stroke, colour combinations, use of lighting, sky treatments, centre of focus. She had spinach quiche for lunch with lemon iced tea and returned to the apartment about six. Sally made dinner – a grilled ham steak, a salad and macaroni with cheese sauce. She answered a phone call.

"Maggie?"

"Um. Yes. Who is this?"

"Meg. Didn't you recognize my voice?"

Maggie emerged. "Oh, yes. I'm sorry. How are you?"

"I'm fine. I thought I'd pay you a visit in the morning. Would that be okay?"

"Yes. Do come. I'll be home." She ate what Sally had prepared without wondering who made it, watched television for an hour, registering nothing, and then drove to the pool. A tiny woman of perhaps forty watched her as she removed her clothing, put on her bathing suit, showered and washed the goop out of her hair.

Maggie faced the woman and said, "Do I know you?"

"I was hoping to get to know you. You're so strong and muscular."

"Oh, so that's it. Sorry. I am not interested."

She walked out of the dressing room slipping on the wet floors and dove into the warm water. She swam laps for forty-five minutes, counting as usual, refusing to think about homosexuality, maintaining her distance between the woman in the next lane and herself, changed in the washroom, and went home with her hair still sopping wet.

Later, she fell asleep on the couch with the television still on and dreamed that she was young and tiny. Brown bars surrounded her bed, like a cage. A light beam pointed at the floor. A big black monster loomed into her room and picked her up roughly in hard callused hands. He stumbled but did not fall on the stairs as he made his way in the dark to the living room. She shivered with the cold as he removed her pink pyjamas and she started to cry. "Ssh, ssh. Don't cry. You'll wake up Mommy." He wrapped her in a knit afghan and laid her in his left arm as if to give her a bottle of milk. He opened the blanket just enough to allow his right hand to touch her, first her face and neck, then her chest and stomach, down farther and farther. He pushed her chubby legs apart. She started to whimper again. "Don't cry," he whispered. "That's a good girl." He changed her sopping diaper, redressed her in clean pair of pink flannels, inserted a plastic soother into her mouth and carried her back to her metal crib.

52

Wednesday, January 17

MAGGIE WOKE UP the next morning aching all over. Tired and groggy, she made coffee and ate two bran muffins with two slabs of marble cheese. She read the *Free Press*, did the crossword puzzle and read the chess article. She didn't bother to shower or get dressed until a few minutes before nine. Meg arrived shortly after ten o'clock. Maggie put another pot of coffee on to brew and they sat down to chat.

"You've changed the living room and now it looks more like you. Those paintings are marvellous. You did those?"

"Yes. I did. I am not finished my interior designing yet. I intend to paint the living room and kitchen."

"So you're not working. I am not surprised. You have a lot of healing to do."

"I have parted company with Jenkins Williamson. I offended a senior partner by placing a restraining order on his grandson – Anton. He is getting angrier and angrier and I know, I just know, he's going to do something stupid."

"Gus offered you a position?"

"Yes. I will take it if he allows me to have some time off first."

"How much time?"

"I don't know. I was thinking I could go back to work by the first of March, but I have no idea really. I can't afford to be unemployed for long."

"Phone him. Right now."

"Okay. If you insist."

She dialled the number, her hands trembling. The receptionist informed her that Gus was out of the office. "Would you like me to page him?"

"No. That won't be necessary. Would you take a message?"

"Yes, of course. Go ahead."

"Tell him that Maggie Barnett has not had a vacation since she finished grade eleven. She would be pleased to join the company on March first."

After she hung up, she turned to Meg. "I hope six weeks is long enough."

"It's hard to know, but you'll feel more secure knowing that you have a job waiting. So tell me. How are you coping?"

"It is really tough. Sometimes I feel as if my head will explode. My body is releasing its pain and I feel it throughout my entire being. I am trying to appease children, a teenager, a boy, an artist. I really don't need job stress right now."

"Relax. You've cut off parts of you for specific reasons. When you were studying to be a lawyer, there was no time for other interests. Now they want their day in the sun too."

"I really don't want to be a girl. That's the biggest problem. I don't want to do girlie things and I don't like women's clothing. Being an attorney means living in a man's world. I don't know how to heal my feminine side."

"It's okay to be a tomboy and a farmer too, you know. Anton didn't bring out the feminine in you, did he?"

"No. He was the wrong guy for me."

"Maybe you need a new boyfriend."

"Very funny. The last thing I need right now is another man in my life. I change from day to day and minute to minute."

"I once met a multiple who had over two hundred personalities, at least so she said, and her boyfriend told her he wanted to make love to all two hundred."

Maggie laughed. "I hope there aren't two hundred in there. It's hard enough now."

"The important thing to remember is that becoming a multiple is a coping strategy, a way for you to survive. Honour that. Thank each one for helping out. Have you tried meditation?"

"Yes. But all it does is bring out more memories. It doesn't give me much rest."

"I have some excellent books on Christian meditation. That should work better for you. We're going back to the farm tomorrow. I'll mail them to you."

"Okay. Thanks."

Maggie was feeling much better by the time Meg left an hour later. She brought her journal up to date, did an hour of yoga to relieve her sore muscles and had a turkey TV dinner for lunch. She also brought her chequebook up to date, opened mail that had been sitting on the counter since Christmas, wrote several cheques to pay her bills, and walked down the street three blocks to the red mailbox on the corner, counting her steps and thinking about buying a dog, a Sheltie, for company, and a spacious house with a yard and a basement storage area. She walked another three blocks, still counting, but the frost was nipping at her ears, so she turned back.

The blinking red light on the phone indicated that there was a message for her. It was from Gus, "Welcome to Borden International. We'll see you on March first."

Maggie wasn't sure whether Gus's reply made her happy or sad. She watched a movie on television which wasn't very good, but she watched it anyway. She read more mail, relaxing on the couch.

She is in grade one, aged seven. It is spring and she doesn't want to go inside the school. She wants to stay outside to play baseball. Mrs. McClure arrives with the Sinclairs and Maggie is curious. Why didn't she bring her own car? The teacher takes her place behind her desk and lifts her head off her chest and faces the class. Her eyes are almost swollen shut. Her right cheek is a mass of purple and red. Another bruise disfigures her left arm just below her three-quarter length sleeve. Out of a cut lower lip, she says, "Alright, class. Please stand for *O Canada*."

Maggie cannot keep her eyes off Mrs. McClure. She wants to

know who did this to her teacher. She tries to do her subtraction problems but she is unable to concentrate. Mrs. McClure slowly, painfully rises to her feet. "Listen, everyone. You probably know that my husband is responsible for my injuries. No man has the right to do this to his wife or to anyone else." She points to her face. "The school board says that I may finish this school year while boarding at the Sinclairs. So that's that. Now let's do something different. I'm going to give you each a large sheet of drawing paper. Yesterday was Thanksgiving. I want you to draw a picture of what Thanksgiving means to you."

Maggie's paper is blank. She sees the other students working very hard on their drawings, but she sits for a long time unable to pick up her crayons. Finally she begins to draw the prairie, its dips and dives, the trees, all golden now since fall is upon them, green grass and a huge cloudless blue sky. She signs it 'M.L. Barnett.' Mrs. McClure hangs all the masterpieces on the back wall and then they play Farmer in the Dell until recess.

Suddenly it was three o'clock and she had to hurry to make it to her appointment with Dr. Dixon at three thirty.

"Come in. Sit down. I haven't much time today."

"I appreciate your seeing me like this."

"I am glad to help." From his cupboard, the doctor brought out a fire-engine about six inches long, with its red paint chipped off, a dump truck with a blue cab and a yellow box, and a John Deere tractor with a cultivator hitched to it. He put the toys on the chair next to Maggie and asks, "Would you like to play with these?"

She immediately slipped out of her chair, picked up the tractor and cultivator and knelt on the floor. A noise exactly like an old John Deere emanated from her larynx as she drove her tractor counter-clockwise around the imaginary field on the floor.

"Did your father have a tractor like that?"

"Yeah," answered a boy's voice. "My Dad is a John Deere man."

"Could you tell me your name?"

"Dick."

"How old are you, Dick?"

"I am nine and I want to play hockey." He wanted to tell all his troubles to this white-haired grandpa.

"Why aren't you playing hockey?"

"My Dad won't let me. He is busy with Rob's team and he won't let me play too."

"Tell me about Rob. Do you and Rob fight?"

"All the time. He thinks he's big and smart and he won't let me do anything. He won't let me play with his toys, even if he doesn't play with them anymore, and he won't let me read his books and he won't play catch with me. He won't let me play hockey with him and his friends during public skating. He's a jerk."

"Does he hit you?"

"No. We just yell at each other."

"What about your Dad?"

"He always takes Rob's side. He tells me to go play with the girls at the rink or help Mom in the house and he won't let me do stuff either. He teaches Rob all about driving a tractor and how to run the machinery and all about the car and truck and how to change the oil and change flat tires and all about fertilizers and growing crops, but he won't even let me listen. He sends me to the house. I hate him."

Dick got to his feet, returned the toys to the chair, and sat down. He wanted to throw himself in the doctor's arms but didn't want to be a sissy. He turned his face away from the doctor but not before Dr. Dixon had seen the tears in the boy's eyes.

Maggie came back to awareness. "Who was that?"

"Dick. An eleven year old. He hates his father because he didn't teach him how to maintain vehicles and operate the farm."

"I'm not surprised. My father allowed me to drive his car but he taught me nothing about looking after it. Sandy and Trish know more about farming than I do. I had an older brother hogging all the attention."

"So you do remember."

"I remember every time I get behind the wheel."

"No doubt. Are you okay to drive home now? I am needed elsewhere."

"I'm fine. I'll see you tomorrow."

With shaking hands, Maggie poured a Styrofoam cup full of coffee and added some powdered creamer and a lump of sugar. She drank it sitting in the Buick before she drove off. On the way home, she bought a set of John Deere toys and three potted tropical plants. When she got home, she arranged the plants on the kitchen table in the light, although she didn't know the names of the plants, whether they liked sun or shade, whether they needed little watering or lots. She always thought houseplants were rather silly; growing geraniums, spider plants, violets, snake plants, dieffenbachia in the house yielded no positive results, but then only utilitarian plants interested her. Like hard red spring wheat. Or malting barley. Or early red potatoes. Or garden peas. Or ears of golden corn.

Setting the farm machinery on the coffee table, she cultivated the field she intended to sow to wheat until she got hungry and cursed her empty stomach before she made a tuna salad with the leftover macaroni for dinner.

At six thirty, Mags went to Sandy's to help with the dance class. To her satisfaction, her students were beginning to get the idea. After the lessons, she had tea with Sandy and Meg.

"So what's the big secret?" Sandy asked. "Why are you two plotting to meet alone like a pair of lovers?"

"Never you mind. You don't need to know everything," answered her mother.

"She is helping me with a problem, that's all. I will share with you when I am ready. I have to get to the rink," said Maggie. She didn't want to discuss the issue with Sandy, it was none of her business anyway, and she changed into her curling gear and left for the rink.

Her skip Bob was waiting for her, drinking a coffee while he stretched out his leg muscles. He introduced her to his team, his second who turned out to be her hockey coach, Kevin, and his third a matron named Pat, a fierce competitor. Maggie found it difficult to sweep up to Bob's fast-moving rocks, and she lost count of the number of brush strokes she made. He asked her to make more difficult shots than Angie did, like a perfect hit and roll and a double takeout, and she was elated that she could rise to the challenge. She happened to glance up when positioning her rock in front of the hack. Anton was standing in the lobby watching her. "Oh shit," she muttered.

"Who is that?" asked Kevin.

"My ex. I don't know what he's doing here."

She did her best to ignore his presence and concentrated on the game. After it was over, she glanced around the lobby, but he was nowhere to be seen.

Bob noticed. "Would you like me to see you home?"

"Yes, if you wouldn't mind."

Since it was late, after eleven, they didn't stay for coffee and Bob followed her home, staying only a car length or so behind her. The Nova appeared out of nowhere and it passed Bob's car and travelled alongside the Buick. Bob honked his horn. Once. Twice. Three times.

Anton slowed a little and twisted his head around to see who was driving the red and black Cherokee Chief. Then he took off.

As Maggie turned into her parking garage, she waved to Bob in thanks. Unknown to her, Bob waited for ten minutes to make sure she was in the building before he drove off. Safe in her apartment, she called the police. The cop who answered had a young voice and she pictured him as a new hire with six whiskers on his chin and a brush cut so short his scalp showed. He was not sympathetic. "We understand that this man is annoying you, but there is no reason for us to consider him violent. However, we will talk to him again."

She banged the black handset on the base, angry at both the police and Anton. Annoying. Yes. It was annoying to be scared to death and it was more than annoying to be looking over her shoulder every time she left the house, every time she went to the swimming pool or to the arena or the curling rink. She didn't understand why Anton wouldn't take no for an answer and give up on her and find another girlfriend – he didn't love her, that she knew. He chased her and Bob escorted her home. What a contrast. Interesting that Bob drove a Jeep.

She had a cup of chamomile tea to help her relax and rested her weary bones in her queen-sized bed. Ball, bell, bill, boll, bull. Bag, beg, big, bog, bug. Fan, fen, fin, fon, fun. No.

53

Thursday, January 18

SHE WOKE UP with the baby doll held tightly in her arms like a security blanket. She carried it while she went to the washroom and put it down on the bed long enough to tug on a pair of blue jeans and a green T-shirt. She laid it tenderly on the couch to free her hands to make a peanut butter sandwich. She spilled an eight-ounce glass of milk on the kitchen floor. "Oops," she said with a giggle. She cleaned it up with a terrycloth tea towel.

With the baby doll in her arms, she turned on the television, leaving peanut butter smudges on the dials, and watched *Mr. Dressup* and *Sesame Street*. Soon she was bored with that and she ran down the hall to the library to find some picture books. Roughly she leafed through *Lassie, Come Home*, tearing a page and smearing peanut butter on the cover. Not finding what she wanted, she threw the book on the floor. She wandered around the apartment as if searching for something or someone. She picked out one of Lynne's long-handled brushes and dry-painted on the table. That didn't work so she threw it on the floor as well. With an HB pencil she scribbled all over the cover of the sketch book. She toddled back to the living room to get her baby doll, climbed on the bed and pulled the covers over her, thumb secure in her mouth, and soon she was fast asleep.

When Maggie woke up about nine thirty, she was hugging the baby doll which she quickly laid on the dresser, a thing repugnant. She didn't remember getting dressed. She walked out to the living room and turned off the television but couldn't remember turning it on. She wasn't hungry but she wanted coffee. On the kitchen counter, she found a loaf of bread and a jar of peanut butter, the lid on the floor, a knife on a chair smeared from tip to tip with peanut butter. Her tea towel was in the sink, wet and sticky, and she rinsed it out and threw it in the washing machine.

"Lord have mercy. Christ have mercy. Lord have mercy."

Dr. Dixon phoned. "Where are you? You missed your appointment at nine. Are you alright?"

"No. I'm not. A child got up this morning instead of me. She made a peanut butter sandwich, spilled milk all over the floor and turned on the television. She ripped one of my books and played with the paints. Dr. Dixon. I can't do this. I can't. I can't cope with this." She sobbed, down on her knees on the rug.

"Okay. Okay. Calm down. There was no harm done. You were abused at a young age so there's bound to be alters who are children. Do you have any sedatives left?"

"Yes. I think so. One."

"Take it and relax. You'll be okay. I'll see you tomorrow."

After she made her coffee, she sat in the living room thinking about this latest development. Safety was her biggest concern. It would be disastrous to leave the apartment in a child state, and her child alters should not touch the stove or any other electrical appliances. She gathered herself together and went shopping at Woolco where she purchased some safety plugs for her electrical outlets, including the ones on the range, and a chain for the exterior door. When she asked the block superintendant to install it for her, he wasn't too keen. He argued she had no need for it in a secure building, but she insisted and finally he complied. Next, she moved all the cleaning supplies from below the sink to the top shelf of the broom closet, knowing that these children were the same height as she was. She hoped they wouldn't think to look in the higher cupboards.

Now then, she needed to do something that would make a child happy. She decided to take her inner children on a trip to the

Museum of Man and Nature, which she vaguely remembered visiting on a grade twelve field trip to the big city years before. Interested in everything historical, she strolled through the exhibits and was awed by a celestial show in the Planetarium. All the while her mind typed, Now is the time for all good men to come to the aid of the party. Now is the time for all good men to come to the aid of the party. Now is the time for all good men to come to the aid of the party. In the gift shop she bought a black T-shirt with 'Manitoba' on the front. Having no desire to cook, she stopped at A&W for a Mama cheese and onion rings. The waiter wasn't too happy that she didn't choose root beer, but she was in need of another coffee.

Later she went to hockey practice which was as much fun as usual. Although there was no body checking in their game, she learned how to poke check the puck away from her opponent and to protect her goalie and the net as well as she could. She now knew Kevin a little better, making someone more comfortable in his presence. Afterwards she felt a bit tired and was slow getting changed.

Singing along with the radio, she turned right off Portage Avenue onto Route 90 on the way home, the traffic light as usual at that time of the night. As she rounded the curve, she was suddenly blinded by headlights behind her. Annoyed, she flipped up the rear view mirror and held up her left hand to shield her eyes from the reflection in the side mirror. The traffic light at Academy Road was red, she slowed down ready to stop, but it changed to green and she sped through the intersection, trying to lose the ignoramus with the high-beams behind her. Without warning, he turned into the left lane, sideswiping a Ford pickup truck. He caromed into the right lane barely missing the rear end of the Buick. With a sickening thud, the car came to rest against an elm tree on the side of the road.

Maggie stopped the Buick and backed up. She ran to the car to see if anyone was injured. She wasn't surprised that it was the Nova. Fearfully she peered inside and found Anton knocked out but still alive, his right leg twisted in an odd angle. Then she ran to the black truck. The driver, a young guy about twenty-five, stepped out with his hands holding his head, blood spurting between his fingers. His girlfriend was unconscious lying on the seat. Fortunately the oncoming traffic stopped without ploughing into them and a stocky man with a curly red beard walked up to her. "I called the police on my CB. They oughta be here soon."

"Oh. Good. The driver of the car is out cold but he's alive. And so is the girl in the truck. We'll need a couple of ambulances."

Abruptly, the mountain man turned and hurried back to his vehicle to radio for more help. Maggie returned to the Nova. The engine was still running and she reached over the inert body and turned off the key. Anton was starting to come to. She removed her sheepskin jacket and spread it on his legs and tried to shield him from the wind. Five minutes later two police cars arrived, red and blue lights flashing, sirens wailing. A rescue vehicle was close behind.

While Anton and the couple in the truck were being loaded into ambulances, a tall blonde police woman interviewed Maggie, "You know the driver of the Nova?"

"Yes. I do. Ex-boyfriend."

"His name?"

"Anton Ballecero."

"Your name?"

"Maggie Barnett." She quietly gave her phone number and address.

The officer stared directly into her face, revealing a pair of frank brown eyes. "Was he chasing you?"

"I don't know. I don't know if he was following me or not. I didn't see him at the rink. I came east on Portage, turned right on Route 90. The next thing I knew a car was right behind me, shining its high beams in my mirrors. Then it changed lanes to pass me and hit the truck."

"Has he ever chased you?"

"Last night he followed me home from curling. I reported it."

"Where were you this evening?"

"I was at hockey practice in the West Town Arena."

"Okay. You can go home now. If we need any more information, we'll call you."

Shaking, Maggie drove the few blocks to her apartment. She was right. He was dangerous. But the crisis had come and gone and she was alive and so was he. She sat at the coffee table and wrote, dangerous, danger, anger, range, ranged, rang, sang, song, sung, rung, rouge, age, aged, ager, rag, rage, sage, sag, dog, rogue, dug, rug, drug, drag, dreg, Reg, nudge, ad, read, red, Ed, gourd, goad, god, gad, grade, road, rod, rode, sod, nod, node, grad, sad, rude, raged, nude, dear, dare, gear, gar, ear, era, Rae, are, near, sear, gore, ore, oar, or, o, nor, sore, soar, soared, sour, soured, our, dour, adore, adorn, rouse, rose, ruse, use, dose, roused, used, user, grouse, groused, sea, re, sue, due, rue, rued, sued, roe, do, doe, doer, goer, us, and, rand, grand, an, ran, Dan, Dane, dean, end, rend, send, sound, ground, round, one, on, don, done, den, gone, Ron, roan, run, rune, groan, drone, son, sun, sane, Sean, gun, dun, dune, nose, nosed, nu, resound, darn, earn, douse, arse, dung, dong, sander, ode, snore, snored, snare, snared, onager, ogre, nag, snag, snug, auger, surge, surged, urge, urged, nard, nerd.

She soaked in bubble bath for half an hour and her heart rate slowly returned to normal. She loved him once but she loved him no longer. Still she didn't want him dead. She couldn't think about it and so she went to bed.

A voice said, "He's such a loser."

Another said, "I like him."

She ignored them both.

54

Friday, January 19

PICTURES OF THE accident were splattered all over the front page of the *Winnipeg Free Press*. Anton's pride and joy made good copy, a mangled wreck whose bright coloured paint job appeared ominous in black and white. Maggie, however, didn't remember any cameras at the scene. The phone was ringing before she had the coffee on.

"It's me. Did you hear about Anton?"

"I was there, Sandy. He tried to pass me and hit the truck."

"Oh. No. Are you okay?"

"A little shaken up. I haven't read it yet. What does it say about the girl?"

"It says she had a mild concussion, and that Anton has a broken leg."

"Oh. Good. I was afraid she was badly hurt. I wasn't worried about him."

"Do you want to come over?"

"Thanks but no. I have a doctor's appointment right now."

In a pair of black corduroy pants and heavy denim blue sweater, Maggie set off for the medical clinic. As she passed by the scene of the accident, she started shaking again.

Dr. Dixon was waiting for her. "Maggie. I was wondering who would come to see me this morning."

"Who was here that time I was wearing the black leggings and white shirt?"

"Lynne."

"What's she like? I know she wore her hair slicked back. It was full of gel."

"She's very confident. Strong. She said she took over when you and Sammy were over-stressed."

"Yes. I'd go hide in my room, behind a locked door. And draw."

"You remember that?"

"Yes. And I remember going on a field trip to Winnipeg when I was in grade twelve. Is this significant?"

"It could be."

"Did you read about Anton? The accident?"

"That was your ex?" He picked up the paper and pointed to the wreckage of the Nova.

"Yes. I think he was chasing me."

"Are you okay?"

"Yeah. Just shaken up a bit and still thanking my lucky stars he didn't hit me on the rebound."

"I'm glad you're alright. That should end the harassment."

"Yes. I hope so. Now, about that little girl?"

"Let's see if we can reach her." He grabbed the doll and sat in front of Maggie holding the baby doll close to her. "Little girl. Little girl who likes peanut butter. Would you like to play with me and my doll?"

"I like peanut butter. Can I play with the dolly?"

Maggie regressed to four years old, shy, coquettish, innocent.

"Yes. Here she is," said the doctor, handing her the doll. "Are you Mary?"

"No. My name's Annie and I'm four."

"Did you spill the milk on the floor yesterday?"

"Yes. I sorry. I'm a bad girl." She pushed back in her chair, clearly expecting a severe reprimand or a slap on the face.

"It's okay. You're not bad. You just had an accident. Why don't you and the baby doll play now while I tidy up?" The doctor edged out of his chair and walked over to the white sink to wash his hands. He put a new paper sheet on the examining table and rumpled up the old one and put it in the garbage can, watching her all the time.

Annie rocked back and forth in the chair singing "Rock a bye baby in the tree top, when the wind blows the cradle will rock."

"Doctor. I want a sucker." The doctor had apparently passed the test and the little girl was comfortable enough to ask for a treat.

"How did you know I have suckers?"

"My doctor in Sampford always has suckers."

"Would you like a purple one or a red one or a green one?"

"Purple."

He offered her a purple lollipop from his desk drawer. She grabbed it without touching his hand, pulled the plastic wrapping off it, threw it on the floor and stuck the sucker in her mouth.

"You should say thank you."

"I fordot. Thanks you."

"Tell me about your doctor in Sampford."

"He's not old like you. He has black hair and a black beard and he doesn't wear glasses. He says that Mommy should take me away from the farm, but she won't go."

"Why does he want you to leave the farm?"

"So I won't get hurt."

"Did you get hurt once?"

"Yes. I had owies in my peepee."

"How did that happen?"

"I was riding Rob's bike. I don't want to talk to you."

"Okay. Bye for now. Maggie. Maggie."

"I heard that," Maggie said as she emerged. She took the sucker out of her mouth and looked at it, then with a grin stuck it back in again.

"How do you feel?"

"Okay, I guess. So I wonder, did Mom know I was being abused? I'm not sure. Is there any way I can reach the children at home? They can't read or write."

"You could talk out loud to them, read children's books out loud, listen to children's music, and watch kids' shows on television. I don't know if they will hear you, but you can try. It worked with Sammy, didn't it?"

"Yes. Okay. I'll try. Meg is going to send me some books on Christian meditation. Do you think that's a good idea?"

"Definitely. And we may try hypnotism at some point. There's still some bad stuff inside that head of yours."

"Okay. One step at a time. If I try to go too fast, I might get overwhelmed."

"Yes. See you Monday."

She had made no plans for the day. She drove slowly back to the high-rise apartment block she called home. The phone was ringing when she opened the door. It was Jared.

"I believe we owe you an apology."

"Accepted."

"You could come back to work."

"No. It doesn't change how you and Brad treated me."

"Well, old dogs can learn new tricks. The offer is open, if you change your mind – in New York if not Winnipeg."

"I'll keep it in mind."

She sat down on the couch to think. The telephone awakened her ten minutes later. This time it was Bob Hunter. "Was that your old boyfriend in the accident last night?"

"Yes, sir."

"Were you involved?"

"Yes. He tried to pass me and collided with the truck."

"So you were right to be leery of him."

"Yes. Don't you just hate it when you're right?"

"I know it's late to be asking, but would you have dinner with me tonight?"

"Okay. Yes. That would be fun."

"I will pick you up at six thirty then. What's your apartment number?"

"Five ten. See you later."

Fully awake now, Maggie wanted a skate. Before she could get changed, however, the phone rang again. This time it was Anton who begged her to visit him. After much cajoling, she agreed. At a local florists' shop she picked up two bouquets of flowers, pink carnations and white daisies with yellow centres, stems of greenery. At the reception desk at the hospital, she left one flower arrangement for the woman in the truck, and then went in search of Anton. She found him reclining in his hospital bed with his right leg on top of the covers, taped, but without a cast.

"You came. That's great."

Maggie laid the flowers on his tray table. "How are you? You haven't had surgery yet?"

"Tomorrow morning. I'll have a cast from my ankle up to here." He indicated a spot halfway between his knee and hip. "Now we can get back together, right?"

"What?"

"Well, you do care or you wouldn't have come. Doesn't the sight of me lying here in pain and agony bring back your love for me?"

"No. It does not. Did you slash my tires?"

"Oh, forget about that. I have proved that I love you. Now come on. Admit you love me too."

"You don't deny you vandalized my car. You whined to your grandfather and succeeded in getting me fired. You disobey the restraining order whenever you feel like it. And that proves your love? Anton. I am not your possession." As she spoke, she looked directly into his brown eyes and realized that he would indeed force her to have sex given the opportunity.

"It is not over. I refuse to accept that."

"It is over." Without saying good-bye, she walked out with the uncomfortable feeling that she'd been flattened into a pancake like Wiley E. Coyote in the cartoons. As she climbed into the Buick, she asked herself, "What happened to my quiet orderly life? My quiet orderly boring life? I want more. That's what happened."

She skated for an hour, helmet on, skating backwards as fast as she could, turning from backwards to frontwards, frontwards to backwards, and the reverse, until she could do it without tripping over her feet, forgetting to count, working with a game scenario in mind. Then she headed home to dress for her date, but when she sat down at the coffee table, someone wanted to write.

'Do you think this is a good idea, going out with him? You don't know anything about him. Maybe he's married.'

'There's only one way to find out. He doesn't wear a ring.'

'So? Not all men do. What's the real reason you don't want to go?'

'Don't you know? I'm a lesbian. Didn't you notice me eying up the girls?'

'Oh, it's you staring at women's breasts. Cut it out. What's your name anyway?'

'I'm Lynne. And I don't have to stop admiring women.'

'Oh. I see. So how do we resolve this? Sammy and that other one are guys and as far as I know they're straight. I am definitely hetero. You're gay. So who is Margaret Lynne Barnett?'

'Beats me. Is there such a person? Do we have to choose?'

'I don't know. Well, I have a date with Bob. Can you plan a painting or something and not bother me?'

'Oh, okay.'

"Lord have mercy. Christ have mercy. Lord have mercy," she prayed under her breath.

Maggie put down the pen, shaking her head in disbelief. Her life was becoming more complicated all the time. She showered, dried her hair using a little gel, applied her new makeup including lipstick and eye shadow, inserted silver dangling earrings into her small ears, and put on her long black skirt, dress boots and a black knit shirt with a scoop neck and three quarter sleeves, another unexplained find. A black cinch belt with a silver buckle completed the ensemble.

Bob arrived promptly at six thirty. She asked if he wanted to come up for a few minutes, but he said, "No, not this time. I am too hungry. I haven't eaten since breakfast."

"What were you doing today that you missed lunch?" asked Maggie as she climbed with difficulty into the Cherokee.

"We had a machine break down in the factory. We finally got it up and running at four o'clock this afternoon."

"I thought you curled on Friday nights."

"I do, but we have a bye tonight."

They went to a roast beef house that was new to Maggie. Bob ordered a Blue and Maggie her usual Brown Cow and for an entrée, they ordered the special. Bob devoured the contents of the bread basket while they were waiting to be served.

"Tell me what happened last night."

Maggie related the whole story once more. "I am lucky. It is a miracle he didn't hit the Buick too."

"So that's over. I was wondering if you were seeing someone. I had a little trouble getting enough nerve to ask you out."

"Really? Why?"

"Well. I just got divorced two years ago and I haven't been dating. My ex has custody of our twin boys and she's an alcoholic and she isn't looking after them properly and I haven't had a chance to think about dating."

"How old are the boys?"

"Eleven. You're the lawyer. Tell me how to get custody."

"Oh, that's why you asked me out – free legal advice."

"Oh, no. Don't take it that way." He looked at her, alarmed.

"Just kidding. Take pictures of the boys when they come to see you – their hair, their clothes, their facial expressions. Go to the school and talk to the teachers and the principal. If they're into hockey or anything, talk to the coaches. Talk to their friends' parents. Talk to their grandparents. Let the boys talk without asking direct questions and tape the conversations. Take them to the doctor and dentist. Document everything you know. Build you case."

"Man. My lawyer told me to forget it."

"If your wife is an alcoholic, there must be some way to get evidence about that, too. How did she get custody in the first place?"

"I'm a man. What do I know about child-raising? I thought they'd be better off with her, but it hasn't turned out that way. Is family law your specialty?"

"No. If you're in need of a new attorney, I can recommend Tom Henton at Jenkins Williamson. He is very good."

"Thanks. Now you know the details of my sordid marital life. Did you ever marry?"

"No. I was too busy with my career. Besides, I like my freedom. I have to admit it, but even so I asked Anton if he wanted to buy a house and settle down and he panicked. He couldn't make a commitment. I realized that I didn't want to live with him or have children with him. He got ugly. I ended it. And here I am, single and fancy free."

They lingered over coffee and dessert until about nine o'clock. Maggie was suddenly exhausted. "Please take me home."

He walked her to the door. "Are you going to ask me up?"

"No. Not tonight."

"You wanted to come home early. I thought that meant you were in a hurry to get to bed."

"I am. In my own bed. Alone. I told you, I'm tired."

"You just broke up with your boyfriend. You must need a little whoop-de-do."

"Good-night, Bob."

She dreamed she was in the eviscerating shed at the farm. She is fifteen. She is candling eggs, washing them, and packing them in wood crates. Grandpa MacDonar walks in. "Hi there, lassie." He tilts her chin up and plants a wet mushy kiss on her lips. They hear Mary Ellen coming. He laughs and saunters out of the shed.

55

Saturday, January 20

THE NEXT MORNING, she was busy playing with her big doll, Tommy, who was eating his breakfast of cold cereal and apple sauce in the high chair. He was making a big mess and she was very cross with him. She told him, "You're a big boy now. You should be able to eat without making more work for me. I have to get the eggs ready. I have customers coming. What day is it today anyway? Saturday?" She peered at the calendar on the kitchen wall. 'Dance' was written on the square for Saturday.

Quickly she donned her kilt and, stuffing her shoes into her shoulder bag, dashed out the door.

Sandy greeted her with, "What's with you, Mags? You were always ten minutes early for everything."

"Getting old and absent minded, I guess."

Sandy of course didn't know that Mags was another person entirely. Mags paid extra attention to detail and precise movements as she worked with her six charges. After the class, she and Sandy relaxed with a pot of tea.

"Are you going to enter Caroline and the older girls in competition this spring?"

"Caroline and Wendy competed last year and I think they'll do well. I don't know about the other two. Are they ready?"

"They could be. Even the little ones could try."

"Man, are you in a hurry."

"Perhaps. Why aren't you charging the parents for these lessons?"

"I am doing it for Caroline. I'm sorry. I'd like to stay and talk but I have to go. Danny's game starts in fifteen minutes. Gus took him to the rink for me."

"Okay. I will see you at the rink on Monday."

Maggie had just filled her face with a bite of her roast beef and lettuce sandwich when the phone rang.

"Maggie. Hello. This is your mother. Grandma MacDonar doesn't want to live alone now that Dad is gone. She wants to live in Winnipeg with you."

"No. Absolutely not." She felt the room closing in.

"You must take her. There is nowhere else for her to go."

"Why don't you take her? She can have my room. I won't be using it."

"I am not feeling well."

"Well, the answer is still no. She can go live with Ross. Or Rob. Or young Mike. Or in a senior's residence. She's not living with me."

"We'll order a bed from the Eaton's catalogue and have it delivered to your apartment. As soon as you get it, we'll bring her in." Her mother hung up before Maggie could answer.

It is the first slaughtering day of autumn. The evening before, she helped her mother capture two dozen chickens to be placed in starving crates for the night. Early in the morning Mike takes the birds one at a time and with a mighty whack chops their heads off. Red blood spurts on his clothes, on the grass and on the chopping block. The headless creatures flop around a minute or two and then lie still. Two women from the neighbourhood wait in the shed among the sparkling clean stainless steel sinks, tubs and tables. All the women including Maggie cover their hair with netting and wrap their middles with white cloth. Mary Ellen scalds the chickens with boiling hot water to release the feathers from the skin. Maggie gags.

They pluck the feathers from each bird and singe the skin to be rid of the last few hair-like feathers. One woman dons a pair of pink rubber gloves and slits open each chicken between the legs and pulls out the entrails. Maggie gags again. The smell is more than she can stand. After the feathers and innards are removed, Maggie washes the birds thoroughly, sets them on their hind legs to drain, headless, featherless and comical, and then she is free to go. She runs to her bed room to get away from the odour.

She tried to swim off her anger and frustration but it didn't work very well, even after a half hour of counted laps. She called the curling rink from the pool to check on practice ice and Brian said it was a quiet day, come on over.

She picked up her curling gear at the apartment and changed her pants and footwear at the rink. Maybe if she stayed away from home long enough her mother would disappear into the great blue yonder. She practiced her in-turn and out-turn guards for fifteen minutes, wishing Brian or Bob would come to help. Then she put a number of rocks in the house, imagined where the broom would be placed, and tried the take-outs, then did it all over again, trying to hit and roll to an advantageous spot. After that she threw eight draw shots, and satisfied, she returned the rocks to their storage spots, still tense and angry. She bought a coffee and a chocolate brownie covered in frosting and relaxed in the cafeteria with her feet on a chair wishing Bob were there, or Kevin, or Sandy. Being unemployed was lonely, but she had a job to do, healing herself. She strode out of the rink.

Back in her apartment, she phoned Rob in Vancouver, and when no one answered she left a message. 'This is your sister Maggie. Would next weekend be a good time for me to visit you and Tracy?'

She pondered a few minutes about what to do next. She wrote on the yellow pad – 'Sally. Sally. I haven't heard from you for a long time, not since New York. Do you want to go out for Italian food?'

No answer.

Maggie tried again. 'Sally, you told me about young Mike. Do you have anything else to tell me? You don't have to carry it all yourself.'

She leaned back on the couch, wondering what else she could do or say to contact Sally. Her hand moved back to the page.

'Okay. Alright. I am Sally. I am twenty and I like to cook. You don't, but I do. What do you want besides more information? Do you want to get rid of me?'

"No. I don't know. This is so weird. How are we supposed to function? What happened to you? Twenty. We were in university then."

'I had a boyfriend, Mark, whom I met in one of my classes. We were parked in his Ford half-ton outside the dorm necking when he grabbed my hand and pushed it down to feel his big woody. I didn't want to touch it. I didn't plan to have sex in his truck right on the street where anyone walking by could see. He said, make me come, right here, right now, whatta you say, babe? I jerked my hand away. He grabbed me by the back of the head and pulled me down towards his crotch. I twisted and turned and got myself free. Then I pushed myself backwards so I could see his face. He looked just like young Mike, slack jawed, bleary-eyed, and I couldn't stand it. I wanted to puke. I got out of that truck as fast as I could and I ran back to my room to study and I never went on a date again.'

"Jerk. You didn't go out with Anton?"

'Never. I don't like him.'

"Why not?"

"He doesn't care about me, or you. All he wants is sex."

"What do you want? What do you like to do besides cook?"

'Nothing. I don't want to go out with Bob. He makes me want sex and I don't want to date any sexy guys.'

"Why?"

'I feel out of control. He might take advantage of my feelings, hurt me somehow. I am really depressed. I don't want to live.'

The pen stopped. She didn't feel like cooking. The phrase resonated, I don't want to live, I don't want to live. Choose life, she thought, choose life. She would have liked Italian food for dinner, but she didn't want to eat alone in a restaurant, not on a Saturday night, with all the lovers holding hands, kissing and staring into each other's eyes, and not with the groups of friends talking and laughing when she had no one. She could have called Rebecca and Sadie and joined them at the Blue Rose but their existence had slipped her mind. She ordered Chinese again and ate it smothered in soy sauce at the kitchen table, with the doll beside her in the high chair.

Rob returned her call. "This is a surprise. Yes. Do come. You can stay with us. There's no need for you to book a hotel room or rent a car. Just tell us when and we'll meet you at the airport."

"Okay. I'll call you back on Monday evening."

She wondered if she had done the right thing. Maybe this was a really stupid idea. It could be the time to talk or the time to stay as far away as possible.

"Well, Lynne, do you want to work tonight?" she said aloud. Lynne was in a playful mood and made three wash paintings before she settled down to work on an oil painting of Mags and Sandy dancing at a competition in their flying kilts and snow white blouses and black vests. She used one of Sandy's photos as a guide, but made the feet and legs blurry to show motion and she placed them on a platform with sky and prairie behind. And just for the fun of it, she added King the German shepherd, sleeping in the shade in the foreground.

56

Sunday, January 21

BOB TELEPHONED EARLY Sunday, while she was reading the morning paper, and it took her a few minutes to register.

"I acted like a real jerk on Friday night. Will you give me a second chance? Will you have dinner with me tonight?"

"I don't know. I have about had my fill of men who take me for granted."

"I really like you. You aren't like other women. Give me another chance."

"I am not that different, Bob. Okay, I'll meet you at Alexander's at seven." She hung up without saying good-bye, annoyed that she'd agreed to go.

To guarantee a parking space, she hoped, she arrived at the gothic church twenty minutes before the service, signed the guest book, and sat in a pew a little closer to the front. She kneeled to pray, "God have mercy, Christ have mercy, Lord have mercy. Give me the courage to face my brother Rob. Give me the strength to resist my mother's unreasonable demands. I cannot look after my grandmother now. I pray for guidance regarding my career and my health. Amen."

On this occasion, she leafed though the *Book of Alternative Services*, and discovered a whole new dimension to worship and she turned to page one eighty-five to follow the service with the rest of the congregation. She also noticed the rood screen that divided the chancel from the nave. It was hand carved, she thought, from the same wood as the chancel and it looked to her like tatted lace or metal filigree. Afterwards, she took a few minutes to examine the stained glass windows, and one of the wardens, a lady by the name of Phyllis, invited her for coffee. She readily accepted and to her delight, her new acquaintance introduced her to a number of parish women and they chatted over coffee and homemade cookies.

After a liquid lunch, a canned smoothie with milk, she immediately went to the pool. Her apartment was too small for her. Lap after lap after lap for forty-five minutes, she swam, counting strokes until another swimmer accidently ran into her. She wanted to drown out the voices of Anton, her mother and her father and young Mike. She didn't want to hear their words but they intruded into her thoughts, leaving her feeling dirty, used and worthless. She knew now why she wanted to be a lawyer. She thought it would give her prestige and status, but it made no difference. To the world she was still just tits and ass and it was infuriating.

Maggie spent the rest of the afternoon reading one of Meg's books on meditation and experimenting with the techniques it described. Meditating even for a few minutes allowed her mind to rest and she felt more at peace as she dressed for her date with Bob. As she turned into the parking lot at her favourite restaurant, she had a strong urge to go to a hamburger joint for a cheeseburger and fries, but resisted it. At least she'd get a free meal of linguini. Bob was waiting for her, already on his second glass of wine. A Brown Cow didn't seem appropriate with pasta, so she asked the waiter for ice water with a slice of lemon.

"You came. I was afraid you'd stand me up."

"I am a lawyer. I say what I mean. And I don't sleep with any guy who winks at me."

"Okay. Okay, I'm an idiot. Can we begin again?"

He talked about his weekend with his sons, still concerned about their welfare. She asked him a few questions about working at Borden's. They discussed curling. They didn't have a lot in common but the chemistry was there, vibrating, inviting and delicious. Maggie, however, wasn't ready to act on her body's urgings because she couldn't. One minute she desired sex so badly she wanted to ravish Bob, the next minute her libido dried up like an old prune, the next minute she wanted to play catch in the parking lot. Perhaps her confusion was evident to Bob. He paid the bill, left a generous tip for the waiter and went home at precisely eight o'clock leaving her drinking her second cup of tea. She didn't hurry off. She wasn't embarrassed to be left sitting alone.

The three of them, Mike and Rob and herself, hide in the basement of the old farmhouse. It is really just a hole in the ground, lined with shelves for Mary Ellen's preserves – beet pickles, dill pickles, rhubarb with strawberries, rhubarb with orange peel, plain rhubarb, bread and butter pickles, stewed tomatoes, peach halves and pears. The air is damp and smells like the rich black soil. They huddle in the semi-darkness. Young Mike has swiped a bottle of his father's rye whiskey and a bottle of Coca Cola. He pours generous portions of the rye into three Tupperware tumblers and adds a smidgeon of soda pop. He hands one each to Rob and Maggie, who takes one sip and says, "Yuck. I am not drinking this." Mike grabs her by the hair. "You will too." He tilts her head back and runs the sweet sticky liquid into her mouth. It spills down her neck and onto her blouse. She squirms and kicks, but he manages to empty the rest into her mouth. She swallows so she won't choke.

"Now maybe you'll be more cooperative," Mike pushes her down so that she lays flat on the dank spider filled floor.

"I'm getting out of here," says Rob, and Mike allows him to leave.

A second or two later, he yells down at them. "Mom and Dad are home."

Maggie jumps up, climbs the ladder to the kitchen, and runs upstairs to her room. She brushes her teeth, washes her face and neck and changes into a clean red T-shirt.

She drove home automatically looking for Anton and his Nova. It really was too bad about the car. She was lonely and wanted to have a friend who was a man, but she hated being hit on. She may have been a bit old-fashioned because she didn't want to have sex on the first date, but for her there had to be something more than sex. She needed someone to love her, to care about her, a friend that she can trust. She had Meg and Dr. Dixon, but that wasn't enough.

57

Monday, January 22

MONDAY MORNING, SHE brewed coffee for breakfast and drank it with a bowl of oatmeal with brown sugar and milk. She called her travel agent, the one who booked all her flights for Jenkins Williamson, and was fortunate to get a return trip for Friday afternoon, arriving in Vancouver at five twenty in the afternoon, and leaving Monday morning at ten after ten.

It was Sally who kept her nine thirty appointment with Dr. Dixon. She hid her body under a bulky turtleneck sweater and Maggie's curling vest and blue jeans. Like a whipped puppy, she slunk into the doctor's office without saying hello.

He looked at her curiously. "Now who do we have here?"

"Sally. I came to talk to you. Would you please close the drapes on that window? I am ruining her life."

The sensitive doctor complied with her request, turned and said, "Whose life? Maggie's?"

"Uh-huh. I am so afraid of men. I believe sex is dirty and disgusting and sinful. I can't bear to touch a man and she wants a boyfriend and I think it's horrid."

"How old are you?"

"Twenty."

"Do you want to talk about that? About relationships with men? Or something from your early childhood?"

"There is something I want to tell you, but you mustn't tell Maggie or anyone else. Promise."

The doctor nodded and she went on, "My grandpa took me fishing in a secluded spot in somebody's pasture near the river. He made me lay down in the long moist grass and he took off all my clothes and put his horny old hands all over me. It didn't feel good. His hands were so rough and he wasn't trying to be nice. He put his long skinny index finger up inside me and pretended to do it. He kept going until my body responded. Then he laughed and laughed and laughed. It was such a big joke that a ten year old could reach orgasm, I guess. Dirty old man."

"Old men need sex too, but not with children. He had no right to touch you."

"Well, every time a man touches me, I feel dirty. I feel ashamed and I wish I could live in a world occupied only by women."

"But you are not gay?"

"No. I am straight, but I don't want women to touch me either."

"My prescription for you is this. You should find a woman who can give you a haircut, a manicure, a pedicure, a massage and a facial."

"No way, never."

Sally disappeared and Lynne, confident and poised, took her place. She removed the vest and set it aside with obvious distaste and ran her fingers through her hair. "That was mean, doctor. I am not happy with you. Maybe we should stop coming here."

"Sally needs to have someone touch her in a safe environment. Sometimes healing feels like torture, I agree."

"Well, this is Maggie's doings. She has upset everybody. She booked a flight to Vancouver to see Rob and she won't be able to meet you next Monday."

"I would like to talk to her before she goes."

"Well, not today. I am going to a workshop on painting the human body and I have to go or I shall be late. I am sure we'll meet again. Good day." She got up and left.

Lynne had a marvellous time at the workshop. Afterwards, she picked up the airplane tickets and a chicken burger and fries and ate her fast food in front of the television, ignoring the urge to write on the yellow pad. She was not interested in curling, but she didn't know how to let Maggie come out. Finally she read several pages in a legal text on the laws pertaining to separation and divorce.

Maggie changed into her curling pants as if nothing unusual had happened and went to the curling rink early hoping to speak to Sandy. As soon as she arrived, Maggie said, "I won't be at dancing on Saturday. There's something else I have to do."

Sandy yelled at her, "How can you do that to me? You promised you'd be there to help me."

"Keep your voice down. Please. I said I would come when I am available and I am not available this weekend and on the tenth of February."

"Some friend you are." Sandy stomped away.

"It's your gig," said Maggie to her retreating back. She enjoyed her game despite Sandy's outburst. After she got home, she lounged on the couch, her mind in a whirl. What was with Sandy? Did she think she owned her? It was such a relief not to worry about Anton lurking in the shadows. Now then, what would she say to Rob? Should she ask him what he remembered? Should she berate him for telling the school she wasn't a virgin, only ten years or so too late? Should she try to be friends? She had no clue. What did she want from him? She wanted to know why he was so vindictive. Sibling rivalry was one thing, being mean was another. Maybe it was all just kid stuff. Maybe it was because the home environment was toxic. Dysfunctional family. What a joke. Hers wasn't dysfunctional. It was completely fucked up.

She felt the urge to write by someone inside so she picked up the pen. It was a child who printed, 'I want to see Rob. He is my big brother.'

Maggie said aloud. "Do you love him?"

'Yeah, I do. He helps me read. He tells me the big words.'

"What else?"

'He plays ball with me. He tells me all about baseball so I can play at school.'

"When you see him, what will you say to him?"

'How come you don't love me anymore?'

Maggie's eyes stung with tears. "Ask him."

The hand stopped writing. Maggie broke down and sobbed. Her heart was broken.

She is in grade eight. She is now thirteen years old. She and David and Sandy are now the oldest children at MacNabb's Crossing School and the teacher is a Miss Shelley Adamson. Her hair is a mass of red curls. Maggie loves her because she is an athlete. Sometimes she comes outside at noon hour to umpire baseball games and to play soccer with the students and to build snowmen with the younger kids. It is early spring, the first really warm day. The baseball diamond is finally dry enough for play to begin. As usual, Maggie has started the day at first base. Trish went out and everyone moved up a position so that now Maggie is the pitcher.

"Wait a minute," says Miss Adamson. "I want a turn at bat."

Maggie stares into her teacher's steady green eyes. She goes into her windup. She chucks a strike right down the middle of the plate waist high. Miss Adamson cocks her bat and smacks a line drive straight back to the pitcher's mound. Maggie does what any major league pitcher would do. She ducks.

58

Tuesday, January 23

ON TUESDAY MORNING, Maggie was on her way to her appointment with Dr. Dixon when the store called about delivering the bed. The woman left a message - her name and number and a request that M. Barnett return her call as soon as possible.

Dr. Dixon's receptionist apologetically informed Maggie that the doctor had been called to the hospital and wouldn't be able to meet with her that morning.

So she drove to Portage la Prairie for lunch. As soon as she was outside the Perimeter, her eyes relaxed as she stared towards the horizon. The sky was high and blue, except for a far away skiff of white clouds, the highway dry, the snow in the fields white and beautiful, a Christmas card view. She didn't want to talk with anyone, didn't want to be a lone female sitting in a restaurant, didn't want to listen to fellow diners, didn't want to see friends laughing and joking together, and had no desire to witness lovers meeting for their noon meal. She chose the drive-through, ate her onion rings and chicken burger in the parking lot, and sipped on a coffee as she returned to the Peg.

Someone from Eaton's called again while she was meandering through the St. Vital shopping centre. She didn't buy anything but she looked at everything. She didn't need anything, she thought. But that wasn't true, she did. She needed new furniture for her new house. She spent the afternoon shopping for a new couch, a bedroom suite and a kitchen/dining room set. She saw some items she really liked, but wasn't ready to buy.

The store called a third time two minutes after she removed her coat and boots. She informed the insistent sales representative that she had not ordered a bed, that she did not want a bed, and that she would not accept delivery of a bed.

She made a chicken Caesar salad and rice for dinner. She spent an hour meditating, felt better, and watched television the rest of the evening, not wanting to think about the farm, her parents, her brothers, Sandy, Anton, or anything else. Dan, den, din, don, dun. Okay, if I allow proper nouns. Ban, Ben, bin, bon, bun. Works except bon is French. Fan, fen, fin, fon, fun. No. Tan, tin, ten, ton, tun. No. Pan, pen, pin, pon, pun. No. Darn, can't find another one. Hack, heck, hick, hock, huck. Is huck a word? Huck towelling. Wasn't Sandy making placemats from huck towelling? Ha, another one.

59

"I WANT TO meet Jane," said the doctor. "Jane. Would you talk to me? Jane."

"I don't have anything to say." Jane looked about the doctor's office warily, as if she expected boogie men to jump out of every corner.

"Are you afraid?"

"Yes. I am afraid of men, especially big men. I am afraid of teachers and I am afraid of policemen and judges and lawyers and mayors. You are a doctor. You're like a teacher. You want to boss me around and make me do things I don't want to do."

"Tell me about one teacher you didn't like."

"Okay. I'll give you a for instance. When I was in grade four, the teacher was Miss Carmichael. She had red hair and freckles and a bad temper. She told me to stop behaving like a boy. She told me that I had to wear skirts and dresses to school and she told me I was a disgrace to the female sex. She told me I should be ashamed of myself in front of all the other kids in school. She sent a note home to my parents. She wrote that I was to stop wearing pants to school and I should learn to cook and sew and knit and keep house."

"How did you feel about that?"

"I don't know. I was angry 'cause I hate wearing skirts. And it doesn't matter whether I wear pants or skirts or shorts, I am still a girl. Girls can play ball and ride bikes and drive tractors. She's a mean teacher."

"What did your parents do?"

"Mom went over to Sinclairs. That's where the teacher boards. And talked to her, but I don't know what she said. I never heard another whisper about it."

"But it hurt."

"Yeah. Other people say I look like a boy."

"You are definitely a girl, a woman."

"But I am ashamed of how I look."

"I have an idea. Why not get a haircut, a manicure, a pedicure, a facial, maybe some new clothes? Get a massage. Do you think that would make you feel better?"

"I do. I do. Maggie has lots of money and we're going back to work in March. I'll do it. I will. Right now - if I can get an appointment."

She jumped up and left, even though there was at least fifteen minutes remaining in the appointment. In the mall she had a thirty-minute facial in a darkened steamy room with soothing music playing. An oriental woman of perhaps fifty applied moisturizers and a clay mask. As her facial pores cleared, the woman massaged her back and shoulders and neck.

"Oh, you are so tense. You should come every week," she advised.

After that Jane walked down the mall to find a hairdresser. She didn't know any hairdressers, but her feet took her to Maggie's favourite. Elana trimmed the hair at the back of her head and her sideburns so that she would have a smooth line. Jane almost fell asleep while she fussed with the nails on her feet and hands.

For lunch, she had mushroom quiche and coffee, and then feeling like a new woman, Jane shopped for some new clothes, just one outfit of her own. She bought a blue denim skirt, a straight skirt that fell just above her knees, a long-sleeved jacket to match, and a dusty pink plaid shirt with long sleeves that could be rolled up to three-quarter. She used Maggie's credit card and felt a little guilty signing

'Maggie Barnett.' It was late in the afternoon before she went home. There was a phone message waiting but she ignored the blinking red light while she made a grilled pork chop, brown rice, and steamed carrots and peas for dinner. She tidied up the kitchen, changed into her kilt and went to Sandy's.

Caroline met her at the door with a big hug. Her mother said, "Oh, you showed up, did you?"

Mags didn't try to appease Sandy. She just ignored the snarky comment, worked with her six charges for the required time and then left.

Mary Ellen phoned again. "Maggie. What have you done? We ordered the bed and you refused delivery. We are bringing your grandmother to you on Friday."

"Mother. I told you that I cannot take her. I don't have room and I don't have the time to look after her. I will be going back to work soon. This is my vacation."

"You have to. I am your mother. I am telling you that you have to take care of your grandmother. And what do you mean – no room? Get rid of all your damn books and your silly art stuff and you'll have plenty of room."

"Yes. You are my mother, but I am twenty-nine years of age and I no longer take orders from you. I said no and I mean no."

"We'll see you Friday." Mary Ellen hung up.

Maggie sat on the floor cross-legged with her back against a chair. "Jesus. Jesus. Jesus. I am lost. I am one of your lost sheep. I am sinking. Lord, I am drowning. Please come to me in my hour of need. Show me that you exist. Give me something to hold onto. You said that you left us with your peace. Lord, give me your peace, I pray you. Give me your peace." Tears rolled down her cheeks.

Slowly she became aware of a feeling of warmth and love, beginning in her heart and spreading to her belly and her shoulders and neck and her head and down her legs to her feet. It seemed to envelope her completely, including the space around her. It was so strong and powerful it made her gasp. She wanted to say, 'Stop. Stop. That's enough. That's all I need.' But the amazing peace strengthened and continued on and on. Her legs were getting numb sitting in that position, but she didn't move and she didn't care. She sobbed. She said, "Thank you. Thank you. Thank you." The feeling ebbed a little, enough for her to climb to her feet and walk to her bedroom. She climbed into bed and fell asleep with her mind at peace.

60

SHE HAD NO appointment with Dr. Dixon the next morning, and she was at a loss for something to do. She had breakfast – several handfuls of Cheerios right from the box and a glass of orange juice. She played with the boy doll for a time, instructing him on his table manners and took him for walks down the hallway. She tried to induce him to say Mary but he would not. She soon tired of that game and brought the baby doll from the bedroom. She pretended that the boy doll Tommy was married to the baby doll, Susie, and in the game, Tommy tells Susie to stifle herself, just like Archie told Edith. She pretended that Tommy was her father Mike telling her mother to hurry up, quit dawdling, no time for rest. By then she was tired and had a nap on the living room rug.

Dick woke up about ten o'clock, hungry as always. He made a sloppy peanut butter and jam sandwich and drank orange juice directly from the bottle. He played with his farm machinery. His cultivator broke down and he spent fifteen or twenty minutes fixing it. That done, he worked on the summer fallow for the rest of the morning. Then he too had a siesta on the living room rug.

Maggie emerged around noon, wondering what on earth she was doing sleeping on the rug. Her body ached from lying on the floor, her head was in a whirl and she had a throbbing headache. She ran a hot bath, filled the tub with Epsom salts, and soaked for half an hour, but she didn't feel any better. She drank two cups of coffee and ate some green grapes.

Time to get ready for Vancouver. She retrieved her luggage from the storage room in the basement, and packed some jeans and shirts, her bathing suit, her new jean jacket and skirt, and odds and ends. She checked her wallet for cash – only twenty dollars. She made a quick trip to the bank and withdrew two hundred dollars. Once out of the house, she didn't want to go back, so she drove to the skating oval. Her skates were cold from being in the back of the car, but she put them on anyway. She skated for an hour, counting the strokes of her skates. Still the fogginess in her head didn't clear. She couldn't think of anything else to do, so she went back to the apartment to finish packing. By the time she left for hockey practice, she was feeling better, but she almost cancelled her flight to Vancouver. She still didn't know what to say to Rob.

61

Friday, January 26

MAGGIE CANCELLED HER eleven o'clock with Dr. Dixon. She didn't know why, but she didn't want to talk with him that morning. Anyway she wanted to be at the airport by noon. She didn't read while she waited for the flight. She wrote in her journal and tried to nap on the way, but failed miserably. She arrived in Vancouver in a state of uncertainty.

As agreed, Rob was waiting for her next to the luggage carousel. They didn't hug. There was too much baggage between them for that. Neither did they shake hands. They were brother and sister, not strangers. They just nodded hello, and turned to watch the moving belt for Maggie's suitcase.

Maggie turned to look at him. She smiled slightly and said, "We still look like two peas from the same pod."

"We do. I hardly recognized you at the funeral - so poised, so professional. You are a handsome woman, Margaret L. Barnett, Attorney at Law. Whoever would have believed it?"

"Professor Robert T. Barnett, Ph.D. Who would have believed that?"

"Touché. I don't know why you came after all these years, Maggie, but you are welcome."

"Thank you."

Rob steered away from emotional topics as he made his way through the Richmond traffic to Burnaby, where he and Tracy owned a two-storey house on the side of the mountain. He introduced Maggie to his wife, who had a delicious dinner of baked salmon ready and waiting.

"Tomorrow," she said, "Rob has a commitment, so you and I are going shopping. I know some neat little shops you'll just love."

Maggie smiled, "Sounds good to me." She already liked Rob's wife. She looked like a blonde copy of herself, tall, slim, athletic, but full of life and energy and it was obvious that she and Rob were devoted to one another.

"And then," Tracy went on, "I am going out in the evening so that you two can talk."

They settled into deep beige leather tub chairs to have coffee and Baileys, Maggie's favourite. "Do remember your childhood, Rob?" She had to start somewhere.

"Yes. Most of it, I think. Why?"

"I do not. I hardly remember anything that happened before I started university. I have blocked it all out. But for the last few months, it has been coming back to me in bits and pieces."

"That must be difficult. Do remember that time I told everybody you weren't a virgin?" asked Rob.

"I did remember that incident recently. I don't understand why you were so vindictive. I understand sibling rivalry and all that, but, man, that was a low blow."

"I was always mad at you because it was your fault Mike left. Mike was my hero. I thought the sun rose and set with Mike. The look on your face, I will never forget it."

"My fault? How could it possibly be my fault? I was only six years old."

"But that time we were down in the cellar with Dad's whiskey, you didn't fight him. You didn't even scream."

"I couldn't fight him. He was too big and strong. And why scream? There was no one home to hear. Besides he threatened to kill me."

"Well, if you had told Dad and Mom when it first started, it never would have escalated as far as it did."

"Oh, Rob. Do you think they would have believed me? I was just a little girl. How could I know what was right and what was wrong? And you had no right to tell everyone. It did a lot of damage. After that, I was branded a bad girl, a loose woman. Other girls and their mothers wouldn't speak to me. Teachers were meaner. Guys hit on me. I went underground and hid in my books and sports."

"And became a lawyer."

"Yes. Nobody stopped to ask who the guy was. I guess that was a minor detail."

"Okay, you two. Let's talk about something else. You can rehash more crap from the past tomorrow. Tonight, let's go out. Let's go to a place we know where there's a great band and the atmosphere is funky and the people are true Lotus Land loony tunes."

Later, on the way back to Rob's house, Maggie started to laugh. "Rob, do you remember that time we got stuck in the garden? It was in the spring. The grass was green and the puddles all dried up. We asked Mom if we could go outside to play, and she said it was okay, but stay out of the garden. That of course was the wrong thing to say. We went directly to the garden and our boots got stuck in the mud. We couldn't move. Mom had to get some planks from the shop to walk on so that she could rescue us."

Rob chuckled. "Yes. I do remember that. Mud? That stuff should be called quick sand."

"Yeah. And then it dried as hard as rocks. Remember? We made ashtrays and vases from that yellow clay. We couldn't break them no matter what we did."

"Yeah. We hurled them at that clothes line post as hard as we could and all we accomplished was chipping the edges a bit. They were really hard."

"Speaking of the clothes line post – do you remember when that kitten climbed up Dad like a tree? We were playing catch near the clothesline, for some reason. You threw the ball to me. I missed it and ran to pick it up. King ran after the ball, but the kitten thought, apparently, that the dog was coming after it, and it climbed the nearest tree, which happened to be human, digging its claws in all the way up."

"It's a wonder Dad didn't kill it on the spot. The look on his face was priceless."

62

Saturday, January 27

TRACY AND MAGGIE went for an early morning swim at a nearby pool. Maggie was right about Tracy's athleticism, she swam like a fish. They both swam laps for forty minutes before they stopped. Afterward, they had coffee and blueberry muffins at the sports facility.

"I think your visit is doing something good for Rob," said Tracy.

"What do you mean?"

"He is so angry and bitter at times. And he doesn't want to have children. He says he'd make a lousy father."

"We have a lot to be angry and bitter about. Our family is dysfunctional. That's the word in psycho babble for completely screwed up."

"Your other brother raped you?"

"Yes. He did. Dad caught him and banished him from the farm. Mike's actually a half-brother. He's Dad's son from his first marriage."

"Oh. Now I understand. Come on. Let's go home. Surely you two can release some more of your pain and anger."

The three gathered in the living room to read the morning papers and drink a pot of coffee. Rob didn't say anything more and neither did Maggie. Tracey warmed up some thick delicious beef stew for lunch, along with hot soda biscuits directly from the oven. They drank a pot of green tea and had fruit salad for dessert. It was eerily quiet as they ate.

As Rob was leaving for his appointment, he continued with his argument about Mike. "But you wrestled with him, played ball with him, and asked him to help with your homework."

"I know, Rob. It was complicated. Maybe I had already blocked out the memory of the attack. Maybe I was just trying to be normal. Maybe I didn't want Mike to hurt me in other ways. He'd done too much already."

"He shouldn't have touched you, no matter what. It was not your fault." Rob turned and walked out of the house.

"Well, that's progress," said Tracy. "Let's go shopping."

They hit all the trendy boutiques that they both loved. Maggie bought an imported silk scarf in purple and mauve to wear with her black coat and a pair of high-heeled tan leather slide-ons. Tracy bought a red shirt trimmed in white and red Capri pants. They had an enjoyable afternoon. Maggie forgot all her woes and relaxed in Tracy's warmth. They ordered in Chinese food for dinner and then Tracy left Maggie and Rob alone.

"So why did you come? What do you want from me?"

"I don't even know. In fact, I almost changed my mind. I wanted to know why you hated me. I guess I have the answer to that. But Dad hates me, too. And Mom. I don't know why. So I have no family. Do you?"

"I have Tracy. I have no idea what makes Ma and Pa tick. I gave up trying to figure that out years ago, and I haven't talked to Mike in years. I'll make you a deal. I'll come to Winnipeg once a year and you come to Vancouver once a year, and we'll get to know each other a bit."

"Okay. I'll take you up on that deal. Would you write to me?" When Rob nodded yes, she continued. "What if we stopped talking about the past and started talking about the present. Tell me about your work at the university." Despite all the years and all the trauma she felt connected to him, connected by shared memories and forgotten familiarity.

They were still talking when Tracy got home. "You two haven't killed each other?" she asked, jesting, she hoped.

"No. We buried the hatchet. For this short weekend, we are just getting to know each other. Maybe we'll get into the past another time." Rob actually had tears in his eyes, and he seemed more relaxed. He rose from his chair. "What do you drink, Maggie?"

"Brown Cows."

"Oh, yeah, you hate the taste of booze. Let me see. You could try a Caesar – that's vodka with Clamato juice - or you could have vodka and orange juice."

"I'll go with a Caesar, tempt fate, live on the wild side," joked Maggie, the first funny she'd cracked for months.

63

Sunday, January 28

To Maggie's surprise, Rob and Tracy were also church goers. They took her to a newly built United Church located in their middle class neighbourhood. Afterwards, they took Maggie to lunch at a seafood restaurant in a high-rise overlooking English Bay and spent the afternoon showing her the sights.

"Next time, come in the spring or fall," advised Tracy. "It is so beautiful then. There will be a next time, won't there?"

"Yes. I will come again - for more than a weekend. Do you ski?"

"Yes. I bet you've never learned. You may have to come more than once a year," said Rob.

They barbecued T-bone steaks and baked potatoes for dinner and talked until midnight.

64

Monday, January 29

ROB DROPPED HER off at the Vancouver airport at nine sharp. He didn't have time to wait with her, but Maggie wasn't concerned. He hugged her and said, "Thanks for coming, Sis."

"I am glad I came. Bye for now."

She picked up her required reading material in the book store, the first in a series of historical novels, *The Kent Family Chronicles*, this one called *The Bastard*, and read until her flight was called. She kept on reading most of the way back to Winnipeg. She felt happier than she had in some time.

A voice said, "I'm going to kill Rob."

Another voice said, "He told me I put out for Mike but not for him."

Maggie didn't want to deal with the voices, so she continued to read. When she got home, she ignored the accumulated mail, the pile of newspapers and the telephone messages. She drifted off to sleep, awakening after five o'clock. She went to the curling rink early and had a grilled cheese sandwich in the cafeteria upstairs where Bob Hunter joined her.

"Hi. Did you vanish for the weekend? I called you several times."

"Hi yourself. I went to Vancouver to see my brother."

"That would explain it. Will you have dinner with me tomorrow night?"

Maggie couldn't think of any reason to refuse, and she was feeling generous, so she agreed. Sandy wasn't quite so forgiving. She was about to snub Maggie until she saw the good-looking man behind her. "So who is this? Found a new squeeze already?"

Maggie winced. "Sandy Borden, meet Bob Hunter, vice-president of Borden International." She left them to figure it out and went out on the ice to take a few practice shots.

After the game, she didn't stay for a drink. She was having too much trouble keeping her eyes open. At home, she listened to her phone messages, which included two irate messages from her mother, checked the real estate listings in the *Free Press*, and sorted through the mail. There was nothing urgent, so she went to bed. She wrote all about the weekend in her journal, noting that she had no flashbacks and no bad dreams for the entire four days.

65

Tuesday, January 30

HER MOTHER CALLED early, waking Maggie up. At the sound of Mary Ellen's voice, she was suddenly afraid and didn't know why.

Mary Ellen yelled into the phone, "Where were you? It's a good thing we called Friday morning or we would have been left sitting in your lobby. Explain yourself."

"I told you. I will not let Grandma live with me. You didn't listen."

"You only think of yourself, you selfish girl."

"Well, no one else thinks of me. Somebody has to."

"What's this about you and Meg? She told me to leave you be. You're having a tough time right now. What are you doing confiding in her instead of your own mother?"

"Mother, why do you hate me?"

"You are the cause of all the troubles in this family."

"Why? Because I'm a girl?"

"You know what I'm talking about."

Maggie had a flash of knowing. "What did your father do to you?"

"Nothing. He was a good father."

"He wasn't a good grandfather."

"Margaret Lynne Barnett. You are a liar. My father would never touch you. I will never speak to you again." Mary Ellen slammed down the receiver.

Maggie recoiled from the phone. Her right ear hurt for half an hour, but she didn't have time to worry about it. Sandy called, inviting her for lunch in the Borden International cafeteria. She wasn't sure she was still talking to her school mate, but she agreed to go. She quickly had toast with a generous spread of three fruit marmalade and a generous helping of apple juice and arrived at the medical centre five minutes late for her appointment with Dr. Dixon.

"So who are you today?"

"Maggie. I am Maggie. I think."

"So how was your trip to Vancouver?"

"Pretty good, actually. Apparently Rob blamed me because Mike was sent away. He said Mike was his hero. Some hero. When we got that out of the way, we just ignored the past and talked about the present. I left feeling really good, but then the voices told me I was wrong – that Rob tried to rape me. I'll have to get to that memory eventually."

"You weren't uncomfortable there?"

"No. I didn't feel threatened, but Rob is not functioning all that well according to his wife. He was raised in the same dysfunctional household after all."

"What else?"

"My mother tried to make me take my grandmother into my apartment. I refused. I just can't handle that right now."

"No. You need your privacy to heal. Don't feel guilty."

"I am pretty sure she was abused by her father."

"That wouldn't surprise me. She's probably powerless when it comes to her father and couldn't have protected you, no matter what. It will come clear in due time. Let's talk to Miranda today. Miranda. Miranda."

The woman squirmed in her chair. She picked at the red cashmere sweater Maggie had chosen to wear. She crossed and uncrossed her legs. She didn't want to be there. "What do you want, Gramps? I got better things to do than jaw with you."

"Why don't you want to talk with me?"

"You can't help us. We're a way over your head. You don't know how."

"There is only one way. The first step is to let all the parts speak."

"I got nothing to say."

"Did Rob try to hurt you?"

"Nah. That wasn't me."

"Who was it?"

"I don't know."

"Tell me about your mother."

"She's a cold unfeeling bitch."

"Tell me."

"Well, I made this swing in the one tree in our yard. I took the baler twine. You know, Mom bought straw from Sam MacNair to bed the chickens, so there was lots of used twine around. Anyway, I braided the twine to make ropes for my swing and I used an old steel seat from a mower or something for the seat. One day I was swinging away in peace and the swing broke. I fell down face first. Knocked the wind right out of me. I bashed my elbow and I had big welts across the backs of my legs where the rope bruised me. I limped to the house crying and she wouldn't even look at my rope burns. She told me to stop bawling and go to my room."

"Was she that unfeeling at other times?"

"Yeah. She didn't nurse me like Meg. She never washed out my cuts and bruises and she never hugged me. I wanted Meg to be my mother."

"Who is Meg?"

"Meg is Sandy's mother. She's a nurse at the Sampford hospital."

"What do you think your mother wanted from you?"

"I don't know. Maybe she wanted me to be like her, heavy into knitting and cooking and chickens. Or maybe she wanted me to be a boy, tough. Or maybe she wanted me to be as mean as she is."

"Did your Mom and Dad fight?"

"Sometimes. Dad was the boss man. What he said went. But other times he asked for her opinion too. I don't know. I ignored them as much as I could. They fought about Mags. Dad didn't want her to dance and Mom wanted her to do it."

"Dance?"

"Mags did Highland dancing, you know, the Highland fling. This is a drag. Talk to someone else." She drooped forward, her head almost in her lap.

"Mags. Mags."

A dancer appeared, her head high, body erect, eyes alert. "Yes. Doctor. Did you wish to speak to me?"

"I didn't know you existed."

"Maggie doesn't know, so how would you?"

"Tell me about you."

"I was a Highland dancer. I even won a competition when I was thirteen. I was so happy. I actually beat Sandy, but Dad wouldn't let me go to Maxville for the finals and I was so mad at him. He and Mom had a big fight. He hit her on the mouth with his fist, so I decided to quit."

"You are helping Sandy teach now."

"Yes. I like teaching, but not having Sandy as my boss."

"What do you remember about your home life?"

"I can't figure it out. I mean. Dad didn't want me to dance, yet he made me put on my kilt and pose for pictures of my bare bottom. And my chest. Who'd want pictures of that? I didn't even have any breasts. Weird."

"Maggie had some memories of pictures too. Where did you go for these pictures?"

"The pink house."

"She remembered that too. Did they hurt you when they took the pictures?"

"Dad did. He put his big ugly penis in me for some of the shots. I don't like to talk about this." She closed her eyes and her head dropped to her left shoulder and she slumped against the chair.

"Maggie." The doctor's eyes were wide with alarm. "Maggie. Maggie."

"I am here. I think." The lawyer returned. "I heard all that. I don't know how, but I did."

"You have some terrible memories to dig out yet."

"I know."

"Are you okay? Why don't you have coffee in the waiting room before you go? I have another patient waiting."

Maggie did as he suggested, since she was somewhat disoriented. She needed a few minutes to digest the new information. She had guessed that Mags existed, but didn't know her name and she remembered the painful welts on her legs but not their origin. After she finished a second cup of coffee, she drove slowly and carefully to Borden International and parked the Buick in the staff parking area. Sandy was waiting, bubbling over like a root beer float. Maggie knew immediately she'd had sex the night before. That glow of satisfaction was obvious.

"Maggie. Hello. Why didn't you tell me you went to Vancouver to see Rob? I am so glad you two are friends again. Come on. Let's get something to eat before the good stuff is all gone."

Maggie wanted to leave. So, Sandy had a hot night with Bob Hunter. And he told her about her trip west. She helped herself to some spinach quiche and a garden vegetable salad and a mug of green tea.

Sandy plunked down on the chair opposite Maggie's. "I would like your tapes of music that you had for competition."

"I don't know if I still have them," lied Maggie. "Maybe they are at the farm. Why don't you use your own?"

"I always liked yours better."

For Maggie the room was getting smaller and smaller despite the high open-raftered ceiling and bright lights. The buzz of conversation around her grew louder and louder, and her ears wanted to pop.

"You're entering the older girls in the spring competition?"

"Yes. I think they will be ready. Are you sure you can't skip the bonspiel?"

"No. I signed up and I intend to curl. Get the older girls to dance with the young ones. It will help both age groups."

"I suppose I could do that. Listen, I have to get back to work."

After she left, Maggie lingered with her hot tea. One of the three young lawyers approached her, friendly, as if nothing had happened the last time they met. "Why don't you join us at our table?"

"Are you taking a long lunch?"

"We schedule our conferences over the lunch hour. We eat and talk and get off work early – some days."

They introduced themselves, Bruce, the one who came to get her, Tom and Arnold.

"So have your heard?" asked Tom. "The old man might be sending you to Ireland."

"Ireland? Really? Where in Ireland, exactly?"

"Dublin. The other attorney, the one who never comes to our meetings, doesn't want to go after all, and none of us want to go. So you're it."

"Oh, man. Gus never mentioned that to me."

"Well, you may be in for a surprise. Hey, we'd better be off."

She was left again sipping a second cup of tea and then took her time driving home. She stopped at the apartment long enough to pick up her skates and a warm toque, her hockey stick and gloves, and a puck. She practiced wrist shots and slap shots until her wrists were sore and she was tired of counting, and she skated forwards and backwards for an hour. By then her ears were cold despite the warm hat and her nose felt as if it might be frozen. She went home for a cup of hot chocolate. When the doorbell rang at six thirty, she and Lynne were busy painting a portrait of King the German shepherd and didn't bother to answer. An hour later the phone rang but she didn't answer that either.

66

Wednesday, January 31

THE NEXT MORNING, she didn't have an appointment with Dr. Dixon and had no plans except for dance class that evening. She sat down at the kitchen table to compose a letter to Rob. She wrote: Dear Rob, Thanks for welcoming me into your home last weekend. It was a good beginning. It seems that Mom also blamed me for all the problems in our family. Blaming the victim is a good way to absolve yourself of any responsibility. I remember being down in the cellar with Mike and the bottle of whiskey. Do you remember the turkey chasing me? Did you ever wonder why Grandpa took me places and left you behind? I am pretty sure he abused Mom too. After I got home, I remembered that you wanted the same benefits as young Mike. Do you remember that? We were some mixed up family. Maggie

She hesitated before she dropped the letter in the mailbox. What if her memories were false? What if this letter stopped their dialogue completely? She let it slide into the slot, quickly, before she could change her mind. She knew she was depressed, but the doctor didn't want to medicate her. She had so much to process, like the fact that she did pose for dirty pictures. Somewhere out there were a bunch of nude scenes with her as the star. Yuck. She wondered how many guys got to drool over her skinny little bottom. Did her father receive money? And she was right about the pink house. To make matters worse, Meg told her mother that she was having a rough time. Could she trust Meg? Ireland? Would she go to Ireland? Oh, man. Sandy took her boyfriend. He wasn't her boyfriend. Not really. She didn't want to be an instant mother to two pre-pubescent boys anyway, but of course he was looking for sex not a wife.

At that precise moment, Bob phoned. "Are you alright? You stood me up last night."

"Wouldn't you rather be with Sandy?"

"Oh. She told you."

"She didn't have to. I don't want to see you, Bob. There is nowhere for our relationship to go."

"Okay. If that's the way you want it."

Maybe she was being a prude. Was she? Did she chase him away? He was a sexy guy and she didn't own him. They had no commitment to each other and she was tired and she couldn't be bothered to figure it out. She lay down on the couch and closed her eyes, but sleep wouldn't come. Dick came out and played with his John Deere equipment. The wheat wasn't ripe enough to cut so he too lay down to rest. Mary played with the Barbie doll until she was tired. She slept for an hour.

Maggie made a liquid lunch of milk and a weight-loss meal replacement. Lynne took over and they worked on the dog's picture until about four. Then she skated for an hour, counting every stroke of her blades. She was restless, needing to move, wanting to run away, but it was too cold outside to skate any longer.

"Mags, do you want to teach tonight?" she said aloud, but there was no answer. She wrote on the yellow legal pad, 'Mags, do you want to teach tonight?'

Her hand moved on its own. It wrote – 'Yes, I will teach. But let's go home right after.'

She changed into her tartan kilt and viewed her reflection in the full-length mirror on the bathroom door. Her stomach heaved. She took the kilt off and put on a light blue denim skirt which was another find from deep in her closet. It was full enough to allow high kicks but longer than her kilt.

Sandy was angry that she didn't wear the regulation kilt and she asked about the dance music but Mags said, "I don't have it. It must be at the farm." Sandy glared at her, but Mags didn't care. She just shrugged her shoulders and proceeded down to the dance studio in the basement. Her pupils were glad to see her and they had a good class together, and then without saying good-night to Sandy, she walked out.

She slid behind the wheel of the Buick and breathed in the new car smell. She shook her head a little and smiled and said, "Mmm." She gazed at the luxurious sand-coloured interior, put the transmission in gear and listened to the engine purr as she drove to Headingly and back to her apartment. She didn't want to stop, so she kept on going all the way to Elie. Finally she went home. She meditated for half an hour and then picked up the John Jakes novel.

She is in grade five at the Crossing School where preparations for the Christmas concert are in full swing. She is in the square-dancing number for the first time. Beth is partnered with George; Sarah is with Rob; Sandy is dancing with David, and Mags with Tom, since he's the only boy taller than she is. The teacher is Miss Jacques, who prefers to be called Ma'mselle Jacques, but none of the students remember. She is a petite, shorter than Meg, with dark brown eyes and long black hair, which she wears in a French knot most of the time, and she speaks with a pronounced accent. The four couples dance to a scratchy record, which begins with 'Honour your partners.' Tom bows to her, sticking his tongue out and wiggling his ears. Mags giggles as she gracefully curtseys. This much she knows.

'Allemande left.' She faces her corner, Rob. They slap their left hands, walk around the each other, and return to their places.

Miss Jacques gives the brother and sister a dirty look, but says nothing. She teaches them to promenade and do sa do and dance through an intricate pattern to a tune that Mags doesn't recognize. She soon has the words memorized - "Allemande left on your left hand, Dance right into a right and left grand, Hand over hand, go around the ring, Meet with your partner, pretty little thing, and Promenade."

She is in love with Tom Bannerman, but he has eyes only for Trish.

67

Thursday, February 1

"DR. DIXON. I have only four more weeks before I go back to work. I don't feel any saner than I did two weeks ago."

"Don't panic. We are making progress here."

"My life is chaos. I black out on a regular basis. I dream. I remember. I am overwhelmed and on top of all that, it seems everyone is against me. Even Meg and Sandy."

"What happened?"

"Meg told Mom she was counselling me, and Sandy took my boyfriend, well, my potential boyfriend."

"So how do you feel?"

"I feel betrayed in both cases. Meg didn't need to tell Mom anything, especially a lie. She isn't counselling me. I told her I was a multiple personality because I needed a friend. As for Bob, it hurts, but he was just looking for sex. I can't get into a sexual relationship unless there's some love involved."

"Can you tell me more about that?"

"I don't want anyone to touch me unless I can feel love in that touch, not just desire. Otherwise, it feels too much like rape and my body turns off like a light switch."

"Was that the way it was with Anton?"

"Sometimes. Most of the time. I should have broken up with him years ago."

"Tell me about Sandy. Were you really close friends?"

"I never confided in her. Yet we played together when we were young. All the time. There were four of us – me, Sandy, her sister Trish, and Sarah – until Sarah moved away. I think that was about grade six or so. In high school, I was always into sports and we didn't spend much time together, yet we were still friends."

"But not best friends."

"No. I don't think I ever had a best friend. I couldn't confide in anyone."

"Abuse does that. It isolates its victims. It affected your relationship with Sandy and probably Anton as well. To be in a relationship means to let the other person in, into your most intimate feelings, desires and hopes."

"I don't know if I can do that. I don't know if I want to do that. I don't like to feel vulnerable and weak. Who is Margaret Lynne Barnett anyway? Is she an artist or a lawyer or something else?"

"You will know that in time. One will dominate, although I suspect you'll be a lawyer in order to make a living, but you'll still be an artist and an athlete."

"What else could I do to heal?"

"You could join a support group. I can set you up if you'd like. It would help you to feel less alone."

"Okay. Let's do that."

"Now could I talk to Dick? Dick. Would you like to play with my toys today?" The doctor reached for his box of boys' toys.

Immediately a snarl appeared on Maggie's face and she slouched down on the chair, knees apart and feet together. "Why should I talk to you?"

"Why not?"

"You told her about me. She even bought some John Deere stuff for me to play with at home. That's okay I guess. But she knows when I've been out and I don't like that. I don't want anyone to know about me." He made no move to pick up a toy.

"Why not? Will something bad happen?"

"I don't know. I just want to stay hid."

"I won't tell but the others know you exist."

"I hate this. I am a boy and I don't want to wear dresses and I don't want to wear pink and I don't want to dance. I don't want to have breasts and I don't want to bleed every month and I don't want any creepy old boyfriends touching me. I don't want to be here at all."

"Why are you here?"

"I don't know. Just to be a brother for Rob. He doesn't like to play with girls. I liked seeing him this weekend but we didn't do any guy things, just talked. I did see where he works. He likes chickens and other birds. Not me. I like tractors and trucks and seed drills and swathers and combines and all that."

"You're a farmer."

"Yup. I am."

"What about young Mike?"

"Mike and I were buds. He played catch with me and hit out flies. I was pretty little but I tried my best to catch them. I was one sad little dude when he left."

"You have hockey practice tonight."

"Yup. I'm all ready. Can I go now?"

"If you wish. Bye for now. Maggie. Maggie."

"I'm here."

"Time's up. You okay?"

"I will be in a minute."

Maggie's arms and legs had about as much strength as a rag doll. She drove home stopping only to pick up a few groceries. By the time she carried them up to her apartment and set them on the counter, she was completely exhausted. She put the milk and ice cream and sliced turkey in the fridge and fell onto the couch. She tried to meditate but her mind kept whirling even if her body was worn out. She turned on the television but could find nothing of interest. She picked up her novel but couldn't concentrate on that either. She took the pen in her hand, twiddling it among her fingers. Someone had something to say.

'I am Jeanie. Do you know about me?'

"Yes. You're the sexy one. Do you have something to tell me?"

'Yeah. Don't worry about losing Bob. He's not the one for you – or me.'

"I'm not worrying. It just bugs me that Sandy waltzed him into her bed."

'Guess her marriage bed is cold. She probably misses sex more than you do.'

"I don't care. Bob was my friend."

'I feel like a real fool. I thought I would be okay if I went along with those creeps but I don't feel better at all. I want to wash my hair a thousand times and take a million showers and buy all new clothes and new furniture and a new car and get a new job and have everything new and clean and shiny.'

"I feel the same way. If I buy a house, I will get new furniture."

'Can't buy a house if you go to Ireland.'

"Then we will have a new life. Do you want to go?"

'No. Not really. We'd be in a different country, in a different culture, with an English surname. It's a bit drastic, don't you think?'

"How about New York?"

'And work with Alex? I don't suppose we'd get many favours from him.'

"Vancouver?"

'You'd have to find a firm there needs you. They do trade with the Pacific Rim countries. Maybe.'

"If I didn't want to see Rob, I wouldn't have to." Maggie laid the pen on the coffee table. She was too tired to continue the conversation.

She picked up the pen again and wrote, countries, count, tries, cot, cote, not, note, nut, cut, cute, cuter, rot, rote, scot, Scott, sot, set, cite, nit, snit, rite, sit, site, net, inset, onset, into, its, it, I, is, rise, cries, risen, siren, rinse, since, one, on, con, cone, scone, tone, stone, Eton, crone, toner, Ron, run, rune, sun, son, sin, sine, tin, tine, stein, Sten, ten, tune, tuner, stun, ice, trice, rice, tic, sic, sec, once, use, us, nice, nicer, sect, insect, section, sector, ire, ore, or, core, score, sore, store, nor, snore, sire, sir, stir, tire, tier, tore, torn, corn, turn, urn, stern, tern, iron, tie, rue, cue, Stu, sue, nu, to, toe, so, roe, no, crest, rest, unrest, rust, crust, nest, incest, course, Norse, nurse, curse, cost, roust, oust, rouse, rose, nose, ruse, true, cruise, scout, out, rout, route, outer, snout, curt, court, escort, sort, user, nicer, sure, cure.

She leaned back on the couch and fell asleep, awakening at seven o'clock, too late for hockey practice. She moved to her bed and went back to sleep.

In her dream she is lost in New York among the high rise apartment buildings and hotels and office towers. She looks up and around, and up and around, and she cannot find the sun and she doesn't know which direction is north or south or east or west. The cars and trucks and buses whiz by at high speed and she tries to hail a taxi but no taxi stops for her, and she cries, help me, help me, but there is no one to answer her call or come to her rescue. She sees a city police officer standing on the curb, a big gun on his hip, and she approaches him but he walks away without seeing her. She is invisible.

68

Friday, February 2

AROUND THREE O'CLOCK in the morning, Maggie woke up with a chest so sore and tight that she could not breathe.

She is in her bedroom in the old farmhouse. She senses that she is four years old. A ray of light from the bright, full moon falls across her bed. A black shadow moves into the room, a strong callused right hand covers her mouth, the elbow holds her arm motionless. She struggles, tries to get free. He undoes the buttons of her pyjama top and runs his left hand over her chest, pinching her tiny nipples. He pulls off her pyjamas bottoms and he plays with her, pokes his finger inside, rubs her undeveloped clitoris with his thumb. The pain is unbearable and reaches all the way to her throat. She screams but the sound is muffled by his hand. Her legs are shoved wide apart. A muscle in her thigh is pulled and now it hurts too. Then all is black.

"Lord have mercy, Christ have mercy, Lord have mercy."

This time she knew it was her father. He smelled of cigarette smoke and the man was too large to be young Mike.

She tried to escape into sleep but it wouldn't come. She got out of bed and drank a cup of chamomile tea. She understood why she might have considered suicide as a child. It was a way to escape the brutality and ugliness of her life. She didn't want to go back to her bed, the scene of the crime, so she took a blanket and her pillow to the couch and curled up there. After a long while, she went back to sleep.

It was well after ten before she woke up. The cobwebs didn't clear until after her second cup of coffee. She had some cereal for breakfast. She didn't want to think so she went into her studio and painted until hunger pangs made her stop, mixed up a liquid lunch, carried it back to the studio and sipped on it while she worked.

Dr. Dixon was busy with another patient when she arrived later that day. While she was waiting, she picked up a magazine and read an article about being your own woman.

"Come in, Maggie, or is it Lynne? Sorry to keep you waiting."

"How did you know?"

"You're dressed like an artist, hair slicked back, earrings, eye makeup, tight leggings, turtle neck, big shirt."

"Hmm. I've become a cliché. While I was waiting, I was read an article about being your own woman. What the hell does that mean? Your mother wants one thing, your father another. Siblings have their ideas. Your teachers have expectations, and so does the priest or minister. Your coaches want performance. If you marry, your husband has his needs. If you have children, they want your all. Bosses want excellent work and a certain attitude. It seems to me society splits women apart. Maybe being a multiple is the best way to handle it."

"It was the way you found to cope. What's going on?"

"Maggie is exhausted, but she has to make a living for us. What should we do? Early this morning, she remembered being raped by her father."

"Well, it's good that it came up. It had to come eventually. Was it your memory?"

"No. I wasn't molested. The only time she's experienced my world is painting."

"She has to decide where to work. Has there been a change in that department?"

"Yes. She might have to go to Ireland if she works for Borden."

"Really? That complicates the decision making. What do you want?"

285

"Me? I am happy anywhere. There are art classes in every city and different things to paint. I am getting tired of painting stuff from my childhood and I want to try something new."

"I'd like to talk to Maggie now."

The woman now before him had black shadows under her eyes and she slumped in her chair.

"How are you, Maggie?"

"Really tired. I have become a nursemaid for all these alters. I have to deal with all their feelings as well as my own and I am overwhelmed and there is no way to take a break. None. Except meditation."

"Let's try hypnotism."

A few minutes later, Maggie slowly opened her eyes. "I don't know what you did, but I feel better."

"Good. Have a quiet weekend."

Later in the evening she pulled on a pair of blue jeans and a University of Manitoba Bisons golf shirt and drove to the Blue Rose. Rebecca and Sadie weren't there, but Paul stood next to a pool table, leaning on his cue.

"Game?"

She nodded and, as she turned to get her cue, she undid the top buttons of her shirt. She grabbed the first cue from the rack and chalked it. He set the balls and she made the break. She ordered a Caesar. They played the first game and he won. She won the second game easily, and he won the rubber match. She didn't get a shot. He ordered Caesars for both of them. She won the next game and he won the second game and the third.

He sidled up to her, hip to hip, and put his lips close to her ear. His moustache tickled her neck. "Maybe we should go to your place."

"Why not yours?"

"My roommate has company."

"Then my place it is. Follow the black Buick."

Trembling, she led the way to the parking lot. He kissed her before she unlocked her car. His lips were cool and searching. He followed her closely all the way to her apartment. He kissed her in the garage doorway and in the elevator. He kissed her at the apartment door. He took the keys from her trembling hand and opened the door. They kissed as they stumbled into the room. He removed her sheepskin and she took off his army surplus jacket. They sat on the floor giggling while they kicked off their boots.

He rolled her onto her back and kissed her again, his right hand caressing her breast. "Where's your bedroom?"

"This way." She took him by the hand and led him down the hall to her room. He removed his T-shirt, unbuttoned her shirt and took it off, admired her black brassiere. He undid it and kissed the nipples that hardened under his touch. They crawled under the covers and lost themselves in their need for the other.

69

Saturday, February 3

THE PRESENCE OF another body in her bed awakened Maggie in the night. She got up to empty her bladder, allowing the light from the bathroom to illuminate the face on her pillow. She wanted to wake him up and tell him to get the hell out of her bed, but she did not. He wasn't her guest, after all. She slipped back into bed and was soon asleep.

Paul was the first to rouse in the morning. He rolled over and kissed her on the ear. "Wake up, sleepy head. It's nine thirty."

Mags woke up with a start. "Oh. No. I have to be at Sandy's in an hour."

"What for?" He pulled on his jeans.

"We are teaching some girls how to dance."

"I'll make breakfast."

Mags dashed some water on her face and brushed her teeth. She combed her hair back in Lynne's style and held it in place with a black band. Her face was red with embarrassment, a man she didn't know or recognize in her bed, seeing her naked, watching her fasten the belt of her robe around her slim waist. She put on her tartan kilt and a white shirt, afraid he'd come back before she was covered.

Paul had bacon sizzling in a frying pan and coffee dripping in the coffeemaker. She took over while he freshened up and then they ate side by side at the kitchen table.

"Why the dolls?"

"I was babysitting Sandy's little girl," she lied.

They finished their meal in companionable silence. He rinsed his plate in the sink, placed it in the dishwasher, turned to her and said, "I have to get going." He took her in his arms and kissed her again. It was no quick peck but long and loving. "I'll be at the pub tonight."

He pulled on his boots and grabbed his jacket off the floor and was gone.

Mags hurried to the coffee table, coffee mug in hand. 'Who was that?' she wrote.

'Paul.'

'How did we meet him?'

'Playing pool at the bar.'

'Okay.'

She gulped down the rest of her morning fix and hurried off to Sandy's. The car slid sideways on the ice, and she almost hit a parked car. Caroline answered the door bell, hugged her and took her coat. Telling her about the new kilt her Grandma Borden was buying for the competition, she led the way to the basement studio. Sandy rushed over.

"Mom phoned your mother about the music. She said you took all the dance music and all the books. You must have them in your apartment."

"Oh. Why did you and your mother call Mom? I am quite capable of phoning her myself. I will double check my collection, but I don't know why you need mine."

"Just because I do."

The dancer Mags didn't stay for tea after the lessons. She stopped at a drugstore and looked in confusion at the array of condoms. The pharmacist, a young guy fresh out of university, came to her rescue and increased her embarrassment. He showed her the two more popular brands and she took a package of each and hastened out of the store.

She had her liquid lunch of a weight-reducing smoothie because she was afraid that she would gain weight; she was always afraid she would gain weight. She wanted to up-chuck all the pork chops and cheeseburgers and chocolate cake and Brown Cows but didn't, only because the others wouldn't like it. She played all the Scottish music she owned, including the competition tapes that Sandy wanted and practiced some steps that she wanted to teach her students. She played several tapes over and over and finally chose two to take to the next lessons. She put the dolls and the farm machinery out of sight in the library.

She enjoyed swimming as much as Maggie did, but she wasn't sure that she'd stay out if she went. She decided to chance it. She swam laps for half an hour, then went home to dress for her date. She showered the chlorine out of her hair and combed it straight back slicking it down with styling gel.

As she made her weight watchers' dinner of a salad and sole fillets, she tried to decide what to wear. Nothing suited. None of the clothes in the closet were hers. She finally put on Sammy's blue jeans, a black tank top, and Lynne's long white shirt, which she tied at the waist. She waited until nine o'clock and then with her heart in her throat, she left for the bar.

Rebecca and Sadie perched on their usual barstools. Anton, with his leg in a cast and his crutches leaning against the bar, held court with his friends and three girls that Mags didn't know. Paul was nowhere to be seen. Disappointed, she took the stool next to Sadie and ordered a Caesar. Her friend looked at her in surprise but said nothing. As the bartender set her drink on the counter, he said in a low voice, "Paul will be back in a few minutes. This drink is on him."

She didn't want to talk with the women, even though she liked them well enough, as far as lawyers go. They might talk about law and she wouldn't know what to say and Maggie might show up. Ten minutes later someone jabbed her gently in the ribs. "Pool?" he asked.

She slid off her stool and followed him to the pool table. They played two games. Paul won them both. "Let's go," he said.

They left the bar. Mags could feel Anton and Rebecca and Sadie staring at her back but she didn't care what they thought. They walked down the street to an all-night diner and ordered hot chocolate.

"Perhaps we should introduce ourselves," he was laughing, "now that we know each other. What is your name?"

"Mags. Mags Barnett. Short for Margaret. You are Paul but I don't know your last name."

"Paul Faulkner. But the girls call you Maggie, right?"

"Yes. Most people do, but I actually prefer Mags."

"What do you do besides dance?"

"I make my living as a lawyer."

"You're kidding. No. That fits. But you've changed somehow."

"I guess I have. I am tired of dressing like an accountant and acting like Mother Theresa. And what do you do, besides hang out in pool rooms?

"I am a commodities trader."

"Are you? Now that is interesting."

He kissed her leaving hot chocolate on her chin. "Your place again?"

"Yeah. My place again."

He kissed her in the parking lot. In his red Mustang, he followed the Buick to her apartment and he kissed her in the garage and in the elevator and in the hall and in the living room and in the hallway and in her bedroom. He didn't know he made love to a virgin.

70

Sunday, February 4

MAGGIE OF THE weak bladder woke up first. She quietly got out of
bed, trying not to wake him.   He looked so young and innocent in
sleep. She climbed back into bed and cuddled up to him, her front
to his back and she put her arm around him. He took her hand and
pulled her arm tighter around his waist. She closed her eyes but
couldn't go back to sleep. Ten minutes later he roused, turned to look
into her eyes and gave her what she wanted.

Afterwards they lay on their separate pillows puffing a little, lost
in the moment. He looked at the clock. "You're not going to believe
this, but I have to go. I always take my mother to church."

"I go to church too. I belong to the Anglican Church."

"Really? One of these days I'll have to take you both. Do you
have a pen and some paper handy?"

"In the drawer under the phone."

"Here's my phone number and address. My roommate and I are
cooking spaghetti tonight. Why don't you come? Six on the dot."

"Okay. Sure. I'll bring the garlic bread."

"Good idea. Okay. See you then."

He dressed quickly and left her lying in bed. Her head whirled.
She wanted to stay in bed but she had to get up to lock the door.

After a shower and breakfast, she went to church, arguing with herself about premarital sex. Was it a sin? How can love be a sin? Is this love? Maybe. She prayed for Paul, for her brother Rob, for Jane and Jeanie, Lynne, Sammy, Dick, Mary, Miranda, Sally and Annie.

"Lord have mercy, Christ have mercy, Lord have mercy."

On this day, she realized that the colour worn by the priest during the Eucharist and the colours of the altar cloth and the one draped over the chalice were co-ordinated and she was curious about what that meant. As always, she was glad she went. She felt so peaceful afterwards and she swore that the wine and wafer had a magical effect on her.

After lunch she swam laps for half an hour, practicing her typing in her mind, When the going gets tough, the tough get going and the weak drop out. When the going gets tough, the tough get going and the weak drop out. When the going gets tough, the tough get going and the weak drop out. Back in her apartment, she picked up the pen. 'Jeanie. Jeanie.'

'I am not talking to you.'

"Why not?"

'You and Mags are in my bad books. I brought Paul home. Then Mags got up Saturday morning and stayed out and she went to the bar to see him. Then you wake up today and have sex with him. Man.'

"Couldn't you feel it too?"

'Yes. Sort of. But for some reason I couldn't take over.'

"I don't understand. This whole thing is weird to me."

'It is weird. It was better before when you didn't know we existed. Now everyone in here is upset and I'm not writing anymore.'

The hand stopped writing for a minute or two, then wrote:

'What the hell do you think you're doing?'

"Who are you?"

'Sammy.'

"I thought you'd left."

'I am here. Paul is my friend and I play pool with him. Now you girls are having sex with him? Geez.'

"He thinks this person is female."

'I bet he knows. He's really sharp. We can't hide from him. You're getting in trouble here.'

"If I continue to see him, I will have to tell him the truth."

'Don't you dare. You are impossible. I am not talking to you either.'

Maggie put the pen down with a bang. Life was definitely more complex, also more frustrating. It had never crossed her mind before that, if and when she found a man to love, she'd have to tell him that she was a multiple, and that she might lose him because of it. She spent an hour in meditation but couldn't reach that deep point that meant perfect relaxation. She changed the sheets on the bed and threw them in the washing machine, emptied all the garbage receptacles, vacuumed and dusted throughout the apartment, and washed her clothes and towels and made a quick trip to Safeway for the garlic bread.

She didn't know what to wear. She couldn't dress like Sammy, and she didn't want to be as blatant as Jeanie. She could be artsy like Lynne or Mags, and she didn't want to be too much the lawyer. She expected Paul and his friends would be in jeans. That was perfect. But what else? She chose a shirt tailored in red poly-cotton. She tucked the tail into her waistband and added a leather belt that matched her jeans and checked her appearance in the mirror. She looked too much like a cowgirl.

She took off the belt and pulled the shirttail out an inch or two giving it a blouse-on look. That suited her better. Wearing her sheepskin jacket and boots, she went down the elevator to her car. She had forgotten the garlic bread and had to go all the way back up to her apartment to get it, laughing all the way. Times, smite, mites, items, emits, time, emit, mite, item, site, stem, mist, ties, tie, sit, set, met, Tim, me, it, is, ti, mi, I.

Paul and his roommate Ross shared an ordinary two-bedroom apartment on Portage Avenue near the Deer Lodge Hospital, with standard white European kitchen cupboards and a U-shaped kitchen. They were busy preparing the spaghetti sauce, but Ross turned to stare at her.

"Ross, this is Maggie Barnett, I mean Mags Barnett. I am sorry. I think of you as Maggie."

"Then call me Maggie. Most people do."

"Barnett? I knew a Rob Barnett in college," said Ross.

"My brother. Looks just like me?"

"Yes. Are you twins?"

"No. He's two years older than I am."

"Where is he now?"

"Vancouver, lecturing at U.B.C. I was just there last weekend."

"Oh, so that's why you weren't in the bar," interjected Paul.

Maggie raised her eyebrows as if to say, 'You've been watching for me?'

Linda knocked on the door and walked in. Ross made the introductions and then said. "Okay, now, all women out of the kitchen. The men are cooking tonight."

Maggie and Linda settled on the director's chairs in front of the television. They talked sporadically, strangers feeling each other out. Maggie found out that Ross was an insurance broker, that they'd been dating for a year, that Linda taught the sixth grade at a downtown school, and that they were getting married in June. Maggie caught the flash of her diamond, but refrained from gushing. She told Linda that she was a lawyer but that was all.

It was a relaxing enjoyable evening, the conversation light, the jokes plentiful, and the wine free-flowing. Maggie as usual didn't partake in the wine but matched the lively mood without it. Ross, however, asked her about her current employment. She told them that she had left Jenkins Williamson and was starting a new job at Borden International on March first. They took it in stride. Around nine her energy flagged.

"Okay, Maggie. Get out. Go home."

She looked up at Paul in surprise.

"You are tired. Go home." He smiled. "I have to clean up the kitchen. No, you can't help. And I have to be up by six tomorrow. So go home."

She laughed. "Okay, okay."

He helped her into the sheepskin. "Are you busy tomorrow night?"

"Curling. I curl at nine."

"Tuesday?"

"Free."

"I'd like to take you to dinner."

"Great. I will see you on Tuesday." He kissed her and held her close for a minute or two. She said good night to Ross and Linda and left.

During the drive home, she typed, The quick brown fox jumps over the lazy dog. The quick brown fox jumps over the lazy dog. The quick brown fox jumps over the lazy dog.

That night she had no flashbacks or bad dreams and she heard no voices. She slept until ten the next morning.

71

Monday, February 5

MONDAY MORNING, SHE made instant oatmeal for breakfast and downed a glassful of orange juice, and she took a cup of coffee in her steel mug to sip as she drove to the medical clinic.

"Maggie. You are Maggie, aren't you?" The doctor wasn't sure. This woman shrank into her chair, shy, perhaps afraid.

"I don't know who I am."

"Oh, dear. What happened this weekend?"

"Well, as far as I can figure out, Friday night Jeanie took Paul the pool player home with her. Mags had breakfast with him the next morning and met him at the bar that night. Maggie had sex with him yesterday morning and dinner at his place last night."

"How do you feel about this?"

"I don't know what to think. I like Paul, but I didn't want to have sex with him."

"Well. I have met Jeanie and Jane and Lynne. Are you Sally?"

"Beats me."

"Were you out in New York City? Did you go for Italian food in New York?"

"Yes. I did. Maybe I am Sally."

"What do you remember about your childhood?"

"Nothing much. I remember going to school at MacNabb's Crossing. I remember my teachers and all my classmates and I remember I always sat behind Sandy. I remember learning to read and to add and subtract. We sang *O Canada* and recited the Lord's Prayer every morning. I remember riding my bike to school in the spring and fall. Sandy and Rob and I rode on a yellow school bus to Sampford Collegiate and I remember studying really hard in high school so I could win a scholarship to university."

"Did you study law?"

"Yes. Maggie did too. I wrote some exams and she wrote the rest."

"You seem tired."

"I am. I am stressed out and I worry all the time about being good enough."

"You didn't get much positive feedback at home. How could you feel worthy? Do you have something you want to discuss?"

"No. I'm rather tired."

"Then I would like to talk with you another time. Today I'd like to have a word with Jeanie."

The change was immediate. The live wire Jeanie sat up to address him, "Hiya, Doc. What do you want of me?"

"I hear you picked up a guy in the bar on Friday."

"Yeah, I did and then Mags and Maggie took him away from me." She groped inside her purse and found a package of sugar free gum. She shoved two pieces into her mouth and lobbed the wrappers into the garbage receptacle.

"Isn't that risky behaviour?"

"No. Heavens no. We met him more than once. He plays pool in our favourite bar."

"But you didn't know anything about him, did you?"

"Well, we're getting to know him now. He's really good in bed, you know."

The doctor's face reddened. "Maggie doesn't sleep with a guy on the first date."

"She could have kicked him out on Saturday morning, but she didn't. She was the one who initiated sex on Sunday. Your Maggie isn't such a prude after all."

"Oh. Really. Who is curling tonight?"

"Sammy. He's really pissed. Paul was his friend to start with. Sammy asked him to play pool with him."

"Sammy's still around? Maybe I could talk to him."

There was no response.

"I don't think he wants to talk to you because he's angry, he's so mad he could eat somebody. He doesn't like being a man in a woman's body and he's not gay and he doesn't want a man to touch him. I wish he'd just go away. He's a royal pain in the butt."

"Well, he'll have to work it out himself then. I have to go now. I'm sorry. I am late for a lunch meeting. Are you okay to drive, or should I call Maggie?"

"I can drive," she lied.

Maggie took over the wheel for safety's sake. A message from Paul was waiting at home. "Come to the curling club at eight. We can have coffee before you go on the ice. I need to talk to you."

She called him back, but he didn't answer his phone. She left a message that she'd see him at the rink at eight, as suggested. After lunch she practiced handling the puck and skating backwards, and skated around the outdoor rink for an hour and as she skated, she typed, abcdefghijklmnopqrstuvwxyz. Abcdefghijklmnopqrstuvwxyz. Abcdefghijklmnopqrstuvwxyz. She was in that mode where she just shifted her weight from one skate to the other and sped effortlessly on the ice. Her mouth and nose felt the frost even though she wore a woollen scarf and she had to give it up for that day.

She wandered into the studio but had no desire to paint. She avoided the yellow legal pad. She couldn't handle any more alters. She was happy. She didn't remember when she felt happy. She read her novel, baked an Apple Brown Betty for dessert, made a ham roast and scalloped potatoes for dinner, washed down her refrigerator and range, the kitchen counters and cupboards. She ate dinner at the table with candle light and her book for company.

She arrived at the rink just before eight. Bob Hunter stood in the waiting room watching Sandy's game, but he didn't see her and she went directly upstairs without speaking. Paul was sitting at a corner table.

"This morning I met someone you know – Rodney Thomason."

299

"Rodney? Yes. He's a client – he was a client."

"He was complaining that his favourite lawyer was no longer at Jenkins Williamson and I promised him I would find out what happened to you."

"It's a long story. The short version is: I was seeing Anton, you know, the guy at the bar with the broken leg. Well, I broke it off, he got ugly, I got a restraining order, he disobeyed it, he whined to his grandfather – Marshall Jenkins. I got fired. Then he cracked up his car while chasing me. One of the partners offered to hire me back and I refused."

"I am going to tell Rodney what you said. It sounds very unfair. I guess you have to go. Walk down with me?"

"No." She pointed to the ladies' room.

"See you tomorrow."

Maggie was late by then and went directly out to the ice surface without talking to Sandy. Every game her skills improved and she enjoyed it more. It was almost midnight when she got home. For once there were no messages waiting for her, no one wanted to write nasty things to her, and she was able to sleep in peace.

72

Tuesday, February 6

TUESDAY MORNING SHE had an appointment with Dr. Dixon as usual. She wore her jeans and a black and white checked flannel shirt and her sheepskin jacket and boots, with her hair curled over her forehead.

"You must be Maggie."

"Yes. I'm Maggie and I have a big problem. I have to decide what to do. If I work for Gus Borden, I am tied with Bob Hunter and Sandy, although I might have to go to Ireland. If I stay here, I could work for Jenkins Williamson and deal with the aftermath of being fired. I could work for J&W in New York. I could start anew somewhere else – Vancouver, Ottawa, Montreal – but I'd be the low man on the totem pole, if you know what I mean. If I leave, I won't have Paul. I don't know what to do."

"What do your feet tell you?"

"Run away. Run away with no plan. Just go. Get in my car and drive."

"Okay. Sit back and relax. Think about that. You're in your Buick. You have a Buick, don't you? Okay. You are in your Buick. The radio is playing your favourite music. You have a full tank of gas and the highway is clear and the visibility excellent. You are leaving Winnipeg. What direction would you drive, east, west, south?"

"West."

"Okay. You are driving west along the Trans-Canada Highway. You go past the gaol at Headingly and the statue of the white horse. You take the bypass around Portage la Prairie. You pass the half way tree and MacGregor and Austin and Carberry. You go through Brandon. You keep on driving past Virden and on into Saskatchewan, Moosamin, Broadview, Indian Head. Do you stop in Regina?"

"No."

"Do you turn north to Saskatoon?"

"Yes."

"Okay. You drive north, past Lumsden, Bethune, Davidson, C.F.B. Dundurn. Do you stop in Saskatoon?"

"No."

"Do you continue west?"

"Yes."

"Okay, you continue through Saskatchewan, past Rosetown and Darcy, past Kindersley, and you are getting closer and closer to Calgary. Are you going to stop there?"

"I am getting tired. Perhaps."

"Okay. You get a hotel room – a room in a Ramada Inn. You walk into the room with your suitcases. What do you see there?"

"Paul."

"Does that answer your question?"

"Yes. It does. But where will I work?"

"My advice is to wait. Now. Let me see. Is there anyone other than Maggie who wants to talk with me today?"

There was no response.

"Sammy. Sammy."

"I don't want to talk to you." The voice was deep and masculine and rough.

"Why? What's going on?"

"You want to get rid of us, and so does Maggie. You want to make us weaker so that eventually only Maggie will remain."

"You understand, don't you, that most people have only one personality."

"So? That doesn't mean anything. We're not most people."

"The natural thing would be a move toward integration – that's what I am saying. But the integrated personality would be a combination of all of you, including Maggie. I don't know what will happen in this case."

"None of us will talk to you then."

"Maggie. Did you hear that?"

"Yes."

"This is difficult. They have to understand that if they integrate, they don't die. They live on in the whole."

"They don't have to integrate. They have just as much right to be here as I do."

"Yes, but the system is unstable now. They have all had a taste of being in control, and it won't be long before a shift of some kind occurs."

"What do I do?"

"Ride it out."

Not very encouraged, Maggie spent a couple of hours at an indoor rink. She skated forwards and backwards and practiced handling the puck. She sang in a monotone, just loud enough to hear herself, 99 bottles of beer on the wall, if one of the bottles fell off the wall, there'd be 98 bottles of beer on the wall, 98 bottles of beer on the wall, if one of the bottles fell off the wall, there'd be 97 bottles of beer on the wall, 97 bottles of beer on the wall, if one of the bottles fell off the wall, there'd be 96 bottles of beer on the wall. She got to 74 bottles before she realized what she was doing and stopped.

The rest of the afternoon, she read the morning paper and her novel and watched Oprah. Again, she couldn't decide what to wear for her dinner date, and she wondered why she worried about it so much. She chose her long black skirt and knitted shirt, hoping she didn't look theatrical or funereal. Paul rang the doorbell at six.

"Do you want to come up for a minute?"

"Yes. I most certainly do."

A few minutes later he was at her door. "I just wanted to do this before we left." He enfolded her in his arms and kissed her. "Okay now, we can go."

Maggie laughed. He helped her into her coat and together they descended to the lobby. "I thought we might try Chinese. Okay with you?"

"Sure. I haven't had it for a while."

The restaurant, with its typical Oriental decor, was almost empty and they had their choice of seating. They both wanted a window seat.

"I talked to Rodney and he is quite annoyed with J&W. Maybe you'll get your job back."

"I don't know if I want it. Unless their attitude towards women changes, I am not sure I want to work there."

"Would it be any different in another firm?"

"Probably not. Maybe I should start my own."

"I don't know about that. I think Rodney has a plan, so hang on for the ride. So, are you close to your brother Rob?"

"No. I hadn't spoken to him for years and I went to Vancouver to clear the air. We made some progress but there are still some issues. Now we have a deal. He'll come to Winnipeg once a year and I'll go to Vancouver once a year and we'll get to know each other."

"I have an older brother who's in the import business. He works out of Toronto and I seldom see him. Guess I should take a hint from you and go to visit him."

"It might be the only way."

"I was born and raised here in Winnipeg, but my grandparents on Mom's side live in Brandon. I spent lots of summers with them and my grandfather took me fishing at MacNabb's Bridge. You went to school in that little white school house?"

"Yes. I did. And do you remember a farmyard south-east of the school with a house that looked like a Swiss chalet? That was my home."

"I do remember it, vaguely."

It was almost eleven when she got home. Her answering machine blinked at her. She was tempted to leave it until morning, but she was glad she didn't. The message was from Meg: "Your mother is in hospital here in Sampford and she would like to see you."

Maggie set her alarm for six and lay down to rest.

A voice said, Comment ça va?

Je vais bien. Vous parlez français?

Ah, oui. J'ai besoin à practiquer le français.
Pourquoi?
C'est necessaire.
Je l'ai oublié. Bon soir.[1]

---

[1]   How's it going? I am doing well. You speak French? Oh, yes. I need to practice my French. Why? It is necessary. I have forgotten it. Good night.

73

Wednesday, February 7

As SOON AS she got up, she phoned Sandy to say she couldn't make it to dance class, without giving a reason why, dressed quickly in jeans and her Arran sweater, fuelled the Buick, and was on the road by seven. It was pitch black, but as always her eyes relaxed as soon as she could see more than a block in the distance. Snow drifted across the highway but her visibility was not impaired and she cruised along, listening to the radio and singing along. She was halfway to Portage la Prairie when a voice said, "What's your hurry?"

She glanced at the speedometer, a hundred and thirty five kilometres. Guiltily she eased up but her foot was heavy and didn't want to keep at the speed limit.

"My mother wants to see me."

Maybe this time, after twenty-nine long years, her mother would open up and talk to her. Maybe this time she'd show that she cared for her daughter. Or maybe not. Maybe she wanted to force her to take Grandma MacDonar into her small apartment, her grandmother whose location she didn't know at the moment. The Buick speeded along far above the posted limit. She removed her foot from the gas pedal altogether and cruised until she was ten kilometres an hour over the speed limit, surely a recommended lower bound.

A voice said, "You're going to marry your father."

Still another, or was it the first one, said, "You're going to kill yourself."

She answered them, "No. I am not." But the voices repeated themselves over and over. She stopped in Portage for coffee with one cream and one sugar and a blueberry muffin, gulped down the baking like a starving Biafran in the restaurant, grabbed a lid for the Styrofoam cup, and hit the road again, coffee in hand. She made the half-way to Brandon tree in record time.

The Skyhawk was getting quite a workout. She slowed it down once more. The music selection on the radio wasn't to her liking so she searched for a better one. Sixties rock and roll was the only genre that kept her awake on a long drive. In Brandon, she picked up a bouquet of red and white carnations at Safeway. The voices were quiet.

Sampford and District Hospital was a single storey building with a white stucco exterior that sprawled across a wide snow-covered lawn. As soon as she entered the lobby, she could smell disinfectant and something else she couldn't identify. Visiting hours hadn't started but the crisp white nurse gave her the room number and told her to "Go on in." She walked down the white hallway admiring the paintings hung for the benefit of visitors and patients and found her mother propped against two pillows, her long grey hair strewn over the white pillow case, reading a *Chatelaine* magazine.

"Hi. You wanted to see me?"

"Come in, Maggie. Here, sit down."

"What's the prognosis?"

"I have a lump on my right breast. It is malignant and they are going to remove it on Friday. They say that it was caught early and it hasn't spread to the lymph nodes. They figure I'll be okay."

Maggie laid the flowers on the night table. "Why didn't you say something?"

"Never mind that. I want to tell you that you were right. My father did molest me and I buried the memory. I refused to see what he was doing to you. Now I have to live with the knowledge that I didn't protect you."

Maggie nodded. She was at a loss for words.

Her mother went on. "But you rejected me, rejected women. You didn't want to learn to cook and sew and knit and help with my poultry business."

"I wasn't rejecting you. I can't be your carbon copy. I was being me."

"I see that now and I wish we had it to do over. You'd better go now. Don't stay for the surgery. Your father will be here shortly. I am sorry, Maggie."

Maggie reached out and held her mother's hand for a brief moment. Then she turned and left the room, tears forming in her dark eyes. She met her father in the hallway.

"What are you doin' here?"

"She wanted to see me."

"You kin stay at the house."

"I guess likely."

"Your poor old Dad."

"Stuff it." She looked around for some hard object to throw at him, a tightly wound baseball, a gray rock, a perfectly balanced hunting knife. She didn't want to kill him, just shut him up and render him incapable of ever hurting her again.

"Well you seen her. Go back to your fancy life. Now git."

She continued down the hall. Meg accosted her at the nurses' station. "Well, Maggie, what did your mother want?"

"That's between us, Meg. I don't want to talk about it."

"Oh. Alright then. Are you staying until after the surgery? You could bunk with us."

"Thanks, but I am going back to Winnipeg."

Maggie sat in the Buick for a few minutes trying to regain her poise. She wanted to cry but she would not. When she finally regained control, she fired up the engine. She drove up one street in Sampford and down another, past the grain elevators lined up like soldiers along the railroad track. She thought of a painting of the prairie sentinels, not as silhouettes against a wild red sunset or as examples of tall objects on flat terrain, but as the places of commerce that they were, with two and three ton trucks lined up waiting to dump their precious cargo of wheat or barley, lethal grain dust and chaff swirling in the breeze. Or a pen-and-ink of the farmers in the office smoking and gossiping and comparing notes and complaining because their wives do the exact same thing. She passed the brick town hall topped by the bell tower and the post office and the business section, its stores with the false fronts, and entered the residential area. She didn't remember any houses in town that were pink, a two-storey or a storey-and-a-half, she wasn't sure. She gave up her search in that town and began her homeward journey. She stopped in Brandon for a large coffee and drove through the older parts of the city, but she couldn't find the pink house. It could have been re-painted by then, green or red or gray or white. Surely such a black building was not painted the colour of purity.

Imagine. Her father asked her to stay at the farm with him, alone in the house, with him. Her stomach hadn't recovered from that one and she rummaged in her purse with her right hand, while keeping her eyes on the road, until she found a package of Rolaids. She took two. Your poor old Dad. He wanted pity? Her fancy life. Her father with a grade eight education and bad grammar had done quite well for himself and his wife, yet he hated his daughter. She had escaped.

In Portage la Prairie she choked down some lunch at a chicken place – two pieces, white meat, with a baked potato and coleslaw swimming in white dressing. She asked the skinny blonde waitress to rinse out her steel mug so that she could fill it with green tea and took it out to the car. She leaned back on the headrest.

She is at a baseball game with her father. They have arrived early and she rushes to the bleachers to watch the pitchers warm up, getting ready for their dual. Her father sits down two rows up to talk to a fat-bellied man wearing a United Grain Growers cap. "Is that her?" says the UGG man.

Maggie turns around.

"Yep. That's her."

The two men don't speak again as they walk away from the bleachers with Maggie in tow. Her father holds her by the neck of her shirt, choking her. They stop behind a non-descript van and the chubby guy unlocks and opens the back doors and Mike forces Maggie inside.

"The ball game'll take about three hours. Have 'er back by then."

The doors slam shut. Maggie's heart is pounding. She is furious with her father and afraid of what might be in store for her. The van backs up and drives off. It seems to her that the vehicle goes in circles. She rides cramped on a grubby blanket. The trip lasts forever. When they finally stop, they are in the driveway of a pink house. The man grabs Maggie by the arm and drags her out. They go into the house and immediately turn right and descend to the basement where she sees a room with a circular bed covered in shiny black sheets and photographers' lights that beam a soft red light onto the bed and two cameras, bigger than she has ever seen before.

"Sit on the bed."

Reluctantly, Maggie climbs on the bed and sits with her arms around her drawn up legs. He takes two photos.

"Okay. Take off your blouse."

"No."

He slaps her across the face. "Don't you know? I'm paying your Dad good money for this. Now do as you're told."

She removes her top and instinctively puts her arms over her nipples. He impatiently pushes them aside and takes two more photos.

"Now your pants."

She obeys, slowly, her face red with embarrassment, her mind asking why, why, why anyone would want to photograph her child's body. He takes two more pictures.

"Now your under pants."

He takes pictures of her with her legs spread wide and on her back and on her front and lying on her side. She is mystified. He goes to a cupboard and brings out a white cotton dress. Maggie's mouth falls open and she gasps for air. Except for the color, it is identical to the one that Sandy wore to Mrs. McClure's shower.

"Here. Put this on."

Shaking, she dons the dress. He takes more pictures. Then he fumbles in a dresser drawer and brings out a pot of purple chalk used by pool players and makes bruises on her thighs and on her arms and on her face. He takes more photos. He gives her a wet facecloth to wash off the chalk and tells her to put her clothes on.

Tap. Tap. Tap. Someone knocked on the car window, bringing Maggie back to the present. She pushed the button to roll down her window. It was an R.C.M.P. officer not much older than she was, a long nose and square jaw protruding beneath his hat.

"Are you alright, ma'am?"

"Yes. Thanks. I was just having a rest before I take off again."

"Where are you off to?"

"Winnipeg."

"Sure you're alright? You look a little woozy."

"I am fine. I'll just drink my tea and then go."

Her whole body ached with fatigue. She felt someone take over the wheel. "I hope that you know how to drive," she said aloud.

Only then did it register that her mother had cancer, a malignant tumour, in her right breast. The dreaded C word had been spoken and acknowledged, the great equalizer had caught Mary Ellen. A suspicious lump had been found, a biopsy performed, surgery scheduled all without Maggie's knowledge, but that didn't surprise her since she was never her mother's confidante. If she died. No. In these situations a person should think positive. But that could have been her last chance to have a positive relationship with the woman who carried her around in her womb for nine months and went through the agony of labour and child birth, for her.

"Jesus wept."

Immediately she felt guilty for the blasphemy. But probably Jesus did weep every time someone caused her pain. 'Suffer the children to come unto me.' The verse. What was the verse that gave her comfort? 'The Lord is my shepherd, I shall not want. He maketh me to lie down in green pastures. He leadeth me beside the still waters. He restoreth my soul. He leadeth me in the paths of righteousness for his name's sake. Yea, though I walk through the valley of the shadow of death, I will fear no evil, for thou art with me. Thy rod and thy staff, they comfort me. Thou preparest a table before me in the presence of mine enemies. Thou anointest my head with oil. My cup runneth over. Surely goodness and mercy shall follow me all the days of my life, and I will dwell in the house of the Lord forever.'

If only Jesus hadn't waited for eighteen years to rescue her from her personal death valley. It occurred to her that Jesus could have saved her from all that torture if her mother had walked out on her father.

She almost hit a support post in the garage. The underground lot was low-ceilinged and too dark for comfort and she hurriedly retrieved her suitcase and shoulder bag, locked the car, and pulling the wheeled piece of luggage, returned to her refuge on the fifth floor.

Her answering machine was blinking red again. "Maggie. Jared here. I would like to speak with you. Would you please come to the office tomorrow afternoon at one thirty, if that's convenient."

74

Thursday, February 8

THE NEXT MORNING, she woke up at eight o'clock. Her bedroom seemed strange to her, as if she'd never been there before. "Who am I now?" She wasn't hungry, only thirsty. She made a pot of coffee. While it was brewing, she glanced at the wall calendar. Written on it were 'Dr. Dixon @ ten' and 'Jared.'

She drank her coffee, black, and dressed in grey woollen slacks and a black sweater, a cardigan with a zippered front. She added an ornate Celtic cross pendant.

"I don't think we've met, doctor," she said.

"Perhaps not. You are?"

"Marie. I am a nun."

"A nun? I didn't know you were Catholic."

"Oh, we're not. I attend the Anglican Church now, but I'm a nun just the same. I gave my sexuality to Christ. I couldn't handle it, so I offered it to Jesus in prayer."

Indeed she had the look of a nun, full of humility, kindness and patience. She sat demurely on the chair with her feet modestly crossed beneath. She kept her eyes on the floor, never meeting his.

"When was this?"

"When I was a teenager. You know, doctor, we would be happy

to supply wooden crosses for you to hang in each room and a larger one for the lobby."

"Thank you, but all my patients are not Christian. We'll leave religion out of it."

"But surely you believe that healing comes from God."

"I do, but not all my patients agree. Now, then. Maggie cancelled yesterday's appointment. Why was that?"

"We had to go to Sampford because Mother is in the hospital. She has breast cancer and she is having surgery tomorrow."

"I see. You didn't stay?"

"No. I didn't wish to stay with my father, subject to his advances. Or with Meg. Or in the one and only hotel. That would start a whole round of gossip. Anyway, Mother told me to leave. She asked me to come so that she could apologize. She admitted she was abused by her father and she told us that she was sorry that she didn't protect her from him."

"What can you tell me?"

"I was not touched by anyone. I was kept separate, pure and unsullied. I retain the ability to love."

"Do you love Paul?"

"Yes. I do. And so I have this problem. Should I renounce my vows and marry him? How do I know if that's what Jesus wants?"

"Did Jesus want you to become a nun?"

"I believe so."

The doctor obviously didn't know how to answer her. "Then you need to spend some time in prayer, or talk to your priest."

"Thank you, doctor. Will that be all?"

"Wait just a minute. What are you going to do today?"

"I have a meeting with Jared."

"Then I should talk to Maggie. Maggie. Maggie. May I talk to you?"

The woman lost her humility and became an alert tough-minded lawyer. "Hi. Who was that?"

"She said her name was Marie. She's a nun."

"I am not surprised. Sometimes I feel that I sinning when I am with Paul."

"But you don't agree?"

"No. Yes. I don't know. In a way, it would be better to wait until I am married. In another way, it is wonderful. How can loving another human being be a sin?"

"Then the question is: should we make a formal commitment to each other before we unite our bodies in sex?"

"I don't know the answer."

"I am on the side of making a commitment, but perhaps I am old-fashioned. Now then, I hear you have an appointment with Jared."

"Oh, yes. Thank you. I had forgotten. Is that why you called me?"

"Yes. I thought you should be the one to meet him."

Maggie laughed. "Good thinking, Doc. One of my former clients is apparently upset that I left the firm. I don't what Jared has in mind, but I guess I'll soon find out."

"Hmm. It seems you have an ace up your sleeve."

"Maybe. Well, time's up. See you tomorrow. I think."

As soon as she got home, she called Paul to invite him to dinner Friday night.

"I thought you didn't cook."

"Well, even I can manage a roast of beef with potatoes and carrots done with the meat."

"That is one of my favourite meals."

"Good. I'll have it ready for six. Come whenever you're ready."

She had a bowl of beef and barley soup and a toasted tomato and cheese sandwich with some Apple Brown Betty for dessert. She took off the cross and put on a crocheted vest. She couldn't remember if it had been made by her mother or grandmother or if she'd picked it up at a craft sale, but the colours were perfect − three tones of green.

In Jenkins Williamson's waiting room, Maxine greeted her with a hug and a broad smile and they chatted for a few minutes before the receptionist rang Jared.

"Thanks for coming, Maggie. Let's go up to my office."

Neither knew what to say while they rode to the ninth floor. Jared took his usual spot behind his desk and motioned for Maggie to sit in the leather chair in front. He hesitated and then said, "It's good to see you. You're looking well. Rodney Thomason and Ted Foxworthy have threatened to take their business elsewhere unless we re-hire you."

Maggie's jaw dropped. "Really?"

"Yes. That means you personally bring a lot of business to this firm, and we don't want to lose it. Besides we miss you around here. Will you come back? It will mean a substantial raise and a potential partnership, but it would mean that your responsibility would still be international law. Did you accept Gus Borden's offer?"

"Yes. I told Gus I'd start work on March first." She didn't tell him that her office could be in Ireland.

"Let's see. This is the eighth. Will you take a week and think about this?"

"Alright." She got up to leave. "I'll see myself out. Thanks."

On her way down, she stopped at her old office. Her name was still inscribed on the door and her plants were still healthy and green on the cabinet by the windows.

She stopped at reception to pick up her coat and Maxine pulled her aside. "Are you coming back? Please say you're coming back."

"I don't know yet. It certainly is tempting."

In deep thought, she drove to Safeway to purchase a sirloin tip roast and the vegetables and milk, and to the Liquor Commission for a bottle of merlot and one of kahlua. On impulse she also bought a bottle of vodka and had to return to the grocery store for Clamato juice. She took the groceries home and left again, with her journal in her shoulder bag. She didn't know where else to hang out, so she went to Polo Park Mall and meandered through the stores, buying nothing, seeing everything. On the second floor, she found a seat in the food court next to some rowdy teenagers and sipped a coffee, wondering why they weren't in school. Teenagers don't seem to care about the future. Perhaps she cared too much. She wondered what it would be like to live day to day, not worrying about tomorrow. That's what Jesus says his followers should do. She doubted that he knew about pension plans. Surely he wouldn't discourage financial responsibility. Did she care about a partnership? It was the reward for good service.

She opened her journal to a fresh page and drew a vertical line through its centre. At the top of one half, she wrote Winnipeg, and New York on the other. She divided the next page in two and wrote Ireland on one half and Vancouver on the other.

Under New York, she wrote - unable to afford a house, lucky to find a suitable apartment with a parking space. Under Ireland, she put housing and big question mark, and under that - have to sell car & furniture & books, under Vancouver - find another company that needs my expertise, expensive housing, sell furniture and books. Under New York, Ireland and Vancouver, she wrote - leave Paul. At the bottom of the page, she put, I still want to run away. Under Winnipeg, she wrote – buy a house, keep car & furniture & books, work for Gus, be more involved with Bordens, Jared turn a new leaf, same old male-oriented thinking, possible partnership at J&W, my office my second home, Paul.

Crap. It was an interesting exercise, but she still didn't know what to do, but she leaned towards J&W and Winnipeg, familiar places. With her mind upside down and inside out, staying put looked the most appealing.

Rather than be arrested for loitering, she drove home, had a bite to eat and phoned the hospital. The nurse told her that Mary Ellen had gone out to dinner, and yes, she was in good spirits, and yes, she would tell her mother that Maggie called. Duty done, she went to hockey practice. In the dressing room, Marilyn hurried over to talk. "Are you really coming back to work?"

"I don't know yet."

"I hope you do."

Exercise was exactly what she needed. She skated as fast as she could, shot the puck hard, scored two goals in their inter-squad game, and wished the practice was an hour longer. Afterwards the team, including the coach, descended on a pizza joint. Maggie appreciated the chance to relax and have some fun without worrying about alternate personalities or voices or jobs or men or her mother.

On her way home though, the voices started again, 'You're going to kill yourself.'

"Playing hockey?" she asked aloud.

'Yes. It's dangerous.'

"I'll be okay."

'You're going to kill Mike.'

'You're going to kill your father.'

Those ideas were too preposterous to answer, so she ignored them.

'I don't like Paul.'

'I think he's sexy.'

"Lord have mercy, Christ have mercy, Lord have mercy."

75

Friday, February 9

LYNNE AROSE THE next morning, ate toast slathered with peanut butter and drank a cup of green tea for breakfast, and went immediately to work in the studio where she was painting a three picture grouping of a harvest scene. Her favourite season was autumn with the complementary colours of golden fields and deep blue sky, offset by green leaves and grasses.

The bonspiel coordinator called at nine to say that her first game the next morning was at eight thirty and that her skip was Bob Hunter. Maggie checked the time. If she hurried, she could be on time for Dr. Dixon, but since it was another bitterly cold day, she had to wait for the Buick to warm up and she made it to the medical centre ten minutes late.

The doctor looked her up and down. "Well, let me see. You are wearing leggings and a long shirt. And your hair is combed back with a band. Let me guess. You must be Lynne."

"Wrong. Sorry. Lynne was up early this morning and laid in a trio of paintings. But I'm Maggie."

"How are you doing today, Maggie?"

She looked up at the ceiling and exhaled. "Mudding it through. My life is so complicated I don't know what to do from one minute to the next. What do I do about the voices? I still can't reach them and they drive me nuts."

"What do they say?"

"Oh, I'm going to kill my father or Mike or myself. Or I'm going to marry my father. Isn't that rich?"

"I don't know. I really don't. You'll meet the owners of the voices eventually. Have you tried writing to them?"

"No. Not yet. I should have thought of that, but they usually come when I am in bed trying to get some sleep. Or else when I'm driving."

"Have any answered you?"

"Yes. One said I was going to kill myself playing hockey."

"Well. Let's see if I can reach that one. Hi. I want to talk to the one who is worried about getting hurt playing hockey. You are worried about your safety. Would you talk to me?"

There was no response.

He tried again. "Who said, 'You're going to kill yourself?' I want to meet you."

No answer.

"Sally. Sally. Would you talk with me today?"

Again there was no answer.

"I don't think they want to talk to you. You want to get rid of them."

"Don't you?"

"I'm beginning to hate them. We have only one body, and we have to share it, I know, but I can't please them all, not at the same time."

"Patience. Patience. You must try to make friends with them. After all, they are parts of this body and what they want to do is just as valid as what you want, but there will be conflicts. I am not a multiple and I have internal conflicts, wanting to do two things at once. Okay. If they don't want to talk, we'll talk. What did Jared have to say?"

"He wants me back. With a raise. And the possibility of a partnership."

"What did you tell him?"

"I have a week to decide. I have thought and thought and thought and I still can't make up my mind. I still want to run away, but mostly I want to run away from myself. I don't like being me right now."

"It doesn't matter where you live. You have to deal with this."

"I know, but I don't want to. I just want to get on with my life."

"You can't. Face the facts. There's no escaping it. You have to accept it."

"I suppose so. Okay. Yes. I have to."

"Keep meditating. That gives you rest. Try writing with your left hand. There might be a lefty or two in there. Ask for their help. Ask Sammy and Dick to help with hockey and curling. Ask for help with cooking, since you don't enjoy it. Talk to the nun about Paul. Keep working on this, Maggie. Don't get discouraged."

"Alright. I think our next appointment is Tuesday. See you."

She drove home via Headingly. The phone rang. "Hi. It's Rob. I just called to tell you Mom came through the surgery well. They think they got it all."

"Glad to hear it. Where are you?"

"Vancouver. Dad called me. So I called you."

"Thanks. I appreciate it. I was out to see her on Wednesday. She asked me to come. She apologized to me, said she was abused by Grandpa too, and then told me to leave before Dad showed up."

"Well, that's progress. I got your letter, by the way. There's an answer in the mail."

"Okay. I'll look for it."

"I have to go. I have a class in two minutes. Bye."

She answered, "Bye," but doubted he heard her. She housecleaned the apartment, although it didn't really need it, meditated for a half hour, read a few chapters in a book on healing from post traumatic stress, watched Oprah, and put the roast in the oven. She sat down at the coffee table and the yellow legal pad. 'Okay,' she wrote, 'Paul is coming for dinner. Marie, I really like this man. Jeanie, we don't need to seduce him. Sammy, Dick, I know you hate this but it can't be helped. Lynne, I know you prefer women, but I don't. Mags, I know you like him too. Can we do this?' She hoped she covered all the bases.

'This is Mags. We'll do this together. Quit worrying.'

That was all. No one else had a word to say. Reassured, she

showered and changed into black jeans and Jane's crisp pink shirt. She fastened a silver chain around her neck and another around her left ankle. She checked the roast, added the carrots and potatoes, threw a salad together and set the table for two with a spotless white tablecloth, matching candles in crystal holders and her new dishes. It was the first time she'd cooked for a man in her apartment, first time since she moved to the city as a student. She was still pondering why she'd never invited Anton for a meal when her guest arrived.

Paul got there at five thirty, a little breathless, still dressed in his gray business suit. He reached for her hand and pulled her close and kissed her lips and her eyebrows and her neck. Maggie struggled free before she smothered and giggling hung his suit coat and jacket in the closet as he removed his striped tie and rolled up his sleeves.

"Mmm. That beef sure smells good. Do you mind if I use the washroom?"

"Of course not. Second door to the right. Would you like some wine?"

"Sure."

Maggie poured a glass of red wine for him and mixed a Brown Cow for herself. She sat in the living room, happiness emanating from her toes.

"This is the oddest apartment. I have to say. How come it looks as if there are two distinct styles in one place?"

Maggie chuckled. "I suppose it does look as if a schizophrenic lives here. I had the whole place decorated in black and white and hot pink with a white rug here in the living room. Then I wanted a change and I hung those pictures and bought this new rug. I made a few changes in my bedroom and the bathroom and I planned to re-paint and perhaps buy new furniture. Well, then I got the idea of buying a house and I stopped. And this is what we have!"

"A house?"

"Yes. I want a yard and a garden. I want to come down to earth."

"What are you looking for?"

"I don't know. I really like Rob's house in Van. It is two-storey and unusually spacious. The bottom level has the most interesting flooring. It looks like weathered red brick, but it's actually tile and it covers a spacious living room with a fireplace also in red brick, a dining room, a U-shaped kitchen with an island in the middle. The patio off the dining room is also in red brick, but the real thing. It is just gorgeous."

"That sounds like a west coast house. Is there anything like that here?"

"I don't know. I haven't started to look, but I like the openness and the continuation of one type of flooring throughout the living area. The walls were off-white throughout, except for feature walls here and there. I really like that house."

"I can tell. I might even move in."

They were both laughing then. "There's one condition," she said. "You have to like dogs. I plan to share my house with a Sheltie."

"Okay," he answered. "By the way, you lied. You are an excellent cook."

"Why, thank you, sir."

Paul helped her tidy up the kitchen. She challenged him to a hot game of cribbage. They fell into bed thoroughly at ease with each other and no voices interrupted her sleep.

76

THE NEXT MORNING he made the coffee and popped in the toast while she set the table and poured the orange juice. They ate without conversation and then left together. "Come to the rink about seven," she told him. "There's dancing after the banquet, or so I understand."

Maggie joined the group of curlers around a flip chart on which she found Bob's name listed under sheet four. The first draw was about to start. He waved to her from the far end of the lobby. "Walk out with us." He introduced the third, a twenty-something girl named Gail, and the second, a stout older man he called Lefty.

The bonspiel began when a Highland piper led the curlers onto the ice. Maggie recognized the tune and she sang along, ". . . the bonnie, bonnie banks of Loch Lomond." The sound of the pipes echoed in the rafters of the curling rink and she felt her usual headache forming behind her left eye. As she cleaned off her rock, she whispered in her sleeve, "Sammy, help me out here."

She thought about being with Paul the night before. What happened with Bob didn't matter. She forgot about Sandy and curled as she never had before and they won that game. After that short four-end game, Bob treated his team to brunch in the cafeteria upstairs. She wanted to ask him if he was still seeing Sandy, but she didn't. She wanted to ask him how things were at Borden International, but she didn't say a word about that either. While they waited for their next game, Gail went shopping with two friends, Lefty and Bob played poker and Maggie went for a walk. Bob still hadn't acknowledged that he knew her. Just before they filed out on the ice for the second game, Bob paused beside her. "I hear you are going back to J&W."

"I hear that Gus wants to send me to Dublin."

That was the end of the conversation. After the game, they had drinks with their opposition and then joined the skills competition. They competed in four categories - draws to the house, take-outs, tap-ups, and hit and rolls. Bob came second. Maggie was pleased with her performance but wasn't in the medal winners.

During the banquet, Maggie sat with her Monday night skip Angie and several other women whom she hadn't met. Bob glared at her from across the room. Paul came at seven, kissed her hello, and asked her to dance. Only a few couples were on the floor. "Let's go," he said.

They watched the movie *Grease*, and then went to the Blue Rose. She glanced around the dimly lit room, searching for her friends, but Rebecca and Sadie weren't there. Anton wasn't present either. "I challenge you to a best-of-three," she said.

They played pool for an hour, drinking Caesars and then he drove her back to the rink to get her car and said good-night. He didn't kiss her good-night. In fact, he hadn't kissed her since he arrived at the rink. Maggie thought that was odd and she was disappointed that the evening ended there. He didn't ask to see her the next day.

77

Sunday, February 11

ON SUNDAY MORNING, Maggie was hardly out of bed when the phone rang. It was Bob.

"There's practice ice available at three. Do you want to come? You need to work on your out-turn take-outs."

"Okay. I'll be there at three."

She had a leisurely breakfast of black tea, two eggs over easy, and toast with marmalade, read the morning papers and went to church in one of her professional looking suits, which fit in very nicely with the clothes worn by the church members. Attending church continued to have a positive effect on her and she was grateful. She stayed afterwards and had two cups of coffee and a man-sized piece of chocolate cake with other members of the congregation. The phone was ringing again when she stepped in her door.

"Where were you?" Paul demanded to know. He seemed far away.

"I just got home from church."

"Church was over more than an hour ago."

She didn't bother to answer. She wasn't operating on his time table.

"I saw why you didn't want me to come to the rink until seven."

"What are you talking about?"

"I came to the rink and saw you talking to that guy."

"He's my skip. Why didn't you say hello?"

"You were angry at each other. There's more to this than you're telling me. How do you know him?"

"He taught me to curl. He's seeing my friend Sandy as far as I know. He works for Gus Borden and I'll talk to him if I damn well please."

She slammed the phone down. Ten minutes later he called back. "I'm sorry. I guess the green-eyed monster caught up to me."

"You're jealous? Well, you'd better get over it. You remind me of Anton. I talk to lots of guys, especially at work."

"Okay. Okay. I'll call you next week."

She didn't have the strength to deal with her inner friends. Her outer ones were causing too much trouble. In reality, she didn't want to think at all and she wrote, president, preside, reside, resident, present, resent, per, side, pied, tied, tide, reed, peed, seed, need, teed, speed, steed, pride, pried, tried, spied, ripe, rip, dip, nip, tip, apt, sip, seep, deep, drip, trip, snip, strip, stripe, tripe, strep, step, steep, sprite, ire, pier, dire, tire, deer, peer, tier, seer, steer, spire, stir, pen, peen, seen, teen, ten, pin, pine, in, I, spine, spin, din, dine, sin, resin, sine, preen, die, pie, pi, pries, rise, risen, siren, dries, pee, see, nee, re, tee, dent, pent, rent, pint, print, sent, spent, tend, pretend, end, spend, spent, send, tarp, stride, ripen, nest, pest, rest, rested, ripened, nested, spider, stein, it, is, its, pit, rite, ret, pet, Pete, Peter, pester, sit, site, nit, snit, spit, spite, priest, tries, net, set, inset, red, rapt, dirt, pert, stern, tern, tired, pined, sired, spited.

She made a grilled cheese sandwich for lunch and two cups of green tea and watched television until it was time to go to the curling rink.

Bob's first words were, "Why did you stand me up that night?"

"We've already been through this. You slept with Sandy."

"So? We're still free agents, aren't we? Anyway, that was a mistake. It is not a good idea to sleep with the boss's daughter-in-law, especially when she isn't divorced yet. Besides, she wasn't interested in me. She just wanted to get her rocks off."

Maggie glanced at him, eyebrows raised.

"That's what you thought of me, wasn't it?"

"Fraid so."

"I'm sorry. I like you. I liked you from the first time I saw you watching curling in that seat right over there." He pointed to the seats in the lobby. "You can't imagine how sorry I am that I came on the way I did."

"Ready, Dad?" Two Bob Hunter clones approached them.

"My sons, Ted and Tom," Bob said to her. "This is Maggie. Come on, let's curl."

Acting as skip, Bob ran down the sheet of ice to the house and called shots for the three of them. They took turns throwing rocks and sweeping until Bob was satisfied they had learned their lessons. As they were returning the rocks to the ledge, he said to Maggie, "By the way, I talked to Gus. He does want you to go to Dublin."

"Oh, no." Her stomach hurt and she almost dropped the forty pound rock.

"I have to get these guys back to their mother. Could you curl for me on Wednesday at nine?"

"Sure. And thanks for the info."

She warmed up leftovers for dinner and took her tea to the studio. She took a scrap of paper and wrote, 'Lynne, what do you think I should do? I have to make a living somehow.'

Lynne responded in an even delicate script, 'Go back to J&W and stay in Winnipeg.'

Maggie didn't write anything else. Lynne continued her work on the three prairie paintings. When she finally went to bed, it was only to dream that Rob was chasing her down the prairie trail leading to the south fields. She ran as fast as she could but he was riding his mountain bicycle and soon caught her. He jumped off his bike like a cowboy bulldogging a calf and knocked her to the ground.

"Now, you little bitch, you're going to give me what you gave Mike." He pulled her slacks down. She panicked. She thrashed around and kicked him hard in the crotch.

"No. No. Don't. Leave me alone."

She woke up screaming, "Leave me alone. Don't."

She crawled out of her warm pit, walked slowly to the kitchen, rubbing her eyes, wanting to sleep. She made a cup of chamomile tea and lay down on the couch while it cooled. She drank her tea and ate a chunk of marble cheese and some Ritz crackers. Depressed, she fell asleep right where she was.

78

Monday, February 12

THE NEXT MORNING, Maggie paced the floor waiting for the mail to come. At five past ten, she took the elevator to the lobby in time to meet the letter carrier, a short brown haired woman who always appeared unhappy, as if she hated her job. In Maggie's mail box there was the letter from Rob, two bills and some junk mail. She opened her brother's letter in the elevator and read: 'Dear Maggie, The therapist I've been seeing for the past two years tells me that all these memories are false. He says that nothing I remember is true in any way, shape or form. So just forget all this stuff. Let's get on with our lives. And keep writing. And remember, we have a deal. Rob'

She sighed and cried. It was intolerable. Not being believed was an insult. She was still trying to come to terms with the letter when Meg phoned to say that she and Sam were coming to the city. She asked Maggie to join them at Sandy's for dinner on Tuesday evening. Maggie agreed to go but didn't understand her reluctance.

For lunch she consumed a cold roast beef sandwich with a bit of hot horseradish and washed it down with two cups of coffee, and to wear it off, she skated for an hour, hockey stick in hand, shooting the puck off the boards and watching the caroms, stick handling forwards and backwards, practicing the slap shot, for which her wrists needed strengthening. Later, for want of something more interesting to do, she sat down at the coffee table and picked up the pen in her right hand. She wrote, 'I am going to put the pen in my left hand. Is there a southpaw in the house?'

'I'm left handed. I am Marie.'

The script was tiny and neat and faint, nothing like Maggie had seen before.

"You are the nun."

'Yes. God bless you child.'

"Child? We're the same age, aren't we?"

'Of course. It's an expression we use.'

"Do you want to stay single?"

'I don't know. I would only marry a special guy.'

"Yes. He has to be special, alright."

'I don't think Paul is the one. He's possessive.'

"Yeah. Apparently so. Tell me. Do you think we should stay in Winnipeg?"

'I think you should go back to J&W and stay.'

The phone rang, interrupting their conversation.

"Gus Borden here. Bob Hunter tells me that you are aware of the possibility that I might ask you to go to Ireland. How did you know that?" The phone seemed hollow, as if there was an echo, perhaps from a speaker phone.

"I met three of your lawyers in the cafeteria when I had lunch with Sandy. They were only too eager to break the news."

"I apologize. I should have discussed it with you. It should have come from me."

"It's true then?"

"Would you consider it?"

"I don't know. It would be an adventure and Ireland is a beautiful country, but I am not sure I want to leave Winnipeg, let alone Canada."

"It could be for two years, five years, or a lifetime if you like it there."

"I will think about it."

"Good enough. March first?"

"Yes. March first."

She didn't know what to do. She could go to Ireland if she didn't go back to the mother ship at J&W. Gus didn't say whether going abroad was a condition of her employment and he had his four lawyers in Winnipeg.

She had more roast beef for dinner, this time between two slices of bread and a generous helping of leftover gravy. Still unable to make a decision, she left for the curling rink. Bob was there already, talking to Brian in the office but he didn't see her and she joined her team. The four had drinks with their opposition after the game, as usual. By that time Bob had disappeared and Maggie was a little disappointed. The phone rang as she walked into her apartment and she briefly considered having it disconnected. This time it was Paul.

"I'd like to take you to dinner tomorrow night."

"Sorry, I can't. I'm expected at Sandy's."

"Oh, how about Wednesday? We could have coffee and dessert or a couple of games of pool after your dance class."

"Ah, nope. I've been asked to spare in the nine o'clock draw."

"Curling? With that guy, I suppose. I really want to see you on Valentine's Day. Thursday you have hockey. Really, Maggie, you are so busy." It sounded like a reproof.

"Curling is curling and has nothing to do with you. Thursday after hockey practice would be okay. I usually get away by eight or so."

"Okay. I'll come to the rink to meet you. And what about Friday for dinner? I'll meet you at Alexander's." She should be available when he wanted to see her.

"Alright, I'll see you on Thursday after practice and Friday at six?"

"Friday at six thirty."

She sat at the kitchen table to write to Rob. She wrote a page, ripped it up, wrote another page, tore it to shreds, wrote a third page, and destroyed it too. She didn't know what to say.

The voice in her head said, You're going to kill Rob.

'Who are you?' she wrote on her mauve stationery.

The voice said, Never mind. I am only trying to protect you.

She wrote, 'Are you Maggie the Cat?'

You don't need to know. I don't trust Rob. Be careful.

'Okay.'

The voice didn't speak again but at least she had made contact. She was exhausted by this time. She meditated for half an hour, wrote in her journal, set the alarm for seven and went to bed.

At some time during the night, she dreamed that she is walking through a field of wheat, which is well out in head and yellow gold and above her head. It smells ready to harvest. She knows she is in trouble because she isn't allowed to walk in the grain because she'll knock it down and the swather will miss it and the wheat will shell out on the ground and her father won't be able to sell it at the elevator and make some money to buy groceries and gasoline and school books. She trudges along wishing she had a drink of icy cold water from the well in the yard and her arms are itchy from rubbing against the wheat stocks and grasshoppers jump at her and spit on her blue dress and she hears little animals running along the ground. She thinks they are mice and she is not afraid. She hears her mother calling her name and then her father. She keeps on going. A cold wet nose touches her elbow and she turns giggling and King barks twice and washes her face with his long tongue and they walk together through the thick crop towards the sun until they come upon a water-filled slough with soft green grass growing around it and she lays down with the shepherd for a pillow and closes her sun-scorched eyes.

79

Tuesday, February 13

ON TUESDAY, HER appointment with Dr. Dixon was early – eight o'clock. She had become so lazy from not working for a living that she didn't arise in time to have a shower or wash her hair and she felt grubby and sweaty and she was embarrassed to appear in public.

"Good morning, Maggie."

"How'd you know it was me?"

"You want to see me. The others don't."

"I have a clue about the voices. I didn't tell you about one of the alters. Her name is Maggie the Cat and she moves like a feline, and she is my protector." Dr. Dixon didn't say a word about her appearance. Surely he noticed that her hair wasn't shiny and it stuck up at the top as if she were spiking it.

"Oh, my God. I hope she isn't dangerous."

"Only to Dad and Mike and Rob, as far as I know. But if she were going to attack one of them physically, I am sure she would have done it years ago. Now she warns me when I am in danger."

"Well, that's a good thing, I guess. Hold on a minute."

He slipped his jacket on over his white lab coat and left the office. A few minutes later he returned with a carton of white milk. "Here, drink this."

She drank it down in one gulp. The doctor took a small rubber ball from his treasure trove of toys and bounced it on the floor. Instantly the woman pounced on it. She sat on her knees and played with the ball, batting it back and forth with her hands as a cat does to a mouse.

"Could we talk, Maggie the Cat?"

She poured herself onto the chair and gazed at the doctor, her head tilted to the right. "What did you want to talk about?"

"I want to ask you. Would you harm anyone?"

"I might scratch their eyes out."

"Their eyes? Whose eyes?"

"Maggie told you – Dad and Mike and Rob. She missed Grandpa, but he's dead now."

"Those men are big, aren't they? And Mike has military training. Are you sure you'd attack them?"

"I tried. Many times. I always fought. But you're right. They always overpowered me, but I'll never stop." She looked about for more milk but there was none. She slunk off the chair and stalked around the room searching for signs of mice or rats but there was no evidence to be found. Disappointed, she returned to the chair and yawned.

"What else can you tell me? How can I help?"

"You are helping. You are helping Maggie and the others cope with all this. Tell Maggie not to trust Meg and Sandy."

Maggie the Cat purred and stretched and closed her eyes. Maggie the lawyer reappeared. "Not trust Meg? And Sandy? I wonder why."

"Maybe they will betray your trust. Does Sandy take you for granted?"

"Yes. She does. And Meg phoned my mother about some music tapes and she told my mother that she was counselling me. That wasn't true. Meg and I did talk a couple of times but she is not my counsellor. I think my mother was actually jealous."

"Take care then."

Later that morning, Maggie and Lynne started a new painting – a pair of mallard ducks, a greenhead and his brownish mate, swimming on a bright blue slough, surrounded by brown-topped reeds under the equally blue prairie sky. She added a red hip-roofed barn and the hint of a white farmhouse in the background and a flock of blackbirds circling overhead. They worked on it for most of the day.

Without much thought, she chose blue jeans and a black tank top covered with a long white shirt to wear to Sandy's for dinner. Sam met her at the door with a hug, "How are you, Maggie?"

"Oh, we're plugging along."

They took their seats in the Borden sunken living room. Sandy and Meg didn't leave their places on the chesterfield to greet her.

"How is your mother?" asked Sandy.

Meg answered. "Mary Ellen came through the surgery with flying colours. The prognosis is good. She will probably go home today."

"Imagine. Not going to see your mother when she has surgery. For cancer yet. Really, Maggie," Sandy said.

"I was there. And I am aware of her progress, thank you, Meg."

"And what did you and your mother talk about – old times?"

Maggie ignored that barb. "How did the classes go last week?"

"Just fine. As if you care."

"How's curling, Maggie?" Sam changed the subject.

"I am having fun with it. I am even sparing the odd time. I can see how people get hooked on it, that's for sure."

Meg called them to dinner. She had prepared a large pan of meat lasagne and a lettuce and tomato salad, garlic bread and apple pie for dessert. The atmosphere was tense and uncomfortable, and all during the meal Maggie wondered why she'd been invited, unless they needed someone to pick on, like a scapegoat, perhaps.

"So are you and Maggie having a secret rendezvous while you're here, Mom?"

"Sandy, for heaven's sake. That is none of your concern."

As soon as she finished her tea, Maggie said, "I don't believe I will come to dance class tomorrow night, Sandy. I have better things to do. Thanks for dinner. Good night."

Smarting, she drove to Elie and back before returning to her apartment, watching her odometer and counting each kilometre as it went by. She spent the rest of the evening absent-mindedly watching television, idly picking up the pen, large, regal, glare, lager, Lear, gear, real, Gael, gale, earl, ager, rage, leg, Reg, era, ear, Rae, are, ale, lag, age, rag, gar, gal, re, la, Al, a.

She dropped the pen and continued to read her book on post traumatic stress.

The voice said, You're going to kill Sandy.

Another chimed in, You're going to kill Mike.

You're going to marry your father.

"Shut up. Shut up. For God's sake, shut up," she cried aloud.

You're going to kill yourself.

She had a hot bath, but it didn't relax her because the voices kept telling her what to do. She collapsed into bed, hoping for the oblivion of sleep.

Two hours later she woke up with an excruciating pain in her crotch. She put her face in her pillow and screamed. The agony went on and on and on and it seemed as if it would never stop. It moved into her abdomen and enveloped her entire lower body. She could not be still. She writhed. She twisted and she rolled. She pounded the bed with her heels. She tried in vain to escape. She hugged her pillow like a teddy bear, but she didn't cry.

The pain stopped as suddenly as it had begun. Out of breath and sweating profusely, she got up and had a warm shower and shampooed her hair and donned a fresh nightshirt. She changed the damp sheets on her bed. Afterwards, as she sipped on a mug of hot chocolate, she felt something let go inside her brain but she didn't understand what it was or what was happening to her.

80

Wednesday, February 14

SHE SLEPT IN Wednesday morning. She didn't want to get up anyway. Dr. Dixon's receptionist telephoned at eight thirty to cancel their appointment. She had nothing to do.

Maggie drank her morning coffee while reading the news and the sports, especially the baseball news, and the economic comments, doing the crossword puzzle, and scanning the real estate listings. She was disappointed that Dr. Dixon couldn't see her that morning and wondered if therapy was becoming her entertainment, her social life, consisting of visits to the medical centre to see her friends the doctors, nurses, technicians and receptionists. She was ready to go back to work, if only to have more contact with people. Curling and playing hockey were ways to meet new people, but otherwise, all her friends were lawyers, not that there was anything wrong with lawyers for friends, but it would be good to have other friends too, more broadening. Friends. She wasn't sure that Sandy was her friend.

She was reminded that it was a special day when a pimply faced teenager delivered a dozen long-stemmed red roses with a card that read, 'Happy Valentine's Day, Paul.' She phoned to acknowledge the gift but he didn't answer. She left a message on his voice mail, thanking him for the roses, but she decided not to send him anything.

She and Anton had never celebrated Valentine's Day, no romantic dinners, no red roses or chocolates, or lingerie or diamonds, barely a kiss. She wondered why she expected him to initiate the date for the special occasion, being a liberated woman she could have invited him to dinner in her apartment or booked a table at fine dining establishment, but she didn't. She couldn't remember her parents acknowledging Cupid's day but that wasn't surprising, since she remembered so little about life before university. She did recall the school at the Crossing, decorated in red paper hearts and cupids and red and white streamers, and the paper cards laboriously cut from a book and addressed to each student, the party with red cinnamon candies and chocolate cup cakes with white icing and more red hearts on top, and spending the entire afternoon skating in the hockey rink in Sampford.

For want of better employment, she composed her letter to Rob. 'Dear Rob,' it said, 'I have been working with my family doctor and he warned me that many therapists deny the veracity of memories such as yours and mine. My doctor does not doubt that my recollections are true, but sometimes the same situation has to come up several times before I get the entire picture. I hope you will find a new counsellor. I have two job offers, one at Borden International and the other back at J&W. Jared's proposal includes a raise and the possibility of a partnership. Gus Borden wants to send me to Ireland. I am having difficulty deciding what to do. My relationship with Paul is foundering because he's the jealous type, or maybe he's just not my type. My relationship with Sandy is in even worse shape. I don't know what her problem is. Lonely in Winnipeg, Maggie'

Despite its brevity she decided to send the note as it was and she stuffed it into an envelope and mailed it before she could change her mind and rip it up. On the way back from the mailbox, she picked up her mail, a child's Valentine's card with a picture of Cupid on the front with the caption, "Be my Valentine." She flipped it over. On the back it was signed, 'Bob.' She laughed aloud. It really was cute.

She skated for an hour and a half, again practicing handling the puck and skating backwards. She wanted to impress Coach Kevin who wanted her to play defence. Afterwards, she couldn't stay at home, so she drove to the mall to buy some Valentine's treats and tried Alexander's for lunch. Fortunately Rebecca and Sadie were there. They advised her to take Jared's offer, but she still wasn't sure. She still wanted to take off for parts unknown.

For want of anything else to do, she returned to her apartment. She sat down at the coffee table and the yellow legal pad but no one took up the pen. She spoke out loud, asking to talk to Sammy or Jane or Marie and no one answered. She retrieved the dolls and farm toys from the library, laid them on the coffee table but no one wanted to play. She picked up a novel and was soon engrossed but the afternoon crawled by. She had a ham and lettuce sandwich for dinner and left for the rink early, where she watched the games in progress, again spending particular attention to the skips' strategies.

When Bob and his team arrived, she handed out her Valentine treats. There was little conversation as they brushed the speeding rocks and coaxed the slower ones into strategic positions in the house. After the game, Bob said to her, "Good game, kiddo. You catch on quick." Because of the late hour, they didn't stay for a drink and Maggie went home, her need for social interaction unfulfilled.

After a long soak in the tub, she climbed into bed where she tossed and turned, unable to get to sleep because of the incessant voices. She woke up screaming but couldn't remember the dream. A little later, bladder empty and thirst assuaged, she rolled over and went back to sleep.

81

Thursday, February 15

Dr. Dixon's nurse telephoned early Thursday morning to cancel her appointment. With nothing else to do, Maggie took her usual seat at the coffee table and picked up the pen, but again no one wanted to communicate with her. She made some oatmeal cereal for breakfast and washed it down with chocolate milk. She wandered down to her studio, but wasn't inspired to paint. She went down to the lobby at ten o'clock. The letter carrier smiled and said, "Good morning. Which are you?"

When Maggie told her the apartment number, the heavyset woman handed her several pieces of mail, including a letter from her mother and a legal journal. She read her mother's note first. It said, 'Dear Maggie, I am still weak but otherwise I feel fine. I don't know yet whether I will need radiation or chemotherapy. Thanks for visiting me. Considering the life we've had together and the things I've said, I didn't deserve it. Could we try again to be friends? Love, Mom'

She read the journal and her newspaper from cover to cover, trying to avoid thinking about her mother. To become friends with her at this late date would require forgiveness, not forgetting the past or saying it didn't matter, just letting it go. Maggie wasn't sure she could let her mother off the hook for choosing her husband instead of her daughter, but it was much more complicated than that. Besides, Mary Ellen had survived being abused and so would Maggie. It was either forgive or forget about developing any kind of a relationship.

In the afternoon, she skated as usual, counting her strides. She didn't know what to do with herself. She went through the Museum of Man and Nature one more time and she watched some television.

She thought about her life. She was Maggie the lawyer. She worked. She read. She dated Anton. Or she did. She patronized one bar, the Blue Rose, and she ate out at one restaurant – Alexander's. She was a one-dimensional person and she was bored. She needed to go back to work because that was what she knew. How pathetic, she thought. No wonder the alters were also bored and angry. To be a whole person, she needed the alternate personalities, but none of them would talk to her and none of them had tried to take over. Was this some kind of boycott? She understood that they didn't want to integrate because she didn't want to integrate either and they had just as much right to be there as she did. It was frustrating not to know what was going on in her own mind.

Her brother Rob was a disappointment. He did verify some of her memories, and he didn't deny attacking her verbally, but he said in his letter that their memories were false. Maggie wasn't sure what she wanted from him, what she expected, perhaps too much, but she didn't doubt the truth of her memories for a second. In her pensive mood, she went off to hockey practice.

As promised Paul was waiting for her after practice and they went upstairs to the restaurant in the curling rink for chocolate brownies covered with ice cream. He had a mug of decaffeinated coffee, black, and she drank green tea without sugar or milk. She felt like a shoulder-heavy athlete, unused to walking about without skates, a bit awkward in a social setting, and not sexy at all.

"Thanks again for the roses. They are lovely."

"Least I could do. There's something I want to talk to you about."

"Shoot."

"Well, you know Ross and his girlfriend are getting married this summer, and that means I won't have a place to live or a roommate. I was thinking maybe, we should live together?"

"So soon? Shouldn't we spend more time together before we set up housekeeping?"

"You aren't ready yet. Well, when are you going to be ready? We had sex on our first date. Doesn't that mean anything?"

"It means the chemistry is there, but does it mean we're in love and ready to make a commitment to each other?"

"Nobody said anything about a commitment. I just want to live with you."

"I don't want to live with you unless there is a commitment. I don't want to live with you unless there's a wedding in the air."

"Why not? Good God, Maggie. This is the seventies. The eighties are almost here. We can live together. Lots of people do it."

"Maybe they can, maybe you can, but I cannot. I need to know that you love me, and I need to know that I love you, and I'm not there yet."

"Okay. Okay. June is a long ways away. We can talk about it again. Okay?"

"I am having some emotional difficulties right now. I need to be alone."

"Did I tell you? My brother was here last weekend and we had a family reunion on Sunday – the whole band of outlaws were there – aunts, uncles, cousins, everybody. It was great."

"So, um, when do I meet this band of outlaws?"

"Oh, I don't know. One of these days, I guess."

She finished her tea and said, "I am tired tonight. I want to go home now."

"You can't be tired. You're on vacation."

"Paul. I know when I am tired."

Later that evening, Maggie lay on her couch thinking again. She was right and she was wrong. Dr. Dixon was right and Dr. Dixon was wrong. She was right that a couple didn't have to be married to have sex. She was right not to have sex on the first date, not because of somebody else's rules, but because it was too soon. Jeanie and Mags changed all that and she was wrong to have gone along with it. If the whole dating thing is going right, she reasoned, having sex should seal the couple's commitment to each other, whether they are married or not. Then living together naturally follows, along with having children, but the dating ritual hadn't gone right with Anton, or with Alex, or with Bob, or with Paul. And it was her fault – at least partially. She was not living according to her beliefs and she was not explaining her value system to her guy. Whatever that was with Paul, it was not working.

And, can you believe it after all these years, her mother wanted to be friends. She didn't know what she is asking.

Too wired to sleep, Maggie soaked her aching body in a bubbly tub of hot water and drank a mug full of chamomile tea in the bathtub. Afterwards, she slathered lotion all over her body, and put on her short nightshirt in a slippery red fabric, which didn't match the blue of her terry cloth robe, but it didn't matter. She leaned back on her soft pillows, still thinking about guys that wanted to live with her, in her apartment, guys that didn't want to provide a home for her.

Her breath slowed. She was breathing as if she were asleep, but she was awake – a strange sensation. She closed her eyes and listened. The sleeper snored gently. Maggie matched her own breathing to the sleeper's and drifted off to sleep.

82

Friday, February 16

IN THE MORNING paper, Maggie read that Dr. Charles Dixon, a prominent Winnipeg physician, had passed away on Thursday. She bent her head in grief. He was such a good man, a kind soul. She didn't know what she'd do without him. She pictured a huge canvass, like the ones she saw in the Tate Gallery, still gesso white, dominating the room, and there she was, a tiny black stick figure in the centre, alone.

Ten minutes later, the phone rang and Sandy shouted into the receiver, "Maggie Barnett, you're a multiple personality. You are clinically insane. You are crazy. You are a bloody psycho. You stay away from my children. And stay away from my dancing students." She banged the receiver in Maggie's ear.

Maggie's left eye throbbed with pain; it spread to her left cortex and into the centre of her brain. She staggered into her bedroom and sat down at the edge of her bed. The middle of her head started to swirl. She sank to the floor and sat with her legs splayed out in front, her head on her chin. A tornado twisted and turned within her mind. Sandy. Meg. Rob. Mom. The whirling deepened. Dad. Young Mike. Sarah. Miss Lindsay. Deeper and deeper it went: Dr. Dixon. Anton. Jared. Paul. Bob. Alex. Trish. She collapsed. She lay on her left side, her head pillowed on her arm. New York. Ireland. Vancouver. Ottawa. Winnipeg. Her office. The church at MacNabb's Crossing. Sampford. The school. The farm.

Farther and farther it continued to spiral. Sam. Abby Sinclair. Ralph. Grandpa. Grandma. David. Turkeys. King. The Highland fling. Drawing. Baseball. The tornado smashed through a barrier - Sammy. Mags. Lynne. Marie. Maggie the Cat. Dick. Annie. Jane. Jeanie. Mary. Sally.

The tornado touched down on a ridge and below lay a deep and black abyss. She knew that if she fell into that crevasse, she would be insane with no hope of recovery. She didn't have the strength to push back from the edge. But she did not panic.

"Lord have mercy, Christ have mercy, Lord have mercy."

Little by little, the force of the tornado diminished. The whirling inside her head ceased. The pain in her head ebbed and finally disappeared and she wiggled away from the rim. She stayed on the floor. The minutes ticked into hours. At long last, she rolled onto her back. She rested a few minutes, bent her right leg and placed her right foot on the floor, bent her left leg and put that foot on the floor. She stretched her arms skyward. Her body hurt. She summoned all her energy and leaning to the left, sat up. She raised herself to her knees. Using the dresser as a crutch, she stood up. She crawled under the covers, still fully dressed, and immediate fell asleep. She slept for fourteen hours.

83

Saturday, February 17

WHEN SHE AWOKE, she stared at the clock. Three fifteen. She expected it to be three in the afternoon, but the sky was dark. She staggered to the bathroom without turning on the light. Bouncing off the walls, she made her way to the kitchen for a glass of cold water. She returned to bed and fell instantly asleep.

The telephone rudely awakened her sometime later in the morning. It was Paul.

"Where were you? Why did you stand me up at Alexander's? I was so embarrassed, waiting there for a woman who didn't show up."

"Our relationship is over, Paul. I no longer wish to see you."

"You are really something."

"Aren't I though."

She nibbled on a chunk of marble cheese and some crackers and drank a full eight-ounce tumbler of orange juice and stumbled back to bed. She slept until about seven in the evening, had a bowl of chicken with rice soup, and returned to bed.

84

Sunday, February 18

SHE WOKE UP and glanced at the clock. It was five minutes to ten, but whether it was morning or evening she didn't know. She glanced through the kitchen window. The sun was shining brightly. She opened the door, picked up the newspaper and checked the date. It was Sunday. Good thing she subscribed to a newspaper. Otherwise she wouldn't know what day it was, like some old crone in a nursing home. She didn't have the energy to go to church, but she was sure that Jesus would understand.

Her stomach clamoured for her attention. She was both hungry and thirsty after her long hibernation. She poured a bowlful of Cheerios. She opened the carton, sniffed the milk. It was sour. "Yuck," she said out loud. She poured the oat cereal back in the box and the milk down the sink. She took out two slices of whole wheat bread. A delicate web of blue grew on the top crust so she threw the entire loaf, or what was left of it, in the garbage. From the freezer, she withdrew another loaf and broke off a couple of slices without mangling them and dropped them into the toaster to thaw. She boiled the kettle and made a cup of chamomile tea to drink with her toast with peanut butter and raspberry jam.

About lunchtime, Bob phoned. "Sandy just called me. She ranted on and on about you being insane and you shouldn't be allowed to work for Borden International. Is she for real?"

"What do you think?"

"I think. No. I know that I want to be your friend."

"I'd like that."

"Then I will see you at the rink tomorrow."

"I'll be there," she answered and put the receiver back on the cradle.

On her way to the bedroom, she stopped at the bathroom to check her appearance in the mirror. Her greasy dark hair stood on end and her face was pale but her skin seemed to be healthy. She looked directly into her eyes, which were bright and steady. She set the alarm and returned to her bed.

85

Monday, February 19

ON MONDAY MORNING, Maggie parked her black Buick in its usual spot. Carrying an odd-shaped parcel and her briefcase, she rode the elevator to reception. Glowing with happiness, she greeted Maxine with a hug and a hearty "Good morning" and marked herself 'In' with a magnetized black dot on the silvery board. As she ascended to the eighth floor, she checked her appearance in the mirror and ran her fingers through her dark hair. At her office door, she stopped a few seconds to admire the brass wording, 'Margaret L. Barnett' and to wipe the dust from it with a white tissue she found in her coat pocket. She placed the black horse's head on the filing cabinet and removed her purple scarf and her long black coat.